CU00684009

DEEP STEAL

Mike Seares

Copyright © Mike Seares 2017

The rights of Mike Seares to be identified as the author of this work have been asserted in accordance with the Copyright, Designs and Patents Act 1988.

All rights reserved. No part of this book may be reproduced, adapted, stored in a retrieval system or transmitted by any means, electronic, mechanical, photocopying, or otherwise without the prior written permission of the author.

All the characters in this book are fictitious, and any resemblance to real persons living or dead is purely coincidental.

A CIP catalogue record for this book is available from the British Library

ISBN: 978-0-9957339-1-6

Cover design by: Jeremy Hopes - www.publishing.graphics
Cover images: Almay/ING Image/Shutterstock

Copy-edit by: Richard Sheehan - www.richardmsheehan.co.uk

For more great titles and to keep up to date with upcoming projects, go to: www.mikesearesbooks.com

For Mum and Dad
Wish you were here

Chapter 1

The gold had lain undisturbed on the seabed for over seventy years.

Until now.

A hundred feet away, a sinister form slithered through the murky water leaving a confused spiral of plankton in its wake. It glided with a rhythmic undulation, its hardened gray-black muscular body perfectly adapted to propel the fearsome creature through the depths.

With eyes scoping the seabed in almost total darkness, the conger eel moved as one with the environment in a domain it considered its own. At over ten feet long it was large for its kind and it was heading home after spawning far from its territory deep in the Atlantic. The journey had taken several days and left it drained and exhausted, but now it was finally back on familiar ground. The deep canyon that rose to a small peak, the sloping seabed that turned from rock to silt, and the wide gulley that led to its lair were all welcome sights.

But then it paused.

Ahead, a dull glow seeped from the blackness, a hazy, indistinct tone in the water coming from above. To the right, where the broken, jagged structure it knew as home was located, a second, more conspicuous light could be seen, only this one was flickering.

And there was something else—something it hadn't encountered before, and that was unusual.

More cautiously now, it moved forward, its protruding upper jaw opening ever so slightly in anticipation. It could make out a long tubular shape lying on the seabed. As it moved closer it felt a tingling in the water, an electrical stimulus its sensors picked up with absolute clarity. It literally sent shivers down its spine—not an unpleasant feeling, but one that needed investigation.

It moved alongside, almost brushing the surface of this strange entity that had come into its world. It was cylindrical in shape, around four inches in diameter, and extended in both directions as far as the eel could see. It lay in a lazy snake-like form across the seabed, occasionally twitching as though pulled by some unseen force that sent small puffs of disturbed silt up off the bottom.

Gaining confidence and moving faster the eel allowed itself to caress the side of the shape, sending a warm, thrilling vibration through its body. It sped up, following the twisting curves and heading straight for the flickering light that grew stronger with every passing foot.

What the eel could not have known was the construction of the strange object in its midst. It consisted of six intertwined cables and hoses. One of the hoses carried a mixture of helium and oxygen at high pressure. A second contained a continuous stream of water at a temperature hotter than a bath. Of the three cables, one carried electrical power, the other two audio and video signals. All were secured around a central line, which provided physical strength and integrity. Its length stretched over eighty feet, from the downward-facing light the eel had seen earlier, to the interior of the rusting wreck of a German U-boat the eel had come to call home.

Approaching its lair, the eel saw the long, meandering object wind inside through a gash in the hull.

The U-boat lay almost upright in a slight hollow in the sea floor. It had clearly suffered a catastrophic explosion that had almost blown the vessel in two just aft of the conning tower, which still reached up into the water as though yearning for the world above. Decades of marine growth covered the surface, and small crabs scuttled over the rusting metal hull in search of morsels of food, frantically scurrying away as the eel approached.

But despite its extreme hunger, the conger's attention was not on small prey. Right now its focus was on the ever-brightening light coming from the interior of the wreck and the intruder that had invaded its home. It started to move cautiously inside.

Apart from the massive gash in the hull, the remainder of the submarine was relatively intact, and as the eel moved forward the sides closed in, forming the claustrophobic interior that had once housed over forty men in appalling conditions during the dangerous days of World War II.

The water was murkier now with silt and plankton hanging in suspension like slow-motion snowflakes. The narrow corridor, down which desperate sailors must have once run in the final moments of their lives, was eerily desolate. Broken shelves and bulkheads hung in derelict disarray, starkly backlit from the light-source that was right ahead. And with the light came a noise, but it was unlike anything the eel had heard before. It was a violent crackling that accompanied the flickering of light.

The eel moved stealthily through the final doorway and hung there motionless. It had followed the strange collection of hoses and cables, and these now led to an apparition of something from another world silhouetted in the middle of the cramped forward section of the sub.

The commercial diver had his back to the doorway and was hunched over, concentrating on cutting into a large metal box with an oxy-arc torch.

The cables fed into his equipment. The large hose, which carried the gas, was secured to a connector on the side of the yellow Kirby Morgan 37 diving helmet. The safety line was attached to the webbing harness around his body by a large karabiner, while the hot water feed flowed into his suit to keep the seven-hour-duration dives tolerable in the near freezing water. Power was connected to the compact light and video camera attached to the helmet and the final audio cable fed into a microphone speaker system inside the Kirby Morgan. All in all the mass of cables made up the full life-support for the diver, keeping him alive and functioning in one of the most dangerous places on Earth.

The eel hovered a few feet behind the diver's head. Below, on the floor of the submarine, was some sort of large, hard plastic basket with numerous oblong metallic objects stacked in the bottom. As the eel moved forward, it could see the diver at work on the rusty metal box, his concentration complete. He was carefully cutting away the top of the box with the tool in his hand.

Oxy-arc burns at a temperature of around 11,000 degrees Fahrenheit, and any metal in its path is literally liquefied. The top half of the box was peeling away, and then, as the searing flame reached the final corner, it fell to the floor as if in slow motion.

The diver paused for a moment and a low whistle could be heard coming from inside his helmet. He gazed into the box briefly before lifting out one of the objects similar in shape and color to those in the basket on the floor. He turned around, holding his prize, and came face to face with the eel.

It could rightly be argued that a human being is superior to a conger eel in pretty much every way, but in terms of reaction time that would appear not to be the case.

As the diver turned, so the light caused a reflection in his faceplate, acting like a mirror. The conger eel found itself staring at ... well, a conger eel. Having a strange apparition in its lair was one thing, but another conger was something else entirely. The eel lunged, hitting the faceplate with its jaws wide open. The diver stumbled back, his helmet smacking the side of the sub hard. He managed to steady himself and stand, but the action caused the helmet safety release clamp to catch on a metal strut on the side of the hull, snapping it open.

As his head turned, so the reflection of the eel seemed to move to the side. The conger darted forward, clamping its teeth around the nylon lifeline that attached the umbilical to the diver's body harness. It writhed in anger, its full length spinning with demented fury in the confined space. The strong, muscular body twisted the line and the sharp teeth did their worst, shredding the braids of nylon that had never been designed to withstand such an onslaught.

The diver tried to maintain his balance, but the eel was thrashing so violently he was smashed against the metal hull again and again. He'd long since dropped the object he'd been holding, which had fallen onto one of his feet. It was clearly heavy and added to the pain and fear creeping into his soul.

He was frantically trying to regain control when he spotted the oxy-arc torch lying on the top of the crate. With a desperate lunge he grabbed it and spun back to the eel, but the animal had backed off, preparing for another attack.

This time though, the diver was ready. As the eel surged forward he brought the cutting tool down in a fiery arc—a dagger of light that would have severed the eel's body in two had it not turned at the last second to avoid certain death. As it was, the burning gas cut through the last six inches of tail, sending the creature scurrying into the bowels of the wreck to lick its wounds and contemplate its newly shortened length.

The diver just stood there, staring in horror into the blackness, daring the animal to return.

"Holy shit!" His breathing rate was in overdrive, heart rate through the roof. They prepared you for just about anything in dive training, but this was one for the manual. A calm but concerned voice sounded in the earpiece in his helmet.

"Everything okay over there, Sean?"

He allowed his breathing to steady for a second before replying. "No problem, John. Just getting to know the local wildlife."

"Your breathing rate was off the charts for a few seconds there."

"Was here too, thanks."

"Just keep it safe."

"Plan to. Me and Sarah gonna settle down after this payday."

John McCready laughed. "You, retire? You love it too much."

"Yeah, well things change."

"Huh, like what?"

"Like you're going to be an uncle." There was silence from the comms. "You still there?"

"Well, well, my little brother finally did something right."

"Yeah, Yeah. Oh, and I think I just got my toe broke by half a million bucks!" He stared down at the gold bar lying across his foot. The solid metal gleamed in the diffuse light, highlighting emblazoned Russian text on the underside of its shiny surface.

John McCready stretched his back and readjusted his seating position, which, given where he was, didn't allow for many options. He was just under six foot tall, with broad shoulders and a rugged, weather-beaten face that had been around the world and back again. He had piercing blue eyes and a hint of stubble that was occasionally allowed to flourish into something greater, but at the moment was tamed to a mere shadow across his face. Behind the subtly handsome features, lay a quiet yet steely determination that was rarely prone to anger, but that right now could well be put to the test. He was hunched up on a small, curved metal seat that had about as much in common with comfort as a barbed wire fence. His surroundings were dripping with condensation that was cold to the touch, and if he leant forward, or stretched out in any direction, he could reach all corners of his current universe, and he had been here for over five hours.

He rolled his head from side to side, easing the tight neoprene neck seal that topped off the DUI hot water suit. It had felt as though it was gradually tightening its grip and wasn't going to let go. He ran two fingers around the inside for the twentieth time until it was in a position that was almost bearable. He wasn't cold, the suit saw to that, but there was no way in the farthest reaches of one's imagination he could say he was comfortable.

For over a month McCready's world consisted of intense concentration and physical extremes in and around the six-foot-diameter metal bell he currently resided in, coupled with boring, exhausting downtime in a pressurized chamber on board the dive support vessel (DSV) *Recovery* that was floating above.

In his early forties, fifteen of which had been in saturation diving, McCready lived for the job. It had seen a marriage come and go, and time since then had been in total dedication to the work. It was, after all, not a profession you could take lightly. Within a couple of feet of his position the water pressure was nearly thirty times that on the surface. The gas in his lungs would on the surface be equivalent to over 160 liters in volume, and his body had to cope with that for a full month, even when on the ship. The continued "saturation" of his tissues with the gas allowed a commute to and from work without the lengthy decompression required when returning to atmospheric pressure. When that time did finally come, it would take over eight days for the pressurized gas in his body to be released safely—or put another way, it would have been quicker for Neil Armstrong to pack his bags after walking in the Sea of Tranquillity and return to Earth, than it would be for McCready to ascend from his current position, go through the requisite decompression procedure and stroll freely on the deck of *Recovery*.

It was a hell of a place to have your office, but McCready wouldn't have it any other way.

He was just about to shift his position again when the bell swayed in the water. A metallic groan emanated from the structure. He wondered what things were like on the surface. To move the bell this deep they must be interesting to say the least. He leaned forward and checked the suit water temperature on a small round gauge. Satisfied, he glanced down at the serpent-like collection of tubes that disappeared into the innocent pool of water in the middle of the floor that was, in fact, eight hundred feet down at the bottom of the North Sea.

Chapter 2

Captain James Radford watched the pair of unfeasibly large breasts slide across the table. They were a light shade of pink and appropriate in size to the somewhat oversized lady they were attached to, and as much as he might have wished otherwise, they were in fact enameled on the side of a well-used white china mug, the inner rim of which sported a dark, engrained stain, indicating numerous refills since the last meaningful encounter with any form of soap and water.

The slide had started slowly, but then suddenly accelerated as the table lurched upwards. Radford had been waiting for it, but the speed with which the mug had reached the edge had caught even him by surprise. However, in a smooth, well-practiced movement, he grabbed it before a single drop of Nescafé's finest could be spilt. Lifting it to his mouth, he took a gulp of much-needed stimulant. It was just what was needed, hitting the spot and reenergizing a body that had not slept for more than fifteen hours.

Radford was late fifties, had a trim waist for a man of his years, and had what would have been a shock of red hair had not age and a recent trip to the barber's— stylist would be going too far—reduced it to a smattering of orange on an otherwise crew-cut scalp. He wore what appeared to be a permanent, affable smirk that was often taken for smugness but was in fact a joy of life, brought about by what he did for a living, which had effectively been playing with boats for the last thirty years.

More precisely, he commanded one of the most sophisticated pieces of floating hardware ever to put to sea outside of the military. At over three hundred feet from bow to stern, and twenty thousand tons, *Recovery* was one of the worlds most advanced deep-water salvage ships, and while she wasn't exactly what you'd call pretty —she was practical. Her silhouette showed a high, angular bow with a stubby bridge and accommodation decks that were almost hidden by the jutting platform of a helipad mounted above and forward of the main superstructure. But her bright red-and-white livery was somewhat striking and she was designed to withstand the battering any ocean could throw at her. All in all she was a formidable weapon in man's arsenal to extract lost or sunken artifacts from the deep.

At this precise moment she was gently rising and falling in a steadily increasing swell, two hundred and fifty miles north-northeast of Shetland in the North Sea. At least that had been until the sudden jolt had sent the mug on its short journey, interrupting the flow of things, but the increasing oscillation was merely a casual workout for the technologically supreme *Recovery*.

While things were pretty much on track, the current operation had had its share of problems, but nothing Radford couldn't handle. Something of more concern was the imminent arrival of Malcolm Mercer, CEO of Global Salvage, the guy who owned the boat and paid for the coffee. A visit from the boss was never good. It meant things were not as they should be, hence the lack of sleep and the requirement for a caffeine infusion.

He stretched, stifled a deserved yawn, and then swept his eyes across the bridge as the light faded on yet another day.

As he took in the low work-lights, adding to the military-like atmosphere of red-and-blue information and navigation screens, he had to smile. At his command were all the high-tech toys to search the impenetrable depths modern technology could provide, and he was paid very handsomely to make them do their thing. There had been many missions with many outcomes, but the current contract, even with the added security implications, had beaten them all. It also had a payday the likes of which he had never known. Of course, with reward came risk, but it was the only way Radford knew how to live, and it was far from over yet.

And that was the problem. At the back of his mind he somehow felt tonight would be different. He didn't know whether it was the worsening conditions, the visit from Mercer, or the fact that every man who lived on the edge had a weakness, but James Radford was fully aware of his and one day he knew it would come back to haunt him. He was prepared. It was just a matter of when.

Beyond the stormproof windows, the sun had started its final dive below the horizon. The plunge sent fingers of crimson high into the air, made all the more dramatic by the punches of black blocking the rays as they headed skyward. The clouds had been gathering for over an hour now, steadily forming into an impenetrable bank that stretched to all corners of his view like an advancing army. Things were going to get interesting.

"The latest from Comsat, sir." Radford glanced up at the letter-sized sheet of paper offered by Carla Sanchez, the young, shapely, but don't even go there, navigation officer. "Looks like it might get a bit choppy."

He scanned the paper, a slight scowl creasing his forehead. "Ever the one for understatement," he muttered under his breath. "Okay, spread the word. Systems checks, storm shutters, and let dive control know. Only halfway through the shift. They're not going to be happy."

"Right away," said Sanchez. "And there are some reports of a container ship shedding its load. We need to keep an eye out for floating debris." Radford considered this for a second and then nodded.

Sanchez turned and grabbed an intercom from a panel at the rear of the bridge. Radford watched her. He liked the way she moved, the mass of brown ringlets that fell around her neck, the plain yet determined and somehow alluring face, and the way her company regulation overalls seemed to be tight in all the right places when they never seemed to fit anyone else. He'd even kissed her once at a very drunken shipboard party at the end of a tough assignment. She'd kissed him back, but that had been it. It was as though she'd been pulling rank in the only way she could. It might have been awkward, but she was unquestionably good at her job, and if there was one thing Radford respected, it was professionalism in the face of adversity, and they didn't come much more professional than Carla Sanchez. His only regret was that there would never be anything else, and he knew it. Even so, he was sure she moved just that little bit more provocatively in his company just because she could. *The bitch!* He smiled ruefully.

Sanchez hit "talk" on the intercom, took a confirming glance out at the gathering clouds, then turned and looked directly at Radford. He could tell she knew exactly what he was thinking, and the hint of a smile almost crossed her lips—almost. Then she spoke into the mike.

Dive control, or DC, was situated twenty feet, or two decks below and aft of the bridge and was the reason this multimillion dollar behemoth had ever left the drawing board. The ship's *raison d'"être* was to access the seabed hundreds of feet below. This could be done in one of two ways: mechanically, using remotely operated vehicles (ROVs); or with human intervention, using divers, either in one-atmosphere suits, a sort of metal, body-shaped submarine, or through the highly complex and dangerous practice of saturation diving. The whole system was monitored and controlled by two guys at a sophisticated panel in DC. However, none of this would be possible if you couldn't control the exact position of the ship above the divers. Any horizontal movement on the surface, and anyone below would have a very bad day. To ensure this never happened, *Recovery* was equipped with the latest in sophisticated dynamic positioning systems. Ten satellites in geosynchronous orbit, twenty-two thousand miles above the Earth, provided a precise position on the surface of the planet. Any movement or deviation from this activated a series of six thrusters built into the hull to automatically move the ship to keep her exactly on station. The system was accurate to within six feet—the result, pinpoint stability on the moving ocean in swells of up to fifteen feet, or a force six. In other words, Mother Nature could pretty much do her worst and the ship would stay "anchored" over a point on the seabed below. It gave the guys in dive control one less reason to worry. So when Sanchez's message came down about the change in weather, it was received with caution but without any undue concern.

Steve Donovan hit a keyboard, and the display in front of him lit up with a radar plot of the approaching storm. Figures down one side indicated wind speed, direction and predicted swell. He was of average build, with short dark hair and a stern but alert face. His demeanor was calm and unflustered and instilled confidence wherever he went. Nothing seemed to faze him, in even the trickiest of situations.

"So is it going to be fun?"

Donovan glanced over at the small, bespectacled man sitting further down the panel. He was in his mid-forties, wearing a gray cardigan and a slightly worried expression. "You may be a technical genius, but you're the sort of guy that wants to know the end of a movie halfway through," said Donovan.

"Come on, gimme a break!"

Donovan was enjoying this. "What you really want to know is, are you going to throw up again?"

Paul Matthews groaned. "That was once. It was a force nine and the bloody cat was throwing up!"

"What gets me is why you work on a tub like this when your guts go on show at the slightest ripple."

"Hey, we all gotta pay the bills. So what are we in for?"

Donovan glanced back at the screen, flicking a pencil

casually between his fingers. He tried to prevent a hint of a smile crossing his lips. "Probably better get the Dramamine. And stay on your side of the shed."

"Oh shit!"

"Preferably not."

The shed, as dive control was affectionately known, couldn't be further from its description. Okay, it was around fifteen foot by twenty, which was pretty shed-like, but beyond that it was the closest thing to a Mission Control outside of NASA. There were no windows, but enough computer displays and closed-circuit TV monitors to provide a view on the only world they needed to keep someone alive in one of the most hostile places on the planet.

A small flashing red light caused Donovan to glance at a section of the display on the left of the screen. As diving supervisor, he was responsible for all sub-surface operations involving humans. It was the second warning light he'd received in the last half hour. The first had been when Sean McCready's breathing and heart rate had spiked briefly. This time though, it was the gas handling system that was at issue. He clicked a button and scanned the readout of pressures that appeared in the middle of the screen. "Okay, time to change the supply over."

Matthews glanced at the figures. "That's earlier than expected."

"Yeah, but it seems to check out. Maybe there's a minor leak somewhere."

The "supply" was the premixed gas that was fed to the divers. It was stored in huge tubes within the hull of the ship and had to be changed at regular intervals to ensure there was no interruption to the flow.

Donovan clicked a couple of virtual buttons to check the integrity levels. "System seems fine. Okay, I'll keep an eye on it. If the usage stays high we can always pull them up early. Looks like, with the weather closing in, we'll have to anyway." He reached for the mouse.

"Okay, your call, but Mercer ain't going to be happy," said Matthews.

"That's his problem. No one's putting my guys at risk."

Matthews looked at him dubiously. Donovan slid a control on the screen and watched as the graphic showed the transfer over to the new storage vessel. A small electronic whoosh accompanied the changeover.

"Jeeez, I hate that!" said Donovan.

"Hey, it's progress," said Matthews.

"Yeah, well sometimes progress is backwards."

Not only was vital life-support data on the screens, but now full electronic controls were displayed alongside. It replaced the old system of physical valves, switches and taps, with the accompanying noise of moving gas under pressure that for years had been what kept the divers below in one piece. Now it was all fly-by-wire, a concept Donovan had taken a while to get used to. Somehow when you made an adjustment to the system, which if you screwed up could kill a man, the reassuring whine of gas flowing through pipes made you feel something was happening. Now, there was just the simulated whoosh of electronic noise to say that anything had changed, and you could even turn that off with a click. It creeped the hell out of him.

Chapter 3

The *Mary Louise* was running for her life.

The small blue-and-white fishing vessel out of Peterhead on the east coast of Scotland had been hauling in her nets when the storm warning had come through from the coastguard. She was about forty miles out, which translated into a three-hour steam, possibly four given the prevailing wind. The skipper had seen the forecast but needed the latest catch to make his quota for the month and so had stayed out. What he hadn't bargained for was the winch jamming with the net still twenty feet below the surface. It was full to bursting and contained a mix of cod, haddock and plaice. His crew had struggled for over an hour to get the machinery working, but to no avail. There was no way in hell he was letting this catch go, so the small boat was currently busting all cylinders to drag the net back to shallower more sheltered conditions.

It wasn't working.

The weight was making her sit lower in the water and list to port, and with every passing minute the waves were increasing. One had already swept over the deck, almost knocking a crewman overboard, and the fact that night was now upon them didn't help the situation.

And then it started raining.

A gentle drizzle at first, but this quickly escalated to massive droplets that stung exposed flesh and was now driving in diagonal sheets across the deck, making any form of work virtually impossible. The outlook was made all the more bleak by the harsh work-lights shining down, highlighting the scene in stark relief.

On the bridge the skipper struggled with the inevitable decision. The clear vision window system was spinning in hyperdrive and he could see the two crewmen, spanners in hand, desperately trying to force some life back into the defunct equipment. He moved over to the cabin door and slid it open. Immediately any warmth was sucked out like the last breath of a dying man, and stinging pellets of rain swept inside. He leant out of the doorway and had to shout against the elements.

"Okay, cut it free!"

His voice could barely be heard above the howling gale, but they glanced up, shielding their faces from the driving rain, their waterproofs running like a liquid sheet as the water cascaded off them. They didn't even bother replying. A simple thumbs up provided acknowledgment, but relief could be seen in the way they turned to the taut cables that were fed over the side of the pitching gunwale.

They were going home.

The larger of the two grabbed an ax and was about to cut the cables when they both stopped and stared forward over the bow.

The skipper followed their gaze and his mouth fell open.

"Oh my God!"

About five hundred yards in front of the boat, a wave the size of a tower block was bearing down on them. It rolled out of the night, an elevated carpet of dread that could not be stopped. The water rose gently at first and then accelerated toward a near vertical wall of impenetrable death.

There was no way they could survive.

On the deck, the large deckhand was galvanized into action. He severed both cables in quick succession and immediately the hull bounced up onto a more even keel, finally free of its anchor of fish. It bobbed there like a toy awaiting its fate.

On the bridge the skipper grabbed the VHF radio, switched to Channel 16 and hit the button. "Mayday, Mayday, Mayday. This is fishing vessel *Mary Louise…*"

Around fifty miles to the south in the warmth and calm of the Aberdeen Coastguard Operations Centre Sandra Adams had just started her shift. She'd driven in from her small flat in the suburbs in the worsening weather and knew it would be a long night.

She was now intently listening to her earpiece to see if the message that had been cut off mid-sentence would continue or be repeated.

But there was just static.

"*Mary Louise*, this is Aberdeen Coastguard, over." She listened for the faintest hint of a reply. "*Mary Louise*, this is Aberdeen Coastguard, over."

The watch commander noted the slight edge in Adams' voice. He moved over to monitor the situation. Adams was concentrating on the radar display in front of her. It showed the Scottish coastline and the north and northeast sections of the North Sea. Across the display various markers with numerical idents showed the respective positions of any shipping that had dared, or was stupid enough, to have braved the elements.

"There a problem?" asked the commander.

Adams never took her eyes off the screen. "Maybe, sir. This target here, the *Mary Louise*. Had a Mayday call, then nothing." The commander moved in closer, scanning the display.

"Nearest assets?"

"Closest chopper is on the west coast, dealing with a freighter that reported taking on water, and the RAF say there's nothing at Lossiemouth that can respond."

The commander looked at the screen. His finger came up, pointing at a target that was moving steadily north-northeast. "What's that?"

Adams watched it closely for a second. The numbers indicated an aircraft of some description and it was heading straight for the *Mary Louise*'s last-known position.

"Not sure, sir. I'll check it out."

"Do that, and keep trying the ship. GPS is reading. She must still be afloat." Adams nodded in acknowledgment and turned back to the screen.

"*Mary Louise*, *Mary Louise*, this is Aberdeen Coastguard, do you copy, over?" There was even more of an edge now to Adams' voice. She lived for moments like this, but at the same time she was fully aware that others may well be dying to provide them.

The wave had hit hard, engulfing the fishing boat like a giant hand coveting a prize. The crest had broken over the mast, and foaming spray and incandescent water had ripped it from its mountings. For a moment water had covered the entire vessel, but then, with a plucky I'm-not-dead-yet attitude the little trawler had burst out of the top of the wave to emerge broken but not beaten.

Inside, the water had cascaded down stairwells and companionways, forcing open unsecured doors and flooding the lower decks and engine room. The engine that had for so long been driving her forward with such gusto was drowned in a single stroke. The water filled the lower cabins, and as it flowed off the sides, she rose slowly to sit with her deck awash with fishing nets and lines floating amid broken planks and old crates. As the wave rolled on looking for more victims, the boat was a sorry sight with her main deck now semi-submerged.

The two crewmen had miraculously managed to grab hold of something and slowly pulled themselves to their feet. The main work-lights had gone out, but the emergency power for the port and starboard running lights had cut in, and they cast an eerie red-and-green glow across the scene.

On the bridge the skipper stood up shakily. He'd sought shelter in the wheelhouse and the mass of water that had crashed through the windows had simply flowed over him, unable to prize his death-like grip from the wheel. He now emerged into the rain to survey what was left of his pride and joy.

He checked his crew were still in one piece and with a feeling of despair he saw the radio antenna was no longer there. Once standing proud at the top of the mast, it was now dangling over the front of the bridge. He went back inside and grabbed the VHF. A crackle of static came from the speaker, but he could just make out something else as well—a distant voice, almost like an ethereal soul that faded in and out from somewhere afar.

"*Mary Louise*, this is Aberdeen Coastguard, do you read, over?"

A ray of hope entered his being.

He pressed the button. "Aberdeen Coastguard, this is the *Mary Louise*, we are taking on water and sinking. Request immediate assistance, over."

He listened and then repeated the message.

Nothing … then …

"*Mary Louise*, Aberdeen Coastguard. We have your position. How long can you …" And then it cut out.

Static.

He tried repeatedly, but it was dead, something he realized could very soon be his own fate—but the woman had said she knew where they were. He put the mike down and hauled himself outside. The crewmen were looking up, the enormity of the situation written in their eyes. He gathered his thoughts and shouted. "They're coming. Won't be long. Just hang on!" If the rain hadn't obscured his face, his expression would have given away the truth.

In the control room, Adams jumped to her feet. "They're alive, sir!" The commander looked up and crossed over to her station.

"Tell me."

"Someone acknowledged my signal, but they're taking on water. I don't think they have long."

"Any ships in the area that could reach her in time?"

"No, sir, but that target you saw. It's a private chopper out of Edinburgh. I'll get them to divert. At least they can monitor the situation, maybe drop some supplies."

"Get on to it, and keep me advised."

"Yes, sir."

Adams turned to her display and looked intently at the small dot that was fast approaching the *Mary Louise*'s position.

It is said that a helicopter can be described as ten thousand nuts and bolts all flying in formation. Right now, the pilot of the sleek white Bell 222 hoped that none of them would fail. He needed every single one to keep the machine from shaking itself to pieces.

Helicopters and storms don't mix, and when he'd filed the flight plan earlier that evening he'd been dubious it was even possible. A conversation with his boss, however, had confirmed that "not possible" was not on the agenda, so they'd taken off at 17:00 and were now around half an hour from their destination.

The interior of the Bell 222 was a calming place to be. She wasn't large. She could take four passengers in leather-seated luxury, and two crew. She had the latest technology to guide and survive in the harshest conditions —up to a point. Things had gone well so far, but the wind was ruthlessly buffeting the airframe and she'd dropped violently on several occasions. The autopilot guidance system was taking them where they needed to go, but he'd had to hold onto the controls to keep the craft from being thrown around the sky on numerous occasions. Also, staring out at an impenetrable blackness of dense cloud, with driving rain beating against the windscreen, was not a comforting experience. As an ex US Marine Corps Apache pilot who had seen action in Iraq and

Afghanistan, it took a lot to phase Mark Shannon, but right now he certainly wouldn't say he was enjoying himself.

He was checking the navigation screen when the message came through.

"Golf Juliet Bravo Foxtrot Hotel, this is Aberdeen Coastguard, over."

Shannon hit the trigger button on the joystick for the radio. "Aberdeen Coastguard, Golf Juliet Bravo Foxtrot Hotel. Copy, over," he said in his laid-back American drawl.

"Golf Juliet Bravo, we have a vessel in distress close to your position. Can you assist, over?"

Shannon paused for a second. "Standby, Aberdeen." He clicked the internal comms switch and spoke into the mike. The system would carry his voice to the headsets of the occupants in the rear. However much comfort might be crammed into the aircraft, you could never get away from the infernal noise the machine made.

Two men sat facing each other in the plush interior of the main cabin. Neither appeared to be overly concerned by the weather raging outside.

Conner Jennings had his back to the cockpit in one of the rear-facing seats. He was dressed in a stylish Paul Smith business suit tailored to fit a sleek and powerful body. The other man, seated at the rear, facing forward, was wearing more relaxed, yet smart clothing. On initial sight you might have thought Jennings was the one in charge. Nothing could be further from the truth.

"Coastguard say they have a ship in distress. They want us to check it out," said Shannon over the comms. Jennings glanced at his colleague, who looked up from a laptop.

The man was in his early fifties, with dark, smoothed-back hair—neat, but not slick. He had a lean, yet somehow rugged face and a physique to match. But it was his eyes that people noticed. They showed a mental fitness that could eclipse most men. There was also an air of menace about him, suggesting that to cross this man would not go well for you.

Outside, the wind had started to calm a little. They were in the eye of the storm. As the helicopter raced on into the night, it skimmed across the top of a sea of clouds, and its rotor wash curled the droplets of moisture into exotic formations as it sped by.

Two thousand feet below, the *Mary Louise* was almost gone. The three men now clung to the top of the bridge, shivering in the extreme cold. The forward deck was completely submerged. The life raft that had been secured to the roof of the bridge had been swept away and had failed to inflate. The loss of hope was clear in their eyes.

But then suddenly a flicker returned to the skipper's expression.

"You hear that?" The two crewmen glanced around.

"There!"

The skipper clambered to his feet on the shifting roof of the bridge, straining to hear. Then the smaller crewman also stood up.

"Yes, there!" he shouted excitedly. Now all three were alert, expectant. On the wind they could definitely hear the far-off whine of a helicopter.

The skipper grabbed the small waterproof emergency

pack he'd managed to salvage from the bridge before it had submerged. Throwing it open he quickly pulled out a flare gun, checked it was loaded and aimed high.

With a loud BOOM the parachute flare sped skyward, and along with it the hopes and prayers of three desperate men.

The Bell 222 was still clear of the clouds. Shannon clicked the comms switch again. "I need an answer guys. Coastguard are getting impatient."

Jennings looked at the casually dressed man. He was glancing out of the side window just as the flare rose through the clouds and hung there illuminating the sky with a brilliant flash before starting its slow drift back to earth.

Then he spoke.

"We haven't time. We're already behind schedule." He looked pointedly at Jennings. He received no argument. When Malcolm Mercer had made a decision, it would be foolish to try to change his mind.

Shannon pressed the radio trigger. "Aberdeen Coastguard, Golf Juliet Bravo. That's a negative. My orders are to proceed to destination. Sorry can't be more help, out."

On the boat there was desolation. The flare had fallen back through the clouds and was heading for the sea about two hundred yards away.

There were now only a few square feet of the bridge left for the men to cling to. They strained to hear, but all hope faded as the whine of the helicopter disappeared into the distance and all was quiet in the brief respite from the storm.

As though signaling the end, the flare landed in the water and after a final defiant spark it fizzled out to nothing. The blackness was complete.

The wreckage bobbed in the waves for a few more moments, then slowly slipped below the surface along with her crew. The dark and unforgiving sea had finally claimed the *Mary Louise* for her own.

Adams sat back in her chair, pulling the comms set from her head. She couldn't take her eyes from the display. She was in total shock. The ident for the helicopter continued northwest just as the GPS marker for the *Mary Louise* blinked one last time and disappeared from the screen forever.

Chapter 4

Recovery was riding the swell with ease, but the frequency and the size of the waves were increasing. Peak to trough on occasion reached up to thirty feet, and as the bow pushed up through the crests, foam and spray was hurled back across the foredeck by the wind.

In the shed, Matthews was feeling far from great. He'd already had two Dramamine but it wasn't exactly helping. Donovan looked over with little sympathy. "Only a week to go. Think you can make it?"

Matthews wore a rueful expression. "Do I have any choice?"

Donovan conceded. "Guess not." He checked over the panel and then glanced back at his colleague. His expression was softer this time. "How's everything at home? Lucy okay?"

Matthews almost seemed to slump in his chair. A sadness crept into his eyes that had nothing to do with his present physical condition. "It's not good. We had the results from the tests and it's definitely cancer. Apparently it's been there for some time, but she never felt anything. Only a routine scan brought it to light."

"I'm so sorry, Paul. Is there anything they can do?"

"There is some sort of experimental procedure, but they're assessing whether she would qualify. If she doesn't, I've no idea how I'll afford it. Just have to hope I guess," said Matthews weakly.

Donovan didn't really know what to say. He was trying to think of something suitably diplomatic when the phone on the desk rang. He picked it up, thankful for the interruption. "Donovan."

A gruff and slightly annoyed voice came over the speaker. "Steve, it's Jerry. We've got a problem with the heave compensation system." Jerry Malone was the chief engineer on the ship. He might be belligerent, stubborn and often irritating, but there was no one with more experience. If he had a problem, Donovan wanted to know about it.

"What's up?"

"If you spin the camera onto the winch, you'll see what I mean."

"Okay, hang on a sec." Donovan clicked a button on the desk and the picture on one of the monitors changed to show a shot of the moon pool. This was the open section in the bottom of the ship through which the bell was lowered and raised, and it was currently a rectangle of choppy water. He grabbed a small joystick that controlled the pan, tilt and zoom of the camera. A small push and the camera tilted up to show the massive drums above the pool. These carried the umbilical and lift cable for the bell. It also showed a series of hydraulics, which made up the heave compensation system. The idea was that, regardless of what the ship did on the surface, the equipment would keep the bell at a constant depth by absorbing any vertical movement. If this failed, the bell would be hauled up and down in time with the swell and anyone inside would be thrown around like a pea in a pod. The problem was that its operating window was ideally a maximum of ten to fifteen-foot swells, and the current conditions were easily exceeding that.

"Okay, on the winch now," said Donovan.

"Right, you see where the hydraulic pipes go into the unit?"

"Yeah, up near the roof."

"That's it. Well, there's a leak. The workload is too great. This swell increases any more, they're going to blow, and you know what that means. Your guys down there are going to be chucking up worse than Matthews." Donovan glanced across at his colleague.

"Thanks, Jerry. Keep me up to date. Juggling a whole lot of stuff right now."

"Will do."

Donovan put the phone down and took a swig of coffee. "And the night is still young." He hated not being on top of a problem. They had a habit of ganging up on you, and before you knew it you had a situation that was out of control.

Eight hundred feet below, Sean McCready lifted the final two gold bars from the rusting crate and placed them into the workbasket. As he did so, he stopped for a moment. The basket in front of him held enough precious metal to set him up for life and then some.

Like anyone working around limitless treasure, the thought had crossed his mind. People in bank vaults, diamond miners, money printers—the list could go on. At some point they'd all had that brief thought—some not so brief—about how all their problems could be solved. But for Sean, it had lasted a mere fleeting moment. That old saying that money can't buy you happiness was so true. He had a beautiful wife, a baby on the way, and he genuinely didn't care about the value of things over and above the place he was in his life right now, and that was a pretty good place.

He smiled at the thought of Sarah and the life they were going to have together—the three of them.

They'd met at a work party several years earlier. She was a close friend of Lucy Matthews, and the second he'd laid eyes on her he knew that if he had anything to do with it they would spend the rest of their lives together. It didn't matter that his brother had been talking to her at the time, or that she was quite clearly completely out of his league. This was one thing John would never beat him at.

He had been bewitched by her beauty, of course—that long blonde hair sweeping down her back, the high cheekbones highlighting a strong, proud face—but it had been her voice that had captivated him. When she spoke it was with a calm, relaxed tone that made you feel you could achieve anything, and if you were with her nothing could ever go wrong—that and the mischievous eyes that hid a wild side he was completely in love with and knew he could never tame.

He now stood calmly, never more sure of anything in his life than that this would be his last job in the dangers of the North Sea. She had never mentioned it, she didn't have to, but he knew this would make her happier than anything in the world—anything, that was, except for the small bundle that was due to arrive in about seven months time.

He turned back to the metal case he'd just cut open and was about to move it to one side when his earpiece crackled.

"Sean, this is Donovan. How's it going down there?"

"Another two crates in here. The rest are further back past the bulkhead. Going to need some primer to shift that lot."

"Okay, get the crates done and then we'll reassess. With the weather coming in we're going to close things down. Let me know when you've finished."

"Roger that. Sounds good to me."

In the shed Donovan leaned back in his chair. The night was turning out to be more of a challenge than he would have wished.

Then things got worse.

The phone on the desk rang. Matthews answered it, spoke briefly and then offered the handset to Donovan. He covered the mouthpiece. "You're not going to like it."

Donovan took the handset and spoke into it. "Donovan."

Malcolm Mercer's voice was even, but there was an implied tone that was plain to hear even above the background noise of the helicopter. "This is Mercer. Give me an update."

Donovan grimaced. "We're slightly behind, sir, and they're already pushing the limits. Also, with the weather coming in, the bell compensation system is working beyond safe tolerances. We're going to have to pull them up."

"You're a week behind. How many more runs to target?"

"Five, but in this weather——"

"Then you'd better make it in three. We land in five minutes." And with that the line went dead.

Donovan stared at the handset as he replaced it slowly. Matthews looked worried. "Trouble?"

Donovan didn't even look up. "Oh yeah, and it's headed right this way."

The Bell 222 sped through the night. Shannon checked their position and then glanced ahead. Through the blackness and the scurrying clouds, he could just make out a Christmas tree of lights on the dark water below. He pulled the mike trigger. "*Recovery, Recovery*, this is Golf Juliet Bravo Foxtrot Hotel requesting landing clearance, over."

There was a brief pause, then, "Golf Juliet Bravo Foxtrot Hotel, this is *Recovery*. The pad is clear but be advised, wind is forty knots, four-zero knots, from the northwest. Swell is averaging twenty feet, peaking at thirty. There is significant pitch and roll of the ship. Re previous transmissions, we do not advise attempting a landing, over."

"Thank you, *Recovery*. Duly noted, but I have my instructions. Golf Juliet Bravo, out." He turned to the rear cabin. "Better get buckled in tight, gentlemen. This is going to be interesting." Jennings and Mercer glanced at each other and then tightened their safety belts.

On the bridge, Radford couldn't believe Mercer was going to attempt the landing. The rain had returned and the wind was increasing again. Coupled with that, the ship was experiencing heavy movement and there were only seconds when the helipad was even remotely stable. He peered out of the side window and could make out the approaching navigation lights in the sky. They were coming ever closer. As he watched, the forward spotlight lit up and he shielded his eyes from the glare.

And then he saw something that was of even more concern.

The beam from the helicopter spilled out across the water, and there, two hundred feet away in the huge swells, was a cargo container. It must have come from the ship they had been warned about earlier.

Radford gritted his teeth and grabbed a waterproof from a hook on the wall. "Okay, I'm going topside," he said. Then he pointed out of the starboard row of windows. "Keep an eye on that container." He strode from the bridge, zipping the waterproof tight around him.

The helipad was about thirty feet square with a large H written across its center. When Radford reached it he could barely make out the far side through the driving rain. Four spotlights illuminated the pad and two crewmen were standing by. They would have the unenviable task of lashing the chopper to the pad once she was on board—IF she was on board. The way things were looking, there was every chance his boss was going to end up at the bottom of the North Sea along with the gold he was so desperate to retrieve.

From the Bell 222 the ship was growing larger by the second. Shannon was an image of total concentration as he juggled the collective, joystick and pedals, to keep the machine as stable as possible as they approached the pitching vessel. The vertical movement of the helipad was about thirty feet at its maximum, reducing to around six feet every few waves.

He hung back, gauging the frequency, trying to find the gap. Finally he saw an opportunity as the waves seemed to lessen for a moment. With total commitment he went for it.

But it was an illusion.

Recovery was at the bottom of a swell and suddenly rose up as the chopper flew in low, hovering where the pad would be in about five seconds time. Shannon peered intensely through the glass portion of the floor, watching the pad as it started its upward rise, but it was coming too fast. At the last second he realized his mistake and pulled hard on the collective, hauling the screaming machine a few feet higher. The pad scraped the undercarriage and then started to drop away. At that instant Shannon cut the lift and the Bell 222 dropped like a stone. It fell faster than the pad was dropping and the relative downward movement of the pad reduced the impact, but still it hit hard. He felt a crunch from the landing gear, but they were still in one piece.

The second the chopper was on the metal the deck hands ran forward to chock the wheels and secure the undercarriage. Shannon kept the rotors at full power until the crewmen had signaled the helicopter was locked down, and then he leaned back in his seat and cut the engine, a small bead of perspiration running down his neck. "Gentlemen, the eagle has landed."

Mercer glanced out at the incessant rain that was

bouncing off the pad and then leaned forward. Pilot and boss locked eyes. Mercer paused for a second and then gave a slight nod, and with that he exited into the storm with Jennings close behind. A wry smile crossed Shannon's lips. "Piece of cake." All the nuts and bolts were still in perfect formation.

Radford greeted the two men and they hurried down a set of metal steps and into the ship.

As the door slammed to behind them, the howling gale and driving rain was shut out, leaving only the permanent background hum of the ship. It seemed like they'd entered a church, the contrast was so great. Calm immediately pervaded the scene. But it didn't last long. Mercer wasted no time. "Okay. Dive control. Let's go."

Radford led off, indicating the way. "Good flight?"

Mercer's look required no further clarification.

Donovan heard the door open, felt a slight breeze enter the shed, and then a feeling that he couldn't quite put his finger on, but that needed no explanation.

Mercer stood just inside the small room. Jennings was to one side and Radford a step behind. "Thank you Captain, you can leave us now. I'll contact you if you're needed." Radford nodded and then left.

Donovan swiveled in his chair. "Mr. Mercer, glad you could make it, sir." He hoped the insincerity in his voice wasn't apparent.

Mercer glanced around the room, his gaze taking in the gas control panel, the row of monitors, and finally coming to rest on Donovan. He looked at him for a moment, then leaned forward and quietly asked, "Where's my gold?"

The consequences of any reply made Donovan pause.

"It's coming … slowly, but the conditions aren't great down there. As I mentioned, the compensation system is beyond its limits, and with waves this size the dynamic positioning thrusters are at breaking point. If we move alignment on the bell—"

"A few waves make you seasick? I don't want excuses. Where's my gold?"

Donovan glanced back at the panel, stealthily activating a microphone that recorded all activity in dive control. "They're at eight hundred feet, sir. If just one of the problems we're experiencing escalates, we could lose someone. And for the record, this has nothing to do with being seasick."

At that instant a huge wave smashed into the ship. It sent the bow high into the air. For a moment the mighty vessel hung there as though frozen in time, but as the wave rolled on, she crashed down on her starboard side in a fountain of spray. The full weight landed on the corner of the steel container that had been swept close to the ship—right where the forward bow thruster was located. It smashed into the propeller, snapping the blades and bending the shaft beyond repair. A massive shudder reverberated through the ship.

Before the hull could level itself, objects flew off tables. Anything not bolted down slid across the deck. In dive control mugs hit the floor. A glass shattered into a thousand pieces. Everyone hung on. Then, as things stabilized, an alarm sounded shrilly from the panel. It was accompanied by an urgent flashing red light.

Matthews was already checking the systems. "Forward bow thruster's gone." Then another warning light.

"Dynamic positioning offline. She's going round."

And with that the ship slewed to starboard and began to roll. At the same time the phone on the desk shrilled. Matthews grabbed it, listened and then put it back down. "That was Jerry. The compensation system's blown."

Donovan clicked the CCTV camera on to the winch above the moon pool. Two of the four hydraulic pipes had blown clean off their mountings. Hydraulic fluid was spurting everywhere.

"Okay, that's it. I'm pulling them up." He reached for the comms, but Mercer moved forward and slammed his hand down onto the desk like a thunderclap. All in the room froze.

"They stay till I say they leave!" His eyes bored into Donovan's skull, leaving no room for argument.

In the depths below, the movement of the ship was now transmitted directly to the bell, making it drop and snatch.

Inside, McCready grabbed hold of the metal seat.

It was a weird sensation.

He could feel movement, but his eyes could see none. It was like being on a blacked-out rollercoaster and it was starting to make even him feel sick.

There was the rise upwards as the ship rode a wave, then a moment of stillness and calm before a sensation of falling as the ship fell into a trough, ending in a sudden, violent jerk as the bell snatched to a stop at the end of the cable and the ship headed up the next wave, repeating the whole cycle.

He hung on as best he could, trying not to be hurled across the cramped interior as it was wrenched dramatically through the water. At the same time he was trying to feed out the umbilical to create some slack, as any movement the bell experienced would be transmitted to Sean down the length of hoses connecting the diver to the bell. After he was sure there was enough umbilical on the seabed, he grabbed the comms mike.

"Surface, we've got a twenty-foot vertical movement on a ten-second interval down here. Any of you guys know what that means in the real world?" He listened intently, but there was no reply.

"Surface, I say again. It's getting—"

Donovan came over the speaker, stress clearly showing in his voice.

"We read you John. Just hang tight. We have a situation up here."

"Oh, yeah, wanna swap?"

Mercer stood over Donovan at the panel. The room was tense.

Donovan stood up, determined to make his point. "With a thruster down he could be dragged from the sub. I'm the dive supervisor on this ship—"

But Mercer cut him off. "And I'm paying the bill, which means, Mr. Donovan, that I own you, and until I say otherwise, they work."

There was a standoff, eyeball to eyeball. Donovan was about to continue when another massive wave hit the ship. More alarms sounded. Matthews looked up.

"Second thruster's gone. She won't take much more of this!"

With the second thruster down, the ship lost all maneuverability and started to turn sideways to the marching waves. The pitching and rolling was such that Matthews wasn't the only one turning green.

Could things get any worse?

Chapter 5

At the bottom of the North Sea things were getting much worse. The umbilical and support cable to the bell were pulled tight as the ship drifted off station. This dragged the bell at forty-five degrees through the water.

Inside, McCready was knocked hard against the metal, causing him to cry out. At the same instant the umbilical snapped tight before he had a chance to pay out any slack.

From the bell the umbilical became a living thing. It leapt up, zipping across the seabed, creating a curtain of silt below. When it reached the U-boat it rose up off the floor until it reached Sean, where it yanked him clean off his feet. He was hurled backward, his helmet smashing into the side of the sub with a massive CRACK.

In the bell, McCready could only imagine what had happened to his brother.

"Sean, you okay?"

There was no reply.

"Sean, are you okay?"

With concern creeping into his voice he tried again. "Come on, Sean, talk to me!"

But there was nothing.

In dive control they heard McCready's desperate voice and watched the monitors. Donovan looked closely at the camera feed from Sean's helmet. Silt and plankton obscured the view, but there was something else, something strange about the image—and then he realized.

"Oh, my God!"

He flicked the comms mike. "John, get in there! It's Sean's helmet. It's come off!"

"Oh Jesus! On my way," came the reply.

Everyone in the shed was now totally engrossed in the drama below. Donovan stared at the monitor for a second, then glanced briefly at Mercer.

"Now you've done it."

He flicked the comms again. "John, we're ready to winch, but make it fast. We're two thrusters down and she's drifting off station."

He stood, pushing Mercer aside. Jennings moved forward, about to intervene, but Mercer waved him back. Donovan checked the winch controls while Matthews flicked a Tannoy mike.

"Paramedics to sat. Full resus," he said urgently.

Many men had died in the coffin-like interior of the U-boat, and the number looked as though it was about to be increased by one.

When the umbilical had pulled Sean off his feet, it had slammed him hard against the bulkhead that separated the cargo section from the main interior of the vessel. His helmet had smashed into a broken shelf, catching it under the collar. As the safety release lever was no longer locked after the encounter with the conger eel, it had ripped the helmet clean off. It was now dangling a few feet away from him.

Fortunately he'd taken a breath just before disaster had struck. He knew he could hold his breath for around two minutes under ideal conditions, but conditions were far from ideal. His eyes were blinking against the stinging salt water, and the shock of the temperature hitting his face had almost made him gasp, but he'd desperately tried to restrain the urge.

It was the only thing that had kept him alive, but the cold was seeping into his brain and he had to act fast.

He had to reach his helmet.

McCready's mind was focused on only one thing—saving his brother's life. His actions in the next few minutes would literally be life and death.

He moved quickly, reaching across the cramped bell to the suit temperature controls. He turned his brother's suit to zero. If he became unconscious, the drop in temperature might just give him that extra chance of revival should his heart stop beating.

Next he grabbed his helmet from the side of the bell, pulled it over his head, and locked it tight. Unraveling enough umbilical to allow him to reach the sub, he jumped into the cold, dark water.

Below, he sank down onto the stand-off frame that acted as a safety stop for the bell to allow the divers enough room to enter and exit above the seabed. He now started the short but slow eighty-foot journey to the U-boat. Every muscle in his body was straining, but to anyone watching it would have been like watching a slow-motion sprinter.

It seemed to take forever.

He leant forward to give his booted feet purchase in the soft silt and moved as fast as he could, but he knew it wouldn't be fast enough. Every second he took was one less second of life his brother had left.

Sean was still unable to breathe. It was clear where his helmet was—the lights were shining straight at him, but reaching it was another matter. When it had been pulled from his head, the umbilical had split. The hot water pipes were still attached to his suit, but the feeds to the helmet for gas and audio/video had become separated. They now hung about ten feet away—not far, but when he started to move, he realized with horror that his left leg was caught under a steel stanchion.

He was going nowhere.

He tried to pull it free, but it was stuck fast. And then he started to feel cold. Out of nowhere, the thought that, with all he was going through, he was going to die cold somehow made him mad.

But then he realized—John.

Even now, when things were as bad as they could be, his big brother was looking after him, like he always had. For a moment he relaxed. Everything was going to be all right.

But then he started to feel lightheaded.

It was the carbon dioxide building up in his system. Quickly his vision began to blur, like he was looking down a long tunnel. He tried his leg again, but it was as though he was feeling someone else's limb from afar. His efforts had no effect. And then in the distance he could see Sarah and their child—it was a little girl. They were all playing by a gushing river in the Highlands. Sarah was smiling, but the smile was getting further and further away, and then the tunnel was too long and he couldn't see her anymore.

He started to gag and choke, his body convulsing violently. There was nothing he could do to stop it, and then the blackness was all enveloping and he felt a strange sense of peace.

Donovan watched Sean's vitals on the monitor. A cold sweat spread over him as the faint sinus rhythm of a heartbeat changed to an emphatic flatline. It was accompanied by a soft alarm of incessant beeping. The true horror was set in stark relief by the image of his lifeless body perfectly recorded by the helmet cam. There was silence in the shed. Donovan loosened his collar and then reached for the comms. He took a deep breath.

"John, you there?"

"Roger, surface. Approaching the sub."

"You need to hurry."

There was a slight pause, then … "Why, what's happened?"

"Just hurry."

McCready was at the large gash in the side of the U-boat. He pulled himself inside and made his way down the narrow corridor, following the umbilical as it led him to he knew not what. With every passing second a growing dread seeped into him.

He reached the final bulkhead and the scene that met

him filled him with pain and agony. His brother was floating upright in the water, one arm outstretched toward the helmet that was only five feet away. McCready was lost in the moment for a mere second before he moved quickly forward and grabbed the helmet. He pulled it over to Sean's inert body and maneuvered it over his head. He snapped the retaining clamp down hard and turned the purge valve. He saw the water evacuated from inside and could now see his brother's face more clearly. He looked hard into the vacant eyes for the briefest of seconds. "I'm not going to lose you, little brother." And with that he moved down to free his leg and started to pull him out of the confined room.

Far above, the massive wave, whose last encounter with mankind had been the *Mary Louise*, rolled out of the night and drove *Recovery* sideways through the water. This was no mere rise and fall, but a full onslaught on the ship that moved it across the surface like a child playing with a plastic duck in a bathtub. There was nothing the crew could do.

The bell was dragged through the water at over five knots. The umbilical snapped tight, and as McCready felt the movement he grabbed hold of his brother as they were wrenched off their feet and hauled fast through the sub. He had no control, and as they hurtled through the narrow corridor his shoulder smashed into a bulkhead, almost shattering the bone. Pain coursed through his body. Startled fish darted out of the way.

In dive control all were transfixed by the confused, jumping images on the screen from the helmet cameras.

"Jesus, they haven't got a chance," said Matthews.

And then on the monitors they could see the two bodies as they were dragged from the sub and out into open water, twisting and turning.

As the wave moved on, the movement slowed, and McCready managed to stand up. He took a second to find his bearings then set off, heading for the small light in the distance—the bell and safety—but it was painfully slow.

Donovan turned to Mercer, all respect and fear of the man gone. "If he dies …"

Mercer nodded to Jennings, a neutral expression on his face. "Take Mr. Donovan below. He's become a liability." Jennings moved forward.

Donovan stood defiantly. "You can't do this!"

Mercer looked on coldly as Jennings grabbed Donovan. He tried to struggle, but the iron grip of the other man was too much for him.

"I'm the dive supervisor. You don't have authority to overrule me – only the captain can do that, and only in circumstances that endanger the ship." He stared at Mercer. Jennings looked questioningly at his boss. Mercer was about to speak, but then he paused for a second. A thin smile crossed his lips.

"Well now, I would say the ship is in quite a bit of danger, wouldn't you? Get the captain on the line. We'll see who has authority." With a slight nod he indicated for Jennings to release Donovan. Donovan pulled angrily from the grip. He stared straight at Mercer.

"That's not what I meant, and you know it." He moved to the panel and picked up the comms mike.

"DC to bridge, over."

A couple of seconds and Sanchez's voice came over the speaker. "Bridge, go ahead."

"Put the captain on."

There was a pause, then, "This is Radford."

"Sir, this is Donovan. We have a situation down here."

"What's the problem?"

"Mr. Mercer and I have a difference of opinion as to who has jurisdiction over diving operations on this ship."

There was a pause. "I see."

Mercer grabbed the mike from Donovan and spoke calmly and evenly. "We go back a long way, James. I know you'll make the right decision."

On the bridge, all watched Radford. The mike was on open speaker. He glanced round at Sanchez and the other members of the crew. He paused, thinking briefly, then closed his eyes. He had known this day would come. His penchant for gambling, the high stakes games in Monaco, the bailouts from Mercer. He knew now that all his failings had been leading to this one moment. When he opened his eyes he gripped the mike and spoke quietly into it.

"I back any decision Mr. Mercer feels is appropriate. Radford, out."

He slowly replaced the mike and turned to face the others. He could feel the disgust, the eyes nailing him to the wall, but the look on Sanchez's face was the one that hurt. He knew he could never remain here and command any respect. Without another word he turned and left the bridge.

Mercer stared evenly at Donovan. "Think we've cleared that little issue up." He nodded to Jennings, who grabbed the dive supervisor. Donovan struggled and held his ground. He stared directly at Mercer.

"You really don't want to do this." There was an implied tone in the voice that suggested Mercer pay attention. Mercer's focus was complete and his laser stare was directed at Donovan. He moved closer.

"That sounds very much like a threat Mr. Donovan." It was clear both men knew what they were talking about. "You really don't want to threaten me." He held the stare for a second and then nodded at Jennings who pulled Donovan away. As he reached the door, Donovan turned.

"You won't get away with this."

Mercer glanced up briefly. "Oh, I think you'd be surprised what I can get away with." And with that, Jennings marched Donovan from the room.

Mercer turned to Matthews, who was watching events with unease. "You've just been promoted. I take it that won't be a problem."

"No, sir. Thank you, sir," he said hesitantly. Then he took a deep breath and turned back to the screens.

At the bottom of the North Sea John McCready was ten feet from the base of the bell and a minute away from having to perform a miracle to revive his brother who had now been dead for over five minutes. The drag on the cable from the movement of the ship had lessened, and as he pulled Sean under the bell he knew the next few minutes would be the most critical of his life.

A minute later he was inside and had winched his brother into the cramped interior. He wasted no time. He pulled off Sean's helmet and then clicked the comms, looking into the helmet camera.

"Get us up, he's not breathing!"

He could almost feel his voice cracking. Without waiting for a reply he immediately started resuscitation.

The human body is an amazing design, but it is fragile. If it goes without oxygen for more than a few minutes it starts to die. The process by which oxygen reaches the organs is a combination of the lungs, where the gas enters the body, and the bloodstream, which transports the gas to where it's required. If the two aren't working perfectly in sync, life cannot continue.

To artificially simulate this, McCready pushed down hard on his brother's sternum. He did this five times in quick succession, with a pressure almost strong enough to break a rib, but it had the effect of compressing the heart, which pushed the oxygenated blood from the lungs to all corners of the body, allowing the oxygen to transfer to the tissues and keep the cells alive.

Once he'd completed the compressions he had to replace the oxygen in the lungs. Tilting Sean's head back to make a clear airway, he sealed his lips on his brother's. Then pinching his nose and ignoring the proximity to the dilated pupils of his lifeless eyes, he breathed out hard to inflate the thousands of small balloons that made up the alveoli of the lungs. Sean's chest rose, and then, after releasing the seal on the lips, it contracted. The compressions were restarted and the process continued.

"Come on, Sean, not now. Please not now!"

He could feel the tears coming. He was powerless to stop them. He knew he would repeat the cycle until either his brother woke up or until someone prized his lifeless body from his arms.

Outside the bell the water was an inky black. The dim light emanating from the small opening in the bottom of the metal sphere and the drama unfolding within moved slowly away from the seabed.

As it departed, a dark, elongated shape slithered through the water below. The conger eel returned to its lair. The intruders into its realm were finally gone. The blackness was complete and life could continue as though they had never been.

But for some, life would never be the same again.

Chapter 6

The funeral of Sean McCready took place in a small church on the shores of Loch Etive.

The twenty-mile-long sea loch stretched inland just north of Oban on the west coast of Scotland, and as if in respect of the occasion, the incessant winds that had been blowing for several days had calmed. A small gap in the clouds had formed and bright sunlight bathed the scene in rays from heaven. The water of the loch was glassy smooth, its mirror-like surface creating a pristine reflection of the surrounding snow-capped mountains in the frosty air. Winter was coming but its full presence was yet to be felt.

The service had been short but moving. The congregation had been kept to close friends and family, and around thirty people had attended. There had been one absence, though, that McCready had found a little odd. He would have to look into that later.

The mourners filed out of the hardy, stone-clad building in ones and twos, and despite it being a positive celebration of Sean's life, these things never felt like or indeed were a celebration of anything. Whichever way you looked at it, whatever you believed in, a good man was no longer there, taken before his time. It was no celebration.

As the last few left the church and McCready had thanked them for coming, he glanced up and saw a small, fragile figure in a black cashmere coat standing by the stone wall at the edge of the loch. The long blonde hair fell in waterfall lines down her back, creating a single streak of light against dark. He took a deep breath and crossed over to her.

Sarah McCready stared out over the calm water. The tears that had flowed freely during the service had dried, but the streaked lines of mascara were still there. She didn't even acknowledge McCready's presence as he stood next to her. Her eyes were fixed on the far side of the loch and her thoughts were far away, maybe in another time—some time, any time before this day. They stood silently for a minute, both lost in memories from the past.

A light breeze brought a chill to the air as clouds started to edge in off the mountains. Sarah pulled her coat tighter around her. "It's so peaceful here … hard, but peaceful," she said.

McCready watched a tern wing its way across the loch, dipping down to the water to whisk a small fish from just below the surface. "That's the way he liked it," he said.

Sarah continued to stare out across the water and then spoke softly.

"With the wind in your hair and the loch by your side,
the love of your life is never far away.
You only have to look in her eyes to realize she will always be here

54

and you will always stay."

McCready glanced at her as she continued. "Sean used to say that to me. He loved it up here."

"My brother reading poetry ... now there's something."

She glanced up at him. "He wrote it, John."

The look of surprise was evident on McCready's face. He was about to say something but stopped, realizing there were things he would never know about his brother, and now was not the time.

As he looked at her he could see how delicate she was right now. When she spoke there was a frustration in her voice—not much, but it was all she could manage. "You know, you guys should have talked more. You lived on top of each other in those horrible tin cans for weeks on end, yet he would always say you never spoke—at least not about anything real. He hardly ever saw you out of work. What happened, John? You used to be so close."

McCready glanced at her briefly. He didn't know what to say. She was right though. Things hadn't been that close between them for some time, and he knew exactly when they had changed. It wasn't something he was proud to admit, and even now the acknowledgment made him a lesser man. It was the moment she had agreed to marry Sean.

McCready had met her first. He'd thought they might have had a future together, but when he'd seen the look of love in his brother's eyes, he'd backed off. He'd told Sarah it wouldn't work out between them—he was too old, relationships never worked for him ... basically anything he could think of. So he shouldn't have been surprised when in time she'd become engaged to Sean. Somehow though, it changed things. He had been, and always would have been, there for his brother, but something was different.

He finally replied to her. "Time, I guess. You guys were always busy. He didn't need me hanging around when we spent so long at work together."

She looked at him curiously, but let it go. They started to walk slowly down the small path between a haphazard array of tombstones to the row of cars parked outside the church. All the other mourners had now left, and they felt completely alone.

But they weren't.

They finally reached Sarah's car, a pale, eggshell-colored Mini Cooper with a black roof. She turned to McCready. "Why John, why?" Her eyes were pleading for answers but knowing there weren't any.

"There are no "whys," Sarah. Life sometimes does that to you. It was always dangerous. He knew it and he still went out there … He lived for it."

"And now he's died for it," she said quietly. He could hear the finality in her simple statement.

McCready looked at her helplessly. What was there to say?

"It was his last job. We were going to be a family." She was almost desperate for him to say she was wrong, it was all a horrible mistake, but he couldn't. He put his arm around her shoulder.

"I know," said McCready. "He told me about the baby. I'm so sorry, Sarah. If there's anything you need. Anything I can do. I'm here for you, you know that."

She gave him a weak smile. He continued. "Would you

like me to drive you, or …?"

"No, thanks. You've been wonderful. There's a lot I need to sort out … by myself, you know?"

McCready nodded and watched her climb gingerly into the car. She started the engine and sat there for a few seconds trying to find the composure to carry on, then she lowered the window and gave him a look with a harder edge to it that said she was going to be okay. "We'll talk. I'll call you."

"Take care," he said.

After a final pause, she looked toward the narrow lane and drove away. As she left, the gold-and-brown autumn leaves that had fallen to the ground curled in the slipstream like some sort of marking of passage.

He watched her go but his mind was elsewhere. Inside, he was in turmoil. He could remember very little about the previous week. From the time the bell had locked onto the chamber on board *Recovery* it had all been like a bad dream, as though he were merely watching the actions of another man.

He could remember being dragged from the bell and a medic taking over Sean's resuscitation. He'd slumped in the corner of the chamber just staring at his brother. Gradually though, the pain of his shoulder had begun to creep in, diverting his attention. He found out later he had a minor fracture, nothing serious, but somehow the pain made it real—as though he deserved to suffer for not being able to save his brother. He'd sought comfort in the pain—he'd liked it.

A car drove past, nudging him from his thoughts. He glanced around and noticed a man standing by the gate into the church. He gave him a brief second glance and then remembered something, or rather someone who hadn't been at the funeral. He pulled out his cell phone, selected a number and hit CALL. The phone rang four times and then went to voicemail.

"Hi, this is Donovan. I'm at sea or in the pub. Talk at the beep."

McCready shook his head in frustration. "Steve, this is John McCready. I need to talk to you, man. Where the hell are you?"

He put the phone away, but his concern was still there. He'd been trying to contact Donovan since he'd been flown back to the mainland and cleared and released from hospital, but no one seemed to know where he was or how he could be reached.

He zipped his coat tighter against the increasing wind and walked down to his car that was parked on a slight slope at the side of the wooded lane. The highly modified Range Rover Sport had been decked out with a fender winch and a snorkel for river crossings. The black snake-like tube extended from the side of the engine and up the edge of the windscreen to the roof. It allowed the air-breathing engine to suck in air to the hungry pistons even if the car was semi-submerged in water. Things could get tough in the Highlands in winter—it was best to be prepared.

As he climbed in, he noticed the man he'd seen earlier. He was glancing his way and talking urgently into a phone. McCready was sure he'd seen him somewhere before but couldn't quite place him. He thought nothing of it, gunned the engine and drove off.

Connor Jennings watched McCready drive away. He held

the phone to his ear. "Yes, sir, he's still looking for Donovan. What would you like me to do?" He listened to the answer and then replied before ending the call.

"Understood."

Chapter 7

The Cayman Islands are located around two hundred miles to the south of Cuba and are one of the jewels of the Caribbean. The group is made up of three islands. The largest, Grand Cayman, lies to the west and slightly south of the two smaller islands, Little Cayman and Cayman Brac. They all sit bang in the middle of the hurricane belt, but for most of the year they enjoy pretty much permanent sunshine and are surrounded by crystal clear waters.

The islands have a renowned reputation for international banking and are the location of many a questionable offshore account, but to most people they represent one of the water sports capitals of the world.

Shaped rather like the profile of a shoe, Grand Cayman is around twenty miles long, is low-lying and fringed with palm trees and sandy beaches. George Town, the capital and home to many of the banks, sits where the heal of the shoe would be, while a massive chunk taken from the instep forms a wonderful shallow bay of turquoise water that has become home to one of the wonders of the underwater world.

For many years, local fishermen would return from fishing trips and take shelter behind the reef at the edge of the lagoon. Here, in only twelve feet of water, they would clean their catch and throw discarded fish parts over the side. The southern stingrays, which frequented the waters, quickly realized a free meal was on offer and have congregated there ever since. It became known as Stingray City, and there was nowhere else on Earth quite like it.

That morning, two female examples of one particular species were swimming with the stingrays. One was multicolored from top to bottom and moved smoothly through the water with a natural, effortless style, while the other had a rich ebony tone with small flashes of blue at strategic points of the body and had fins that flapped somewhat haphazardly without providing much propulsion. Both were at this moment tracking closely behind a large stingray as it swam gracefully around a coral head. They weren't perfect specimens of their kind. One had an inexplicable love of Rod Stewart albums and the other a propensity for pot plants of a dubious nature, but, even so, they would turn the heads of most male members of the species, and, as one of them would wish, some females too.

Clare Kowalski squirted a puff of air into her Oceanic buoyancy compensator (BC) and rose slightly above the seabed. She glanced at her companion and indicated for her to swim around the coral after the stingray. Jade Mancini gave the diver's okay signal and followed her friend.

As they rounded the coral they were met by five giant stingrays coming the other way. Like a squadron of

Vulcan bombers, the animals breezed up over their heads, before one peeled away, spun on a dime, and circled a few feet above them. For years the animals had been fed by divers and this one was clearly expecting a treat for its display.

Jade's eyes widened and she squealed with delight as she felt the underside of the ray brush across her head. Clare laughed through her mouthpiece at the sight of her friend wearing a stingray hat and almost spluttered as the smile lines creased her face letting water into her mask. She expertly cleared it away before she could sniff any up her nose, and then she took a piece of squid from her BC pocket to feed the ray. She held it up in a clenched fist with a small portion protruding so she didn't lose any fingers and watched the ray detach itself from Jade's head and glide over to her. It nibbled the squid for a few seconds before moving off and coming round for a second pass.

Clare was just about to take out another piece when she felt a tap on her shoulder. She glanced over and saw Jade indicating she was low on air. She acknowledged with an okay signal and gave the thumbs up to ascend the short distance to the surface. The rays would just have to find some other suckers to feed them.

Clare rose vertically, circling round with her hand above her head, checking for overzealous tourists on jet skis and other modes of aquatic transport that could run them down. Once she was above the water, she completed another three-sixty to make sure.

Just then, Jade burst through the surface with a WHOOP, pulling the mask from her face and resting it on the top of her head. Her mouthpiece fell into the water and spluttered away until Clare turned it face down to stop the free flow. Then she rescued the mask as it dropped off the back of her head.

"Whoooa! You see those babies? Follow you round like damn puppy dogs!"

Clare had to smile. "So you liked it, huh?"

Jade's eyes were shining. "Liked it? Best darn crazy thing you got me doin' yet, girl!"

Clare grinned, but she was also checking the location of their boat. She spotted the sleek Baja 26 Outlaw powerboat about twenty yards away bobbing patiently in the water. "Okay, now inflate your BC, then on your back and follow me to the boat."

"Yes, sir!"

The girls rolled onto their backs and, with extra air in their jackets giving them support, they gently finned back to the boat.

Clare looked up at the cloudless sky, feeling the water lap around her ears. "You know, this is just what I needed."

"Yeah, thinking time away from the jerk," said Jade.

"What jerk?"

"Atta girl."

A couple of minutes later and Clare climbed the small ladder onto the platform between the twin 300 horsepower Verado Mercury Marine outboards and the rear of the Baja. Once she was on board she unclipped her left shoulder strap and swung the aqualung and BC carefully onto the deck. She then turned to the ladder to help Jade on board. A minute later, Jade was standing next to her free of all her gear.

Both girls were dripping wet, and while Clare peeled

the top half of her dive suit to her waist, Jade stood there with the water glistening on her dark skin. She was still beaming and Clare had to laugh. "Not bad for your third dive. You're gonna be spoiled."

"You can spoil me all you want if that's what it's like!"

"Yeah, pretty cool, huh. How many years I been trying to get you to do this?"

"Too many. Don't worry, I'm sold!"

"Okay, go get the anchor and we'll head on back." Clare pulled her dark, shoulder-length hair into a ponytail, threaded it through the rear of a baseball cap, snapped some Wayfarer shades over her eyes and turned the key in the ignition. Immediately the massive black engines spluttered into life. She gently revved them to warm them up while Jade climbed onto the small foredeck and hauled up the anchor. She let the chain rattle into its plastic crate and was about to return when Clare mischievously gave the engines a slight kick, nearly sending her friend over the side.

"Oh, no you don't! Now I owe you!" Jade stumbled back behind the console and gave Clare a friendly shove. Clare grinned and pushed the throttles smoothly forward, easing the boat slowly away from the other divers' bubbles that were rising in small clusters from the seabed below.

She was just about to open up the engines when she spotted a banana boat approaching at speed. There were six screaming tourists bouncing around on the giant yellow inflatable towed by an aging Glastron speedboat with a faded white Evinrude engine. Four of them were kids and none were wearing lifejackets. The driver, who had the wheel in one hand and a bottle of Budweiser in the other, was spending more time laughing at the antics behind than on where he was going.

They were heading straight for the dive site.

Clare shook her head. "Idiots." And with that she gunned the engine, sending the Baja up onto the plane as six hundred horses dug into the clear waters, propelling them forward at breakneck speed.

The boat skimmed across the water, the hull crackling over the gentle chop that had appeared on the surface.

The banana boat was fifty yards away when the driver looked up and saw the Baja. He yelled something unintelligible, but certainly not friendly, and waved his arm for them to get out of the way. Clare turned smoothly away from the boat, while at the same time glancing sharply at Jade.

"Hang on!"

Jade took her friend's advice, gripping the handrail on the side of the speeding craft.

In one controlled movement Clare eased the wheel round and powered the boat through a full circle to come up just behind the Glastron.

The tourists on the inflatable watched the Baja and clung on as their ride bounced precariously across the waves. Clare nudged the throttles forward and drew alongside. They were doing about thirty knots, but the engines were merely cruising.

The driver of the Glastron looked over, shouting above the scream of the engine. "What the hell you doing? Get out of the way!"

"Hey, you need to slow down, there's a dive area ahead," Clare shouted back. The driver clearly didn't give a damn, continuing to wave at her with hostile hand gestures. He pushed the throttle forward.

Clare glanced back at the tourists. The kids were not having fun anymore. In fact, the frequent screams were no longer shouts of joy.

She quickly assessed her options. They were now only about a hundred feet from the dive site. To the right was a shallow sandbar. She gave a wry grin and edged closer to the Glastron.

The driver wasn't going to slow down.

Suddenly there was a cry from behind as one of the kids was thrown into the water. Now even the parents were shouting to STOP. But the driver was deaf to the calls. He kept glancing at Clare and accelerating. There was nothing for it. She moved closer until the two sides were almost touching, then sharply turned the wheel to the right.

The two hulls collided.

There was a wrenching and squealing of fiberglass, but the larger powerboat easily pushed the Glastron off its course and away from the dive site, but Clare didn't stop once they were clear. She kept on going until she was sure they were dead in line, then she throttled back.

The banana boat sped on. The driver was clearly convinced she'd given up and flicked her a "get lost" sign with his fingers. He was still convinced she had given in, right up to the point where the boat hit the sandbar, slowing to a dead stop in about half a second. He was somersaulted clean over the windscreen to land with a splash of flailing arms and legs in the shallow water beyond.

The yellow banana glided up behind the Glastron, bumping gently into the rear of the beached boat. The remaining tourists slid slowly off the side, visibly shaken by their ordeal.

Clare checked the driver was in one piece. "Think he's learned his lesson for one day," she said, and then she circled round to pick up the kid who had been thrown into the water.

Jade looked at her with affection and respect, "Damn, girl, you always gotta do the right thing."

An hour later and the girls were again staring up at a cloudless sky, only this time from a couple of wide canvas hammocks strung beneath lush palms in the grounds of the exclusive Cayman Palm Resort.

The luxurious hotel was located just along from Rum Point on the north side of the island. It was a secluded slice of paradise, well-away from the more densely packed establishments along Seven Mile Beach in the west. The rooms were made up of individual villas furnished in a rustic style with open decks and personal infinity pools that looked out onto the sea. It was all set in grounds of pristine lawns sprinkled with strategic palms to provide much-needed shade from the burning sun.

The girls had arrived two days earlier and were just starting to relax and enjoy the laid-back ambience.

Jade had insisted Clare needed to get away from it all after the end of a disastrous relationship. So while Clare had chosen the Caymans as the destination, it had been down to Jade to find the accommodation. The girl had done good.

They had met in the tenth grade at high school and at first had loathed each other—they had both been interested in the same boy. That had quickly passed though when they realized he was cheating on both of them with a cheerleader from the school football team. They had then become firm friends after realizing there was a common enemy and were soon over their differences.

After that they were inseparable. Even when they were eighteen and Jade had realized she actually wasn't interested in boys at all and had drunkenly propositioned Clare after a late-night end of term party, there wasn't an issue. Clare remembered feeling really strange for about thirty seconds, then breaking out into a huge smile and hugging her friend for all she was worth. She'd told her it would never happen but that she was incredibly flattered. She'd felt wonderful inside and knew she would have a friend for life and there would be a bond between them that could never be broken. Instead of the moment being really awkward, they'd both ended up in fits of laughter before ending in a tearful hug.

So where one went, the other tended to follow, and that had led to right now, fourteen years later, and the idyllic setting next to the sparkling Caribbean Sea.

Clare was just trying to nod off when Jade nudged her with her foot. "Refreshment time." She propped herself up on one elbow.

Heading their way from a small bar at the edge of the sand was a young, smartly dressed waiter. He wore a tight white cotton shirt and neatly pressed black trousers. He made his way among the palms and carried two tall daiquiris topped with refreshing ice on a small tray. As he approached, Clare noticed Jade looking him up and down. Beneath the shirt was a well-toned body, which was covered in a rich mahogany tan that simply oozed sex appeal. He was in his early twenties and had a boyish charm that didn't scream arrogance or predator.

The waiter, whose name was Marco, according to the small badge on his chest, finally reached them and set the glasses down on the table between the two girls.

"Here you go ladies—long, soft and cold."

"Forget that," said Jade. "You got anything long, hard and warm for my friend here?"

Clare gave her an embarrassed kick and desperately looked for a place to hide, but when you were wearing a black thong and not much else, there weren't too many places you could go.

The waiter hesitated for a second, gave a sheepish smile, then blushed and disappeared as fast as he could.

"What?" asked Jade innocently. "You know you need it, honey. Just trying to help."

"You're too bad, girl."

"Someone has to be."

Jade reached for her glass and sipped the cool drink. Clare grinned and was trying to think of a smartass reply when her phone rang. Jade gave her a dark look. "And I thought we agreed, no phones on vacation."

Clare picked up the device and checked the screen. She groaned. "I have to take it, it's the office."

Five minutes later, Clare clicked off the phone, took a deep breath and turned to Jade.

"Oh no, don't tell me, girl!"

Clare's face was pleading. "They've moved the trip forward. There's nothing I can do."

"So when we talking about?"

"I have to be in London on Tuesday, so that means a flight out of LA, Monday afternoon latest."

It was now Saturday.

Disappointment was written across Jade's face, but then she sighed and tried to hide a smile. "You so owe me, girl." Clare looked desolate. "And I am so going to love thinking of ways for you to make it up to me!"

Clare grabbed a pillow from the hammock and threw it at her friend.

Jade continued. "So, London, huh. Sure you're ready for the culture shock?"

Clare looked at her and grinned. "Hey, it's not like it's the first time, and it's not that bad—they got princes and all."

"Thought you were done with dysfunctional families."

Clare smiled and lay back in the hammock, staring up at the gently swaying palms. The sun sparkled through the fronds, playing across her body as they moved in the warm breeze.

She stretched out like a cat and allowed herself to relax as the hammock soothingly rocked her to and fro. She was determined to enjoy the last few hours of freedom. She knew the trip to London would be no picnic.

Chapter 8

It had taken McCready over three and a half hours to drive from his home on the west coast of Scotland across the width of the country to the approaches to Edinburgh. That was half an hour longer than usual, but a lorry had spilled its load on the A84 just south of Callander and traffic had been at a crawl while cars negotiated the single-file restrictions in place. A second incident had completely closed the M9 south of Stirling and had meant he had to divert along a route to the north of the River Forth. Must be those Monday morning blues.

He'd received the request to meet with Malcolm Mercer at the company headquarters the day following Sean's funeral and he was curious about what was to unfold.

He was now crossing over the Forth Road Bridge and as ever was taken aback by the view.

To his left, the iconic, rust-colored rail bridge that had been standing since 1890 jutted out of the water. It looked for all the world like some sort of metallic prehistoric monster, and he could almost imagine that one day it would stand up and march off across the Forth to the North Sea beyond. Today though, it was standing still and conditions in the estuary were good. He was able to make out a number of small fishing boats bobbing over the light swell as they headed out to the fishing grounds.

His attention was brought back to the road by the officious-sounding voice of his sat nav. It was female, no-nonsense and directed him in no uncertain terms to take an upcoming left turn. He kind of liked it when she talked like that.

Once over the bridge it didn't take him long to reach the turn, and after a final instruction that he wasn't prepared to argue with he headed down a newly tarmacked road that had only one destination.

He drove for a couple of minutes with fields and rambling hedges on either side and then eventually came to a security gate that blocked his way. He gave his details to a guard in a small hut, and after his name had been checked with the system, he was handed a coded key card with an LCD screen. The guard explained it would allow him access to wherever he needed to go and also provide directions within the compound. What he failed to mention was that the card also tracked his location.

The security barrier lifted and McCready drove into the grounds of the complex.

The parking spaces were attractively arranged in a series of landscaped layers among trees and grass banks on the side of a gently sloping hill.

He found his allocated spot, N54, pulled the Range Rover smoothly in, then climbed out into the crisp morning air and scanned the key card on the sensor at the side to register the vehicle. The card blipped and the small GPS-enabled display lit up to show the route he should follow to the main building.

Two minutes later he was approaching the spectacular entrance.

Sixty thousand square feet of glass covered the strikingly designed corporate headquarters of Global Salvage. The curved sides of the building towered either side of the massive double entrance doors, giving the impression of power and prestige. They were made up of a series of large diamond-shaped panes of glass, each around eight feet in height and held together by a latticework of metal struts. These stretched up to the top of the building where they wrapped over to meet in the center, forming the roof. Each pane was arranged at a slightly different angle, creating a myriad of reflections across the surface and causing the building to glitter in the morning sunlight like a giant diamond in the rough.

In all his years of working for the company McCready had never been to its headquarters, and he couldn't help but be impressed. He'd passed it many times on his way to Edinburgh, but seeing it up close with the backdrop of the Forth gave it a whole new perspective.

He was glad he'd decided to wear a suit. It felt appropriate for the place—corporate, intimidating. He wished his shirt collar were looser though. Wearing a tie was somewhat alien to him, and although the effect was almost as bad as a tight neck seal on a drysuit, that was worn hundreds of feet below the surface and could be excused. Somehow, walking around in daylight above water should not involve having your neck constrained.

On either side of the entrance were two striking exhibits. One was a full-size commercial diving bell. McCready noted it was a Unique Hydra model, one he'd spent many hours in and which represented the sharp end of Global Salvage's activities. The other was a fully detailed replica of the *Esperanza*, a Spanish galleon that had sunk in 1806. It was this wreck that had made the company what it was today. McCready was a few minutes early so he wandered over to take a look.

It had been created solely out of stainless steel, complete with features that were represented as embossed highlights across its surface. These included an array of canon down each side, an exotic figurehead at the front, and the rigging and sails above the deck. It was an impressive sight, even at quarter scale, and represented a fitting tribute to the source of the company's success.

As the story went, Malcolm Mercer, along with his business partner Clive Farley, had found the galleon off a small coral atoll in the Philippines in the late nineties. It had been known to be carrying a fantastic treasure and had been one of the last great undiscovered shipwrecks of Spanish heritage that every treasure hunter had been desperate to find. But nothing could have prepared them for the haul they would uncover when they eventually located her and brought the contents of her cargo to the surface.

At the time, Mercer and Farley were enthusiastic amateurs. Farley had access to family money and Mercer had sold his house, throwing everything into the ring to help fund the project—putting it all on black, so to speak. But it had paid off handsomely, as the jewels and precious metals recovered had resulted in a $1.6 billion payday.

The venture hadn't been without controversy and tragedy though. During the diving operation, Farley had lost his life when a lift bag carrying a canon to the surface had split. The canon had fallen back into the depths, hitting Farley who had been helping to survey part of the wreck. It had knocked him unconscious and ripped the regulator from his mouth, leaving him without a breathing source. The controversy had stemmed from the fact that this was the only time Farley had been diving with a regular face mask and separate regulator, rather than a full face mask. If he'd been wearing a full face mask it would have allowed him to keep breathing even when unconscious and given another diver time to reach him. The reason given was that all the spare masks were down for repair or servicing, but later a brand new one had been found in the gear locker of the dive boat. As with all controversies, conspiracy theories were born and foul play was suspected, but nothing had ever been proven.

Mercer, who had been on the support vessel at the time, had merely commented that "accidents happen," and then calmly taken control of the operation.

The end result: the greatest financial find in underwater history and the birth of Global Salvage.

McCready took one final look at the elegant ship and then headed for the entrance.

Four floors above, and in an office that covered the entire fourth and top floor of the building, Malcolm Mercer dropped a report sheet on his desk and looked pointedly at Connor Jennings.

Mercer's office was a grand yet restrained space. The reason your jaw dropped when you entered was that the entire sides and roof were made up of the exterior glass diamonds rolling over and coming together as one in the center. Each diamond was made up of light-dimming glass, which automatically tracked the sun to ensure light intensity and temperature in the room remained at an acceptable level.

Looking out to the front, you could see over fields to the city of Edinburgh several miles away, while at the rear the view stretched over a back lot, complete with helipad, to the Firth of Forth beyond. The road and rail bridges were to the west and the sea to the east. It was a good view from which to conduct international business.

The other impressive feature was the central section of the floor, which was made of reinforced glass and looked down into the main atrium below.

The rest of the room was smart, modern, and had clearly cost a fortune in a stylish sort of way. A large glass-topped desk resided at one end, and in the corners, artifacts from previous projects had pride of place.

There was an actual canon from the *Esperanza*, the requisite hard-hat diving helmet that no collection should be without, and an anchor from a German battleship that had to be lifted in by crane during the construction of the building. At the opposite end to the desk, a bank of video monitors stretched from floor to ceiling, displaying Global Salvage operations from around the world in real time, as well as security camera feeds from the complex. For casual meetings, a number of leather couches were arranged in a semicircle looking out over the Forth. Entrance to the office was accessed via an escalator that rose through the floor close to the video wall.

Jennings eyed the report on the desk and knew what was coming. He walked over from the glass at the rear and waited for Mercer to speak. When he did so, he was all business, but he clearly wasn't happy.

"With *Recovery*'s bow thruster down, she's been pulled off site. Looks like the repairs could take weeks." Mercer looked directly at Jennings. "That was a mess, Connor. We need to recover at least eighty percent. I can't get another ship on site for days, and the new inspection team will be all over her. It's bad enough having snoopers from the Treasury, but a bloody Russian! Can you handle it?"

Jennings thought for a second before replying. "Once they're on board things will be more tricky. We had it set up nicely on *Recovery*, but we'll do it. No problem."

Mercer looked at him sharply. "The divers know what to do? We have to go with a three-man team now. After the McCready incident there are eyes on us. We can't afford any more screwups."

"Fisher, Rizby and Stringer are fine. You could see dollar signs in their eyes when I went through it with them. They won't be any trouble. It looks like McCready's accident was rather timely. Those two were never going to play ball."

"You'd better be right. As my head of security I need to know these things are handled. I'm going to send him on leave. Keep him out of the way for a while."

"Probably a good idea."

"If he gets too inquisitive there's a backup, a press release, but I don't want to go there unless I have to. Just make sure he doesn't talk to Donovan."

"His phones are tapped, but we're not sure where Donovan is right now."

"Then try to find him … and Connor …"

"Yes, sir."

"Don't let this get out of control."

"No, sir."

McCready walked through into the main entrance.

As the automatic doors moved smoothly closed behind him, he found himself in a tall, air-conditioned reception area. It stretched almost the full height of the building, and as he looked up he could see the curved glass rolling over above him.

To either side were minimalist reception desks manned by three staff. Both desks channeled you toward a large white arch, which everyone had to pass through to gain further access to the building. He could see it was clearly a security scanner. The guard at the gate had told him to just walk straight through, as his key card would identify him to the system. He wouldn't even need to remove it from his pocket.

He took it out just in case and proceeded through the arch. A soft beep announced that he'd been verified and a glass barrier slid smoothly into the floor allowing him to proceed. Once through, he glanced at the screen on the card. It showed the layout of the interior and an arrow indicating he should head straight ahead toward the main atrium in the center.

Four floors above, the haptic feedback on the underside of Connor Jennings' Apple Watch tapped twice, causing him to glance at the display. He tapped a round app in the center of the cluster and a small map appeared. It showed McCready's position within the building moving toward the central atrium. "He's here," he said, looking over at Mercer.

"Okay, remember what I said and keep me advised on

the Donovan situation."

"Yes, sir." And with that Jennings turned and headed for the small escalator that disappeared into the floor. Mercer hit an intercom.

"Marian, you can send John McCready up when he arrives."

McCready stepped out of the elevator on the third floor and followed the guidance on the key card around the galleried level that overlooked the atrium. It took him to a desk with an efficient-looking secretary who glanced up at his arrival. She smiled pleasantly and spoke with a soft Scottish lilt. "Good morning, Mr McCready, you can go right up." She indicated the escalator, and after thanking her, McCready walked over and started the short ascent to the floor above.

He was halfway up when he noticed a man heading down the other way. He glanced over. There was something familiar about him. He watched his back disappear below, and then he had it—the man at the church. But then he was rising up into Mercer's office and his attention was elsewhere.

As he looked around the room he was taken aback by the style and form of the space he was in. The sun was higher now and the dimmed glass formed a barrier across the central section, seeming to divide the area into two. He was on one side, and, as he looked across the room, Mercer was on the other.

The head of Global Salvage glanced up and gave him a second to take in the surroundings. Then he rose casually and walked over to greet McCready halfway.

"John, good of you to come in. I'm sorry about your

brother."

McCready was still looking around the room, but then he turned his gaze to Mercer. The man was smaller than he'd imagined, probably four or five inches shorter than himself, but there was that air about him that everyone commented on—something serious, something you didn't want to cross.

He returned the even stare he was receiving and shook hands with the man who had been his boss for over ten years. It was a strong grip, but one that didn't last long, as though merely a gesture that had to be entertained but meant nothing more. No friendship, only protocol.

"Won't you sit down?" Mercer indicated the semicircle of couches that framed the windows at the rear.

Once seated, Mercer looked out briefly across the water and then turned to McCready. "That was a bad business out there. The weather can be so cruel." McCready looked at the man.

"Yes, sir it can, and thank you for your condolences. No one ever said it was a safe profession. You minimize the risks and then what happens, happens."

Mercer absorbed this for a second and then replied.

"I can see you're a pragmatist. How long have you worked for us, John, eight years?"

McCready was pretty sure Mercer knew otherwise but corrected him anyway. "Ten actually, sir."

"Ten …" Mercer seemed to mull this over. "That's a long time. Shows loyalty."

He seemed to be coming to a decision. "In light of recent events I'm going to do something I've never done before. I would like you to take two months' leave on double pay. I know it's not much, but you need the rest.

You deserve the rest, and it's the least I can do for your commitment over the years and the loss you've suffered."

Suddenly the phone bleeped on Mercer's desk. A flash of irritation crossed his face.

"Sorry about this, I have to take it."

McCready raised a hand as if to say "by all means," and Mercer went to answer the call. While he was speaking, McCready noticed a small black spec out over the Forth that was growing larger by the second. He stood up and walked over to the glass.

A Jet Ranger was approaching the complex. He watched as it approached. It was aiming straight for the building. As it came closer it circled to the right and then came in to hover about a hundred feet in front of him and at around the same height. McCready could feel the vibration through the glass of the extreme forces at play required to keep the machine in the air. For a second the pilot glanced over and they locked eyes, then his concentration was back on the landing. The machine descended smoothly to the ground and took its place next to a white Bell 222.

McCready glanced back at Mercer, but he was still embroiled in an animated conversation on the phone. He turned to the rest of the room and walked over to the bank of video screens.

The video wall was an impressive sight. There were twelve screens, arranged in three rows of four columns. Any one of them would have made a great home cinema display. Eight were currently showing Global Salvage projects from around the world.

McCready moved closer to one of the screens.

The mechanical arm of an ROV was turning a wheel

on a pipe fixture on the seabed. He checked the information running in real time in the top right-hand corner. It showed a depth of four hundred and sixty-five feet and a location that would put it somewhere in the South China Sea just off Singapore. The camera was clearly mounted on the ROV, and as he watched, the arm finished turning the wheel and the machine backed off to reveal a large complex of pipes and valves. Even though it was an everyday occurrence, he still marveled at the ability to stand in a room in Scotland and watch live pictures of a machine working at the bottom of the sea half a world away.

Other screens showed a wreck survey in the Mediterranean off Sardinia and a filming job using rebreathers in the Caribbean. The remaining screens showed CCTV security cameras from around the complex in Scotland.

One of the cameras showed a large flatbed truck carrying a damaged propeller on its trailer. He checked the information in the corner of the screen. It said HQ – BACK. The truck must be entering a rear entrance to the complex.

As he watched he could make out some large gas cylinders on the flatbed, but as it approached he noticed there was something odd about them that he couldn't quite put his finger on. He was about to move closer to get a clearer look when Mercer returned from his desk.

"Sorry about that. Major problem with a South African contract. Now, where were we?"

McCready turned from the screens and walked over to Mercer.

"You had just made me a very generous offer."

"Ah yes. As I said, it's the least we can do, John."

"It is very generous, Mr Mercer, but I'm afraid I'll have to decline." Mercer's stare hardened. "It's just that I'd prefer to get right back to work," McCready continued. "To sit around kicking my heels for two months, or whatever, would be frustrating. Too much time to dwell on things."

Mercer looked at him for a second and then walked over to his desk. It seemed he wished McCready to join him, so he followed him over.

Mercer took a sheet of paper from a side drawer and placed it on a small pad that faced McCready. He swiveled it round so McCready could read it. "I can understand how you feel, but I'm afraid it's not an offer. I don't think your mind would be on things right now, and with recent events I can't afford any more mistakes." His tone seemed to have changed slightly and any inclination toward friendliness or sympathy was rapidly disappearing. McCready was taken aback for a second and was about to speak when Mercer continued. "This document covers all the details—you know, legal stuff, saying you accept the terms—and at the end of the two months an assessment will be made in determination of your future."

"My future?"

Mercer looked at him coolly in a way that implied McCready should understand what was going on here. "I can't have my divers screwing up, getting killed and bringing negative attention on the company. You understand?"

McCready was stunned. "That's what you think happened, that Sean screwed up?" He could feel the anger growing but managed to keep it under control.

Mercer looked bored.

"Well someone did, didn't they?" The stare was piercing.

"Yes, sir, they did."

"So, are you going to sign this?" McCready could see Mercer's mind was already turning to other matters—more important matters.

He picked up the document and checked it over. It was pretty much as described. The offer was for two months. The pay was more than generous. There was a certain amount of legalese, nothing serious. But there was something else—a commitment for him to stay away from Global Salvage premises, which he found somewhat strange.

The room suddenly lit up as the sun emerged from behind a bank of clouds, and before the auto tint roof glass could do its thing, the shadows of the latticework of metal stanchions seemed like a giant cage enclosing the room. He finally put the sheet down and looked across at Mercer. "It looks fine to me, but I think I should get my lawyer to check it over, just to be sure."

The irritation in Mercer's voice was barely concealed. "The offer expires today. I'm being more than fair. If you don't accept it, okay, but it could be a problem where we go from here." His gaze looked straight through McCready.

McCready sighed. There had been enough complications in his life recently. Maybe the break would be what he needed. "What have I got to lose?" He grabbed the paper, pulled out a pen and was about to sign, when Mercer stopped him.

"On the pad."

He indicated the padded mat on the desk.

McCready hesitated for a second and then put the paper on the pad and signed and dated at the bottom. He passed it back to Mercer, who checked it over, and then clicked a mouse. A printer whirred and an exact copy spewed out of a Canon desktop printer, complete with McCready's signature on the bottom.

"Scanner built into the pad. Makes things easier," explained Mercer.

He passed the copy to McCready, who folded it and slid it into his jacket pocket without even looking.

"Well I think that about wraps it up," said Mercer. "Once again, I'm sorry for your loss. Have a good rest, John. You never know what the future will bring." He made no move to shake hands or even get up.

McCready glanced around the office one more time. Out of the rear windows he noticed that the flatbed truck he'd seen earlier on the video wall had made its way onto the back lot. He could see it more clearly now and more specifically the row of high-pressure cylinders on the back, but again there was something not quite right. Mercer noticed the hesitation and followed his gaze. McCready turned back to Mercer.

"Thank you, sir. The visit has been quite an eye-opener."

Mercer looked at him thoughtfully for a moment, nodded, then turned his attention to his computer and started typing.

McCready took a final look out of the window and then made his way to the escalator. Before he stepped on it, he looked back. "By the way, sir, I've been trying to contact Steve Donovan. You wouldn't happen to know if anything's happened to him, would you?"

Mercer looked up. "Donovan no longer works for the company. I have no idea where he might be."

McCready looked confused. "No longer works for the company?"

"His actions were largely responsible for the incident on *Recovery* and your brother's death. He insisted you stay down and work in the face of worsening conditions."

"But Donovan is one of the best dive supervisors in the industry."

"That wouldn't appear to be the case, would it."

McCready didn't reply, unable to believe what he'd just heard. He stepped slowly onto the escalator.

As he disappeared through the floor, Mercer watched him thoughtfully. Then, following a confirmation beep from the computer, he clicked the mouse on his desk. The printer whirred again and another document spewed out. He picked it up and looked it through. It was very different to the one McCready had signed earlier, but there, in a distinctive scrawl at the bottom of the printed text, dated with today's date, was McCready's signature, clear as day.

Chapter 9

As McCready stood in the elevator heading down he thought back over the encounter with Mercer. To be honest he hadn't known what to expect, but by any measure it wouldn't have been what had just transpired. If nothing else, he now believed every story he'd ever heard about the man. It also put a number of other things into perspective. Firstly, he'd been shaken by what Mercer had said about Donovan. Frankly, he didn't believe a word of it. He'd known the man a long time and he would never put his divers at risk, particularly when conditions were so extreme. Secondly, there had been things he'd noticed on *Recovery* between shifts that in isolation meant very little, but in the context of what had happened put them in a whole new light. Something that sprang immediately to mind was that often when the other team of divers, Fisher and Rizby, had been caught in conversations, they'd suddenly shut down, not wanting to talk when he and his brother had been around. This all led to the inescapable conclusion that something was going on that wasn't exactly above board.

The elevator arrived smoothly at the entrance level and

a muted BING announced its arrival. The doors slid open and McCready walked out into the main atrium.

The other thing that was bothering him was the stack of cylinders he'd seen on the flatbed truck that had driven onto the back lot. He still couldn't put his finger on what it was precisely. It was something he'd noticed on the metal surface, some sort of anomaly. There was only one way to find out—take a closer look.

He glanced around the large central atrium.

It was striking—oval in shape, and on the narrower sides, two wide walkways led out to the glass diamonds that made up the exterior of the building. The inner walls on all sides extended up toward the glass in the ceiling, which was the floor of Mercer's office. In the center, water cascaded over a feature surrounded by tall, exotic plants in a calming, soothing manner as it flowed over several levels. The remaining space was filled with a seating area scattered with pockets of tables and chairs. There were a number of people seated at the tables. Some were drinking coffee, reading a paper and relaxing, while others were involved in intense discussions, clearly using the space for ad hoc business meetings.

As McCready looked around, no one seemed to be paying him any undue attention. He spotted a door at the far side that looked like it might lead outside. He headed over, and once there, he glanced through the small glass window in the door and saw a short corridor that did lead to a door that led outside.

He pulled out his key card and touched it against the scanner at the side. There was an angry beep and the words NO AUTHORIZED ACCESS appeared in red on the screen.

He stepped back and considered his options.

Glancing around, still no one was paying him any attention. He decided to wait, and sure enough, it wasn't long before someone exited the door. He pulled out his phone, put it to his ear, as though deep in conversation, and moved quickly through before the door could bang shut, nodding at the woman who had just walked through as he went.

Once in the passage beyond he had to smile. Whenever he'd seen someone do that in the movies, it had always seemed so contrived, but it was true—wait long enough by a closed door and someone would eventually walk through it.

In an office on the first floor, Connor Jennings received an urgent tapping on his wrist from his watch. He glanced down and frowned. The display showed McCready had accessed an area at the rear of the building. He pulled out his phone and hit a speed dial number.

"Yes," answered Mercer.

"McCready's heading out to the back lot. What would you like me to do?"

Mercer paused before answering. "Make sure he finds his way back to his car … sooner rather than later. And Connor …"

"Yes, sir."

"Play nice."

Jennings put the phone away and headed to the rear of the building.

McCready was about to take the exit that led outside when he spotted a label on a door further down the corridor that said "Armory." *Armory?* Why on earth would Global Salvage need an armory? But then he remembered that part of the empire involved marine protection and security. Piracy at sea had rocketed over recent years and insurance companies were no longer prepared to insure vessels in certain parts of the world unless they had adequate personnel and firepower on board to protect themselves.

He wandered over and tried the handle. As expected, it was locked. He returned to the exit that led to the back lot and peered through the glass. The coast was clear, so he opened the door and stepped outside.

Immediately in front of him were a number of large metal shipping containers stacked two high in two rows of four. He walked past them and found himself in a large open area about half the size of a football pitch. As he'd seen earlier, the black Jet Ranger was sitting on a helipad on the far side next to the Bell 222. A couple of mechanics were working on the undercarriage of the Bell, which had been jacked up. Parked to one side of the helicopters were three black Toyota Land Cruisers. Over to the right was a small office, in front of which was the flatbed truck. Someone was checking over the load on the back of the flatbed. The guy took a couple of photos with a digital camera then headed back into the office.

McCready made his way over to the truck.

On the carrying deck the large propeller lay in a sorry state. It had *Recovery* written on a label on one of the blades and was clearly from the dive support vessel. One of the blades had been completely sheared off, and there were large cracks in the other two. It must have struck something with great force to do this sort of damage.

What he really wanted to see, though, were the large gas cylinders stacked alongside the propeller. Each was about six feet in length and similar to the ones arranged around the outside of a diving bell, and which provided a separate gas supply in case of emergencies. About two feet from the top of each of them was a mark that encircled the entire cylinder. It was as though they'd been welded together. This didn't make sense. Any weld of this type in a cylinder would render it useless and unable to be pressurized. He was about to move closer when he heard footsteps on lose gravel.

Someone was behind him.

"Mr. McCready."

McCready turned slowly and saw the man he'd seen on the escalator standing by the end of the flatbed. He was smartly dressed, perfectly still, legs slightly apart, and he was looking straight at him.

"I believe you're in a restricted area. I'm afraid I'm going to have to ask you to leave." His tone was friendly, but matter of fact, and left no room for argument.

McCready hesitated for a second. "Really? Sorry, I got a bit lost. Then I saw all this gear and just wanted to take a look." He indicated the propeller on the truck. "The prop took quite a beating."

Jennings glanced briefly at the propeller and then back at McCready. "My name's Connor Jennings, Mr McCready. I handle security for Mr Mercer. Sort of troubleshoot situations for him. I think we both know your statement isn't entirely true, now don't we?" McCready wasn't fazed by this.

"You were at my brother's funeral, weren't you?"

Jennings gave a nod of acknowledgment. "Just showing

the company's presence. Mark of respect."

McCready half smiled, returning the stare. "I think we both know that statement isn't entirely true, don't we?"

Jennings smiled. "Come on, John, this way." He indicated the direction back to the main building. He turned, not even bothering to check if McCready was following.

Four floors above, Mercer watched the scene play out from his office. His expression was grim but other matters were pressing and he returned to his desk.

McCready followed Jennings all the way back to the car park, where he climbed into the Range Rover, closed the door and started the engine.

Jennings stood back and watched as McCready reversed out of the space. Before he drove off though, the head of security tapped on the glass. McCready glanced at him and lowered the window. "Remember the statement you signed, John. Stay away from Global properties, okay?"

"News travels fast."

"Well, big organization like this. Need to be on top things," said Jennings.

McCready raised the window and drove off without another look. Jennings watched him go. Somehow he knew he'd be seeing him again, and probably sooner than he would have liked.

Chapter 10

The Grampian Mountains cut a diagonal swathe through central Scotland and were one of the main geographical features of the region. They provided a truly breathtaking backdrop to any journey and a scenic route that was both beautiful and dramatic, but McCready's mind was elsewhere.

The beauty of the country was embedded in his brain. The sloping mountains, the high waterfalls, the impressive rock faces were all subliminally taken in as the miles rolled under the car, but he was thinking of Mercer, Jennings and his current position within Global Salvage, if indeed he even had one anymore. It had all happened so suddenly, and he couldn't quite work out why.

He was negotiating a particularly tight hairpin when his phone rang. He was concentrating on the turn and let it ring a couple of times before clicking the button that linked the phone through the car speakers via Bluetooth.

"McCready."

A breathless voice came over the speaker and immediately had McCready's attention. "John, it's Steve."

"Steve, I didn't recognize the number. Where the hell

—?"

But Donovan broke in. "Just listen. I don't have much time. I had to ditch the phone. Using a disposable. Where are you now?"

"Er, just west of Crianlarich, heading home. Look, Steve, we really have to talk."

"I know. How long will it take you to get to the viewpoint on Lomond where we met after that ferry job?"

"I don't know. Not long, half an hour or so I suppose. Depends on traffic. What's this all about?"

"I can't tell you now, but bad things are happening. I'm leaving the country. I'll explain when I see you. I'll be there in about an hour. And be careful, your phone is probably hacked."

"Steve …"

But he was gone. McCready gripped the wheel in frustration. That was completely unlike Donovan. He was always so calm, whatever the situation, but something had spooked him and spooked him badly.

Standing in the atrium at Global Salvage, Jennings played back the phone conversation between Donovan and McCready. He thought for a second and then pressed a name on the contacts list. The phone rang four times and then was answered. Jennings spoke quickly. "Take Rizby and Stringer and cover the viewpoints on Lomond. Donovan must have ditched his phone, but we can track McCready. Use access code DC943J on the trace. McCready will lead you to Donovan. Whatever happens, make sure they don't speak. You have less than an hour, and the gloves are off. Now move!"

He ended the call. Things were getting interesting, but

he had confidence in Fisher. He'd come through for him on more than one occasion with certain "off-book" tasks he'd asked him to perform.

He'd get the job done.

In a modern detached house on the outskirts of Glasgow, Steve Donovan threw the last of a few belongings into a medium-sized rucksack. As he moved through the rooms, it was as though he was walking through a war zone.

The place had been ransacked.

Every piece of furniture had been turned upside down. Bookcases had been pulled over and cabinets smashed. He was under no illusion as to who was responsible, and once he'd grabbed the final few items he needed, he ran out of the back door, across a small yard, and in through the side door of a large double garage.

He was dressed in full racing leathers and carried a helmet in his hand. He flicked a remote and the garage door slid smoothly up into the roof.

In the middle of the floor stood a bright red Suzuki 500cc racer. He threw the rucksack on his back, climbed on the bike, pulled on his helmet, revved the engine and sped out onto the street, narrowly missing a car coming the other way.

The car blared its horn, but Donovan was already a hundred yards up the road and only looking forward. His past life lay behind him and he was heading for an uncertain future, but he knew what had to be done and he knew what was right.

Chapter 11

Five thousand miles away, in the heat and humidity of the California sunshine, another bike headed down a street, but this one had slightly less horsepower, being propelled by one human power.

Clare Kowalski pedaled up the small hill and rode into the back yard of Jade's apartment block in Malibu Palisades, just along the coast from Los Angeles. Although the hill wasn't very steep and Clare considered herself to be in pretty good shape, the humidity was high and she was sweating buckets before she'd even reached the shelter of Jade's property.

This was the last thing she needed, as she had a flight to catch in less than three hours and she had no time to shower. She'd just have to use the facilities in the airport lounge. At least she was traveling first class and would be able to relax once on board.

The earliest flight they'd been able to catch back from the Caymans had landed at LAX late the previous evening, and since then things had been in a state of controlled chaos to get everything ready for the trip to London. Clearly, though it hadn't been controlled enough, given Clare's recent excursion on the bike. She was sure she'd thought of everything, but the ten tins of dog food in the panniers was proof she had not. Retrievers eat a lot at the best of times, but when you're a growing puppy, your whole life seemed to revolve around the next edible input.

She lugged the tins up to the second-floor apartment and plonked them on the kitchen table, then checked her watch. The cab would be there in fifteen minutes and she still wasn't completely packed.

She'd been staying with Jade since the recent end of a five-year relationship. Her ex-partner had been younger than her and ran his own tech company. She'd been wowed by his ambition and success and had moved into his grand mansion just outside San Francisco with the starry-eyed belief that they'd be together forever. They'd never married as he didn't believe in it—something that should maybe have set off a few alarm bells. It had all ended when she'd caught him cheating on her with his dentist, of all people—and in their bedroom.

She'd come home early from a business trip and had wanted to surprise him. Instead, it was she who had received the surprise, and she'd rung Jade the same night. There was no way she could stay in the place another minute.

Subsequently she'd moved in with her best friend. It wasn't ideal. Most of her things were in storage and Jade did have her idiosyncrasies, but she loved her dearly and there was nowhere else she would rather be while going through this difficult time.

That had been two months ago.

She heard the door bang downstairs and Jade appeared

shortly after in a tight lycra running suit. She was out of breath and looked flushed. The heat had got to her too. She quickly spotted the cans.

"I coulda got those, girl. You got a flight to catch."

"Yeah, well, had to make sure you got the right ones. I don't want my baby starving now, do I?"

"As if he would."

Clare retreated to her bedroom to cram the last few things into her suitcase. Despite the shortened trip to the Caribbean, the break had done her a world of good—made her forget things she wanted to forget and given her a new positive attitude for the future. Now though, she had to concentrate on the trip ahead. It was going to be hard work.

She was trying to force the suitcase shut when Jade walked in sucking an ice cream. Immediately a small bundle of white fur ran up to her, yelping. The retriever puppy jumped up at her legs, his tongue hanging out, tail wagging.

"Oh no you don't. This is mine." Jade waved the ice cream in circles in the air above the fluffy head. A few inches below, two desperate eyes followed her every move.

"Don't tease him," smiled Clare. "You know how he hates it."

"He's a puppy. Life's all a big game."

Clare turned to the dog. "Now, Maxicles, you be good for your Aunty Jade now, won't you?" Max looked at her with a gormless expression. Jade looked insulted.

"Aunty? Oh no, this is Queen Jade, and you, little puppy, are my subject to command and control and to do what you're told when you're told, capiche?" Max looked even more gormless if that were possible.

Jade looked up at Clare. "You gonna hate it. You need the water, girl."

"Hey, it's an island. They're surrounded by the stuff. Max, out the way!" Max ran out from under her feet and woofed disgruntledly.

"And the cold—it's so damn cold, girl!"

Clare was still trying to close the suitcase.

"Will you do something useful?"

"Oh, okay."

Jade climbed onto the bed and sat on the case, still eating the ice cream. Clare just managed to close the catches. Jade picked up a hardback book lying on the bedside table. She glanced at the cover and then screwed up her face. "*Fluid Dynamics for an Ever Changing World*. Girl, we gotta sort out your bedtime reading!"

"Hey, we all got to earn a living, and I need that. Off!" Clare shooed her off the case, opened the catches again and indicated for Jade to put the book inside.

As she tossed it into the case she knocked a photo off the bedside table. It was a beautiful picture of a man in his fifties with his arm around Clare. Clare was standing dripping wet in a red swimsuit. She was in her teens and holding up a medal that hung around her neck.

But it was the look of sheer joy on Clare's face and the look of sheer pride on the man's that made the photograph special. It exuded the love both clearly felt for each other.

It landed on the floor with a crash.

The glass splintered into small fragments. Clare gasped. "Now look what you've done!" she cried. She slowly started to pick up the jagged pieces.

Jade moved to help clear it up.

"Just … leave it!" There was an edge to Clare's voice that showed real stress. Jade backed off, but didn't take offense. She knew time was short and she also knew what the photo meant to Clare.

Clare put the pieces of glass on the small table and then looked wistfully at the photograph. "I was fourteen. Just won the Montana junior high-diving championship. He was so proud of me." She managed a smile. "He used to call me 'Starfish.'" Clare looked up at her friend and sighed. "Hey, I'm sorry. I'm a bit stressed at the moment." Her eyes were begging forgiveness.

Jade smiled back. "No, I'm sorry. It's not fair what he's doing to you."

Clare looked into the distance for a second and then straight at Jade. "Yeah, but he's still my dad."

"I know, but you don't have to prove anything to him. He has no right."

Clare took a deep breath then checked her watch. "Jesus! The cab'll be here any minute."

Jade put her hand on Clare's and looked into her eyes. "Hey, we good, girl?"

Clare smiled weakly and stared back. "Yeah, we're good, girl."

Jade grinned mischievously. "Oh, and I almost forgot, it rains all the time. Never stops raining."

Clare threw a pillow at her. "Enough already!"

"Only tryin' to warn you. Don't say I didn't warn you. You're gonna miss LA."

"I'm gonna miss the flight if you don't stop."

Clare locked the catches on the case and then heaved it next to the pile of others by the door.

"There, now, what have I forgotten?" In the

background the doorbell rang.

"Your mind."

"Will you shut up, and make sure you take care of Max, okay? And remember he hates storms. Any thunder and you have to hold his ears."

Jade looked at her. "Hold his ears? For how long?"

Clare looked at her as though she was stupid. "Until the storm passes."

Jade looked indignant. "So I'm an ear muffler now?"

The pup looked up soulfully. Clare glanced down at him and paused for a second. She was really leaving very soon. "I know, pumpkin. I'll be away for a couple of weeks. Just got to go help a few Brits out with their plumbing."

"And running away from a broken heart," added Jade.

Clare looked at her seriously. "Don't worry. One more guy messes with me, I'll screw him so bad." A flick of aggression crossed her face, but then it was gone. "Now I really have to go."

They hugged and then Jade helped her down the stairs with the cases and waved her off as the cab departed.

Once Jade was back in the apartment she heard the patter of tiny feet and Max ran into the room. He looked up at her and then ran round her looking for Clare. Jade picked him up off the floor and gave him a huge hug, almost squeezing the life out of him.

He yelped with alarm.

"Now, honeybun, she's gone, and you know I love you really. We're going to have a whale of a time together, aren't we? Just the two of us, but don't tell your mummy. I got an image to maintain!"

Max looked at her with unease. "Missing you already" suddenly took on a whole new meaning. It was going to be a long few weeks.

Chapter 12

During the summer months Loch Lomond played host to hundreds of thousands of visitors from across the world. They came in their droves to experience the breathtaking scenery around the largest inland stretch of water in Great Britain. Even during winter its stunning beauty attracted visitors to its shores.

But today it was overcast.

The sun that normally made the location sparkle and provided a backdrop for all those holiday snaps and selfies was nowhere to be seen. Instead, a thick layer of cloud hung low over the loch and a creeping mist was rising off the water.

There had been a slight drizzle, which had cleared, but the roads were wet and slick and there was a freshness to the air which required a thick coat for comfort.

McCready had been at the viewpoint car park for half an hour and there was still no sign of Donovan. A few other cars had come and gone. A young couple had stopped briefly and walked along the length of the viewing area, but they were so wrapped up in each other McCready doubted they'd even noticed the view.

He was parked facing the water, with the fender of the Range Rover up against a railing that topped off a twenty-foot drop to the loch below. He'd left the engine running, allowing the heater to try to cope with the cold from outside. On any normal day his gaze would have been sweeping the water and the spectacular view down the length of the loch, but today, the mist and the call from Donovan had made things different. He had no idea what had happened to the diving supervisor or why he was so worried, but he could feel events were about to unfold that were going to impact his life, and not in a good way.

He was adjusting the temperature control when something caught his attention. He could hear a distant whine from outside, like the sound of a high-powered engine far away. It came and went on the wind.

He turned around and glanced out through the rear window.

Beyond the car park, a long, straight road led away from the loch. At the far end he could make out a small red speck heading his way. As he watched it grew larger, along with an increase in the sound of the engine. It was about halfway to him and passing a lay-by on the right, when a black shape pulled out behind.

He could now see that the red speck was clearly a bike. The black shape followed in close formation. It looked like an SUV of some sort and it seemed dangerously close to the rear of the bike. McCready had a flashback to the back lot at Global Salvage and the black Toyota Land Cruisers he'd seen there—but if his memory served him right, there had been three of them.

McCready grabbed a pair of binoculars and climbed

out of the car. He could now see the bike and SUV more clearly. It was definitely a Land Cruiser. As he watched, the 4x4 nudged the rear of the bike. He could see the rider glance back briefly before accelerating away. The SUV would be no match for the bike on speed, and he saw the gap between them quickly widen.

The bike was closer now, and McCready put down the binoculars. He watched as it approached the viewpoint. The Land Cruiser was about two hundred yards behind. As the bike entered the curve bordering the car park, the rider turned to look at McCready. Even through the half-raised visor he knew it was Donovan and he could see the fear in his eyes. All he had time for was to open his palms in a questioning gesture before the bike was round the corner and powering down the road that led along the side of the loch.

Then the moment was gone and the Land Cruiser was now entering the corner.

Through the semi-blacked-out windows a figure turned to stare at McCready. He was talking rapidly on a phone, but McCready couldn't make out who it was, and then it too was past and heading after the bike.

A second later and McCready was back in the Range Rover. With the engine already idling, it only took another second for him to hit the accelerator, but he cursed as he lost valuable time turning the big car round before he could head off in pursuit of the Land Cruiser.

Ahead, Donovan was hitting eighty miles an hour on the straights. The road twisted and turned as it followed the contours of the loch. On either side a forest of dense trees covered the steep slope.

He flew round a corner and thought he was going to die.

Straight ahead a small van was overtaking a tractor. How the driver had thought there was enough room before the corner was anyone's guess, but he was on the wrong side of the road and their closing speed was over a hundred miles an hour.

There was only fifty feet between them.

Donovan slammed on the rear brake. The bike fishtailed, leaving a slick of rubber on the tarmac, but he wasn't slowing much on the damp surface.

The driver of the van saw him and froze. Donovan steered the skid to the edge of the road, and as he shot past the van, he twisted the throttle, powering the bike along the drop to the right. Leaves flew in his wake. Gravel spun off into the void. And then he was past. Several beads of sweat dripped from his forehead and smeared the inside of his visor. He dropped the throttle down a notch and took a breath.

A quarter of a mile back McCready threw the Range Rover round blind corners in a desperate attempt to keep up. It was a large car but it was powerful. He was slowly gaining on the Land Cruiser which he could see disappearing around a bend ahead of him.

Donovan was now a quarter of a mile clear and the pressure was off slightly. He came to a fork in the road—one went high, the other low. He sped up the upper road, hoping the Land Cruiser would go low, but a second later he realized it didn't matter what the Land Cruiser did.

The road ahead followed the loch in a sharp turn to

the right. As he glanced at the curve, there on the other side racing almost parallel to him was a second black Land Cruiser. It was closing fast and heading straight for him. He knew beyond doubt it was no coincidence.

The Land Cruiser following Donovan had seen which way he'd gone and headed up the upper road. Five seconds later, McCready arrived at the fork and had no idea which way to turn. With the speed he was carrying he had a split second to decide and headed down the lower route. He pushed the accelerator, hoping to close the distance.

On the upper road Donovan had to make a decision. The Cruiser heading for him was only seconds away. He skidded the bike to a screeching stop. He didn't have long to think.

Then he decided.

With a one-eighty of smoke and rubber, he spun the bike around and headed back the way he'd come. At least the driver of the Cruiser that had been following him wouldn't be expecting this and he might be able to get past with the element of surprise. It would depend on what type of section of road they met on—corner or straight. If he could just get past he would be home and dry. It would take a while for the Land Cruiser to turn round on the narrow road. He headed off at breakneck speed, wondering where he would encounter his nemesis.

It didn't take long. It was round the second corner and on a short straight when he saw the Land Cruiser heading straight for him at over seventy miles an hour. There was plenty of time for it to line up on the bike. The element of surprise was gone. The Land Cruiser moved to the middle of the narrow road. There was no way round.

He didn't have a chance.

He tried to slew the bike into a sideways slide to minimize the impact, but he still hit the fender of the Cruiser at over fifty miles an hour. The bike was shunted back down the road across the rough tarmac with Donovan still gripped around the seat. A second later and the second Land Cruiser rounded the bend. It hit the bike head on, sending it spinning out over the eighty-foot drop at the side of the road.

Far below, McCready heard the impact from above and glanced up in time to see Donovan cartwheeling through the air. He slammed on the brakes and could only watch in horror as his friend arced across the sky. Bike and rider parted company in midair and both hit the trees on the steep slope about fifty feet up. They crashed down through the branches until they smashed into the ground a hundred feet in front of McCready. The bike exploded on impact, sending flames high into the sky. What had happened to Donovan, McCready could only imagine. He drove as fast as he could, slewed the car to a stop, then ran over to the inert form lying at the foot of one of the trees.

On the road above, the two Land Cruisers pulled up to the edge of the drop, inches apart, like expectant predators after a kill.

When McCready reached Donovan's crumpled form he almost threw up. His helmet was split down the middle and one leg lay at an impossible angle. The thighbone had punctured right through the leathers and the white bone shone in the diffuse light.

McCready winced and was aghast to hear a cough and splutter coming from the broken body. He quickly pulled up the helmet visor and cradled Donovan's head the best he could. There was no way he was going to try to remove the helmet. He didn't want to risk damaging the spinal cord—that would have to wait for the emergency services, but deep down he knew they were never going to be there in time.

Donovan was barely alive, but his eyes flickered open, and through a gurgle of blood and groan of pain he tried to speak.

"John, I'm sorry about Sean ..."

"Jesus, not now, Steve. I have to get you to hospital," said McCready.

"There's no time. You have to know it wasn't my fault. *Recovery*—"

"I know. I've got to—"

"No. The ship. Dive control—"

"Steve, there's something going on at Global Salvage. Something's not right there."

A certain sadness and confliction came over Donovan. Even in his condition, McCready could see it is his eyes. All life seemed to go out of them, but in one last gasp he made a desperate plea.

"Dive control ... Evidence ... Rec ... Rec ..." And then he slumped in McCready's arms, all life gone from the shattered body.

McCready just stared at him for a second before carefully lowering his head to the ground next to the tree.

He was still deep in thought when he heard the revving of engines from above. He slowly turned to look up through the trees and the mist that had started to form. The noise was growing louder and then the tone changed to a higher pitch, and then out of the mist two mechanical wraiths appeared like ghosts in the sky.

The Land Cruisers flew through the air, freefalling as one to land on the steep slope below, cracking and smashing branches as they drove through firs and saplings and heading straight for him.

In a second McCready was up and running for the Range Rover. There was no time to do anything about Donovan.

He'd made it to the car and started the engine when the SUVs skidded down on either side, blocking the road in both directions.

There was a moment of calm and then they charged.

Without hesitation McCready reversed wildly at the closest Cruiser. At the last second he shot up the earth bank at the side of the road and slid through a reverse one-eighty at forty-five degrees. As the car spun on the slope above the Land Cruiser, McCready caught a brief glimpse of the driver—Fisher. He'd recognize the balding head, fine stubble of a beard and nose that looked like it had been broken more than once, anywhere. Now he knew for sure that Global Salvage was behind today's events and, ultimately, Steve Donovan's death. It made him even more determined to find out what the hell was going on.

He also realized something else. He wasn't in any game.

This was for real.

But he didn't have time to think. Behind him, Fisher accelerated backward, spinning sideways and using the immovable trunk of a tree to complete the turn in the confined space. The other Land Cruiser overtook him during the turn and then both accelerated after him.

The chase was on.

McCready pulled his seatbelt and clicked it firmly into position. Somehow he felt he was going to need it. He was heading back the way he'd come and knew the road well enough to take the corners at speed, but when he suddenly rounded a bend and found a large lorry in the middle of the road, his only option was to take a steep gravel track that headed up the mountain to his right.

As he drove higher there was a precipice to his left and a tree-lined hill to the right.

He suddenly felt a bump from behind.

The second Cruiser was on his tail. As the slope of the hill to his right lessened, the Land Cruiser raced alongside, driving at forty-five degrees. McCready glanced across, and through the window he saw the driver suddenly throw the wheel to the left.

He braced for the impact.

The Land Cruiser smashed into the side of the Range Rover, threatening to knock it over the edge, but McCready had been ready and had thrown the wheel hard right. The wheels dug into the gravel on the track, throwing small stones in all directions as the two vehicles thundered along, locked in a titanic battle, neither willing to give an inch.

Finally the Cruiser moved to the right, slightly up the hill, then turned to run down at full speed, aiming to smash the Range Rover over the edge. McCready saw him coming and at the last second braked hard, skidding the two-ton vehicle across the loose stones, but it had the desired effect.

The Land Cruiser shot in front, and as it cut across its path, McCready accelerated, hitting the tailgate. The added momentum shunted the Cruiser forward at an angle, hurling it over the edge and into oblivion.

As McCready sped on, he watched it tumble end over end down the steep slope, to eventually smash into a stone wall and explode in a massive fireball below. The flames licked up into the cold Scottish air, but McCready had no time to relax. Within a few seconds the Cruiser driven by Fisher loomed large in his mirrors.

Ahead, the track headed down to join the main road again. McCready put his foot flat on the floor and hit the tarmac, barely missing a coach coming the other way.

Behind, the Cruiser was still tracking his every move.

He had to think. How could he shake him?

He turned on the sat nav and checked the map for their location. He knew the area reasonably well. Then as he scanned the map an idea came to him.

Over the next two miles he let the Cruiser come up close behind. Finally he saw the turn he was looking for. They were about twenty yards from it when he slammed on the brakes.

Behind him, Fisher yanked the wheel to the right, trying to avoid a collision, but he was too close. He hit the rear of the Ranger Rover hard, smashing the right-hand taillight and sending the Cruiser spinning out across the road.

McCready hurled the Range Rover to the left down the side road. Fisher overshot and spun the car one-eighty to slew it to a stop. In the mirrors McCready saw Fisher speaking into a walkie-talkie, but at least he'd gained a breathing space. It would be hard for him to catch up now.

The road headed through large green fields and then up into some low-lying hills with mountains beyond. He continued along the route for around ten minutes. In his mirrors he could see the Land Cruiser trying to keep up when the road was straight enough, but it wasn't gaining.

They were now heading higher into the mountains and the road was twisting back. He could see Fisher lower down as he negotiated yet another hairpin, but still he was comfortably in front.

A mile further on and McCready drove fast through a rock gorge. It led out onto a metal bridge which spanned a ravine. There was a fast-flowing river way below. He was halfway across the bridge when he skidded to a halt. He sat there staring ahead, and then the sweat started to form on his brow. He now knew who Fisher had been speaking to on the walkie-talkie.

He now knew where the third Land Cruiser was.

It was parked on the far side of the bridge, waiting, watching him. He could almost feel it breathing, realizing it had its prey cornered and there was nowhere for it to go. A minute later Fisher drove up to the end of the bridge behind him.

He was trapped.

The bridge was a hundred yards long and he was bang in the middle. It was eighty feet to the raging river below and he was fresh out of options.

He'd been thinking for about ten seconds, his mind in turmoil as to what to do, when suddenly, out of nowhere, a crazy idea came to him. It was completely off the wall, but right then that was as good as he was going to get.

He glanced at the structure of the bridge. The main support was a curved metal arch made up of reinforced steel girders, but the side rails were thin metal railings and they looked pretty rusty.

When he'd been a kid his parents had taken him to the cinema, and before the main feature there had been an advert for Land Rover. The vehicle had driven along the side of a river, only to be confronted by a massive, almost vertical dam. Not deterred by this trifling obstacle, the daring Land Rover driver had merely attached a harpoon to the cable winch on the front of the vehicle, then fired the harpoon up to the top of the dam, where it had stuck fast. He'd then calmly sat in the cab allowing the winch to pull the vehicle up the near vertical dam wall. He remembered it so well because once the driver had reached the top and driven off, the whole audience had spontaneously burst into applause with accompanying whoops and cheers.

So, as the saying went—what goes up must come down.

He slewed the vehicle across the road in the center of the bridge close to one of the metal girders. He then climbed out and pulled the winch cable free. He wrapped it twice around the girder and then reattached it to the cable. He then pulled a further thirty feet of cable free and was about to climb back into the car when he heard a far-off drone from above.

He instinctively glanced up to look for the passenger jet that would no doubt be high in the sky, but there was nothing. Maybe it was behind the mountains somewhere. He thought no more of it and realized he'd just wasted a few precious seconds.

He climbed back into the Range Rover and pulled the door shut. He glanced briefly at the Land Cruisers. It wouldn't take them long to figure out what he was doing.

Hopefully by then it would be too late.

Fisher watched McCready, wondering what he was playing at, but when he saw the Range Rover reverse wildly and hit the railing on the right-hand side of the bridge, he knew exactly what was happening. He lifted the walkie-talkie and pressed TRANSMIT. "Rizby, get to McCready! Now!" He didn't wait for a reply and floored the accelerator heading for the center of the bridge.

McCready had hit the side railing twice and it still hadn't given way. A few rusty bolts had sprung loose, falling to their fate in the river below, but the main railing was still in place.

He glanced to either side.

The Land Cruisers were almost on him. One more go. That would be all the time he would have.

He drove as close to the left-hand side of the bridge as he could. His fender nudged the railing. He then dropped it into reverse and floored it. The vehicle tore backward, hitting the railing with the force of two tons of stampeding metal going at thirty miles per hour.

It never had a chance.

This time the railing splintered as the Range Rover shot out backward over the void. Now all he had to hope was that the cable wouldn't snap as the full weight of the vehicle was suddenly upon it.

The car soared into space just as the Land Cruisers skidded to a halt inches apart where the Range Rover had been seconds before.

Fisher and Rizby jumped out and raced to the side. Below them the Range Rover was suspended in midair by the cable. It was slowly swinging in a gentle arc beneath the bridge. Fisher thought for a moment then turned to Rizby.

"Saw!"

In the Rover, McCready could see movement above him on the bridge and could only imagine what was going on. His hand was firmly on the winch control, but it only had one speed and that wasn't fast.

The car was descending slowly and was now fifty feet above the river. The good news was that the swinging had almost stabilized. All he could do was hope he reached the water in one piece.

What happened then would be interesting.

Rizby had grabbed a large hacksaw from the trunk of the Cruiser. He was a small man, but his lean, willowy figure was etched in muscle, and he was sawing feverishly at the cable with a demented fury. It twitched and shuddered with the tension as the car dropped ever lower toward the river.

Fisher watched over the side of the bridge. "Come on! Come on! Faster!" He kept glancing at Rizby, who was breaking into a sweat, but it was paying off. The cable was nearly through—and then it was.

With a loud CRACK the severed cable scythed its way through the air as it shot over the side. Fisher and Rizby dived for cover, keen to avoid decapitation from the flying metal.

A second later the Range Rover hit the water from a drop of around forty feet. It went deep, the water completely covering the bonnet for a second, but then it bobbed up, rising like a leviathan from the depths and settled in an upright position, the water lapping around the windows.

Inside, McCready had heard the crack of the cable even above the roar of the river and had braced himself for the impact. It had all happened incredibly fast.

As the car went into freefall the bridge above him disappeared at an alarming rate, but even so he seemed to drop forever. When the impact did finally come there was a mighty shudder as he hit the river. Suddenly everything had gone a dark green as the churning water frothed around him, covering the windscreen and obscuring the sky.

That had been the scariest moment, but McCready had faith.

When he'd had the conversion done by the Land Rover Special Vehicles Operation Team, he'd asked for the car to be weatherproofed to the highest possible degree. You never knew when you might need to wade through a river in Scotland or when driving snow would completely cover a vehicle in a drift. The elements could turn on you in a moment. He'd hardly had this scenario in mind, but it seemed to have done the trick. No water seeped into the cabin, except where the driver's window had been open a crack. A problem he'd quickly rectified.

And then he was back on the surface and bright light filled the interior. Once he had his bearings he could see he was heading downstream. The river had been deep enough for the car not to hit the bottom, but now he needed it shallow enough for the wheels to get a grip and be able to haul him to the side. He tried to steer but it had no effect. Somehow he had to get closer to shore.

He revved the engine hard, trying to spin the wheels in the hope they'd propel the vehicle toward the river bank, but to no avail—they just turned aimlessly. He checked the terrain settings dial on the center console just to the rear of the gear lever. As he turned it the different modes displayed on the screen in the center of the dashboard— SNOW—MUD—SAND.

"What, no RIVER!" he yelled in frustration.

He was about to give up when he felt a jolt from behind. He checked the rearview mirror and saw that a large log had bumped into the back of the car. It edged him toward the bank.

A few seconds later one of the tires skipped across something. The river was easing in its flow the closer he got to shore and the tires were bumping up against pebble and rock.

He carefully applied power, not wanting to push the car back into the main flow of the river. Even though only one wheel was in touch with a hard surface, the intelligent traction system fed the power to that wheel and the differential lock ensured it didn't spin.

Inch by inch the car clawed its way toward the bank. Then two wheels had traction, then three and four, and then finally the car slowly pulled itself out of the water, the level dropping below the glass of the windows.

With a huge sigh of relief McCready drove up onto a small pebble beach. Ahead was a grass slope and beyond that a road. Tarmac had never looked so good.

He stopped the car and took stock. Little water had entered the cabin but the carpet was more than slightly damp. The main thing was that everything seemed to be working.

He climbed out and saw the trailing winch cable running beneath the car. He quickly cut it free and was about to climb back in when he glanced up at the bridge. Two small figures were standing on the edge watching him. He made a gun out of his fingers, took aim and fired. Then he climbed back into the car and drove up the small bank to the road.

He grinned. It really was the best 4x4 by far.

On the bridge Fisher and Rizby watched the Range Rover make its way up onto the road and drive off. Rizby hurled the saw over the side into the water below.

"Arrrrgggghhhh!"

Fisher's response was more measured but his expression was hard. "You were lucky this time, mate, but it's not over yet."

He took a final look and then turned away.

Chapter 13

Clare Kowalski pulled out a crisp twenty pound note and handed it to the driver of the black cab. "Keep the change."

"Thanks, luv. Hope you've got an umbrella. It's cats and dogs out there."

Clare glanced out of the window, smiling at the cockney slang for a description of the weather. "I'm not an umbrella kind of girl, but thanks." And with that she opened the door, pulling the hood up on her quilted North Face climbing jacket.

The second she stepped out of the cab just off the Fulham Palace Road in Hammersmith, West London, Clare knew that Jade had been right. It rained a lot in England. It wasn't heavy at the moment but the gusting wind drove it into her as she clutched her laptop bag and hurried up a short flight of concrete steps at the front of a large, modern five-story building. The entrance had revolving glass doors, and a polished metal sign to the left said: *LONDON WATER—serving the capital since 1885*.

Once inside, she pulled down her hood and crossed over to a receptionist seated at a table on the far side of the modern entrance lobby. He'd been expecting her, and as he prepared her security pass she put her bag on the visitor's couch and took off her jacket. Underneath, she was wearing a dark blue stylish pant suit with black leather shoes.

She glanced around at the familiar surroundings she hadn't seen for more than three years. On the walls were six-foot high prints of a London Water project she'd been intimately involved with.

As chief designer for International Pipe and Flow, she'd overseen the development and initial construction of the largest metropolitan water distribution system in Europe. She had only been involved on the construction side initially, as a larger more important project had come up requiring her services in Shanghai, so she'd been pulled off the job. This, though, had turned out not to be the full story. London Water had decided they could get a better deal with a third-party project management company and had dispensed with Pipe and Flow's services, so Clare had had to go. This had been much to her chagrin, as she'd enjoyed her time working with the team on the ground in London. It was a decision the management at London Water had lived to regret. The man from the company that had taken over had eventually been fired for corruption. He'd been caught taking backhanders from the suppliers, and now a year after launch, she was back to pick up the pieces and fix a system that basically didn't achieve what it had originally been designed to do.

She was looking closely at a shot of one of the massive thirty-foot diameter pipes which dwarfed the design team in the foreground—one of which was herself—when the receptionist informed her the pass was ready.

She crossed over, picked it up, assured the guy he didn't need to give her directions, and headed down a corridor she knew would take her to the heart of the facility.

She pushed open the double swing doors and entered a world few people realized existed. Water utilities were hardly the sexiest subject on the planet, but the technology and infrastructure that ensured when you turned on the tap every day, clean, safe water came out would amaze most people.

The room was large, about the size of a university lecture theater. Along one wall was a giant display, which showed the layout of the whole system—a bit like a subway map but without all the bright colors. In front of the screen were two banks of consoles at which technicians worked to monitor and control proceedings. At present there were six people on the main consoles and two at a separate console on the far side of the room. One of these was an elderly gentleman wearing a white lab coat.

Clare looked for familiar faces. Most of the previous team she had known would be gone, but she spotted an old friend, Kelly, at one of the desks. She had looked up when Clare came in through the doors and now wore a big smile on her face. She was about to say something when Clare put a finger to her lips and grinned, indicating the guy in the white coat at the end. Kelly gave a nod of understanding and mouthed *talk later*, before returning to her work.

Clare was now halfway across the room and approaching the two people at the desk. She could see one was clearly a new technician who was listening avidly to the elderly gentleman in the white coat, who had his back to her.

Clare couldn't help smiling at seeing Jason Smythe again. She was now almost behind him and could hear the conversation. Smythe was totally absorbed in what he was saying to the young technician.

"No, Benson, not the large dial. That overloads the pressure in SW1. We don't want Her Majesty having a fright on the loo, now do we?"

Clare listened with amusement. She was still behind Smythe but knew exactly what he was going to say next.

"You know, it took me forty years, man and boy, but if you try hard and listen and learn …" As he repeated the mantra she'd heard many times before, Clare couldn't help but join in with the last line.

"… I'm sure you'll get there in the end."

Smythe started to turn. "Now who on earth …?" And then he saw Clare. His whole face lit up. He was about sixty-five, with a kindly, weather-beaten look and fair, wispy hair. He had the air of a favorite uncle about him, but Clare had always seen him more as a second father figure, and she was thrilled to see him again.

"My God! Clare. It's been so long," he said.

Clare beamed back. "Too long. You'd do anything to get me back here you old goat!" They embraced and held the hug for a while.

"Now that's not fair. You know how we hate it when you know more than we do. How was the flight?"

"Oh you know, long, can never sleep properly, and whoever let that kid into first class should be put in an early grave."

"You poor dear."

Clare glanced at the lab coat. "Still wearing that old

thing."

"Professors need to wear something appropriate, sort of makes it official."

"But you're not a professor."

Smythe backed away and indicated Benson with a flick of his head. "Shhhhhh. They don't know that."

Clare laughed. "So how are Mary and the kids?"

Smythe looked at her quizzically. "Oh, Mary's fine. Always going on about when I'm going to retire. I think she imagines her elder years cruising round the world on some yacht. Doesn't seem to understand I need to keep working for her to fulfill this dream."

Clare smiled.

Smythe continued. "And the 'kids' are great. As you well know, Joshua is thirty-five now and Patrick is thirty-seven. Josh still has a crush on you." Clare blushed and glanced up at Smythe. "And Patrick would have done if he'd met you. Whenever I get out that photo of the team in the tunnel, he always asks how come I get to work with this beautiful woman."

Clare grinned. "Yeah, yeah!"

"I told him he could come in and meet Kelly any time, but somehow he wasn't interested."

Clare punched him playfully on the arm. Smythe pretended to be hurt. "That, my dear, in your part of the world, could be construed as assault."

Clare smiled. "I'll show you assault!"

"Come on, let's go somewhere we can talk," said Smythe.

He started to lead her over to a small office at the far end, but before they'd made it halfway, a rather rotund woman followed by a gaggle of what looked like tourists burst into the room.

The woman, who was clearly some sort of guide, led them to the open space in the middle where she proceeded to talk ten to the dozen and point out the various features of the control center. The group, made up of six adults and four children, stared around in fascination, though it didn't take long for the kids to lose interest and wander off to look at a bank of video screens. The harassed guide tried in vain to round them up.

Clare looked at Smythe with a questioning expression. He glanced around the room and was clearly irritated. "They're running bloody tours of the place now!"

"When did that happen?" asked Clare.

"Oh, about six months after you left. Uh oh ..." The guide had spotted Smythe and was making a beeline for him.

"Quick, let's get out of here," he whispered, ushering Clare faster toward the office. "I'm not a performing monkey and this isn't Disneyland!"

Once inside the office, Smythe didn't relax until he'd checked through the small glass window in the door that the guide wasn't following.

Clare smiled. "I don't know. I could just see you with a peg leg and a parrot in the *Pirates of the Caribbean* ride!"

"Don't laugh. I think that woman fancies me. Every time she's there with a group she heads straight for me."

"Ah, but that would be for your professorial demeanor and unrivaled expertise," Clare said with a grin. Smythe looked at her for a second and then burst out laughing.

"Well, of course, I know that!"

The office was fairly cramped, with a single desk, a couple of chairs and a large computer screen with a series of external hard drives daisy-chained in. A single window streaked with rain looked out onto a dreary side street. Smythe switched on the computer, and while it was starting up his expression turned serious. He paused before continuing, as though deciding what to say. "Now, my dear, how are you coping?" His face showed real concern.

Clare sighed, and for a second couldn't look at him, then she looked up and her face was full of sadness. "It still haunts me every night. I can see the road, but I never saw the truck."

"But it wasn't your fault."

"My mother is dead, Jason." There was anger and despair in her voice. Smythe put a hand on her shoulder.

"There was nothing you could have done."

"Try telling my dad. I was driving. We've still barely spoken."

He looked at her sadly. "I'm so sorry, my dear. I'm sure he'll come round. It'll just take time."

"Maybe, but how long is he going to need? It's tearing me apart inside. If he leaves it too long there may be nothing left between us."

There was an awkward silence. Clare wiped away a tear before it could make its way down her cheek. She took a deep breath. "Okay, guess you'd better show me why you've dragged me halfway round the world."

Smythe smiled softly and then was all business.

"Yes, that's a good idea. So, did they brief you?"

"I've had the official version, but I'd rather get it from the sharp end."

He suddenly looked weary. "It's bad, Clare. Let me show you." He opened a program on the computer and brought up a series of schematics and data spreadsheets.

"Now, here we are. The five hundred thousand gallons a minute you designed into the system works fine, but we're just not getting the flow rates in the lift tunnels. When we increase the turbines, we're into the red before the rates even come close."

Clare looked at the data on the display. "And you're running the excess tolerance?"

Smythe looked even more despondent and then replied. "We've tried, but we're still not getting the figures."

"Okay, I have the original pump specs and lift tunnel designs, but I'll need details of any changes that were made after I left, as well as the flow records for the last six months. Oh, and a deal breaker—coffee, black, nothing fancy."

The coffee came, the hours ticked by, and by the time it reached 5pm Clare was shattered. The jet lag was catching up and she could barely keep her eyes open. It looked like the situation was actually worse than she'd feared. She told Smythe they'd pick it up in the morning. She wanted a day or so to do a full breakdown of where they were at, and then she would have to head into the tunnels to see for herself.

She grabbed her things, managed to hail a cab in the London rush hour and almost nodded off on the short trip back to her hotel. Once inside, out of the rain, she didn't even bother to eat, but headed straight for her room and crashed out.

There was no danger whatsoever of her not getting a good night's sleep.

Chapter 14

The City of Aberdeen lay between two river mouths, the Dee and the Don. It had a population of around two hundred thousand and was often known as The Granite City, due to the number of properties built from the locally mined gray granite. On sunny days the buildings can be seen to sparkle as the rays glint off the mica embedded in the stone. Over time it's relied on many industries, including shipbuilding, fishing and textiles, but in recent years it's come to survive on only one thing—oil.

Since the boom days of the 1980s when the city had grown to accommodate the expansion of the industry, every aspect of the place had been enlarged. From the roads and the hotels to the number of restaurants and the number of escorts. It could even lay claim to the busiest commercial heliport in the world—all catering to the men and women required to keep the black gold flowing ashore.

Its location close to the oil fields, combined with the natural deep-water harbor made it the perfect choice. But with the expansion, the city had changed, and to many, not for the better. Like anywhere with a proud past, when big business and the infrastructure surrounding it moves in, something has to give, and that's usually character, charm and a sense of identity.

McCready pulled to the side of the road on York Street and parked the Range Rover a hundred yards short of the entrance to the docks. It was early evening, but it was as black as the night was going to be. He clicked off the lights and watched the security gate for a few minutes. He was still haunted by Donovan's last words and what they could mean, and there was only one way to find out.

He'd spent most of the day with the police going through the details of Donovan's death. He hadn't told them anything about the involvement of Mercer's men. There was too much in play right now and he needed to find out for himself exactly what was going on. Instead, he'd said he'd arranged to meet with Donovan and had been traveling to the agreed location when he'd come across the bike lying at the side of the road. Clearly some dreadful accident had occurred, because when he'd arrived at the scene Donovan was already dead. He hadn't been able to call the police immediately because the battery in his phone was out. Once he'd finally done so he'd been told that another member of the public had already reported the incident. Even so, he'd been advised that he should come in the following day to give a statement. This he had duly done. They had seemed happy but he'd been told not to go too far as they may need to talk to him again.

As he now stared at the entrance to the docks, he wondered what he would find when he finally got on board *Recovery*.

The fog that had hung around for most of the day still

lay across the sprawling dock complex. High arc lights shone down, creating striking patterns in the swirling mist like the landing lights of some intergalactic spaceship. There was no rain, but a biting wind swept in off the North Sea. It was not a night to be out and about.

McCready thought over Donovan's last words and what he was supposed to be looking for in dive control. He knew *Recovery* would be in dry dock, having seen the bow thruster at Global Salvage. What he wasn't sure of was the security around the ship given earlier events, and whether or not anybody would be aware that his presence on Global Salvage property was *persona non grata*. Either way, he had to get on board if he was going to find any answers.

After a couple more minutes, when several trucks had come and gone, there appeared to be no undue extra security that he could see. He started the engine and drove up to the gate. While checks were the norm, he knew the night shift tended to be more lax, particularly on a night like this.

At first no one came out to question him. There was a small gate office and he could hear the sound of a football match coming from a TV. He was about to climb out and go over to the window, when a portion of the glass slid sideways and an elderly security guard looked out. He had a streaming cold and didn't seem happy at the disturbance.

"Yes?"

McCready held up his Global Salvage security pass. He doubted anyone had been told about him personally. The docks covered a large area and there was a lot of coming and going. Also, the guy behind the window didn't seem particularly interested in anything other than getting back inside his cocoon. "Just going down to the dry dock. Late-night meeting."

The man squinted at the pass. It clearly looked official. He raised the gate and waved McCready through without another word. A second later and the window slammed shut and he disappeared from view.

He drove slowly along the fence that bordered the dry dock. As he rounded the corner he could see *Recovery* sitting high up behind the massive gates that held out the sea. It was strange seeing any ship in this condition. They somehow looked neutered—an object without a purpose —the proverbial fish out of water. What he also saw were two cars parked close to the gangplank that led onto the ship. One was a graphite-colored Porsche 911 Turbo and the other a black Toyota Land Cruiser.

McCready stopped the car and considered his options. He had to get on board and see what he could find, but it would be playing with fire. He flicked off the lights and drove to a space next to a large shipping container that was in shadow from the lights that illuminated the ship. He also turned the car around in case he needed to make a hasty exit.

He walked slowly over to the gangplank.

There was no one on the dockside and the ship looked deserted, except for a lone figure wrapped up against the cold. The man was walking to and fro on the deck close to the gangplank. He looked somewhat overweight and every now and then McCready could see the bright glow of the burning embers of a cigarette being inhaled at regular intervals. There was only one guy on the ship that fitted that description, Jerry Malone, but what the hell was the chief engineer doing on sentry duty?

McCready walked up the gangplank as if he had every right to be there. As he reached the top, Malone, who had thrown his cigarette butt over the side walked over. His coat was wrapped tight around him and he had what looked like three scarves clinging to his neck. He looked frozen to the core. McCready thought he'd get the first word in. "Hi, Jerry, what the hell you doing out here? You look like a block of ice."

Malone looked like he was trying to disappear into the thick parka hood that covered his head. "Freezing my nuts off, that's what, John. I'm just trying to pull some overtime helping out, what with the ship laid up and all. By the way, real sorry to hear about your brother. He was a good man."

McCready paused for a second. "Yes, yes, he was. Thanks." So far, there wasn't any hostility from Malone.

Malone continued. "So what brings you out here? She's real quiet at the moment."

"Just need to pick up a few things from my locker. With all the chaos, some stuff got left behind."

Malone looked hesitant for a second. "Not sure why, but I'm not supposed to let you on board, John." McCready looked at him, his heart sinking. Malone continued. "But seeing as the order came from that prick Jennings, take all the time you need. I'm here all night."

McCready breathed an inward sigh of relief. "Thanks, Jerry. I can't go into it now, but you're doing the right thing. Just know I really appreciate it." Malone nodded through the circle of scarves.

McCready headed for one of the watertight doors. Before he entered he stopped and turned. "Anyone else on the ship tonight?"

"Yeah, a few. Those two little bastards, Fisher and Rizby. Never could get on with them. Oh, and Jennings. Thinks he runs the bloody place. But don't worry. I see them, you were never here, never have been."

"Cheers mate." And with that, McCready disappeared inside while Malone lit another cigarette, muttering to himself.

"May as well die of these as the bloody cold."

The interior of *Recovery* was dark. There were only dull safety lights on in most of the ship. In the background there was the hum of a generator, but not the reassuring low end vibration of the engines, or the slow, steady movement of a ship alive on the ocean. It all seemed somehow kind of sterile—dead. It made McCready uncomfortable.

He headed deep into the ship. If Fisher, Rizby and Jennings were here, he wanted to know what they were doing at this time of night.

He was two levels down when he heard a clanging sound to his left. He paused, glancing around. He carefully made his way along a short corridor to a watertight door that led to the moon pool. It was firmly shut, but a grimy reinforced circle of glass allowed a limited view of the area beyond. He could hear voices now and more clanging.

He took in the scene.

Bright lights illuminated the entire area. It was quiet and calm after the normal action that would be the center of operations during a saturation dive. A diving bell stood on the floor to the side of the rectangle of water at the center of the open space.

Fisher stood next to the bell looking up at Rizby, who was perched on top of one of the large high-pressure cylinders that encircled the metal sphere. These would normally provide emergency gas in case the umbilical to the surface should ever be severed, but as McCready could clearly see, these cylinders would never be providing gas for anyone. One was already lying on the floor with its end removed.

Fisher looked around nervously and then back up at Rizby. "Come on we haven't got all night."

"She's jammed. Give me a wrench," replied Rizby.

Fisher passed up a wrench and Rizby applied the tool to unscrewing the bolts that held the cylinder in place. Then from out of his view McCready heard Jennings' voice.

"Move it! We're running late." He walked in through a door behind Fisher. "And that business with Donovan— very messy, guys."

Fisher looked up, annoyed. "You said make sure he doesn't talk to McCready. He didn't talk to McCready."

"Yeah, but you can't be sure, can you?" replied Jennings.

"He'd never survive that fall, and we almost got McCready. Even smashed one of the bastard's taillights, I was that close."

McCready had heard enough and headed off down the passage to dive control.

There were two ways into the control room. McCready entered from deep within the ship, while the other door led to a corridor that in turn led out onto a companionway at the side of the ship.

It was dark inside when he entered.

He stood there for a moment, thinking, taking in the room. None of the displays were up and running and the whole place had the feeling of a blank computer screen— a lot could go on but nothing was happening. But he knew full well that what went on in this room kept him alive when he was hundreds of feet below the surface, and he would treat it with the respect it deserved.

He took out a small Maglite, twisted the beam on and shone it around in the darkness. *What were you trying to tell me, Steve? Dive control. Rec … Rec what? And what evidence?*

He walked around the room shining the narrow circle of light over the equipment. As he moved across the main panel on the desk, the beam played over the CCTV control joystick. He thought for a second, then put the torch down and switched on the CCTV cameras.

Immediately, black-and-white views of different areas of the ship sprang to life on the bank of monitors above the main panel. He clicked a switch until a view of the moon pool was up on the main screen in the center of the array.

He could see Fisher was still arguing with Jennings. There was no audio so he couldn't hear the conversation, but it looked pretty heated. As he watched, Fisher crossed over to the bell and helped Rizby lower the cylinder he'd been working on to the deck. It was now lying at Fisher's feet. Jennings walked over as Fisher unscrewed the top of the cylinder and withdrew a brick-like object from the interior.

McCready zoomed in the camera, and despite the rather grainy black-and-white image, he was left in no doubt the true color of the small brick Fisher held in his hand. Fisher carried the bar and put it into another large cylinder that had been cut in two. This one had the same dimensions as those McCready had seen on the flatbed truck at Global Salvage. All it needed was to be welded together.

He followed him with the camera.

In the moon pool Jennings watched Fisher put the gold bar in the newly cut cylinder. "Make sure the weld's secure." He was about to continue when he was distracted by something in the corner of the room. He looked up and caught a slight movement of the CCTV camera.

He looked sharply at Fisher. "Who's in the control room?"

The two men exchanged glances and shook their heads. A look of concern flashed across Jennings' face as he ran for the door and exited the moon pool.

In dive control McCready watched Jennings run beneath the camera on the monitor. "Shit!" He had to get out of there fast, but he was still none the wiser about what Donovan had been trying to tell him.

He shone the torch around the room one last time.

As he was sweeping the beam across the panel on the desk, he suddenly stopped and backtracked the light to a button with an unlit red light next to it.

It was labeled, RECORD.

He froze, then quickly moved forward and lifted the cover to the USB drive recorder. He unclipped the cable and removed the drive, stuffing it deep into his jacket. He then pushed the cover down and ran from the room.

If he had stayed a second longer he would have seen that the cover had not properly located on the closure clip and had risen up to lie in a half open position.

A moment later and Jennings entered from the other door. He snapped the lights on and saw the second door swinging to. He ran over and lunged through it but stumbled on the high lip at the bottom of the opening.

McCready burst out of the door leading to the companionway and ran for the gangplank. As he approached he saw Malone throw another cigarette over the side. "Didn't find your things then, John?"

"Actually, Jerry, think I found more than enough." And with that he sprinted down the gangplank and over to the Range Rover.

A couple of seconds later, Jennings tore down the deck. He reached the gangplank, totally ignored Malone, and watched a car disappear into the fog. He didn't get the number plate, but the right-hand taillight was missing.

"Nice evening for it, Mr. Jennings."

Jennings suddenly noticed Malone. "Who was that?"

"Who was what?"

Jennings shook his head, a steely expression across his face, then headed back into the ship, leaving Malone again muttering to himself.

"Yes, indeed, lovely evening for it."

Jennings stood in the middle of dive control and glanced around, looking for anything out of the ordinary. His attention eventually came to rest on the half-open drive cover. He moved over to it, flipped it all the way up, and saw the drive was gone.

He pulled out his cell, hit speed dial and waited for it to

be answered. "It appears McCready didn't take that leave after all. He may have seen more than he should, and the USB drive's missing from dive control."

He listened.

"No, sir, no knowing what was on it, but we should assume the worst."

He listened again.

"Yes, sir, I'll see the press get it right away."

Chapter 15

McCready's house was located at the end of a half-mile dirt track in a small bay about ten miles south of Oban. It had taken him around four hours to drive back from Aberdeen, and he'd kept an eye on the rearview mirror the whole way, but no one had followed.

As he turned off the A816 onto the unmarked track he eased his neck from side to side and rolled his shoulders. It had been a tiring couple of days and an eventful evening. Despite all that he still didn't know if he'd found anything of any importance, but he felt sure the USB drive would have some answers. The drive was there to record what went on in dive control, and something serious must have happened if this was in fact what Donovan had been trying to tell him.

If it wasn't, he was back to square one.

He still didn't believe Mercer's comments about Donovan's actions, and with everything else that had happened he was unlikely to believe anything Malcolm Mercer ever said again. It was clear they were covering up the amount of gold that had been brought up, right under the noses of the inspectors, and as much as he might not wish to believe it, it was likely Donovan had in some way been complicit in this. But he'd seen something in his eyes before he died—a realization that he'd somehow become involved in a situation that was way over his head.

He braked suddenly as a rabbit shot out of the dense bracken that grew on either side of the track. He just missed its little bobbing tail as it disappeared into the undergrowth on the other side. A minute later and he turned the final bend. The full beams of the headlights lit up the entrance to his home.

The house was built over several levels on a gently sloping hill at the side of a sweeping bay. It was a work in progress and the location was remote and wild. Just the way he liked it. Being a commercial diver might not produce the most conducive lifestyle for family life, but you earned a considerable amount of money. He'd spent the last five years building a home he could feel comfortable in and which allowed him the peace and quiet he enjoyed away from the rest of the world.

He parked the car in front of a double garage on a granite-slabbed parking area that was on the middle floor of the building. He climbed out, stretched his tired limbs, and then crossed over to a large oak door set into the solid stone wall. He opened the door, walked in and punched in the code to disable the alarm. It was unlikely there would be many people this far out who'd wish to rob him, but by the same token, if anyone did decide to, there was no one for miles around to hear them. The alarm was linked to the nearest police station, which was over ten miles away, so there was hardly going to be any rapid response. As a backup it alerted McCready's smartphone, which also had the ability to monitor security cameras around the premises so he could at least see what was going on, and there would be a record of any illegal activity.

He hung his coat on a rack in the corner and then walked through into the main part of the house.

An open-plan hallway flowed into a split-level living area. To the left was a cozy nook with a log fireplace, low comfy chairs and a TV. At one end an old-fashioned oak bar protruded from the wall. To the right, a larger space contained a dining table and six chairs, while further to the right was the way through into the kitchen. Just past the dining table, a set of French doors led out onto a patio.

The center of the room continued on through to the main living area via a split-level drop of two steps—all open-plan. Once on the lower level, the room opened up to a thirty-foot-wide space. It had another fireplace at one end surrounded by low couches and a TV in the corner. At the other end a round table and easy chairs provided an optional seating area. Wherever you were in the room though, the breathtaking aspect was the thirty-foot spread of glass across the back. It was made up of four panels, the center two of which could be slid back to open the room up to a deck that in turn had a glass surround and looked out over the bay at the middle-floor level. A wooden stairway led from the deck to the ground below, where a second garage and storage area made up the lower section of the house.

The floor above the living area consisted of three bedrooms, all with en-suite bathrooms, and in the roof was McCready's office. It couldn't quite boast the dimensions and shear wow factor of Mercer's, but it did have a spectacular view across the bay.

The "work in progress" aspect of the property was an extension beyond the patio that included a barbecue as well as a games/hobby room. At the moment there was only a new wall a couple of feet high, but it gave an indication of what was to come.

The house was decorated in a minimalist but comfortable style, and there were mementos from travels to far-flung lands in strategic corners and on many of the walls.

In pride of place in the main living room was a spear from a Masai tribesman. The man had insisted he accept it after saving his daughter from a raging river in Kenya—though getting it back through customs had been an event in itself.

There was a brown poncho made for him by a Peruvian girl from his backpacking days after leaving school. The simple gift with its red, green and yellow bands meant more to him than he had ever told anyone.

And then there were the matching antique gold pistols, presented to him by a Saudi prince after a salvage job in the Red Sea. The outcome had resulted in the prince saving a huge amount of face and he'd sworn he would forever be in McCready's debt—at least to the tune of two matching pistols, which were probably worth more than the house itself, but to the prince it would no doubt be merely the equivalent of a tip for a waiter. McCready kept them on display to remind him of the real value of things. He knew which of them he prized the most and which were truly worth the most.

His parents had always instilled a sense of wanderlust in him, having traveled extensively throughout their lives themselves. He would hardly have called them Bohemian, but their values and beliefs were more for living for the moment with what you had, rather than the acquisition of wealth and material possessions. He'd always been taught that so long as you did your best no one could ask any more of you. And while having dreams was all well and good, the notion that anyone could do anything if they tried hard enough was treated with a dismissive sigh that implied that that way of thinking was espoused by those with no true understanding of the real world.

He had been fifteen when his mother had died.

He always referred to it as when his mother had been *killed*, but his father had never allowed him to say that out loud. It had been when she had *died*.

She'd been volunteering with the Sea Shepherd environmental organization. The expedition had been in the Southern Ocean, trying to prevent a Japanese whaling ship from completing its mission. Something his mother had known was dangerous. Something his father had known was dangerous, but it was so close to her heart that his father knew that if he'd ever tried to stop her he would lose her forever.

She'd been in a fast RIB in six-foot swells, trying to position the boat between a whale and the harpoon gun. After an hour of cat and mouse, the captain of the whaler had lost patience and rammed the small craft, sending it crashing over and throwing the crew into the freezing waters.

He'd then proceeded to run them down.

There had been no survivors.

When McCready had reacted with anger and revenge in his heart, his father had, with calm and dignity, explained that nothing could bring her back and his anger and grief should be channeled into something constructive. McCready had listened and respected his father's words but inside he'd known there would always be something dormant that would one day surface, and when that day came he would not be responsible for his actions.

Although his father had never spoken of the event again, he'd been a changed man. His mother had meant everything to his father and McCready was sure that was why he'd retreated from the world and died several years later.

It had hit Sean particularly hard, and it had fallen to McCready to help his brother through the difficult times. It was probably this more than anything that had made him back away when he'd seen Sean's love for Sarah.

He threw the keys down, grabbed a bottle of whisky from the bar and poured himself a shot. He then pulled the USB drive from his pocket and plugged it into a laptop on the table in the lower living area. He found the file on the drive, took a swig of Ireland's finest and hit PLAY.

There was a brief crackle and hiss from the recording and then he heard his own voice. It was slightly altered as the electronic wizardry corrected the helium-induced distortion that anyone breathing the gas suffered from, but it was clear enough.

As he listened, the initial warmth garnered from the quality malt disappeared and he found himself clenching the glass harder and harder.

MCCREADY: Surface, we've got a twenty-foot vertical

movement on a ten-second interval down here. Any of you guys know what that means in the real world? … Surface, I say again. It's getting—

DONOVAN: We read you, John. Just hang tight. We have a situation up here.

MCCREADY: Oh yeah, wanna swap?

DONOVAN: With the thruster down, he could be dragged from the sub! I'm the dive supervisor on this ship—

MERCER: And I'm paying the bill, which means, Mr. Donovan, that I own you, and until I say otherwise, they work!

Alarms sound.

MATTHEWS: Second thruster gone! She won't take much more of this!

But McCready had heard enough. He clicked off the recording, then stood and took his drink out onto the deck overlooking the bay. The wind had blown the fog away, and a starry night and a full moon shone down, illuminating the scene with a flat, beautiful light that only the moon can provide. The sea was calm, and gentle waves lapped along the beach that stretched the length of the curved bay.

But he didn't see any of this. He just stood there oblivious to the temperature that was close to freezing. Then he hurled the glass into the night and with composure and power said three words, the implication of which was to change the course of his life.

"You bastard, Mercer."

Chapter 16

What the hell is that noise?

It was like a jackhammer splitting his head in two.

He looked up and could see an image of Mercer hammering the nails into Sean's coffin—then it changed to Jennings nailing his own coffin shut. Then the two images merged and both men were coming at him with the hammer.

The noise went on for a minute then stopped—*relief*.

Then it started again. It jolted him awake. He was sprawled across the bed. Sheets in a tangle. A warm sweat on his skin.

Where the hell am I?

He couldn't remember the night before. He opened his eyes and bright light lasered into his brain. He shut them quickly, squinted, then tried to open them slowly. An empty whisky bottle swam into focus on the floor.

The noise continued.

He opened his eyes further and they came to rest on the phone beside his bed—*the noise*.

He pushed himself slowly up onto an elbow, and a splitting pain speared through his head. He reached for the phone and lifted it off the cradle—*heaven*—the noise stopped. He held it in his hand for a second. A disembodied voice came from the earpiece.

"Mr. McCready, are you there?" It paused and then repeated, "Mr. McCready are you there?"

McCready put the phone to his ear, collapsing on the bed and closing his eyes. He managed to get out a mumbled, "This is McCready."

The voice continued. It was male, young and intensely annoying. "Ah, Mr. McCready, there you are. I'm glad I've reached you. My name's Matt Stevens from the *Tribune*. Just wanted to know why you let your brother die in that wreck."

McCready opened his eyes sharply and the pain returned.

"What did you say?"

"The death of your brother. Just wondered if you had any comment?"

"Yeah, fuck off!"

He slammed the phone down and rolled over, rubbing his face. With a great effort he sat up slowly, trying to acclimatize his eyes to daytime. He glanced at the phone and took it off the cradle. The clock on the side table said 9.30am. He eased into a sitting position on the edge of the bed and caught a glimpse of himself in a mirror. He looked like shit—but what he was more concerned about was the phone call.

Five minutes later and a hundred needle-like jets attacked his body in the large walk-in shower. He let it run at maximum temperature for as long as he could stand it and then switched to cold and stayed there for longer than he could stand it. The pain had the desired effect. It woke him up and made him contemplate the day ahead and what other surprises might be in store.

Breakfast was coffee, toast and a large glass of orange juice. He was standing on the upper level looking out through the panoramic sheets of glass and chewing his second piece of wholemeal when the doorbell rang.

McCready opened the front door and was met by a small, waspish-looking woman in her late forties. She was smartly dressed, had short dark hair and wore a pair of steel-rimmed glasses. She had a bright red laptop bag over her shoulder, which seemed at odds with the rest of her. Parked next to the Range Rover was a white BMW 1 Series coupé. It was covered with mud down the side he could see. He turned his gaze back to the woman.

"Mr. McCready, Tania Briscoe, *Sunday Times*. My card." He took it automatically. "You're a hard man to find. Been trying your phone all morning." McCready glanced back at the mud on the Beemer and a wry smile crossed his lips.

"Seems like not hard enough. Why would you want to find me anyway?"

"Why were you fired from Global Salvage?"

McCready sized her up. The tone was professional, but there was an edge to it.

"What?"

"You used to work for Global Salvage, correct?"

"I do work for Global Salvage. I'm on leave at the moment."

"Not anymore. I understand it was your fault … the incident that caused your brother's death." She looked at him expectantly.

"Lady, I've no idea what you're talking about. I have

not been fired and I wasn't responsible for my brother's death. Now if you wouldn't mind …" He slammed the door in her face and was about to walk back into the kitchen when he heard her voice through the door.

"The reports say different. The press release"—he opened the door again—"issued last night. It says you take full responsibility for the incident and that you've resigned—effective immediately."

"What press release? That's bullshit!"

She offered him a sheet of paper. He glanced at it briefly. "Can I keep this?" And before she could answer he shut the door on her again. There was a pause, then Briscoe threw him a parting shot.

"Look, I'm not going to beg but if you have any comment … or there's something you'd like to say … your side of things …" She let that hang for a moment. "You know where to find me." She turned and headed for the car.

McCready watched her through a window as she climbed in, gunned the engine and disappeared up the track. The other side was equally muddy.

He poured himself another coffee and then took the press release into the living room to take a closer look, but not before propping her business card on a side table by the door.

The release was typed on Global Salvage stationary, and as he read through it he became more incredulous by the minute. It effectively said he was responsible for Sean's death through negligence and poor working practices, whereby safety regulations were ignored and procedures carried out in breach of guidelines. It went on to say that in light of these revelations being discovered by the company he clearly could no longer remain in their employ and subsequently resigned from his job. He took full responsibility for his actions and no legal claim would ever be made against Global Salvage with respect to any matter. The most disturbing thing, though, was the signature at the bottom of the release—it was his.

McCready screwed the paper up into a ball and threw it across the room.

"That son of a bitch!"

In the small office at London Water Clare sat with an almost empty mug of coffee and her head buried in schematics and computer programs.

It was now 10am and she'd already been in for several hours. She had, in the end, not been able to sleep due to the jet lag, and never one to sit around idly, she'd made her way into the office and was wading through the production reports from the ring main construction. Things were actually stacking up to be far worse than she'd imagined.

She was just about to go and pour herself a third coffee of the morning when Smythe poked his head around the corner. "Good morning, young lady."

Clare glanced over her shoulder. "I'm afraid it isn't, Jason. Come and look at this."

Smythe crossed over and sat down next to her. She pointed at the screen. "There seem to be two areas where costs have been cut. The first is with the figures for the width of the lift tunnels. They're smaller than the original specs I designed. The result of this is a lower capacity for volume movement. The second is the size and power of the pumps in each tunnel. Again, lower spec than design.

The end result is less water movement and at a speed that doesn't meet your original requirements. There's no way those pumps are going to pull that volume of water up those pipes. We'll have to go check on the ground, but it's not looking good."

Smythe looked at the data on the screen. "And there can be no mistake?" he said glumly.

Clare looked straight at him. "You got problems, Jase old boy. It's going to need a full system-wide shutdown, else you run at existing pressure and flow rates permanently. Only way round it is to upgrade the pumps and/or enlarge the pipes, which is going to cost."

Smythe took a deep breath and suddenly looked very tired, even though it was the start of the day. "I don't suppose you have anything else on right now, my dear?"

Clare looked serious and thoughtful. "Well, there is this contract in the Bahamas …" She saw Smythe's face drop. She smiled and gave him a "just-kidding" look. His face immediately brightened. "First though, we need to check for any more screwups and I'll need access all areas twenty-four seven. There are going to be a few all-nighters on this one."

Smythe looked worried, but there was also a certain amount of relief on his face.

Chapter 17

The knife-like bow of the sea kayak cut through the calm waters of the bay. McCready paddled fast with a steady, rhythmic stroke that powered the small craft through the water at several knots. He was dressed in a lightweight drysuit and thin neoprene gloves. Immersion in the water at this time of year wouldn't be a pleasant experience, and while you tended to sweat more in a drysuit, the thickness of wetsuit required to keep out the cold if he'd capsized would have restricted his movement.

He always headed for the water when he needed to clear his head and think. It was a very raw experience—just you and the elements, the wind on your face and the smell of the sea all around. It was one of his favorite times. It also meant he had no need for the gym he'd originally considered in the design of the house. The kayaking sorted out the upper body, and running the local trails sorted out the lower body. Both saw to cardiovascular issues—throw in a few sit-ups every day and you had a made-to-order fitness program— he should do a video.

He'd reached the line of rocks at the edge of the bay

and slowed the stroke, finally coming to a stop. He allowed the kayak to drift slowly with the tide. It was just turning so he wouldn't travel too far.

He gulped in the refreshing air, getting his breath back and calming his pulse rate. He glanced around. His gaze was focused close to the shore near a narrow inlet with rocks and small pools at its edge. If he waited long enough he hoped he'd receive visitors.

He'd been drifting for about five minutes when the first small head popped above the surface about twenty feet away. A moment later and two more joined the first. They were covered in thick fur and had dark, alert eyes that darted hither and thither with an insatiable inquisitiveness. Their noses were small and black like a dog's, and either side sprouted long white whiskers. They were checking out the area and in particular the new arrival.

McCready had known the otter family for just over a year. He'd watched the mother, whom he'd named Mira, bring up the two pups without a father, who'd been run over by a car soon after their birth.

Naming the youngsters, who were brothers, had been easy. The first time he'd seen them, one was on the surface and the other under the water. When underwater pup had come back to the surface, a stream of bubbles had foreshadowed his appearance and the other pup had squeaked in fear before his brother's head had appeared —so, of course, they immediately became Bubble and Squeak.

He watched now as they porpoised through the water like quicksilver. They seemed to flow with the medium and were totally at one when they were in its embrace.

He'd snorkeled with them many times and the pups had joyfully chased him through the long kelp forests close to shore. He felt humbled to be treated as one of the family.

They swam up to the kayak and then dipped and dived around the bow, chorkling and muttering to themselves as only otters could. One of the pups tried to climb onto the shallow deck using a twist of rope at the bow, but fell off halfway up with a squeal. He returned for another go but was pulled away gently by his mother.

McCready couldn't help but smile in their presence. It took away a lot of the stress that had been building over the last few days.

He enjoyed their company for another ten minutes before checking his watch. There was somewhere he had to be and he didn't want to be late.

Reluctantly he took a final look at the family he'd grown to love. Then spun the kayak around and stroked powerfully back to the house, leaving the otters cavorting in his wake.

An hour later, McCready drove into the car park of the Highland Arms pub just off the A816 near Lochgilphead.

He'd been looking forward to and dreading the meeting in equal measure. He still didn't know how he was going to feel or what he was going to say as he pulled into a space next to the eggshell-colored Mini Cooper. He paused for a second before climbing out. The air was calm and clear, but there was a light dusting of snow on the ground and it was still bitterly cold.

As he opened the thick wooden door to the pub a wave of welcome warmth washed over him. He quickly entered and shut out the wintery weather behind.

There were about ten people inside. The pub had low oak beams and a cozy, friendly feel to it. A crackling log fire was nestled in an alcove on one side of the room and the landlady nodded a welcome as he walked past the bar. A few people were eating typical pub fare for their lunch as McCready scanned the faces.

He found her sitting in a corner away from the other customers. A window with sprinkles of frost was behind her head and the backlight from the sun gave her a diffuse halo. She was wearing a thick white turtleneck jumper with sleeves that were way too long, almost covering her hands in that endearing way that only a woman can seem to achieve. She was cradling a cup of coffee and the steam flowed up across her face making it appear as though through a haze. As he moved closer, her eyes glanced up and locked onto his. There was a weak smile and then she put the coffee down and stood quickly. They hugged and clung on to each other for a long minute. When they did finally break, there were tears in her eyes.

It was the first time McCready had seen Sarah since the funeral and he hadn't realized he'd be so emotional. Although she was still frail, a certain composure had returned and he could see a trace of the inner strength of the girl he'd known before.

But standing there looking at her, he knew two things. One, he would do everything in his power to always protect her, and two, the love he felt for her was as for a sister and no more. Something had shifted within him, and with all that had gone on, her relationship with his brother, the brief moment they had shared several years previously, it felt right and it lifted a weight he wished had been removed when Sean had been alive.

He sat down across the small table and he felt a lightness to his being, as though an obstacle in his life was no longer there. She was looking into the half-empty cup in front of her.

"How are you coping?" he asked.

She stared at the coffee for a second. "A moment at a time"—then she looked up at him—"and they're long moments, John. I wake up every morning and for that brief instant everything's right with the world. Then it's like a wave rolling over me, and I know life will never be the same again. Then there's the post, phone calls from people who don't know—even dry-cleaning, for God's sake!"

McCready could feel her pain but he knew it must be far worse for her. "It'll take time. It always does, but you have to hold on to the memories, Sarah. You have to have something for the baby."

Sarah looked at him briefly and then back at the coffee. She seemed to find solace there and then said simply. "Shauna. She's going to be called Shauna."

"You had the scan?"

She looked up and the frailty was back. "I had to have a name I could talk to when I tell her about him. Every night I tell her something new." A weak smile crossed her face, while at the same time a tear ran down her cheek.

McCready put a hand on her shoulder. "That's wonderful."

She looked up with more of a smile this time, as though she was happy the admission had been met with acceptance. Then her brow crumpled into a crease of concern. "How do you deal with it?"

He didn't answer straight away, but when he did it was

without emotion. "I try to shut it out. I have to for now."

"But how can you?"

He was again silent and then his face turned serious. "Other things are happening, Sarah." There was a pause. "Steve Donovan was killed."

She threw a hand to her mouth. "Oh my God! What happened?"

"I'd been trying to reach him since the accident. Something was going on on the ship and he was scared. He said he was leaving the country. By the time we met up he'd been run off a cliff by two of Mercer's men. Before he died he tried to tell me something about a recording."

"A recording? Of what?" she asked.

"If there's an emergency, all conversations in dive control are backed up. Sort of like a black box. It turned out Mercer kept us on the bottom when the thrusters went down. He even had Steve removed from the panel to stop him bringing us up."

McCready could see that Sarah's mind was turning over. Then she said slowly, "So he's responsible. That man's responsible for Sean's death."

McCready paused before he replied. "Yeah, you could say that."

Her mind was clearly focused on his previous statement as McCready continued. "And there's more. I saw two divers removing gold bars from a dummy cylinder on the bell. The same guys who ran Steve off the road."

She looked up at this. "They're stealing the gold?"

"They're trying to get around the inspectors. Think about it. Most of what comes up goes back to Russia; then a sizable chunk goes to the Treasury. If you can sideline a few bars here and there, that's a very nice sideline."

"But what happens when there's a shortfall? There must have been an original manifest."

"Mercer'll just say he couldn't bring it all up—the weather, too dangerous. You name it. He can say what the hell he likes. I mean, who's going to go and check?"

"But surely you can take what you know to the police?"

McCready took a deep breath. "It's not as simple as that. I found out today that Mercer issued a press release. A journalist even turned up at the house. You'll probably hear about it—it's not pretty."

"What does it say?"

"Basically that I was responsible for Sean's death. It was my fault and I've resigned from the company in disgrace. If I say anything now it's going to look like I'm making things up—trying to get back at them, otherwise why didn't I say something before? It's Global's word against mine. No one would believe me."

"But they can't do that. You can sue them."

"Unfortunately they are doing it, and that's a minefield I really don't want to get into right now." He paused. "And anyway, it's personal now. It's way beyond the police and lawyers."

She looked at him, and when he met her gaze he was taken aback. There was something different about her, as though the information about Mercer had changed something within her. The frailty he'd seen earlier was gone. In its place was a heightened presence, like someone had taken a Photoshop sharpening tool to the cells in her body and realigned them in a harsher way. He was looking at a different woman, and when she spoke she used a tone he'd never heard before. It came from a dark place. Her voice was low, almost a whisper. She looked straight at him, and he was left in no doubt of the implication of her words.

"Get him, John. I don't care what you have to do, just get the bastard!"

Chapter 18

When he arrived home that evening Sarah's words were still racing around his head. He'd never seen her like that and it worried him. He had to do something, that was obvious—his whole career was on the line. And then there was the fact that Mercer was ultimately responsible for Sean's death, and for that he would pay dearly, but exactly what to do—that was the question.

He switched on the TV in the nook by the fireplace, grabbed a beer from the fridge and flipped on a news channel. The headline of the hour was the near miss of a satellite that had prematurely returned to Earth and nearly hit a cargo ship in the Pacific - what were the odds? There were the usual reports of famine and hardship in far off countries, back to back with a cat and her kittens rescued from a storm drain in Mexico. He never could get his head around the way the world's dramas and tragedies were treated like soap opera sound bites. But then something came on that did catch his attention. A picture of Malcolm Mercer filled the screen. He turned up the volume.

The picture was a posed publicity shot, taken outside

the HQ near Edinburgh. It moved from full to quarter screen and to one side of the newsreader. The woman was clearly in excited mode as she relayed the story.

"And more now on the extraordinary news of the lost Russian gold. Global Salvage's maverick CEO, Malcolm Mercer, has said it will be taken to a secure vault at Wellings private bank in Frederick's Place in central London, before going on display at the new Mercer Wing of the British Museum, due to open shortly. The gold, which has been salvaged from a German U-boat eight hundred feet down in the North Sea, was found by Mercer's company three years ago and has only now been raised. It was stolen from Russia by the Nazis at the end of World War II. The Russian ambassador will be at an upcoming ceremony in central London before returning a portion of the treasure to Moscow. When asked if he was nervous about the responsibility of the gold's temporary stay at the bank, Wellings' director Steve Branning had this to say."

The screen was filled with a shot of Branning, a short, balding man with a serious face.

"We're confident our newly completed deep vault is up to the task. It's the deepest in London, took two years to complete, and anything that goes in will certainly be staying there."

The screen changed to show graphics of the position of the vault beneath London, while the newsreader explained, "The vault has been constructed deep among the network of tunnels and systems beneath London's busy streets. One of the major challenges was to avoid hitting any existing tube tunnels, or the London Water ring main, which carries an underground river around the capital. Let's hope that doesn't spring a leak!" The newsreader was back on screen. "And now the weather with Trish."

McCready took a swig of beer and carried on staring at the screen. His mind was whirling.

He was suddenly jolted out of his thoughts by a loud bang from outside, like a gunshot. It was quickly followed by a second. He glanced around and then ran through to the back and out of the glass doors that led onto the raised deck.

He listened for any movement. The bay was dark, but all he could hear was the gentle lapping of waves on the shore. He wasn't taking any chances, though, after the events of the previous day.

There was another bang off to the right down by the beach. A few more seconds and there were shouts and a torch was shone in a wild arc. There was the sound of bottles clanging.

He watched for a few more minutes. There had been some problems with a local motorbike gang who occasionally came out onto the hills with shotguns. It sounded like they were drunk. They'd taken over a derelict building on the far side of the bay. McCready had told the local authorities about them but nothing had been done. That had been over a year ago. He'd even offered to buy the building—it had, after all, pretty much fallen into disrepair—but again he'd met with no response. He was convinced drug dealing was carried out at the property and one day he vowed to take matters into his own hands if things continued as they were. For now though, he couldn't be bothered with them and returned inside. At least they couldn't do any real harm.

He sat down in the nook and watched the television for another hour, but he wasn't seeing the pictures. In his mind he kept on playing the news report over and over.

He awoke with a start. It was dark. His watch said 2.30am. He listened but there was nothing. Had it been another gunshot? Then there was a scuffling sound outside his window. A dustbin clattered over.

He jumped out of bed, pulled on a sweatshirt and jeans and headed for the front door. He kept a baseball bat behind the door and grabbed it as he pulled on some sneakers.

Outside it was dark. He made his way along the side of the house. The lights for the security cameras flashed on as he moved into their zones. He couldn't hear anything, but as he reached the corner at the rear there was more scuffling. He took a deep breath, tensed his muscles, then whirled around, bat in hand, ready for anything— anything that was, except for what he saw.

He stood there in shock and gently lowered the bat. In the middle of the slab terrace outside the lower garage, Mira and Squeak were trying to get through the small gate at the bottom of the steps that led to the upper deck. They'd been here once before when they'd followed him as he carried his kayak up from the water. What was truly shocking, though, was the small bundle of fur in the middle of the slabs.

It was the other otter pup, and it was barely moving.

As he rounded the corner, the two otters froze. Then as Mira recognized him, she ran over to her pup and ran around him in circles, snuffling and muttering. Then she ran to McCready and back to her pup.

McCready walked over and gently picked up the small animal. He wasn't dead, but it wouldn't be long. There was a bad wound on his left side and he squealed pathetically every now and then, his little paws trying to grasp at the air. He was missing one leg and there was blood everywhere. McCready gently put him down on the grass at the edge of the slabs and looked at the other two otters. They were looking up at him expectantly, as if he could perform a miracle. Mira ran to the small pup and then back to McCready, becoming ever more frantic, but there was nothing he could do.

The shotgun pellets had done their worst.

A minute later the little otter gasped, and then, with a quiet sigh, moved for the final time.

McCready sat there with mother and son for half an hour, beyond the point of shivering. During this time Mira had calmed a little, but Squeak kept nuzzling his brother, confused as to why he wouldn't wake up.

Finally McCready had had to leave. He went into the garage, grabbed a spade and dug a small grave at the edge of the rear garden. Mira and Squeak followed him everywhere, and while they clearly didn't understand what he was doing, they seemed to trust him and accept his every move.

As the last of the earth covered the small body, man and otters looked at the newly dug patch of ground for a few moments. In that time something coalesced inside McCready. Parents shouldn't lose sons, and brothers shouldn't lose brothers. There had to be consequences.

He let them into the garage where it would be warm for the night and where they could be close to the little pup. Then he headed back inside and to bed, though he knew he would hardly sleep.

A plan was forming in his mind. It was pretty crazy, but right now "pretty crazy" seemed pretty good. He didn't even know if it would be possible, but he sure as hell was going to find out.

Chapter 19

Clare sat at the rear of the small inflatable boat and started the electric outboard motor. It didn't cough and splutter like a petrol-driven engine, but there was a brief high-pitched whine and then it settled down to a quiet hum as it idled away. She wore a neat red Crewsaver life jacket around her neck and had a walkie-talkie in a waterproof case strapped across her chest.

She watched as Graham Collins, one of the London Water technicians, helped Smythe into the small craft. He was also wearing a life jacket and wobbled for a moment before plonking himself down on the bouncy side tube. Clare grinned at him. "You sure you're up to this?"

He gave her a pained expression. "I'm not past it yet, my dear. And anyway, any chance to get out of the office."

"Yeah, guess you could say this is 'out of the office.'"

The boat was sitting on a fast-moving river of water that disappeared into a tunnel at either end of the vast underground chamber they were in. They were twenty-five feet below the control center at London Water, and if the center was the brains of the operation, then this was

166

the circulatory system—the arteries and veins.

Access was by an elevator from the floor above, and the space itself was massive—more like a small hanger than a room. It had been hewn out of the ground, and much of the ceiling and walls were still exposed clay strengthened by a plastic sealant. Where any infrastructure had been added, it was secured against this backdrop.

The main feature was the raised half-pipe that divided the room. It was thirty feet in diameter and the sides rose up to form the top half of the curved pipe before it entered the walls at each end. Suspended above the open section was a massive cowl on the end of a hydraulic arm that could be lowered into place. This would allow the pipe to be filled to the top as the water flowed around the system and was the default position. When work or maintenance was required, such as now, the water levels were lowered, the cowl raised, and it was possible to enter the pipe. A metal walkway straddled the structure to allow access to the other side, where large shuttered doors led to a ramp, which in turn led to the outside world. The space was large enough to handle a large flatbed truck. On the near side of the pipe there was a glass-windowed office, a number of maintenance rooms, and a control panel with monitors covering half of one of the walls. This provided basic control over the system in case there were problems in the main center above.

Collins crouched down to check Smythe had his life jacket secure, then stood up. He untied the bowline. "The level's as low as she'll go without disrupting services too much. You guys should be okay."

Smythe looked up and took the line that Collins threw to him. "Thanks, Graham. We'll see you later."

Collins couldn't resist a parting shot. "And no water-skiing under Piccadilly!"

Clare smiled and waved as she maneuvered out into the middle of the flow and they headed off into the tunnel.

The boat had just disappeared when the elevator doors in the corner of the chamber opened and the tour guide stepped out with a gaggle of eager tourists in tow.

There was much gasping and excitement as the group stared around in amazement at the facility. A father had to restrain his son as he headed for the pipe and the water, while two Japanese tourists couldn't help but start photographing everything in sight. The guide seemed to have her work cut out to keep everyone under control.

Everyone seemed to be awestruck by the space, except for a man at the rear who glanced around with more than a passing interest. He was clearly thinking deeply about something. He moved to the front of the group and took in everything around him—assessing, calculating, absorbing.

After a couple of minutes John McCready smiled to himself.

It had been worth the trip.

The small inflatable was doing about four knots and was going with the flow. It was when they headed back that things would be slower.

Clare had spent the whole of the previous day working out all the inspections she would need to do to confirm her worst fears about the system.

Number one on the list was to check the diameter of

the lift shafts that drew the water up from the main pipe to the tributaries that fed into smaller pipes and eventually delivered clean, fresh water to the millions living above.

The top of the pipe moved past about three feet above their heads. Both of them were carrying powerful torches, which lit up the surface of the pipe in an eerie way.

"Shouldn't be far now," stated Clare. They shone their beams along the side of the tunnel as Clare dropped the throttle. A minute later and they saw the opening of the first shaft that carried the water off to the side. Smythe took over the controls as Clare carefully leaned over to take the measurements.

With the boat stationary next to the shaft, she placed a laser rangefinder on one side and shot the pencil beam of red light across to the other side. A quick look at the reading and she glanced at Smythe.

"Just as I thought, six inches too narrow. To get the flow rates, you're going to have to widen the tunnels and upgrade the pumps. You might get away with just the pumps to save costs and downtime, but you're never going to get the original specs with these diameters."

Smythe looked resigned to the fact and was about to suggest they move on to the next one just to make sure, when Clare's radio crackled. It was Collins. "Clare, it's Graham, over."

Clare pressed TRANSMIT. "Read you, Graham, what's up?"

The reply carried a certain level of concern. "An alert's come through from the Brentford pumping station. There's a surge coming down. Something to do with a faulty flow gate. There's nothing they could do. It should be here in a few minutes. You guys need to get back here … fast!"

Clare was thinking. "Okay, thanks. We'll be quick as we can."

Smythe looked at her anxiously. "That's not good."

"No, that's not good," replied Clare. "Hang on!" And she spun the boat, heading back as fast as the little outboard would go.

How she wished she had the Baja 26, but somehow she didn't think London Water would appreciate the pollution the twin Mercury outboards would spew into their pristine water.

In the access chamber Collins checked the console and saw the marker for the surge move down a graphic of the pipe. It had almost reached them.

He crossed over to the tour guide and her group. "Could you all please move back away from the water. We're expecting a surge at any minute. It's nothing to worry about, but it might get a little wet around here."

They all complied and seemed to be more excited than worried as they watched the tunnel. They clearly assumed a massive tidal wave would flood the room and put on a display. To them it was just another theme park, not a working facility, and they expected to be entertained. McCready, who was now standing at the side of the group, watched with interest.

A moment later a growing roar could be heard coming from the tunnel mouth. While the group were staring into the black hole in anticipation, Collins glanced nervously into the opposite tunnel down which Clare and Smythe had disappeared.

He grabbed his walkie-talkie and was about to transmit when the little boat shot out of the opening. They had twenty feet to go to get to the side, but at that moment a wave of water surged out of the west tunnel, flooding over the edge and spilling up to the flood barriers built into the floor that surrounded the open pipe. But the wave itself carried on, little of its energy having been dissipated.

Clare swung the boat in toward the side of the pipe, but the wave hit them on the turn. It picked up the small inflatable and flipped it over, spilling Clare and Smythe into the water. They were dragged toward the gaping mouth of the tunnel.

Collins reacted fast. He ran forward, grabbed a lifebelt from the wall and threw it toward Clare, hanging on to the trailing line. It landed close to her with a splash but Smythe had gone under. She dived down after him, totally ignoring the safety of the lifebelt.

The freezing water stung her body. It felt like a vice-like grip was crushing her head. Her mind started to numb, but at least the water was clear and she could see Smythe just below her.

She swam hard and managed to grab hold of his jacket. Then she turned to swim back up but the flow was taking her further toward the tunnel entrance. She grabbed for the inflation toggle on his life jacket but her movements were becoming sluggish and she was unable to find it.

She had to get him to the surface.

Kicking hard, she finally managed to reach air. They both gasped desperately, but they were almost into the tunnel and Clare was struggling. She was exhausted from the cold and the exertion needed to bring her colleague back to the surface.

Collins was frantically pulling the lifebelt back in, ready for another attempt.

Behind him at the side of the group McCready could see where this was going. Without further bidding, he pulled off his jacket, kicked his shoes loose, and before the protesting tour guide could stop him, he ran for the pipe. He took a running dive and used the side of the pipe to launch himself into the air.

He flew the first fifteen feet before hitting the water cleanly.

After he surfaced he stroked hard to where Clare was struggling to stay afloat.

He reached them and yanked the cord on Clare's life jacket, giving her instant buoyancy. He then did the same for Smythe, and started to pull him towards the side. But Clare seemed reluctant to let him go.

"Hey, I'm fine," she said, her speech slurring with the cold. "Please get out of the water, sir."

McCready looked at her curiously. "Yeah, right!"

Collins had finally retrieved the lifebelt and sent it sailing across to them. McCready grabbed hold of it and let Collins pull them to the side. Smythe was almost unconscious and Clare was panting, sucking in large amounts of air with every breath. She glared at McCready. "I really was okay, thank you."

Collins stepped forward, having heard Clare's remark. "Hey, Clare, the guy was just trying to help."

Clare was still breathless, but managed to speak between gasps. "Yeah, and before you know it Health and Safety are crawling up your ass cos a member of the public fell in, caught a cold and is suing for negligence!"

McCready looked at her and had to smile as he climbed out and then helped Clare and Smythe onto the side. Clare wasn't amused. "It's not funny, pal!"

He offered his hand. "John McCready." But he also couldn't help noticing her wet T-shirt and the effect the cold had on the profile beneath. She followed his gaze and hostility flared across her face.

"DOCTOR Kowalski, and if you think—" But McCready cut her off.

"Well, doc, maybe you could help out with that cold then."

She glared at him and moved to check on Smythe, who was gasping for breath and shivering.

The tour guide was quite flustered by events and corralled her brood, ushering them toward the elevator. "Okay, folks, show's over. Let's move on."

McCready turned to Collins. "Hey, there anywhere I can warm up, get these clothes dried off?"

"Sure, follow me. We've some showers at the back. And by the way, thanks for your help."

"Not everyone thinks so."

"Ah, don't worry about Clare, she's all right. She's just got a lot on her plate right now."

McCready watched her as she helped put a space blanket round Smythe's shoulders. She shot a glance in his direction but quickly looked away.

Collins led him to an area that had a changing room, showers and drying facilities.

As McCready thanked him and walked inside, he realized he was shivering almost uncontrollably. The adrenalin that had kept him going was leaving his system, and all the usual bodily actions were taking over. He quickly stripped off, threw his clothes into a dryer and climbed into the shower. He generously soaped himself down and then over the next few minutes slowly warmed up his body. Eventually, when he felt almost human again, he walked out of the cubicle with a towel around his waist. He checked the dryer and felt like the guy in the jeans ad who took his clothes off and sat in a launderette in his boxer shorts.

A few minutes later he dragged the clothes out of the rotating drum and started to get dressed. He had his pants and shoes on and was just pulling his shirt on when Clare walked in.

Her mind was clearly elsewhere, and seeing McCready half-naked threw her completely. She did a double take of his slim torso and well-defined muscles and tried to leave before he noticed her, but she moved back too quickly, tripping over a broom that had been lying against the wall. It clattered to the floor. She hastily bent to pick it up. McCready glanced up. "Sorry, is this your ... the guy showed me in here."

Clare was still dealing with the broom, and when she spoke her tone was somewhat harsh. "Hey, don't mind me. You seem to do what you want anyway." She stood there defiantly.

McCready looked at her curiously and then spoke softly. "You know you wouldn't have made it back there."

Clare was again quick with a comeback, but she realized even as she spoke that it was too much. "Well I guess there's always a hero with something to prove."

McCready smiled and walked past her to the door. "Yeah, you might just be right about that. All yours. See you around."

"Somehow I doubt that," she retorted. She stared after him, again regretting her words, but he was gone. She was just about to strip for a shower when Collins came in carrying some supplies.

"Oops, sorry, Clare, didn't know you were in here."

"No problem."

Collins turned and was about to leave when Clare called him back. "Hey, Graham, you didn't by any chance get that idiot's name and number—the one who jumped in the water—did you?"

"Yeah sure," he replied. "Thought it might be useful in case he needs to fill out a form for the incident report. Er, why do you want it?"

At this, Clare blushed slightly. "Oh, you know, just in case we get any letters from lawyers trying to sue us. Always good to be prepared."

Collins looked at her strangely. "Okay, I'll put it on your desk." And with that he left, closing the door behind him.

Clare sat on a bench for a second, feeling for all the world like a giddy teenager. She felt herself blushing again and she hated herself for it.

Mercer had been fielding calls from the press all day. While the task would normally be beneath him and would usually be handled by a press officer, the situation was so delicate it required the full support and credibility of the CEO to back up the veracity of the stated facts.

He'd seen some of the online copy and was satisfied Global's statement had been accepted. McCready wouldn't have a leg to stand on, which was why when

Jennings called with some concerns he wasn't too worried.

"I've spoken to Paul Matthews and he says Donovan could have activated the voice recorder in dive control, though he can't be certain. If he did, it could be incriminating," said Jennings.

Mercer leaned back in his chair and thought for a moment. "It's our word against his. The press is on our side for the moment, but it could make things difficult if some reporter starts digging. It all depends how McCready reacts. He may just lie down and go away."

"I wouldn't count on it, sir. He doesn't strike me as the type. Do I need to take care of it?"

Mercer thought for a moment. "There's too much media interest right now. Let's see where this goes. We don't want to rock the boat. It was regrettable Donovan was killed. Someone might start putting two and two together. Your men were overzealous, Connor. Keep an eye on McCready and keep me informed.

"Yes, sir."

Chapter 20

McCready had spent the night at an over-priced airport hotel and then caught the early Friday morning flight back to Aberdeen.

During the flight he had had time to do a lot of thinking.

From what he'd seen at London Water his plan might just work. But as in any project, taking an idea through to reality took time, and a million problems could come up that you'd never envisaged. And when that plan was illegal and could very well get you killed or put in prison, the problems would be even greater.

The plane landed at Aberdeen airport about twenty minutes late. There had been strong headwinds for most of the flight and some rough turbulence just before they touched down.

He picked up the Range Rover from the car park and was now heading for the city center. He stared out of the windscreen as he entered the outskirts and put his negative thoughts aside. The sky was overcast, but the major chill of the last few days was gone and a blustery wind enveloped the city.

He managed to make it through the congested city center, and on down past the main dock entrance. About a quarter of a mile further along the road, he turned into the entrance to Ocean Oil Exploration. He was expected, so he passed through security without any dramas and drove down a tarmac road to park next to the main construction building.

As he climbed out, the massive structure loomed large above him. It was fifty feet high and a hundred and fifty feet from front to back. He flagged down a company truck with scaffolding on the back. The driver lowered the window and looked at him inquiringly. McCready shouted up. "Craig Richards?"

The driver indicted behind him. "Out by the dock."

McCready waved in acknowledgment and headed down by the side of the construction building to the rear. As he passed one of the massive sliding doors that extended all the way to the roof, he could hear the noise of heavy machinery. Arc welders crackled away. Metal clanged on metal and sparks flew from grinders. Business was clearly good, which made him happy. He had a major shareholding in the company.

Ocean Oil Exploration was a service support business for the oil industry. It was also involved in the design and development of small submersibles and other underwater-related equipment. Aside from being of interest to the oil companies, these also had the military sniffing around on occasion. Either way, the company was known for using cutting-edge technology and materials in its products and for thinking outside the box when it came to a design philosophy.

McCready was here to see the director, Craig Richards.

Richards was an old friend, and if his idea was to have any chance of working, this was one guy he had to convince. He knew Richards would say he was crazy and immediately balk at what he was proposing, but he also knew he was always up for a challenge, and the guy did owe him—big time.

Behind the construction building was a large open area about the size of an out-of-town supermarket car park. It was clearly a dumping ground for defunct equipment and a storage area for consumables such as metal plate and girders. Scattered around were the rusty cast-offs of failed experiments in rig and sub design, as well as old buoys and anchors which looked like derelict guards from some far-off mechanical planet.

To the left was a massive dry dock with a section of an oil rig leg parked high and dry. Part of it was rusted through, and where it had originally been attached to the rig there were broken pipes and metal supports. It looked like the dismembered leg of a gigantic terminator.

The dockside itself was lined with cranes, which could reach out across the full width of the dry dock facility. McCready was walking along the side of the dock looking at the rig leg when he heard a voice he knew well.

"Well, if it isn't Scotland's most wanted!"

McCready looked around but he couldn't see his old friend. He'd completed a full circle when he realized and glanced up. There, thirty feet above, Craig Richards was suspended in a small cage hanging from a tower crane. Stockily built and with a direct but amiable personality, Richards waved at McCready and then signaled the crane driver to lower him down. When the cage reached the ground, he unlocked the gate and McCready climbed in.

They shook hands and Richards put a hand on his shoulder.

"John, good to see you. It was real tough about Sean. If it helps any, none of the guys believe the reports."

"Thanks, but you don't know the half of it. That's why I'm here."

Richards looked intrigued. "Okay, we'll talk as we go over. I need to check out the jacket on the far side. We're trying to work out why the leg failed in a storm it should easily have survived." He paused. "By the way, how's Sarah holding up?"

"She's strong. She'll pull through, but it's not easy for her."

Richards nodded and then lifted the walkie-talkie, looking up at the crane driver. He pressed TRANSMIT. "Okay, take us up."

The driver gave a thumbs up and they started to rise into the air. When they were at a height of about eighty feet the crane swung them out over the dock. Richards looked at McCready. "So what can I do you for?"

McCready paused for a second, refining his thoughts. "Submersible mating collars. You guys working on anything?"

Richards grinned but remained coy. "Always working on anything. Been a lot of interest since the Kursk disaster. Need to mate to different surfaces, variable angles. The Deep Submergence Rescue Vehicle (DSRV) our boys have—same as the Yanks—only mates straight down or else at an angle of forty degrees, which is pretty restrictive. Problem is, if the target's at a more acute angle, you're screwed."

McCready remembered the Kursk disaster. The

Russian Oscar-class submarine had been on a training exercise in the Barents Sea in August 2000 when a torpedo had exploded on board. The sub had crashed to the seabed but there were sailors still alive in the rear compartments. What followed had been an almost farcical delay as the Russians refused Western help to rescue the crew until it was too late. One of the big issues had been the angle of the submarine on the seabed and the fact that none of the DSRVs that were finally allowed down were able to dock with the Kursk's hatch because of the angle. All the crew had died. It was one of the Russian Navy's darkest hours.

"So, did you come up with anything?" persisted McCready.

The cage was now directly over the rig leg. Richards signaled to stop and the movement slowed and then halted. The cage swung gently in the light breeze. Richards pulled out a camera and started taking a variety of shots of the leg. "Well now, that might just be classified. What do you want it for?"

"Can't say right now, but it's to do with Sean's death, and Steve Donovan."

Richards stopped and looked up. "Nasty accident that, I hear."

"You hear wrong."

Richards looked at him curiously and then carried on with the camera. "We've made some progress with the collars, but everything's at prototype stage. Nothing I'd send out with a guarantee."

McCready pulled his coat tighter against the wind that had started to pick up and was making the cage sway a little more. "I don't need guarantees, Craig. Just something that won't let me down."

Richards finished with the camera and signaled for the crane driver to take them back down. As they swung away from the dock, he continued. "Oh, she won't let you down, boyo. It's just not—how shall I put it—lawyer friendly right now."

Ten minutes later and they were sitting in the main design studio at Ocean Oil. It was on the upper floor of a large test tank facility and was fitted out with the latest CAD software with a bank of large 5k monitors connected to Power Mac computers. Two designers were concentrating on their screens on the far side of the room.

Richards led McCready to a display in the corner. They sat in comfortable high back chairs designed to relieve the fatigue of long stints at a computer screen. Richards searched the files until he found one marked *Sophie*. He clicked on it.

McCready glanced at him. Richards shrugged. "Name all the prototypes. This one's complicated, won't do what I ask and throws a tantrum when we try something new."

McCready looked at him. "I seem to remember you were married to a Sophie."

Richards stopped, thought for a second. "Yeah, you're right, so I was." He grinned and turned back to the computer.

A second later and a series of 3D graphics appeared on screen, clearly showing the outline of a submersible, but unlike any McCready had seen before.

Richards typed into the keyboard. This brought up a new menu. He then moved the mouse on the table. The sub graphic immediately rotated in 3D, showing three-sixty degrees around the design.

"Okay, this is the prototype of the next-generation DSRV. She takes four at a pinch and is good for three thousand feet. The final version will carry up to ten, but we're just making sure the technology works as a proof of concept before scaling her up. She has all the latest technology we can fit in her: automatic equalization in the cabin in case of pressure breach; auto rebreather monitoring to cope with deco—you name it, she's got it."

He maneuvered the graphic round to the side. The overall profile was similar to other small submersibles. There was a large glass dome at the front, where the driver sat. This led into the standard cigar-shaped rear, but that was where the similarities ended. The first thing McCready noticed was that it wasn't clear where the hatch was to enter and exit the sub.

Richards continued. "But this is the real breakthrough. What we've done is insert this frame here in the mid-section." He used the cursor to point out a large collar that ran around the full circumference of the sub at the midpoint. "It runs three-sixty, allowing the mating collar to rotate and attach to its target at any angle."

"So, effectively, you can have the hatch at any position. Clever. So how do you get her to swivel and seal at pressure?"

Richards gave him an inscrutable glance. "That, my boy, is why people like you come to see people like me."

"And this actually works?" asked McCready skeptically.

Richards threw him a disapproving look, stood up and walked to a door at the side of the room. "Come on, I'll show you."

McCready followed him outside, which was actually

still inside as the design studio was merely an elevated gallery within the massive test tank building. A metal staircase led down to the main floor of the facility.

The space was dominated by a large water tank. It was over a hundred feet in length and fifty feet wide. For most of its area it was around twenty feet deep, but a section in the middle extended down to forty feet. Across the full width of the far end was an array of hydraulic plates that could rise and fall to the instructions of a sophisticated computer model. It allowed the creation of realistic waves up to two feet in height. That might not sound much, but when put in context with models of ships and other structures that might be placed in the tank, it could simulate waves of up to fifty feet in the real world with full control over their amplitude and frequency. Around the side was a work area that at the moment had the support infrastructure for the submersible. To the side of this, against the wall, McCready could see the sub, but it looked slightly different to the design on the computer.

When they reached the bottom of the stairs, McCready headed towards it, but Richards called out. "Oh no, this way, John. That's the Mark One. You go anywhere in that, you'll be springing a leak at fifty feet!"

Richards led him down to an observation window that was below ground level and allowed a view into the tank from underwater. Beyond the glass McCready could see another sub and this one was an exact reproduction of the 3D model he had seen on the computer.

At present the rotating hatch was docked to a metal plate that was skewed over at an angle of forty-five degrees. As he watched, the plate moved around the sub, stopping at intervals before rotating further.

Close to the sub were two support divers who were recording the test with video and stills cameras. They were both wearing drysuits. The massive volume of water in the tank would have been too expensive to heat.

Richards picked up a mike next to the window. "How's it going, Chris?"

One of the divers stopped taking photos and pressed a button on the wireless comms unit built into his full face mask. "Not too shabby, boss. Had some leakage at one-forty, but we're working on it."

"You do that," replied Richards. Then he clicked off the mike and glanced at McCready. "We've had some teething problems, but that's to be expected. Nothing we can't handle."

McCready thought for a second. "Okay, if I needed it, how long till she'll swim?"

Richards was taken aback. "Steady, John. It's never even been in the sea, for God's sake. We've a whole series of tests still to run. You don't just put this sort of hardware into the field. Too many things to go wrong. People could get hurt. Like I said, she's not lawyer friendly right now."

"For the record, I don't know many lawyers, and don't worry, it's not going anywhere near the sea."

Richards sighed. "I really don't know. I'd need more details of what you have in mind. Then I can assess the risks, go over the areas we haven't smoothed out yet. Know what I mean?"

"There are some things I have to check out first. Take a few days, but trust me, Craig, it'll give you the best goddamned test dive you're ever gonna get!"

Richards looked at him skeptically.

Chapter 21

The London skyline at night was a beautiful sight. The iconic new wave of buildings from The Shard and the colloquially known Cheesegrater and Gherkin sat at opposite ends of the design spectrum to the historical outlines of the Houses of Parliament, Tower Bridge and St Paul's Cathedral, but somehow they all seemed to work, reflecting the character of an ever diverse and changing city.

From a height of two thousand feet on a clear evening, all this history and futuristic architecture was laid out like a model village as McCready started the descent into Heathrow.

The River Thames was a black ribbon surrounded by twinkling lights, and many of the buildings were clearly recognizable from the plane. He knew the journey was nearly over as they passed the floodlit Wembley stadium, standing proud beyond the starboard wing, its white girder-like arch curving high over the famous pitch. There must have been a match on, as a zillion megawatts of light spewed up into the night sky like a cauldron of fire.

The late Monday afternoon flight from Aberdeen had

been uneventful, and over the weekend he had been working on refining the next stage of the plan.

Richards and his sub were at the core of things, and nothing could go ahead without them—that was a given. With the right approach and just the right amount of pressure, he was sure Richards could be persuaded. The next phase, however, was a shot in the dark—the complete unknown. It would mean taking a serious risk, and for most of the flight he'd been thinking that the sensible decision would be to just turn around at the airport, get right back on the next flight north and forget the whole thing. However, he wasn't someone to give up once he was set on a path, and as the cab pulled up at his destination, he found he was more than looking forward to the challenge ahead. He paid the driver and walked up the steps and through the revolving doors of London Water.

The reception area was quiet at that time of the evening. As he entered, some of the staff were leaving and chatting among themselves as they headed home, pulling their coats tight against the cold they knew would greet them through the revolving doors. McCready took a deep breath and walked over to the reception desk in the corner. The receptionist looked up.

"Can I help you, sir?"

"Yes, I'm looking for Clare Kowalski." He was taking a gamble that she'd still be there, as most of the staff would have left, but the technician he'd spoken to previously had said she had a lot on at the moment, so it was likely she'd be working late.

"I'll just try her line. Who shall I say is calling?"

McCready thought for a moment, then smiled. "Just

say, her hero!"

The receptionist gave him a curious look, but dialed the number anyway.

McCready crossed over to the other side of the lobby and looked at the large prints on the wall. They showed some impressive engineering, and the more he looked at the massive tunnels and the scope of the system, the more he thought his plan might work.

As he moved along the wall he caught sight of the photo with Clare in the group. She even looked good in a set of overalls and a hard hat. He was taking a closer look when he heard footsteps behind.

"You!" Clare's voice showed irritation, but also a certain amount of curiosity.

McCready turned and smiled broadly. "Hi, doc, I've got this real pain, just here at the back of the neck, and was wondering whether you could help me out."

Clare sighed, as though the last thing she needed right now was to be dealing with an idiot, but she didn't leave. "I'm not that kind of doctor. Anyway, what are you doing here?"

He looked directly at her and continued with a completely straight face. "Well, I was thinking about the other day and it's only fair I give you a chance to apologize. So I thought you could show me around."

Clare looked incredulous. "Apologize? I really haven't got time for this." She started to turn.

"You always have a problem with people trying to help you?"

She stopped. "I have a problem with … never mind."

"Look, for what it's worth, it took a lot of guts to go after that old guy. I just don't meet many women who would do something like that."

That blindsided her.

She paused. "So what are you saying?"

"Well some people might call it a compliment."

That seemed to give her something to think about.

He persisted "So, will you show me around?"

"You've already taken the tour."

"Well, things often look different on a second viewing, don't you think?"

She paused again. "You're very presumptive," she replied.

McCready smiled. "One of my annoying habits."

"One of many no doubt," she said under her breath. Then she hesitated for a moment. Finally she said "Well, I guess you'd better follow me then." And with that she turned and strode off down the corridor. McCready followed.

When they entered the control room the lights were dim and there was a skeleton staff on duty. Two technicians were working at a console on the far side. One, who was putting on her coat and looked as though she was about to leave, glanced up and waved at Clare. She then looked at McCready and her face seemed to light up. She dropped everything and came over, reaching out to shake McCready's hand. "Mr. McCready, I'm Kelly, it's so great to meet you after what you did for Jason. Everyone's talking about it. It was so wonderful."

Clare rolled her eyes. McCready smiled, shaking her hand. "Oh it was nothing really." Then with a glance at Clare. "Least that's what I'm told."

Clare steered him away and toward the main display. "Come along, Mr. McCready, wouldn't want you believing your own press now, would we?" Kelly raised her eyebrows and gave Clare a wicked look.

"Goodnight Kelly," said Clare.

Kelly smiled and left.

Clare joined McCready at the display. The thirty foot by twenty foot screen dominated the room. The focus of the display was the massive oval tube representing the ring main. There were labels at strategic points around the oval showing the geographical position of the pipe around London. The oval was linked by two tunnels, one crossing from left to right and another from top to bottom. They intersected in the middle. Other smaller tunnels led off from the main oval at various points around the display.

McCready looked at every detail with interest. "Impressive. So go on, I need the full tour here." He glanced at her. She glared back, and then rather awkwardly started to explain what was on the screen.

"Well, the large oval, or giant doughnut as we call it, is the ring main—kinda simplified—and you're looking at half a million gallons a minute right under your feet. The lines in the center represent the crossover tunnels which link the main pipe north-south, east-west, so the flow can be diverted when required … Look is all this really necessary?"

McCready looked intently at the display, but then glanced at her. "Go on, you're doing great. How deep is it?"

Clare took a breath. "Well at a maximum the crossover tunnels hit about a hundred feet, but the ring is a lot shallower, about forty feet. This was required to be able to lift water up through these lift shafts." She pointed out the connections that led from the ring main oval.

McCready took a step back. "Must have been some job building this little lot."

"No kidding. Took five years, and it was like threading a needle through a ball of wool without touching any of the strands. You have any idea of the number of tunnels and structures beneath London? Here, take a look at this."

She crossed over to one of the computer screens and was clearly becoming more enthusiastic the more she explained the system. She searched through a pile of DVD data discs on the desk and then pulled one out and loaded it into a slot drive. A few seconds later a 3D graphic appeared on the screen. A move of the mouse and the graphic rotated, a bit like the sub McCready had seen at Ocean Oil, only this was far more complex. It showed the layout of the whole Tube system, London's underground rail network. Most people were used to seeing the different lines as colors on a simple 2D map, but to see a three-dimensional imagining of all the tunnels, stations and linking passages was simply breathtaking, and then to see it rotated was something truly impressive.

McCready let out a breath. "Wow. I never knew there was so much down there."

Clare grinned. "That's just the Tube lines and support structures. How about this?" She clicked a menu and brought up another layer. This one was electrical and gas systems. Then she added buildings, basements and other subterranean infrastructure, much of which extended down many floors. Finally, she clicked the mouse and the London Water system was overlaid on the screen. It hardly seemed possible that it would all fit in there. Clare rotated the graphic and it showed what a truly remarkable place the world beneath London's streets really was.

McCready was stunned. "Unbelievable."

He looked closer at the screen and pointed out a number of shaded areas that seemed to run through many of the structures indicated on the graphic. "What are these, here?" He pointed to one in particular that passed right across the ring main and stretched down to the Thames.

"Oh those, they're dead tunnels—underground rivers. The ground beneath London is riddled with them. That big one you're pointing at was found during the excavations. Its all dried up now, but the ring main passes straight through it.

Clare tapped on the keyboard and glanced at him. "Now comes the fun part." She clicked some virtual controls and the view changed to inside the ring main itself. Another click and the point of view started to move forward until it was zooming through the tunnel. Initially the walls were solid, but with a slide of a control they became semi-opaque. You could see all the other infrastructure flying past as the camera sped onward.

McCready was mesmerized. "Can you find any specific location?"

"Sure. You just enter the street name and you're in. Have a go if you like."

McCready moved to the keyboard and typed "FREDERICK'S PLACE". Immediately the view jumped out of the tunnel and moved to another point in the system. The surface was simulated as a thin transparent layer above the graphic, and the name

FREDERICK'S PLACE appeared, while at the same time showing the street above the layer. Below ground, the network of tunnels, pipes and systems was as dense as ever, but there, slap bang in the middle, was a massive square block. It protruded sixty feet below ground level and came within a foot of one of the crossover tunnels. McCready pointed it out.

"Whoa, that's a bit close. What on earth is that?" But he knew exactly what it was.

It was the vault at Wellings Bank.

Clare looked closer. "Oh yeah, I remember that one. It was real tricky. When the crossover links went in it was still on the drawing board—one of those private banks, I think. Ended up with only a foot clearance between the tunnel and their structure."

McCready was incredulous. "A foot? You're kidding. Is that safe?"

"You wouldn't think so, but when they were digging Crossrail their main tunnel came within six inches of the Central Line. Talk about cutting it fine!" She paused and then glanced at him, looking curious. "So why'd you look there?"

McCready hesitated for a second. "I work at offices round the corner and they were removing earth from that street for what seemed like forever. Just wanted to see what the hell they were doing."

McCready looked at the graphics for a few seconds and then turned to Clare. "Okay, so what about the access chamber?"

"Thought you'd have seen enough of that?"

"Hey, full apology—full tour!"

Clare frowned. "This is not an apology. In fact, I don't

even know why I'm doing this. I'm backed up to the eyeballs with work and it's …" She checked her watch. "Oh my God, is that the time?"

McCready was worried she'd call it a day. "Okay, just five minutes, then I'll be out of your hair for good."

She weighed things up and then sighed. "Okay, come on. Five minutes." She turned and headed for the elevator. "Follow me."

As she crossed over to the elevator, McCready checked no one was looking and then quickly ejected the DVD and pocketed it. He caught her up before she even knew he was lagging behind.

She pulled out a security card and scanned it on a reader at the side of the elevator door. It beeped and McCready could hear the whirring of the elevator machinery. Clare glanced at him. "It's usually unmanned down there this time of night, unless there's something on in the pipe. They like to keep it pretty locked down."

The elevator doors opened and they stepped inside. They closed smoothly when Clare hit the button and the elevator started its descent.

"So, security's pretty tight, huh?" he asked.

Clare waved the card at him. "Yeah, you can only get down here with one of these. Lets you use the elevator or the loading tunnel to bring goods and equipment in from the road."

The doors opened smoothly and they walked out into the now quiet access chamber. Clare crossed to the light switches and threw some of them on, but not all of them. There was enough light to see by, but there was also a certain atmosphere or mood as well. "Okay, kiddo. You've got five minutes. What do you want to know?"

McCready walked out into the large open space. The cowl was in place, but there was a background throb of the flow of water from behind the steel cover. It felt like the bowels of a ship, like there was a living, breathing monster just behind the thin steel plate.

He looked at the large control panel on the wall. "So what's operated down here? I thought everything was controlled from upstairs."

"We can maintain the network from here. There are lots of duplicate controls in case something goes down from the master control upstairs. From a practical point of view the pipe gives you access to any part of the system."

"And the water flow?"

"Five pumping stations around the loop. Fly-by-wire from up top, but we've some safety overrides down here. Type what you want, computer does the rest."

Clare spent the next five minutes showing McCready the intricacies of the system and how it worked.

When she'd finished McCready stepped back and looked at her.

"So where do you fit in?"

"Hydrodynamics." He looked blank. "Water flow profiles?" Still blank. "If you want to move a mass of water from A to B …"

"Oh right. Fluid exchange, pumped under pressure," said McCready innocently.

"Well …"

"So you don't just look good in a wet T-shirt!"

"Oh come on, McCready, you can do better than that," she jousted.

McCready smiled. "Yeah, I probably can."

"So what about you? What keeps you off the streets when you're not looking for phone booths to change in?" she asked.

"Oh, very boring really—stockbroker in the City. Small office in Old Jewry, just near Frederick's Place. It pays the bills."

Clare looked at him curiously. "Funny, didn't take you for the City type."

"Well, you never can tell." He checked his watch. "Look, I've taken up enough of your time. I know you're very busy. I really should be going."

Clare hesitated. For some reason she was disappointed. "Oh right, well okay. Hope you enjoyed the tour."

He smiled again. "Yeah I did, thanks … and apology accepted."

Ten minutes later Clare had escorted McCready to the entrance. He had said goodbye and waved back at her before climbing into a cab.

He instructed the driver to head for Heathrow and pulled out his phone. He also pulled out the DVD from his pocket.

After three rings the gruff voice of Craig Richards answered. "Okay, cowboy, what you got?"

McCready glanced at the DVD. "Craig, that information I was after. You've just gotta see this."

Chapter 22

The DVD drive spun up to speed with an angry whine and a few seconds later the 3D graphic of subterranean London appeared on the computer display.

It was early morning the next day and McCready and Richards were back in Ocean Oil's design studio. Richards watched with interest but also with the tired resignation of a father humoring a persistent child. He'd known McCready a long time and in these situations it was usually better to let him get it out of his system rather than try to stop him in mid-flow.

When the graphics came up on the screen though, Richards couldn't help but be impressed and stared in fascination at the sight of the intertwined networks beneath London. McCready maneuvered the location to Frederick's Place, and the bank vault appeared right next to one of the crossover tunnels.

McCready started his pitch. "Okay, you know my position with Global Salvage. You know what I've told you about how Steve Donovan died, and Mercer's role in Sean's death. Putting it as simply as I can, I'm not going to let him get away with this. That son of a bitch is going to pay and pay in the only way he knows how. I'm going to take his gold away from him."

Richards was about to say something, but thought better of it. He suddenly had a very bad feeling about this.

McCready continued, indicating the graphic. "This large block is the vault at Wellings Bank. It's where Mercer is going to store the gold before it's put on display at the British Museum in January. This round tunnel is the London Water ring main. It's large enough to drive three double-decker buses through side by side. It connects to this crossover tunnel that runs within a foot of the bank vault. I've been in a room where you could launch the DSRV. From there you fly down the pipe to the vault, lock onto the wall, blow through, and it's all yours—$5 billion in gold bars—tax free." He paused.

"So what do you think?"

Richards was quite literally stunned. McCready had come to him with a lot of hair-brained ideas over the years but this was on a completely different level. Most of them were usually somewhere within the confines of the law, but this was in a whole other league. "Are you completely and absolutely freaking nuts?"

McCready looked at him with a lopsided expression. "Okay, but it's got potential, yeah?"

Richards sat back in his chair, tried to think of what to say and then looked directly at McCready. "Not only would you need access to the system undetected, you'd have to control the flow rates in the pipe, know exactly, and I mean precisely, where to blast through, have an escape route if something went wrong—have an escape route if something didn't go wrong—and, oh yeah, in case you hadn't realized, it's breaking the law!"

McCready didn't look fazed. "But apart from that?"

Richards looked incredulous. "You're serious, aren't you?"

McCready leant forward and stared at Richards intently. "I'm thinking about my brother, Craig. I'm thinking about Sarah, whose baby will never know her father. I'm thinking about Steve Donovan, and I'm thinking about justice for that bastard, Mercer. What do you think about every night when you go to bed?"

Richards sat there wearily for a moment. Then he looked at the graphics on the computer and sighed. "Okay, hypothetically, if you were going to do this you'd definitely need the DSRV—there's no other way, and a support sub, probably Deep Rover. But you'd have to sort out entry and exit, and somehow you'd have to find at least three other nutters who were certifiable. But, Jesus, John, I'd be putting the company on the line if I get into this."

McCready's expression was uncompromising. "And the start-up cash?"

Richards froze. "You're kidding?"

"I'm calling it in, Craig."

"You really are serious, aren't you?" McCready didn't answer.

Richards sighed and pushed back in his chair. He shook his head. "Okay, we need to talk to some people—hypothetically."

The Yorkshire Dales were wild and beautiful places during the day. At night in a howling gale and driving rain they were not so hospitable. It had taken McCready and Richards over five hours to drive down from Aberdeen and as they headed into the night along a mud track, McCready was thinking that this hadn't been such a great idea. Richards had assured him it would be worth the trip though, and that the guy they had come to see was hard to pin down, so to catch him when they knew where he was, was their best option.

The place they were heading for was a wonder in itself. The Gaping Gill cave system included the largest cavern in Britain and linked into a number of smaller caves and passages that were explored by visitors throughout the year. Richards had made some calls and his network of contacts had tracked the man they were looking for down to this location.

The Range Rover lurched over a small landslip on the side of the road and McCready glanced at Richards. "He'd better be worth it, Craig."

Richards grinned. "Oh, Mac is definitely worth it. Used to be a sub skipper, though how he crams himself into a mini sub at over six foot I've no idea. He was doing that till he discovered 'holes in the ground.' Guy's a legend in the cave-diving world. First one to make it a mile underground on heliox—solo."

"So what the hell's he doing here?" The rain increased, if that were possible, and he flicked the wipers on to full speed. The blades tore across the windscreen in a desperate attempt to remove the water and allow a view ahead.

"Some kids got stuck down a pothole in a side part of the cave system. That's why we're not heading for the visitor area. They were with their parents, who were exploring an off-piste section of the caves, totally off limits to the public, when they became separated—that was thirty-six hours ago. With all the rain, the tunnels are starting to flood. Mac was in the area, heard about the situation and came down to offer his services. Not sure the authorities are too happy though—he has a reputation." McCready glanced at him. "Oh, don't worry, it's the sort of reputation you're going to need if your half-arsed scheme is going to have a hope in hell's chance of working."

"Okay, but can he be trusted?"

Richards nodded. "We go way back." McCready wasn't convinced.

Twenty minutes later they pulled up next to a cluster of vehicles parked close to a large gash in the rock on the side of a hill. There was a mountain rescue 4x4, an ambulance and about five cars. There was also a TV news satellite truck. A long wheelbase Land Rover Defender that had seen better days was parked to one side all on its own. The area was lit by high mobile arc lights. A bright pool of light moved among the twenty or so people as the news crew roamed around looking for sound bites and background material.

McCready and Richards climbed out of the car and made their way over to the group. The cameraman had now steadied his shot on the reporter, who was just fixing her hair and listening to her earpiece. As the two men approached, she went live on air.

"Thank you, Martin. Now, as you can see, the weather is hampering all efforts to bring the two children up from deep underground. It's thought that, with the excessive rain, the cave will be like a waterfall, or worse. In fact, one of the UK's top cave divers, Mac Logan, known in the diving community as Mad Mac, has offered his services to help try and reach the trapped youngsters. As of now the authorities have declined the offer. When asked for an explanation, one of the mountain rescue team said, and I quote, "We've enough cowboys down there already. We can handle the situation." This, in fact, remains to be seen, as the search is now into its second day and there's still no word."

McCready and Richards had reached the brightly lit hole in the rock that disappeared vertically into the ground. There wasn't much to see except for the top of a metal ladder protruding from the entrance. The rain had turned everything else to mud. McCready pulled up his hood to keep the rain off. "Thought you said this guy was a legend?"

"Oh he is," replied Richards.

Suddenly there was movement from the side of the hole, and one of the cops started to move everyone back. "Okay, everyone please make way, rescuers coming through."

At that moment three rescue workers climbed wearily from the hole. They looked exhausted and were covered in mud. The lead rescuer looked up and shook his head.

The reporter spotted them and ran over with the camera crew following closely behind. She reached him and pushed the microphone in his face. He didn't look too pleased. The reporter enthusiastically asked the burning question. "So what progress so far? Have you found them?" She looked expectantly at the guy, who was clearly unimpressed.

"We went as deep as we could but the water level's too high. I doubt they've got a chance. Two of our guys are still down there, but it's hopeless."

McCready noticed a couple standing quietly at the side of the group listening intently. They looked emotionally drained and physically shattered. At the final words, the woman, who must have been in her early thirties and was clearly the mother, burst into tears. The man put his arms around her, holding her close. McCready felt for them. The uncertainty must be unbearable.

The reporter persisted. "Wouldn't it have been helpful to have Mac Logan on the rescue?"

The rescuer's face turned hostile. "Are you kidding? There are rules, procedures. People like that—" but he was cut off by a shout from a man at the edge of the group.

"There, up there!" The man pointed up at a dirt track that led round the side of the muddy hill. Immediately the camera and light swung away from the rescuers to illuminate the path.

At first it wasn't clear, but gradually the form of a large man walked into the beam of light. He was massive, and his body-hugging black wetsuit was covered in mud. A large tear stretched down the side of the torso. A small SCUBA cylinder was slung across his back.

But in his arms he carried the two youngsters.

Mac Logan knew how to make an entrance.

The kids were exhausted, but the little girl giggled and pulled at his beard. He laughed with them, but it was clear he'd been through an ordeal. As he came closer the reporter and camera crew dashed forward. The rest of the group surged behind them. The mother and father pushed through to reach their children.

Logan dropped the kids and they ran to their parents.

The mother flung her arms around both of them and hugged them till they could hardly breathe. She was sobbing freely. The father joined in and the reunited family were in a world of their own. As Logan passed, though, the mother looked up and a moment of deep understanding and gratitude passed between them. But then the reporter pushed in as Logan moved on toward his Land Rover at the edge of the field.

"Mr. Logan, Mr. Logan! How did you manage to rescue them?"

Logan was calm and almost oblivious to all the fuss. He didn't even glance down when he answered. "Well, there are those who think they know these caves and then there's me."

The reporter pressed on. "Right. Did the emergency services help you bring them out?"

At this, Logan did briefly glance down, still in mid-stride. "Were they here?"

The reporter realized she wasn't going to get any more out of him and turned and went in pursuit of the family. The rest of the group were gathered around the happy reunion. Logan walked on alone toward the Land Rover. Richards and McCready moved away from the chaos and followed him over.

When he reached the Defender, Logan stood silently for a second leaning against the vehicle, then he dropped his weight belt to the ground and was about to ease the aqualung off his back when Richards stepped forward. "Here, let me help you with that."

Logan stopped and his body stiffened slightly. Then without turning, he replied, "Aye, that you could."

Richards reached up, eased the aqualung off his back,

laid it on the ground and then stood back up.

Logan turned and took a lingering look at Richards. He had a slight smile on his face. A second later and Richards was lying on the floor six feet away having been hit by a sledgehammer right hook. He was too stunned to move and McCready wasn't sure what to do. He instinctively moved forward in defense of his friend, but Richards waved him back. He shook his head and looked directly up at Logan, confusion written across his face.

Logan stared down at him. "That's for Betsy."

Richards looked even more confused. "Thought you two were over."

"We are now. Just making my point."

"You finished?"

"Aye."

Logan walked over and reached down. He helped Richards to his feet and then threw his arms around him, giving him a massive bear hug. "Craig, good to see you again."

"You too, I think." Richards was still slightly bemused and was rubbing his jaw in pain. Then he nodded over at McCready. "Mac, this is John McCready. He's got a proposition for you."

Logan looked McCready up and down. "Has he now?"

Chapter 23

The Range Rover sped along the A556 to the south of Northwich in the northwest of England. It was nine o'clock in the morning and McCready and Richards had spent the night at a bed and breakfast just north of Manchester. The weather was clear and McCready had finally accepted Richards' assurance that Logan would be a necessary member of the team. He had the right skills, and his temperament was actually an asset. You needed someone bloody-minded for a job like this. McCready had taken some convincing, but time was short and he trusted Richards with his life.

They were now on their way to meet someone else Richards had said would be required if the whole scheme was to have any chance of succeeding. When asked about him, Richards had remained tight-lipped and just told him to wait and see. This hadn't filled McCready with confidence, but right now he didn't have much choice.

They were about five miles from their destination, which was an ordnance company called Magma Explosives. Richards had assured McCready that the guy they were coming to see could make things go bang in ways you never knew existed. McCready had been trained in the use of explosives underwater, but he wasn't up to speed with the cutting edge of the science. Today would hopefully open his eyes.

He reached over to the central touch-screen on the dashboard, clicked the phone app and then speed dialed Paul Matthews. While he was waiting for it to be answered, he glanced at Richards. "Paul Matthews should be fine, after what Mercer did in dive control. And he's a great technician. He could be useful."

"That would make up the three, if you can get him."

The speaker suddenly came alive. "Hi, this is Paul."

"Paul, John McCready."

"John, hi. I'm so sorry I missed the funeral, but Lucy had to go in for some more tests," replied Matthews.

"How is she?"

Matthews' voice dropped, and he suddenly sounded extremely tired. "It's as we thought. The cancer's spread, and the experimental procedure won't be covered. We're talking tens of thousands, maybe hundreds. We just don't have that kind of cash. So that leaves us with conventional therapy. There's still a chance, but you hear all these stories. It doesn't look good."

"I'm so sorry, Paul. I'm sure things will work out okay in the end." He paused, as though choosing his words carefully. "Look, I've got something on—high risk, high reward. If it comes off, you could probably buy a hospital. Might solve all your problems. Oh, yeah, and it'll screw Mercer for good. You interested?"

Matthews didn't even take a second to reply. "Where do I sign?"

"Great, I'll be in touch." And he ended the call.

Richards glanced at McCready raising two fingers.

They left the main road and drove down country lanes for another two miles. Then Richards said, "It's just up here on the left." McCready saw the turn at the last minute as it was obscured by a high hedge. He had to brake harder than he would have liked and a lorry behind blared its horn and then was gone. Ahead, the lane continued straight for about a mile then disappeared into a forest in the distance.

A couple of minutes later and they were approaching the trees at the start of the forest. "So, this explosives guy, he does know we're coming, right?"

Richards hesitated.

McCready glanced at him.

"Well not exactly. Not always a good idea to give him a heads-up."

McCready was getting that sinking feeling. "And why not?"

"Well, he's a great guy, Eugene Porter, but he's kind of, well, unpredictable."

McCready shook his head and drove on. A hundred yards further and they disappeared into the trees. The lane had become a track and they carried on for about half a mile with dense forest on either side. The trees cut out most of the light, but occasionally the sun sparkled through the high branches, dazzling McCready with a strobe-like effect. Finally, the trees thinned and they came to a large clearing about the size of a football pitch.

There was a security gate that blocked the way. Richards spoke to the guard, who checked a list and then waved them through.

McCready drove into Magma Explosives' test ground.

A number of cars were parked to their left. Slightly ahead and to the right was a small grandstand. It was full with around twenty people spread across three rows. A wooden roof stretched out over the seats and it looked out onto a demonstration area that covered the majority of the open space.

McCready parked next to a silver Nissan Qashqai and then paused to take in the scene.

Spread over the area were a series of concrete walls and metal structures. Some were designed like houses, others were more basic shapes with a mixture of materials set up one behind the other. A network of colored wires led from the structures to a control panel in front of the car park. It looked like a film set lighting rig with all the cabling linking the structures to the panel. About twenty feet to the left of this, and at the edge of the clearing, was a small wooden hut. The sound of raised voices came from within.

The first was male, very harassed and somewhat high-pitched. There was severe tension in the tone. "This had better go well, Porter. There are multiple contracts at stake!"

The second was deeper and calmer and was delivered in a thick East End accent. "Don't fret yourself, Mr. Streetly. It's all in hand."

And then the door to the shed burst open and two men strode out. The first to appear was Eugene Porter, a small, mean pitbull of a man. He was dressed in a sweatshirt and jeans and in his hand he carried a detonator box. He strode across to the panel near the grandstand. He was completely absorbed in what he was doing and paid no attention to anything that was going on around him. He was lost in his own world, muttering to himself as he went.

The second man, Cyril Streetly, hurried after Porter. He was tall, very thin and wore a pressed suit and tie and an expression that matched the tone of his voice. He didn't look happy. He was trying to catch up to Porter's striding pace.

"I've heard that before. Last time you blew the bloody roof off the grandstand and turned Mr. Stanner's poodle white. He's never got over it."

"What, Stanner or the poodle?" replied Porter without looking up.

"I'm warning you!" Streetly looked like he wanted to throttle Porter but knew that he couldn't.

"Ah, but that was an 'off' day. Today, everything's hunky dory."

Streetly was clearly nervous, and he followed Porter closely, watching his every move.

"Look, go brown-nose your clients or something, will you. Just let me do my job," said Porter.

Streetly backed off a fraction. "I'm watching you. Any screwups and it'll be your job."

Streetly started to walk across to the grandstand when a top-of-the-range Audi pulled up. The driver couldn't find anywhere to park and so pulled in next to a tall concrete wall. To do so he had to cross a demarcation line on the ground. Porter glanced at the car, the line, back at the car and then looked at the retreating Streetly.

"And I'd tell Mr. *Vorsprung durch Technik* to back up a bit."

Streetly replied with a superior air. "That's Mr. Viner. He's a VIP. He can park wherever he likes."

Porter looked at the car and then the wall and shrugged. "More like RIP if he leaves it there," he said under his breath.

"What was that?" asked Streetly.

"Nothing, Mr. Streetly, you know best," replied Porter as he continued to attach wires and check over the control panel. He hummed to himself as he went.

Streetly crossed to greet Viner and led him to a seat in the grandstand. He then made his way back down and glanced at Porter. Porter smiled insincerely and nodded to indicate he was ready.

Streetly walked to the front of the grandstand and looked up at the group who were talking among themselves.

"Ladies and gentlemen. Ladies and gentlemen." The noise quietened and everyone turned their attention to Streetly. "Thank you for coming today. We hope this demonstration will show you the awesome power of Magma Explosives, and the quantum leap in controlled destructive technology this represents. Before we start, you might want to place the ear defenders in your ears—it gets kind of loud—then just sit back and enjoy the show. It's a blast!"

Streetly nodded to Porter to proceed. Porter took another glance at the Audi and then turned to the panel. He interlocked his fingers, stretched them like a conductor, then inserted a set of keys in the panel. He flicked a series of switches, waited for a light to go from red to green and then turned up the volume control on an amplifier. Immediately "Mars" from *The Planets* suite by Holst thundered out.

The show began.

What followed was an incredible display of controlled explosions. Objects were blown up with no damage to others close by—fixed weapons fired limpet explosives onto walls which then blasted perfect holes through several walls, one behind the other.

It all built to a finale of a machine on a small track panning across the wall of a dummy house, blasting the letters of MAGMA EXPLOSIVES clean through the front and rear walls. This would all have been great, apart from the fact that this was the wall Viner had chosen to park his Audi in front of.

As the letters of the company worked their way from left to right, each one accompanied by a deafening BOOM, all eyes followed their path to the Audi. It was parked where the final "S" would go.

Streetly started to look worried. He kept hopping nervously from foot to foot, glancing at the wall and then at Porter, then back at the wall. As the "E" before the "S" blasted through, Viner looked nervous.

It was too much for Streetly. He ran down toward the panel.

"Porter!"

Porter watched calmly, pointing his finger at his ear and shaking his head to show that he couldn't hear. Viner looked desperately at Streetly as the machine lined up on the Audi.

"Porter, NO!" screamed Streetly.

But it was too late. With a massive final BOOM, the explosives blew a perfect "S" clean through the Audi. A gasp went up from the grandstand. A whimper came from Viner. He stood there staring at Streetly as if he could undo what had just happened.

Streetly leapt up and ran at Porter. "Right, that's it. You're history!"

Porter stood his ground, looking innocent and slightly bemused. "What's all the fuss about? Bloody good demonstration of the product if you ask me. Have you seen how clean the—?"

But he never got a chance to finish.

"You're fired!"

Streetly was literally shaking with rage, but even though he was about a foot taller than Porter, he didn't intimidate the smaller man. Streetly could have run full tilt at him and would probably have just bounced straight of the solidly built explosives expert.

Porter looked up at Streetly and then beckoned for him to come closer. Streetly wasn't sure, but it looked like he was going to get an apology. He leaned down. Porter moved closer and whispered in Streetly's ear.

"I know where you live, Mr. Streetly. That wall by the hibiscus? Always thought it could do with a bit of remodeling."

Streetly stared at him in shock as Porter turned away and walked toward Richards and McCready. He tossed the control panel keys over his shoulder as he went. They landed with a plop in a muddy puddle. As he approached the two men, he glanced at McCready and then looked at Richards. "Hey, Richards, what the hell you doing here? Enjoy the show?"

Richards grinned. "Always knew how to bring the house down, Eugene. There's someone I'd like you to meet. He might have a job for you."

Porter stopped walking and looked at McCready. "Well, what do you know? And they say my timing sucks!"

* * *

Half an hour later McCready and Richards were back in the Range Rover heading north. Richards pushed himself back in the seat, reclining it halfway. "Okay, so that's three, but you're still going to need access, John."

"Don't worry, I'm working on it," replied McCready.

Chapter 24

The shower jets eased away the aches and pains from her body like a cleansing massage that always made her feel better, even at two o'clock in the morning.

She stood under the hot water for ten minutes, the steam rising around her. The jet lag was long gone and she'd confirmed the problem at London Water. It just needed her to write up her report and get things in motion to upgrade the system. She had even had a relaxing weekend, much of which had been spent in the luxurious spa in the hotel, so why did she feel so bad?

Clare knew very well. It was McCready.

She thought back over the events of the previous week, and wasn't proud of herself. She knew deep down he'd been right. She would never have made it to the side of the pipe without his help. If he hadn't intervened, Jason might have died. She shuddered at the thought, but what concerned her more was why she was behaving like she was. It was so unlike her.

She put it down to two things.

Firstly, the relationship she'd thought was going to end up in a lifelong commitment had resulted in betrayal and recrimination. He'd complained that she took him for granted—that her career always came first, but she'd been over and over it in her mind and she knew she hadn't. What she had taken for granted was that he'd have told her if there was a problem. Yes, her career was important, but she'd been committed to him. She just didn't think she should have needed to be analyzing every little reaction, comment and statement. Life was too short, and if that was what relationships were about, then what was the point? You should be with someone because you wanted to be with them, to make life easier and more fun. All those people that said you had to work at a relationship were clearly in the wrong type of relationship. She'd hated men for a while, concentrating on her job and shutting out any thought of involvement.

And that was what had annoyed her. She'd been attracted to McCready and she was blaming him for that! How nuts could you get? She half smiled, and it would have been funny if it hadn't been her pigheaded attitude that was making her feel so bad.

The second issue, though, was more serious and seemed in its own way to be affecting her whole outlook on life right now—her father.

She had woken half an hour earlier in a cold sweat. It had been the dream again. It was the same every time, and while it was a dream now, two years ago it had been reality.

"Hey Mom, do we really need that much wine?" Clare glanced at the beautiful sixty-year-old woman who didn't look a day over fifty. Melina Kowalski looked radiant. Her auburn hair flowed around her shoulders and she smiled with a sheepish grin as she loaded the second crate into the back of the car.

"Your father would never forgive me if we ran out. You know how he likes a good party."

"But he doesn't even know he's getting one," replied Clare with a grin.

Melina pondered this for a moment. "I know. That's what worries me. I haven't said anything and he doesn't know you're coming back. He usually pesters me all the time around his birthday. He's like a little kid. I'm sure he knows something."

Clare laughed. "Well that makes two of you. If ever there were a couple made for each other, it was you guys."

Melina stopped loading the provisions and looked at her daughter with love and affection. "And look what came of it all—our gorgeous daughter." She gave her a hug and kissed her on her forehead. Clare laughed and helped load the rest of the bags into the trunk. She was then about to walk around to the right-hand side of the car.

"Oh no, darling," said Melina. "Can you drive? I have too much to think about for tonight."

"Sure thing." Clare changed sides and climbed into the Taurus. When Melina was strapped in, Clare started the car and they drove out of the Walmart car park and onto the freeway.

The weather was clear, though there had been some light drizzle earlier creating a sheen across the roads. Traffic was sparse and they made good time. Clare's father wouldn't be home till 6pm and they had all afternoon to prepare for the party. Ten friends were coming over and Clare was looking forward to seeing her dad again after three months.

She'd idolized him when she was a kid. He'd always been there to pick up the pieces, whether it was a mere fall and a scrubbed knee, trouble with boys, or disappointment with exams or job interviews. He'd been the rock in her life. Not that her mother hadn't been, but for whatever reason she'd been more concerned with everyday things that were happening right now, rather than the behind the scenes problems that had more effect on one's life—a best friend as much as a mother. But her father had always been the one she could call upon and know that everything would be all right. He was simply that sort of man.

She had just turned off the freeway and was thinking back over all the great times they had shared together. Ahead was a set of red lights at a junction. As she slowed down, her mother undid her seatbelt and climbed into the back to find something in her bag.

"Mom, seatbelt."

"I won't be a sec, honey. Just have to find a list of who's bringing what tonight."

As the Taurus approached the lights they changed to green, and after a quick check Clare again glanced at her mother. She pulled out onto the road, turning right.

And that's when the truck hit them.

It was doing sixty miles per hour straight through a red light. Clare would learn later that the driver had been texting at the time. But the reason would never matter.

The forty-ton truck was fully laden with farm machinery and hit the Taurus on the front wing before it had straightened up. The speed of impact and sheer weight of the vehicle smashed the car into a spin, causing the rear to connect with the trailer wheels. This catapulted the car up into the air. It completed three barrel rolls before coming to rest on the grass embankment at the side of the road a hundred yards away. The truck didn't even stop. Later the driver would say he'd never even seen the car and that he'd felt a slight bump and thought he'd driven over a dead animal. Again, whatever the reason, it would make no difference.

Clare's seatbelt had held firm. She'd been violently shaken and her head had smashed into the side window, requiring stitches, but the front airbag had done its job. Melina had died almost instantly. As the car had spiraled through the air, she'd been thrown around like a rag doll. Her head had smashed into the roof and floor and her left leg had broken in half when it had caught between the two front seats.

When other drivers had come to help they'd found a scene of carnage. Blood was splayed across the interior of the rear window and the roof was completely caved in. One of the occupants was very much dead. The other had been barely conscious and groaned occasionally in pain.

She had faintly been heard asking for her mother.

Clare found herself gripping the doorframe into the en-suite bathroom. She was shaking and she was cold. Her hair was still damp and she clung onto the door for support. She took a deep breath and wiped a tear from her cheek. She looked around the room and then crossed to the mini bar. She glanced at the contents, selected a small bottle of brandy, twisted the cap and took a shot of the amber liquid without even looking for a glass. She felt the warmth spread down her throat and into her inner being. It felt good. She knew it was artificial and wouldn't last long, but right now she needed all the help she could get. She took another swig.

Ever since that day, her father had barely spoken to her. Initially she had put it down to shock, but as time had passed, now she wasn't so sure. She'd explained everything, but it hadn't seemed to make a difference. The trouble was that inside she blamed herself. She should have checked the road longer—she should have made her mother wear the seatbelt—she shouldn't have been distracted by her mother in the back. She also knew that this was what her father thought, and the fact that she'd lost the rock of her life—the one person who made everything right—so unsettled her that at times she didn't know what to do. It was as though she'd lost both her parents.

She savored the brandy for a while and then started to pull herself together. There was no way she was going back to sleep now. She switched on the TV to let twenty-four hour news do its thing, then grabbed her phone from the side table, searched contacts and hit speed dial. If this wouldn't cheer her up, nothing would.

The phone rang five times and then was answered.

"Hello, this is the dog pound. We are currently full at the moment."

Clare smiled, which was good. "So how is my little Maxicles?"

"Well, girl, he was great but then he started acting real funny," said Jade.

"Don't tell me he's been near those plants of yours?" Clare asked with concern.

"Now what plants would those be? He might have had a little nibble. Could have been what made him lie on his back and try and run for miles with his little paws in the air going ten to the dozen."

Clare groaned. "So what did you do?"

"Well, a small nip of brandy and it calmed him down no end. In fact think he's dropped right off to sleep." Clare heard her friend move away from the phone, presumably to check on Max. "Yep, out like a light."

"Yeah, well it would have that affect. Please keep him away from the plants and no more brandy." She glanced at her own small bottle and shrugged. "I'm going to come home to an alcoholic, junkie puppy!"

"Okay, girl. I'll do my best, but you know how he gets when he wants something. Now, how's it goin' over there? Met any princes yet?"

Clare smiled again. It was good she had called. "Hey, I'm here to work you know."

"And?"

"And what?"

"I know that tone."

"And, well, there is this one guy," she said sheepishly.

"Yeah?"

"He's ... well he's really annoying actually."

"I thought so," said Jade triumphantly. "You just can't go anywhere, can—"

"Hey, it's not like that," Clare interrupted rather too quickly. "But I think he's interested. He even made up some lame excuse to come and see me at work, so I might have some fun. Damn, men are so predictable. You can read them like a book."

In the background the TV changed from a story about

a fraudulent bank in the City to a scene of a stretch of water with mountains beyond. The caption read *Loch Lomond*. There were pictures of a crashed racing bike and then a picture of a diver in full professional gear appeared. Initially Clare let the images wash over her, but then suddenly she found herself focusing on the man.

It was McCready.

She turned up the volume.

"Hey, hang on a sec, can you?"

"Sure, girl."

The reporter was talking to camera with the loch behind. McCready's picture was now in the background. "… reports put McCready's Range Rover close to the scene of the accident, and it's thought the diver may have held Donovan responsible in some way for his brother's death. Police are asking for any witnesses to come forward and have stated that McCready is currently helping them with their enquiries. We'll keep you posted on this developing story …"

"Hey, you still there?" asked Jade.

Clare held the phone up to her ear, still staring at the screen. "Yeah, I'm here, but I was wrong."

"About what?"

"Predictable men."

Chapter 25

"Steady! Steady!" Richards voice was firm but showed a touch of annoyance. He watched as the submersible swung out over the water, suspended from a moveable gantry in the roof of the Ocean Oil test tank building. The movement had been too quick and the sub was now swinging out in an arc away from the side of the tank. "Just let it slow before dropping her down."

The sub in question wasn't the DSRV—that was already in the water. The vehicle suspended from the gantry was called Deep Rover and it looked like a fish bowl with mechanical arms and thrusters stuck on the side and back. She was smaller than the DSRV, but had pretty much three-sixty degree visibility from her spherical polycarbonate cockpit, and the arms gave her great dexterity, something the DSRV just couldn't match. She only had room for one pilot and could usually be found employed on scientific and filming expeditions. She would be a valuable addition to the project and also a backup to the DSRV if anything went wrong, and the way things were stacking up, the list that came under that category was growing longer by the minute.

The whole team had assembled earlier in the day. As well as Richards and his support staff at the tank, there was McCready and Paul Matthews, which was fine. And then there was Logan and Porter. The two men had taken an immediate dislike to each other and were staying as far apart as possible, which given that they were required to operate in an area of about twenty square feet could only spell trouble.

Deep Rover eventually stabilized and was lowered carefully into the water. Richards would normally pilot the small sub himself but today one of his crew was at the controls. Richards felt he needed to supervise everything, at least until he saw how the team worked together. He watched as the machine slipped below the surface and moved slowly off around the tank to go through a series of checkout procedures. He turned his attention to the DSRV and walked down to the observation window.

Through the glass he could see everything more clearly. The visibility in the tank was usually about fifty feet, but with all the movement of the subs and other activity this could drop significantly, sometimes to less than ten feet, particularly if an outbreak of algae took hold. Today it was an acceptable thirty feet.

About twenty feet from the window he could see the DSRV maneuvering to lock onto a dummy wall. Small spins of the propellers, like the jet thrusts on a spacecraft, brought it slowly in line with the metal hatch it had to dock on to. He had to admire Logan; he certainly knew how to control a sub. The movements were delicate, yet precise, and as he watched, the sub made contact with the metal plate directly in line with the hatch.

He watched as the locking mechanism on the sub hatch

interlocked with the connector on the plate with a reassuring clunk and they were mated together.

When they did this for real, explosive bolts would fire into the wall of the tunnel, sealing the two securely as one, but for now they were using a reusable locking mechanism.

The hatch on the metal plate was attached to a physical profile of the distance and makeup of the ground between the ring main wall and the bank vault. First there was the concrete side of the ring main. This was followed by a foot of best London clay, another layer of concrete, and finally the steel sides of the bank vault. Porter had been calculating all morning the size and shape of the charge required to blast a hole cleanly through the clay sandwich.

From the observation window everything looked smooth as silk to Richards. He dreaded to think what was going on inside the DSRV though. The presence of a large Scotsman, a belligerent East Ender and explosive charges in a confined space did not bode well.

To say the inside of the sub was cramped was an understatement. As it was still a prototype there was test equipment and multiple wires and pipes down the sides measuring a whole range of parameters of the machine's performance. The cockpit was filled with the giant form of Logan, who had somehow managed to insert his huge frame into the small space. Turning round was difficult, which he was beginning to realize was going to be a necessity in order to deal with his co-worker.

Porter was in his element and didn't seem to give a toss about the cramped space. He also didn't seem to give a toss about Logan. In fact, he seemed to relish winding the big guy up. As Logan was effectively trapped in the cockpit, Porter felt secure enough that he wouldn't be able to get to him inside the sub, and once they were back on dry land he felt confident he could easily outrun the Scotsman should it become necessary.

Right now he had his head stuck up the swiveling collar. The inner hatch lay open and he pulled down the outer hatch door revealing the concrete pseudo ring main wall. He reached down to a shoulder pack and pulled out some small charges. He started to attach them to the surface of the wall, whistling "Mars" from *The Planets* as he went.

In the cockpit Logan listened with a face like thunder. "Will you cut out the singsong and concentrate, laddie. We'd all like to make it out of here alive."

Porter carried on with his work, but he didn't miss an opportunity. "Hey, Jock, at least it's not the bloody bagpipes, then our ears really would be shot!"

"Why, you little …"

Outside the sub McCready was listening to the exchange on the comms in his full face mask. He swam closer to the DSRV.

"Hey guys, settle down. We're here to do a job okay, so let's just get on and do it."

An instant reply came back from Porter. "I'm tryin', guv. Just keep the hairy haggis out of my hair!"

Inside the sub, Porter fixed the last charge to the wall. He closed the inner lock hatch and checked a handheld remote.

"Okay stand by. Clear the pool."

McCready swam to the side and climbed out. He pulled off his mask and dropped his SCUBA set to the floor. The other support divers made their way up a ladder at the side of the tank. Even Deep Rover surfaced and watched and waited.

Over the comms came a "3 … 2 … 1 …"

In the DSRV, Porter jabbed the small button on the remote.

There was a massive BOOM as the explosion ripped through the water sending a fountain of spray high into the air, almost hitting the roof of the building.

Watching through the window, Richards instinctively lurched back as the shockwave hit the glass in front of him with a mighty CRACK. A jagged fissure of glass splintered out from one of the corners. Richards held his breath, hoping that the window wouldn't give way. After a couple of seconds he relaxed, but then a thunderous expression crossed his face and he headed for the floor above.

In the tank the blast wrenched the DSRV off the dummy wall, hurling the sub backward. It almost rotated onto its side before rolling back into an upright position.

Inside, Porter was thrown against the hatch. Logan's head was smashed into the dome, causing a string of expletives. Water jetted in from the inner hatch. Porter lay on the floor, a slightly dazed expression across his face. He shook his head and glanced around, looking quizzically at the jet of water that was spraying over him.

"Unreal," was all he could manage.

Logan was rather more expressive. "Porter, you fucking maniac!"

"Keep your shirt on, Macky. It's only a little bang."

McCready's opinion was somewhat weary. "Okay guys, we need to talk about this."

* * *

Clare was shattered from hardly sleeping the night before, but she was overall in a better place for two reasons. One, her chat with Jade had cheered her up, and two, the mystery of McCready.

On the one hand, the implications of the new development were hardly good news—the guy had lied to her, but on the other, she now had a mission—to find out what the hell was going on. It focused her mind, and if he turned out the way she thought he would she'd give him more than a piece of it.

She was just finishing up her report for London Water when a thought came to her. She stopped what she was writing and walked out of the office and into the main control room. The area was buzzing with activity as a full shift was on the floor. She crossed over to the computer where she'd shown McCready the ring main graphic and she looked for the DVD. The desk was cluttered with papers and small boxes of supplies, but there was no DVD. She glanced around to see if anyone was likely to have moved it, then noticed Kelly at her station. She walked over and sat down on the desk beside her. Kelly looked up and smiled.

"So, how's lover boy?"

Clare rolled her eyes, something she seemed to be doing a lot where McCready was concerned.

"There's nothing going on—at least not in that way."

Kelly looked curious. "Okay, in what way?"

"Have you seen the master DVD of the system? The one that shows the networks under London?"

"Thought you had it to show Mr. Wonderful the other night."

"So did I." She thought for a second. "You're a hotshot with computers."

"That's why I'm here."

"Do you know anyone who could set up a location track on a cell phone?" She looked at Kelly innocently. Kelly looked intrigued.

"Now why on earth would you want to do that?"

"Something's come up I need to check out."

Kelly thought for a second. "There is this guy, real nerd, but if he can't do it, no one can."

Clare pulled out the piece of paper Collins had given her with McCready's number on it and gave it to Kelly.

"I owe you one."

Chapter 26

The Ford Mondeo was a standard hire car used by many rental companies, and this one had over 90,000 miles on the clock. It was supposed to be a pale shade of blue, though it was so dirty you could hardly tell. It hadn't been cleaned since the previous client, but it was all they had at short notice and Clare hadn't minded. She wasn't going far and she wouldn't need it for long.

The previous day she'd finished up her report for Smythe, so had now been given the Friday off, while the company digested her recommendations. They would go through things the following week to confirm the way forward, and to work out the most efficient way to restore the system to full capacity.

Kelly had also come back to her about the cell phone trace—her friend had come through. She'd given Clare the details of a website with a pass code she could access. All she had to do was enter the phone number and the device would appear on a map wherever it happened to be at the time. Clare had assured Kelly there would be several crates of whatever she wanted whenever she wanted and had then immediately checked McCready's location on her phone. It had come up with a facility in Aberdeen, Ocean Oil, and it had remained there the whole day.

So now, a day on, she was approaching the security gate and hoping it wouldn't be like Fort Knox. What she needed was a young, impressionable guy on duty who would be dazzled by her charms.

The gate was attached to what looked like a large office-cum-reception building. She pulled up at the barrier and smiled up at the guard. It was a devastating smile when it needed to be and right now it needed to be.

Unfortunately the guard was mid-fifties, had short dark hair and didn't look the slightest bit impressionable. She also looked like she'd climbed out of bed the wrong side that morning.

The smile notched down a bit.

Clare held up a dummy package she'd thrown together earlier. "Hi, I've a delivery for John McCready."

The woman looked over at her, her expression neutral. "Okay, you can leave it with me. I'll see he gets it."

This was not what she needed. "Er, actually it's a personal delivery item. I have to get a signature, otherwise more than my job's worth." The smile was back.

The woman sighed. "Okay, I'll ring through, see if he's there."

At that point another car drove up behind Clare and waited in line. Clare watched the guard on the phone. She spoke into it, replaced the receiver and then turned back to Clare.

Behind, the other car was getting impatient and revved its engine. The guard looked irritated. "He's in the test tank but he's unavailable right now." She glanced at the car behind. "But if you're quick, go over to that large gray building." She pointed it out. "Take those outside stairs to the design studio and someone will be able to sign for it or find McCready for you."

Clare breathed an inward sigh of relief. "Thanks, you've saved my life." She drove off before the woman could change her mind.

She parked next to a Range Rover with a broken taillight and stepped out into the cool, fresh air. The sun was out and there was a light breeze. It was definitely colder than London though.

As she climbed the exterior steps to the studio, the door above opened and a man walked out. He noticed Clare and held it open for her. She hurried the last few steps.

"Thanks."

"No problem," replied the man.

"Hey, is John McCready around?" she asked.

"Sure, he's down in the tank at the moment. Just go through the studio, take the far door and you can't miss it," he replied.

"Great. Thanks again." And she walked inside. There was no one else in the room so she glanced around, taking in the various work stations, the large window on the far side and the door close to the window that must lead down to the tank. She dropped the dummy package on the closest desk and then walked through the studio looking at the computer screens and getting a feel for where she was.

She was at the second row of monitors when she suddenly stopped and the anger started to rise. There on the screen was the graphic of the ring main and the service facilities beneath London. She stared at it for a moment and then took out her phone and snapped a photo. She quickly closed the application and ejected the DVD. She put it in her pocket and crossed over to the large window that overlooked the tank.

Below, she could see two submersibles under the surface. A few people were standing around the edge watching.

One was McCready.

She felt her fists clench and took a deep breath. She took some more photos and then had a last look round before heading for the door.

McCready watched the subs through the surface. It had been a long day but progress had been made. Porter seemed to have managed to find the right balance in the size of the charge, and it was blowing a perfect hole through the mock-up in the tank. Porter and Logan were still hardly talking to each other, but at least there wasn't the barrage of rapid-fire slingshots being hurled every five seconds. Things were starting to look promising. He picked up the comms mike, which fed through to the loudspeaker in the tank and the sub communication systems.

"Okay everyone, that's enough for today."

He put the mike down and watched as the divers and subs started to make their way to the surface. He was about to head down to the observation window when he heard someone approach behind.

"You bastard!"

He froze and then turned slowly.

Clare stood there, her fists balled and the friendly demeanor he'd experienced on their parting in London was nowhere to be seen.

"I bet I'm the last person you expected to see," she said with barely restrained hostility.

Before he could reply, she slapped him hard across the cheek with all the force she could muster. He lifted his hand to his jaw, surprise written across his face.

"What was that for?"

Behind, the subs had surfaced and the divers were watching the performance.

Clare glanced around at all the high-tech gear and the submersibles that were bobbing in the water.

"Looks like you've relocated since London. And correct me if I'm wrong, but stockbrokers don't spend a whole lot of time at the bottom of the North Sea, or did they just get your picture wrong on the news, John?"

He could see she was almost shaking with rage. His immediate thought was why would she really care? He was just someone who had been a pain in the butt to her —unless of course there was something else.

He glanced around at the audience that now included Porter and Logan, who had climbed out of the DSRV. He put a hand on Clare's shoulder. She shrugged it off. "You'd better come with me."

She stood her ground, real anger in her eyes—and hurt.

"Come on, I'll explain everything," he said gently.

He led her to the rear of the facility and the changing rooms. He pushed the swing door open and held it for her. She walked past into a small area with lockers and a row of showers at the end. Once the door had closed she just stood there staring at him, waiting for him to speak. McCready turned his back so she could reach his drysuit zip. "Here, can you help with this?" She reached up and jerked the bulky waterproof zip with brass teeth to one side. "Hey, careful. You yank it, you could make it leak."

"I know," she said, staring straight back at him.

He started to pull off the suit. "So why are you here?"

She seemed barely able to contain her anger. "You seem to be quite a celebrity. Even the police want to talk to you." She pulled the DVD from her pocket and waved it in front of him. "And just what the hell are you doing with this?"

McCready glanced at the disc as he sat down to remove the outer layer of the suit. He left the undersuit on and then pulled on some work boots. Then he stood. "Come with me."

She followed him reluctantly outside.

The sun was slightly lower now and the air was cooler, but it was still bright. They walked over to a quay at the side of the estuary. He took a deep breath and then stopped and looked at her. "It's complicated."

"Fine. I've got time. Come a long way to hear this."

"Yeah, you have." There was still that puzzlement.

Clare seemed to be thinking something through and then she started. "I don't like people lying to me and stealing from me, and I'd like to know why someone I was beginning to think was a good guy is a bad guy." Her expression challenged him to have a bloody good answer.

"I'm not a bad guy," he replied.

"I'll be the judge of that."

He looked around at the quay, the water beyond, and for a second followed the contrail of a jet high in the sky. She waited.

He took a deep breath.

"Okay, my brother was killed on a salvage job recovering gold for a company called Global Salvage. He died because the CEO, Malcolm Mercer, stopped the dive supervisor, Steve Donovan, from bringing us up before things got too dangerous. I dragged his body from the wreck of a sub eight hundred feet down at the bottom of the North Sea. There was nothing I could do to save him."

She continued to stare at him, but an edge to the harshness seemed to have gone.

McCready continued. "I was fired, blamed for my brother's death, and Donovan was killed to stop him giving me information about what Mercer had done."

Clare had definitely calmed down a bit, but it wasn't everything. "That doesn't explain the DVD."

McCready hesitated, not sure where to go with this. "I'm sorry, but you really don't need to know about that."

"Oh, I think I do. You lied to me, weaseled your way into my confidence and stole from me! It wasn't a wet T-shirt you were after, it was information."

He looked at her, still unsure. They started to walk slowly along the quay. In the distance a fishing boat made its way into the harbor, a flock of eager seagulls surrounding its stern, hoping for easy pickings. Then he seemed to come to a decision.

"Okay. What I'm going to tell you means I'm going to trust you more than you could possibly know." He took a deep breath, really not sure he was doing the right thing. "Mercer's bypassing the inspectors on the ship— siphoning off some of the gold. Effectively stealing from the British and Russian governments—potentially millions of dollars' worth. Now, that's reason enough for what I'm trying to do, but there's no way I'm going to sit back and let someone get away with my brother's death. No way!"

They had reached the end of the quay. McCready stopped and looked down at the water, wondering if he'd said too much. He looked up at her again. "Mercer's going to store the gold at a bank vault in London—the one on the plans. I'm going to relieve that son of a bitch of some inventory."

When he looked at her there was shock in her eyes, but the aggression of earlier had gone. "That's what you're doing here—testing, training, whatever?" He nodded. "It's one thing stealing a DVD, John, and playing in these tanks, but how the hell are you going to get in there?" He didn't say anything, just looked at her, and then a certain realization seemed to come over her. "Oh this just gets better and better!"

McCready started to speak slowly and assuredly and with real emotion.

"My brother had a wife. Her name is Sarah. She's expecting a baby in about six months, a little girl called Shauna." He paused. "Have you ever lost someone close to you? Your own flesh and blood? Then have someone blame you for it? You couldn't possibly know how it feels, or what you would do to put things right."

He waited for her to say something, but her eyes had taken on a faraway look. They were suddenly filled with tears and she seemed riveted to the spot. She couldn't speak.

"You okay?" he asked.

She just stared at him, and then with great effort stumbled for something to say. "But, but it won't put it right."

"Yeah, but it just might make it more bearable."

She continued to stare at him, but seemed to regain some composure. "Why on earth would I help you?"

"Because you're the sort of person that does the right thing."

"You don't know anything about me."

"I think I know enough."

She paused. "I have to think about this, John. What you're asking—it's a lot … I think it's too much."

"I know, but it's the right thing to do, and I am trusting you."

She looked pointedly at him.

"Yes you are."

"So what are you going to do?"

"Sleep on it."

Chapter 27

Clare lay on her back on the large queen-sized bed at the Holiday Inn. Moonlight spilled into the room through half-open curtains.

Despite saying she was going to, she'd hardly been able to sleep at all.

When McCready had told her about being blamed for his brother's death earlier that day, a connection had happened between them in a split second that she had never felt with anyone. It was illogical. It was dangerous. She had no control over it and it was the last thing she had expected.

Now, many hours later, her mind was spinning like a fairground ride and she felt unable to get off. One minute she went with it, allowing herself to be swallowed up by the emotion she'd felt in that moment—the next she was looking for a way out, even if it meant getting hurt. But one thing was for sure. To go down the path she was considering could put everything she'd worked for in her life at risk. What she couldn't fathom was why she was even hesitating, even considering a path that could only lead to somewhere bad—but she was considering it.

She knew she had to make a choice and she had to make it soon. In fact deep down she realized she'd already made it. And she needed no more proof than when she rolled over to see McCready's naked body lying next to her.

She was still covered in a light sheen of sweat from their earlier exertions, and she rubbed it into her skin, remembering the feelings she'd experienced. She watched him sleep for a while, then leant back and stared at the ceiling.

They had come to McCready's hotel in Aberdeen and had dined in the hotel restaurant. They had talked about many things but she'd never mentioned her father, even though it was that situation which was drawing her to the man now lying a foot away from her. Somehow she felt it would be giving away a secret, but she also thought that if she told him it would break a spell, a spell that bound them together. It was a feeling she liked, and she didn't want to do anything to jeopardize it, at least not right now.

She turned back to gaze at him, and normally she might have jumped, but she didn't. His gorgeous blue eyes were open and watching her. Somehow she found them calming, reassuring, and she luxuriated in their gaze. Then she smiled.

She took her hand and rubbed it across his chest, playing with the thick black curls that covered most of the broad expanse.

"You okay?" he asked.

"Mmmmm. I'm more than okay," she murmured.

"You know, that slap really hurt," he said mockingly.

She grinned. "I should hope so, you big wimp!"

He grabbed her by the waist and pulled her on top of him. Her hair fell down into his face and she propped her arms on his chest, looking into those eyes again. He ran his fingers lightly down her spine and she shivered at his touch. He then moved down the side of her stomach and gently tickled her soft skin. She squealed and squirmed in his arms. "Stop it!"

He pulled his hands away from her with open palms. "Stop what?" he asked innocently.

"You know what," she grinned.

He looked at her. "What are you thinking?"

She paused for a second and then looked semiserious. "I'm thinking, John McCready, how does a guy like you end up at the bottom of the North Sea? I mean, I love diving, I love being in the water, but at those depths and in those chambers for weeks on end …" She shuddered.

He looked back at her. "Guess I sort of fell into it really. I learnt as a kid when I was at school, and from then on it was all about being in the water." Clare smiled at this. She could relate. "Marine biology was the goal, but I flunked the exams. So I had to look for something else to do. I worked in a number of dive schools—the Med, Red Sea, six months on the Barrier Reef. But that was only a stop gap. It was never going to pay the bills long-term. The only other real option was the commercial sector. Back then the oil boom was on and they were crying out for guys in the North Sea. It just seemed the logical path.

"But saturation diving?" she asked.

He looked up at the ceiling for a moment. "A big part of it was the money. It's very well paid. Screws up your personal life, but that's another story." She looked at him, wanting to know more about that side of the man, but now wasn't the time. "Once I was there, just sort of stayed I guess. Sometimes when something's working, you just don't want to rock the boat."

He looked straight into her eyes and she melted. She dropped down onto his chest and basked in the warmth of the body beneath. She wanted to stay there forever, but then she remembered what he'd asked her to do and she almost shivered.

Was she really going to be that stupid?

Connor Jennings handed Mercer an iPad. The photo application was open and it showed a grid of ten photographs.

They were standing in the living room of Mercer's opulent penthouse in Edinburgh, as the rays from the early morning sun cast long shadows across the room. The view of the famous castle was one of the most prized in Scotland's capital.

"We just got these through," he said.

Mercer clicked on the first one. It was a shot of the test tank at Ocean Oil. In it, the two submersibles were floating in the water. The second showed McCready and three other people. One was tall and had a beard. One was short and somewhat mean-looking, and the third looked like he was in overall control. He flicked through the other photos and all showed the submersibles. Three were taken underwater through a viewing window.

"And you're sure this is what they're planning?"

"That's the information coming through, sir. Shall we change the location for the gold?"

Mercer looked out through the window, across to the castle.

He was calculating options.

"No, let them try. This could be one way to take care of McCready for good." Then he looked directly at Jennings. "But we need the date, Connor."

"Don't worry, our source is well placed. We'll have it soon."

Clare finished showering. McCready wolfed down a room-service breakfast, still in bed. She walked naked across the room and started to dress. McCready watched her lithe body move as she pulled on her clothes.

"I like the way you sleep on things," he said. "Hate to think of the energy you'd have if you were awake."

She grinned, toweling her hair.

"You're really going to go through with this?"

"I have to. There's no other way to get to Mercer. He's too well connected, too powerful."

"So when's the big day?"

He looked at her seriously. "I can't tell you that."

"Oh come on, John. You need my help. I know those systems backwards. You'll never do it without me."

McCready thought for a second before answering. "Look, I may have screwed you for the information." She gave him a look. "But I've seen too many people hurt that I care about. There's not going to be another."

"So you care about me?" she asked playfully.

He replied, completely deadpan. "Some people will say anything to get what they want."

She paused, looking at him for a moment, genuinely unsure if he was serious.

"All I have to do is lift a phone."

"So go on," he dared her.

"You think ... because of last night? Don't bet your cute ass on it!"

McCready smiled but he was thinking.

"Okay, it's Thursday."

"Jesus! That's less than a week," Clare blurted out.

"You asked."

"I have to get back to London, and John, you do need me."

Chapter 28

The blues and twos on the lead police motorcycle ensured cars and other road users cleared out of the way as the convoy sped through the normally congested streets of central London.

It was classic street clearance protocol.

Two police outriders would alert traffic ahead of the convoy and ensure all junctions were clear for the remaining vehicles to move through. As the main convoy passed, the rear outriders would move to the front and the clearance bikes would take up the rear, and so on.

This sort of procedure was normally reserved for state visits of politicians and other dignitaries, but, ever the showman, Malcolm Mercer had used his connections to ensure a dramatic entrance.

The convoy was headed by a Range Rover with blacked-out windows, containing the best security guards in the business, all ex-SAS. This was followed by a five-ton armored car containing the Russian gold, which in turn was followed by Mercer's Bentley. Bringing up the rear was a second blacked-out Range Rover. Surrounding all the vehicles in a protective cocoon were the police outriders, who continued their coordinated dance all the way to the destination. In the air above, a police helicopter added support. The whole spectacle was designed to draw as much attention as possible to the movement of the gold to the secure vault at Wellings Bank. This was born out by the two news helicopters both vying for the best shot of the action below as well as the TV satellite trucks waiting at the bank for the arrival of the convoy. The Global Salvage publicity machine had been in overdrive.

Ten minutes later, the lead bike stopped at the entrance to Frederick's Place to allow the convoy through into the small cul-de-sac. The first Range Rover pulled over and the ex-Special Forces occupants formed a suitably impressive protective shield as the armored car drove in and parked next to the bank. It was followed by the Bentley, which drew up close to the press cordon at the end of the street that had otherwise been closed off to all traffic.

Inside the Bentley, Mercer checked to see that the rear security men had exited the Range Rover, then he climbed out to a barrage of flashguns and rolling video cameras. At the same time the gold was being unloaded behind him. It made the perfect publicity shot— foreground CEO with bars of shining gold on small pallets behind, all to the backdrop of intense security. Mercer made sure he walked close to the barrier that was keeping the press at bay. He wore a big smile as he headed for the bank's entrance. He stopped though, as a microphone was thrust in his face. A disheveled reporter in a beige raincoat coat asked the first question.

"Mr. Mercer, how does it feel to be sitting on five billion

dollars?"

Mercer smiled, but then he became solemn. "It's the heritage of the gold, the story behind it, and the return to its homeland, that's the real treasure here."

He was about to move on, but the reporter persisted. "But it'll make you a very rich man."

"I'm already a very rich man. Now are there any other questions?"

A small waspish woman eased herself through the throng. "Mr. Mercer, Tania Briscoe, *Sunday Times*. This is, I believe, the second diving operation you've been involved in where a man has died. The first being the *Esperanza* project. Do you think the recovery of the gold was worth a man's life?"

At this, Mercer hesitated. A flick of irritation crossed his face but he was in front of the world's press. His expression turned serious. "Any great endeavor has its risks. The loss of any life is tragic. Unfortunately, people make mistakes and accidents happen. That's all I'll say on the matter." He tried to move on, but before he could leave, Briscoe continued.

"I hear the dive supervisor, Steve Donovan, was also killed recently after the incident in the North Sea. Is that merely a coincidence?"

Mercer smiled grimly to himself. "Thank you, ladies and gentlemen, for your time. I'm awaited inside." And with that he strode into the bank surrounded by his security guards.

A reporter tried a parting shot.

"Are you worried about security, Mr. Mercer?"

In a hastily converted storage room at the back of the

Ocean Oil test tank, a large screen had been set up. It was currently showing the schematics of the London Water ring main.

Before Clare had left on Saturday, McCready had appealed to her to at least think about what he'd said and to let him copy the plans of the system. She'd reluctantly agreed, but she wasn't promising anything.

Now, two days later, seated, looking at the screen, were Porter, Logan and Matthews. McCready and Richards faced them. On the screen was a diagram of the ring main that had been enhanced from Clare's original.

"Okay, we go Wednesday," said McCready. "Everything has to be tight by then, and remember, when we have the gold, it stays secure till things die down."

"How long?" asked Matthews.

"We've talked about this Paul and I know it's hard with Lucy, but it's going to be six months, maybe more. I'm sorry, but we can't take the risk."

Matthews didn't look too happy at this.

Richards moved forward. "And once we're in we have to work as a team, or we're not coming out in one piece. Anyone has a problem with that"—he looked pointedly at Porter and Logan—"now's the time."

No one did.

McCready turned to the screen. It showed the large oval of the main pipe itself. In the center of the oval were the crossover tunnels that formed a cross in the middle, with an intersection between the two. Also marked on the plan was the position of the access chamber on the lower left side of the oval; the old sealed-off underground river on the lower right of the oval; and the vault itself, which was located about halfway along the right-hand side of the horizontal crossover tunnel.

"Okay, the main concern is these doors here," said McCready. He pointed out the doors that led from the ring main into the crossover tunnels, as well as doors at the intersection of the tunnels in the middle of the diagram. He then showed an animatic of the doors closing. "As you can see, the doors are of an iris design."

They all watched as the animatic showed the blades of the doors closing like the iris of a camera, forming a smaller and smaller circle until the door was completely shut. "We have to get through three of them to reach the vault. The one from the ring main into the first crossover tunnel, the one into the intersection of the crossover tunnels, and the one leading to the right-hand crossover tunnel where the vault is located. There's then a fourth one to exit back into the ring main tunnel. They can only be controlled from the control panel in the access chamber. Paul, that's you. If you can't open them for any reason, let us know fast." Matthews nodded.

"What if we're compromised?" asked Porter.

"Then we have to play it by ear. We can't bluff our way out, so we'll just have to return to the access chamber, come clean and take our chances."

Nobody looked particularly happy.

"Aye, but what if we're 'really' compromised," asked Logan with a knowing look.

McCready paused. "That's pretty unlikely, guys. There's no way Mercer could find out." He paused. "But if things have gone that far then we're in trouble. We'll have no option but to go to Plan B." He glanced around the group. "Let's just hope it doesn't come to that." There was silence. Then Porter added cheerfully.

"Don't worry, Macky, I'll look after you."

"And that's supposed to make me feel better?" retorted Logan.

McCready ignored them. "If it comes to it, it's every man for himself, and we'll meet at my house in a month. Okay, has anyone anything they would like to add?"

"Yeah, who's the girl?" Porter asked the question, but everyone was thinking the same thing.

Four pairs of eyes were fixed on McCready.

"She works there. That's how we can do this, guys. She'll get us in."

Porter was again in sync with everyone's thoughts. "Yeah, but can she be trusted?"

Mercer's Bentley sped through deserted London streets. It was late at night and it had been a long day, but worth it. The gold was safely in the vault at Wellings Bank and he'd been more than impressed with the security at the facility. It was the next stage that was the unknown. He couldn't believe McCready would have the balls to try what he'd been told he was planning but he believed the man sitting next to him in the rear of the car. They'd been through too much together for him not to, and Connor Jennings had rarely been wrong. He turned to him now.

"So, we have the date?"

"Yes, sir."

"And the equipment is in place?"

"Yes, sir, and Shannon will be at Battersea Heliport with the Jet Ranger as backup if necessary. But don't you think we should involve the authorities? It could get out of hand."

Mercer watched the buildings speeding past outside the

window.

"Right now, McCready knows too much, but he's going to be taking a hell of a risk. He's going to break the law. Once he crosses that line, he's nowhere to go, whatever he knows. We're clear, but we have to let it start. Then we finish it. If he wants to play games, so be it."

Jennings looked at his boss. He had that look that made him remember that this man was capable of anything and the choices he made were never conventional or indeed necessarily rational. He considered his next words carefully. "But by our actions we'll be breaking the law as well, and possibly very publicly."

Mercer looked straight at Jennings. "The law is there for people who have constraint in their lives. You should that know better than anyone, Connor."

The Bentley sped on through the streets of the capital.

Chapter 29

The interior of Wellings private bank was in complete contrast to the high-tech promise of the new super-secure vault three stories below.

Its high ceiling with oak beams was a throwback to yesteryear. Clients would meet advisers at desks positioned across the large floor area, which was covered in a luxurious thick pile carpet that exuded quality. It also dampened any noise and gave the building a feeling of a house of prayer—calm and peaceful. Nowhere was rushed or cluttered and the sense of space led to a relaxed, good-place-to-do-business kind of vibe which was designed to put people at their ease, something that was preferable when dealing with large sums of money. There were also private cubicles on a raised section of the floor, which provided privacy for more intimate financial matters.

McCready had spent the last two days going over every detail of the plan, but now, Wednesday morning, he was sitting on a thick-cushioned sofa waiting for an adviser to come and attend to him. When he'd arrived, a receptionist had taken his details and told him he'd have to wait around ten minutes. Nine of those minutes were almost up.

He was dressed in the same suit he'd worn for his visit to Global Salvage, and he still hadn't managed to sort out his tie problem—it was still too tight. Thank God he didn't work in the City; he'd last less than a week. By his feet was a black leather briefcase with one very important item inside. He was just thinking back over his night with Clare when a small man in his early thirties breezed up to him.

"Now then, Mr. McCready, I believe it is, how can I help you?" He looked younger than he was and seemed to have a permanently excited expression, as though the world was completely wonderful and nothing could change that.

"Well, I was hoping you could sort me out with a safety deposit box for a short while."

This seemed to really please him. "Oh splendid. Not a problem at all. Now what size would you be looking for? Is it for documents, jewelry, other small items, or something larger altogether?"

"Small items will be fine," replied McCready.

"Splendid. If you could just follow me." He led McCready up to one of the cubicles on the raised level and indicated for him to take a seat. He then sat across from him behind a small desk with a computer and pulled some forms from a carousel next to the screen. He placed them in front of McCready. "Now, if you could just fill these in." McCready glanced at the set of papers that seemed to go on forever and then started to write.

Five minutes later he'd finished and handed them back. The adviser checked them carefully, and even this seemed to bring him pleasure. Once he'd entered the details into the computer, McCready watched as two USB electronic keys were coded by a small module plugged into the side. When a blue light flashed accompanied by a BEEP to say they were ready, the adviser pulled them from the sockets. He stood up and smiled. "Shall we?" He proffered his hand to indicate the direction and McCready stood and walked across to the elevators on the far side of the room.

They were in a bank of three and consisted of small capsules completely surrounded by glass. They extended up two floors on open tracks, but once they were inside, the adviser put a security card against a reader and the capsule went in the opposite direction, down into the floor. The shaft of the elevator was also transparent, and it was fascinating to watch the earth and clay scrolling past just beyond the glass tube through which the small elevator descended.

Music played in the background. And as if every minute had to be filled, the adviser remarked on the day's activity. "It's been very hectic here, what with all the excitement over the gold."

"Yes, I heard something about that," replied McCready.

"Never been so much attention." Clearly this was one of the most exciting things that had ever happened to him.

A moment later and the capsule arrived smoothly at the basement level. The door slid to one side and the adviser walked out first, with McCready following behind.

They were in a small atrium with more carpet on the floor and discreet art on the walls. The background was a pleasant pastel color and the music that had been playing in the elevator continued to make its presence felt. It was, again, all designed to provide a feeling of calm, which pervaded the whole establishment.

The adviser led the way down a short corridor to a large circular door that was clearly the entrance to the vault. At the side was a scanner on which he placed his card. He also positioned his forefinger over a fingerprint recognition sensor. A second later and a beep confirmed that he'd been accepted by the technology. Another second and the massive door split into three sections and slid silently into recesses out of sight in the walls.

They walked through into the main vault. It was impressive. To the right there were rows of secure boxes of all shapes and sizes spread around a semicircle in a number of tiers. In the center was a computer terminal. However, on the left-hand side of the room—you didn't really think you were in a vault, it was more like a living room in a house—was the gold. It was stacked on the floor behind a wall of steel bars. The three walls behind the gold were also made of steel, and McCready could almost hear the water running a foot or so beyond.

He stopped, staring at the oblong ingots that only a few weeks ago had lain at the bottom of the North Sea. In fact, he would probably have handled some of them himself, and then he realized—and a lump formed in his throat—that Sean would have handled some of them also.

There were a lot.

They were going to have to move fast the next time he saw them. For a second he thought they were going to need a bigger sub.

The adviser was also taken with the pile of innocent-looking bricks, but for completely different reasons. When McCready glanced at him he saw he was almost in a trance, the golden light reflected in his permanent smile.

McCready coughed.

The adviser came out of his reverie. "I'm so sorry, but it's so beautiful. Five billion, they say."

"They don't?" said McCready in mock surprise.

"They do indeed. Now, if you'll cross over here, sir."

The adviser led him over to the console in the middle of the semicircle. Here he passed one of the USB keys to McCready and pushed the one he retained into one side of a double socket in the middle of the console. He asked McCready to follow suit, and when he'd done so, a quiet electronic whirring could be heard and one of the boxes in the circular wall slid smoothly out and sat there like a metallic tongue hanging from the wall.

The adviser walked forward, pulled the box clear and laid it on the table. "Take your time, sir. I'll be over here. Just call if you need anything. I'll be guarding the gold."

"You do that," replied McCready.

McCready picked up the box and carried it into one of the half-height cubicles at the side of the room. Inside was a low desk with a chair. He pushed the door to behind him and then placed his briefcase on the table next to the box. He opened the box and checked the size —it would be fine. Next he opened the briefcase.

Inside was a small electronic device about the size of a large calculator. It had a series of lights above an LCD screen which took up most of the central section. Across the top of the unit was a curved solid antenna, like you'd find on a GPS receiver. Below the screen was a small QWERTY keypad.

He switched the ON button and the screen lit up. It showed a map of London and their exact position, triangulated using the building's WiFi system, which it had locked onto. The map also showed the position of the London Water ring main.

As he rotated the device, so the map oriented itself to the new direction. He pulled the door open a fraction. There was no danger of the adviser snooping on him as he was standing staring at the golden pile.

McCready reached into his pocket and pulled out a silver metal rangefinder about the size of a large cigar. It had a button and a small display screen on the top. He turned it so one end was facing the gold. He waited until the adviser was looking away and then pressed the button. A pencil-thin line of red laser light stabbed across the room to the solid wall on the far side of the gold. McCready flicked it off before the adviser turned back and saw the telltale pinprick on the wall. A look at the display showed a distance of twenty-seven feet. He typed the figure into the calculator-like device while orienting it in the direction of the gold. A compass reading showed on the display as well as the distance he'd just entered. When the compass stabilized, he clicked a RETURN button and the device beeped. The words POSITION LOCKED appeared on the screen. A red light pulsed slowly away.

The exact position of the gold could now be detected by a scanner they would have on board the DSRV. It would pick up the location of the device in the secure box and the error of the position he'd just entered would be calculated automatically, taking into account the difference between where he was now and the location of the box when it was put back in the wall. It would provide the scanner in the sub with the exact position to blow through into the section where the gold was being kept.

McCready placed the device back in the box and emerged from the cubicle. He walked to the table in the center of the room. On hearing movement, the adviser turned and came over.

"All okay?" he asked.

"Perfect," replied McCready. The adviser took the box and slid it into the empty slot on the wall. There was more electronic humming and a light on the front of the box blinked red with a beep to show it was locked in. The final act was for both USB keys to be signed out of the system. Once this was done, the adviser turned to McCready.

"There we go, sir. Watertight!"

He then led McCready back toward the elevators. As they passed the gold, McCready couldn't resist.

"Oh, and I'll be back for that later."

The adviser gave him a condescending look. "Of course you will, sir."

As McCready walked out of the bank in central London, a few miles away in Hammersmith, Clare was going over the report she'd received with regard to her recommendations to resolve the issues with the ring main.

She'd returned to London with her mind conflicted. She'd had a great time with McCready and she had felt a connection she'd never felt before, but now, in the cold light of day, reality had reared its ugly head, and she wasn't so sure. What he wanted her to do was so out of line with who she was that she knew she'd have to call him and tell him she couldn't help and he would just have to call it off. In some respects she'd been glad he hadn't contacted her as she had needed the time to think.

She was just finishing a section of the report when the phone rang. The receptionist said it was John McCready for her. She took a deep breath and picked up the receiver.

"Hi stranger, how are you?"

"I'm good," he replied. "And sorry I haven't been in touch. A lot on at the moment. How are you after the other day? And I mean day, not night."

She smiled. "I had a great time, but I've been thinking —" Before she could continue, he interrupted.

"Can I see you tonight? I'm in town."

"Well I'm up to my eyes in it, but actually that would be great. We can talk."

"Okay, when's good?"

"It'll have to be late. I've got to finish going through a report. Should be here till around ten. Place'll be pretty quiet by then."

"Perfect. I'll see you then."

She put the phone down and leaned back in the chair. She had absolutely no idea what she was going to say to him.

Chapter 30

The five glasses of champagne moved swiftly through the room perched precariously on a silver tray. They ducked and dived between the groups of elegantly attired guests as the penguin-suited waiter expertly maneuvered between them. The champagne was the best, Dom Pérignon, and the bubbles rose at just the right speed. The light from the room glowed seductively through the liquid aperitif.

The Golden Hall at the Russian ambassador's residence in Kensington Palace Gardens in central London was an ornate affair. The high-ceilinged room led off the main hall of the residence, which was accessed from the grand staircase. If it hadn't been winter, the large windows behind a wide arch would have revealed a view across Hyde Park.

The residence was one of three properties that represented Russia's diplomatic presence in the United Kingdom. It was located at 13 Kensington Palace Gardens, while the embassy itself covered the adjacent 6 and 7 Kensington Palace Gardens, and the consular section, number 5. But the ambassador's residence was by far the grandest of the three buildings and had been the location of many an extravagant reception over the years.

Tonight was to be no exception and the opulent affair had been laid on in honor of the return of the gold to the motherland after so many years lost beneath the waves.

There were about forty people in the room. It had been billed as black tie, and so all the men were in smart evening wear, while the ladies shone in expensive dresses and gowns from the best designers. There were many foreign dignitaries among the specially invited guests.

The focus of the room was at one end below the sculptured fireplace, where a raised dais with an old oak table in the center had been set up. The table was covered in red velvet and in the middle was a strategically placed oblong block. On top of the block, a black velvet drape covered a brick-like object, the identity of which was hardly a secret.

Talking among themselves on the dais were the Russian ambassador, Anatoli Petrov, the British ambassador to Russia, Sir Richard Hawkins and Malcolm Mercer.

Hawkins was a small man with a filled-out body and a lived-in face, but his sixty years were of a sprightly nature and his expression wore the relaxed veneer of experience brought about by years of diplomacy on the international stage.

He checked his watch, indicated the time to the other two, and then moved forward to the front of the dais. He looked out over the room, and as people noticed his presence, the noise of numerous conversations slowly subsided.

"Ladies and gentlemen. First of all, thank you all for coming this evening on this auspicious occasion. For over sixty years a king's ransom has lain hidden, lost at the bottom of the cold North Sea, stolen in a vengeful act in the dying days of the Second World War, and tonight I am delighted to be able to preside over the return of this historic property to our friends and allies in Moscow."

There was a smattering of applause. "It has been down to the hard work and dedication of the now infamous, if I may use that word"—laughter rippled throughout the room—"Malcolm Mercer, who has made this night possible."

Mercer took a slight bow, at which there was more applause. The British ambassador continued. "Through his zeal and courage, five billion dollars' worth of gold has been raised from the hostile depths, and it is now my great honor to ask the Russian ambassador, and my good friend, Anatoli Petrov, to receive an initial deposit of what is to be the start of a final journey for the lost gold."

Much applause spread throughout the room, and there were excited exchanges among the guests as Petrov walked to the front of the dais.

In his late sixties, it was clear that time had not been kind to Petrov. His leathery face, framed by a diminishing crown of silver hair, showed the strain and weariness of many years of political struggle. But for tonight there was a slight gleam in the eye, mirroring the duty he had to perform.

"Thank you, ladies and gentlemen, and first I must apologize for littering your seabed with our property, but it was not us who left it there!" More laughter. "So it is with great pleasure that I hand over this first payment"— he removed an overly large check from his inside pocket —"to Mr. Mercer for his extraordinary efforts in recovering our treasure."

Mercer stood, moved forward, and with a big smile, took the check from Petrov. "Thank you, Mr. Ambassador, and in return may I present you with a small sample of what is to follow."

And with that, he theatrically swept back the black velvet drape to reveal a gleaming, freshly polished bar of gold. There was a massive gasp from the room as all strained to try to find a better view of the ingot on the table. A number of flashguns on cameras and mobile phones fired as Mercer lifted the bar and offered it to Petrov.

Mercer continued. "And while I'm reluctant to give it up"—he playfully pulled it away, to laughter—"I always knew someday it would have to be returned."

He finally passed the bar to Petrov.

The members of the press moved in to record the moment for posterity. Flashguns fired. There were handshakes and smiles all round.

Two miles away in Hammersmith, two large trucks drove past the entrance to London Water and parked in a side street. Craig Richards was at the wheel of the first, while Mac Logan drove the second. Both had tarpaulins covering their load sections. Paul Matthews was with Logan. It had been considered best not to have Logan and Porter in a confined cab without supervision. Consequently, Porter was with Richards, and the older man was starting to see Logan's problem.

They killed the engines and lights, not wanting to draw attention to themselves. Even so, Richards hoped McCready wouldn't be too long. They were on double yellow lines, and traffic wardens seemed to operate at all hours of the day and night in the big city.

The clock on the wall above the reception desk at London Water said 10pm. The lights were low and there was a late-night security guard sitting at the desk playing a game on his smartphone.

He was suddenly disturbed by a loud knocking on the full-height glass pane next to the revolving door. He glanced up. The knocking persisted. He could see a man through the glass. He was dressed casually in jeans, had a thick weatherproof jacket zipped tight and a dark shoulder bag slung over his back. The guard waved him away, not wanting to interrupt his playtime.

But the knocking persisted.

Eventually he put the phone down and walked over. He indicated for the man to leave, shooing him away with his hand and pointing at his watch. "We're closed, mate."

McCready was growing increasingly impatient. He shouted through the glass. "Sure pal. I'm here to see Clare Kowalski. She's expecting me."

The guard sighed. "Okay, hang on." Then he walked back to his desk. McCready threw a look to the heavens.

Richards was watching his mirrors. A couple of minutes earlier a police car had driven down the street. He'd noticed the officer glance up at the truck before he drove on. Now, though there were lights approaching from behind and they were slowing down. He glanced at Porter. "Don't say a word!" Porter looked like butter wouldn't melt in his mouth and drew a zip across his lips.

Richards looked back in his mirror and saw the Ford

Focus with POLICE written on the bonnet drive slowly past the truck and then pull up and stop in front. The rear lights died and a second later the officer climbed from the car and put on his hat. He looked the truck up and down and then crossed over to the cab. Richards lowered the window. The cop looked up.

"You do know this is prohibited parking here, sir."

"Sorry, officer, but we're making a delivery to London Water and waiting for clearance to enter."

The cop nodded. "What are you carrying?"

"Oh, just some experimental gear they need for a test. Nothing fancy."

"Okay, don't be long. I come round next time and you're here, I'm going to have to give you a ticket."

"Okay, understood," said Richards.

The cop started to walk back to his car. Richards checked his watch. "Come on, John."

The security guard walked back to the glass door. McCready could see he had a key in his hand. As he reached the door, he inserted the key and pulled the door open. "Your lucky night, mate. She's over in the control center."

McCready thanked him and made his way down the now familiar corridor.

Clare was working at one of the computers in the central row of workstations. The atmosphere was quiet, with only a couple of other technicians on duty.

He crossed over to stand just behind her. She was dressed casually in a sweatshirt and jeans and her hair was pulled back into a neat ponytail. He watched her for a few moments, realizing they might be the last he would have with her as a friend.

"Workaholic, huh?"

She kept on typing but smiled. "Someone's gotta keep this place running." She finished what she was doing and then swiveled her chair round. Her face was serious. "John, I've been thinking. You have to find another way."

He grimaced slightly. "I'm afraid it's a bit late for that."

"But you can still call it off. There has to be another option."

"Well, you know when I said Thursday …?"

She looked at him, realization suddenly dawning. "Oh no. No, you're kidding, right?"

"I need you to open the shutters right now, Clare." He looked straight at her and she slowly shook her head. She glanced round at the other technicians.

"But it's too risky."

"Is there anyone in the access chamber?"

She hesitated. "Er, no I don't think so. It's shut down for the night."

"Then we're fine. Once we're down in the elevator no one will know."

She looked across at the others. "I can't do this, John. We have to talk, but not here. Give me a second." She stood and walked over to the other workstations, which included Kelly's. "Hey guys, I've some things to check over downstairs. Don't wait up."

Kelly glanced at McCready, then Clare. "I wish I had me some of that kind of checking over to do."

Clare gave her a look and then walked toward the elevator. McCready followed.

Clare said nothing as they descended. When the doors opened she walked over to and entered the small office with a glass window that stretched across the front. Inside, she turned to him. But before she could say anything, McCready appealed one last time.

"All you have to do is open the shutters. We'll do the rest."

"John, I like you, maybe more than like you—God knows why—and believe it or not I do have an idea what you're going through, but this isn't the way. I can't let you do this. I'm sorry."

He looked at her but knew it was her final decision. He moved in closer and held her arms, pushing her back against the metal upright of a protruding shelving unit. It looked like he was going to kiss her.

"No, no, that won't help," she said. But then there was a metallic click from behind her back. She stared at him.

"You gotta be kidding me!"

He backed off as she lunged forward, coming up hard as the handcuffs secured her to the metal upright. He held up her security card.

"I'm sorry, but you left me no choice." And with that he left the office.

"John!" yelled Clare. "McCready!" and then more quietly. "You never trusted me. You knew I'd back out."

But he was gone.

In the lead truck, Richards was tapping his fingers on the wheel when the walkie-talkie crackled. McCready's voice came through loud and clear. "Okay, we're on."

He started the engine, and with a glance at Porter, he put it in gear and drove forward. Matthews and Logan followed close behind in the second vehicle.

* * *

McCready ran over to the control panel. He scanned it, trying to remember what Clare had told him when she'd shown him around. He pushed her security card into the slot and the screen came alive, giving him access to the system. He hit the button that raised the cowl and watched as the ton of metal moved slowly upwards revealing the water flowing beneath. Next he hit the shutter switch and the wide metal shutters clattered up on the far side of the room. As they rose, the headlights of the lead truck flooded into the chamber.

Richards drove in and parked next to the open pipe. Matthews pulled in behind. They would have to unload the first truck to allow the second to get close enough to the water.

McCready ran across the small metal walkway that spanned the open pipe. Richards jumped down from the cab.

"You have any problems?" asked McCready.

"A cop showed some interest, but we should be fine now we're inside."

"Okay, get the trucks unloaded and I'll get Paul up to speed with the system."

McCready led Matthews back over the walkway to the console where he explained how everything worked. Once he'd finished he glanced at Matthews. "Okay, we need the flow rate at zero. Things are going to be tough enough without having a river to contend with. And update me on anything that goes down."

"Will do," replied Matthews. He pulled out a laptop and switched it on. While it was firing up he crossed over to the pipe and placed a small device against its side. Part of it was submerged in the water. On the top was a small snub aerial. He clicked a switch and a red light pulsed on the side. He returned to the laptop and opened a program. A graphic of the ring main appeared.

McCready looked over at Richards. The tarpaulin had been pulled back to reveal the DSRV. It had been slightly modified since the test tank and there were now storage lockers that ran along the length of the hull on each side.

Richards stood next to the controls for the small crane on the back of the truck. He skillfully picked up the sub and lowered it into the water with the help of Porter and Logan holding lines to steady any movement. Once in the water they secured the lines to the side to prevent the sub from drifting off in the flow, which was slowing but not yet stationary.

Richards then jumped back in the cab and the whole procedure was repeated with the second truck, lowering Deep Rover into the water. When the process was complete, the two subs sat there ready for action.

McCready checked Matthews' laptop. Two red blips now marked the position of the subs on the graphic of the ring main. He nodded with satisfaction. "By the way, Paul, how's Lucy?"

"She's just waiting on a date for the surgery," said Matthews. "Hopefully she'll be fine, but it's a new procedure so you never know."

"That's great," replied McCready. "But thought you needed the cash from this to make it happen."

Matthews was hesitant for a moment. "Yeah, I did, but managed to sort something out, thanks."

"Nice one. By the way, take this." He offered him the key to the handcuffs. "Keep an eye on the girl. She's in the office. She stays put, but treat her gently."

Matthews took the key. "Will do."

In the office Clare watched the activity with concern. She had calmed slightly and was in the process of going over the current situation in her mind. At least if anyone found her she could genuinely claim to have been locked in and so couldn't be held responsible. And she did have proof that she'd been getting to know McCready and he had seemed like a genuine guy—he had saved her and Jason, after all. She still felt sad though. She'd thought it might have gone somewhere, but now, where could this possibly go?

The office itself was fairly small and full of all the usual paraphernalia. There was a desk in the corner. It had a swivel chair pushed underneath and a computer on top. Around the walls bookcases reached to the ceiling and were filled with box files and stacks of paper and documents. Two room-high bookshelves extended out into the room between the door and the end wall. It was to one of these that she was currently secured. The post she was locked around was at the end of the unit, which extended out about five feet from the wall. It was made of metal, and however much she tried, it was solid. She wouldn't be freeing herself by bending or breaking it in any way.

She took a closer look at the other bookshelf that was identical to hers. The metal upright consisted of three interlocked sections. They appeared to be just slotted into each other and held in place by the weight of the shelves. She glanced at the top of the frame and saw there was about six inches clearance to the ceiling. If she could just manage to lift the shelves up, she might be able pull the section of frame out from the lower section. If she could do that, she might be able to get free. But she needed to be higher off the ground in order to push the shelves up.

Over to her right she spotted a small plastic-molded step used for reaching the higher shelves. It was about five feet away. She slowly started to walk herself toward it, trying to hook a foot around the side, but it was just out of reach.

She slumped back, cursing.

As she did, the shelf frame wobbled and a broom that had been propped against it fell to the floor by her feet. She stared at it for a second and noticed the word SHOWERS written in blue felt tip down the handle. She gave a wry smile as she remembered it was the one she'd fallen over when she'd walked in on a half-naked McCready.

She stared at it for a second and then managed to hook her toes under the handle and raise it up so she could reach it with her hand. The first two attempts failed, but on the third she managed to grab hold.

Now with a firm grip she twisted her body and extended the broom out toward the plastic step. It was right at the end of her reach and she had to strain against the handcuffs, causing the hard metal to grind into her flesh. But then the broom-head was over the step and she started to pull it toward her.

A minute later she had the step pushed back against the shelf frame next to her feet. She let the broom clatter to the floor and took a deep breath, feeling the welts on her wrists. If she ever got out of this, McCready was going to get more than a slap around the face.

Next she climbed onto the step, positioned her back

against the frame and pushed up with her hands. This had the effect of hooking the chain connecting the cuffs under the shelf above the cuffs, so when she lifted, it started to move the section of the frame upwards. She hoped only an inch or so would be needed as the cuffs were seriously biting into her flesh.

She'd moved it about half an inch when she noticed a shadow cross the room. She glanced out of the window and saw McCready walking round the side of the office. She quickly lowered the frame, climbed off the step and pushed it to one side. But at least now she knew she was nearly free.

A second later the door opened and McCready walked in.

She was still trying to get her breath back from her exertions. He looked at her curiously and then glanced around the room, as though trying to work out what she had been doing.

She had to distract him.

She struggled against the cuffs, fiery resistance in her eyes. "Will you let me out of these things?" she shouted.

He looked at her kindly.

"Look, I'm sorry, but you left me no choice. So much planning has gone into this. I can't let you stop us." He hesitated. "And I can't let anything happen to you. It's better this way."

Although she understood what he was saying, it didn't calm her down. "You know there's no way you can get away with this, and when you're sitting in a jail cell you'll wish you'd listened to me."

He took a deep breath. "Maybe, but it's in motion now. What will be will be."

He turned to leave, but as he did so he paused. He turned back and glanced around the room again. He noticed the plastic step.

He glanced up.

He looked straight at her and a slight smile crossed his lips. Then he reached over to a shelf and grabbed a couple of box files. She closed her eyes in frustration, and when she opened them he'd jammed the files between the top shelf and the ceiling.

Nothing would move it now.

"Nice try," he said, before turning again for the door.

Clare had to make one last attempt, and this time her tone was completely different. "John, I really do care about you, you know. I don't want to see anything happen to you."

He turned back to look at her. "I don't want anything to happen to me either." He paused. "See you around, Kowalski." And with that he left, closing the door softly and locking it behind him.

McCready walked over to the pipe. Richards was standing next to Deep Rover. Logan and Porter were waiting by the DSRV. All looked up as McCready approached. Matthews glanced over from the panel.

McCready stared around the group.

"Okay, this is it guys. Let's go!"

Chapter 31

McCready was the last to climb into the DSRV following Logan and Porter. Richards was already at the controls of Deep Rover going through the pre-dive checks. As McCready stood at the hatch he could see him through the acrylic dome. It was strange being able to see in through the dome and then down below the water level to take in the interior of the cockpit, as though a hole had appeared in the water.

Before he closed the hatch he took a final look across to the office. He could make out Clare in the middle of the room. She was still secured to the bookshelf and she was staring straight at him. For a moment they locked eyes and he felt a pang of guilt, but he knew it was better for her this way.

He dropped down into the sub and with a reassuring CLUNK pushed the hatch closed above him. He spun the locking wheel and then moved to a sitting position in the cramped interior. All was calm and quiet, but he knew things wouldn't stay that way for long.

"Hatch secure," he said.

"Roger that," replied Logan. "Repositioning."

Logan pushed a lever and the collar moved around so the opening was at the bottom of the sub. This was a safety precaution in case the hatch started to leak. In the down-facing position the water wouldn't be able to enter.

While Logan finished the pre-dive checks, Porter arranged his bundle of explosives. As usual he was humming away to himself, a habit which drew the occasional irritated look from Logan, but he held his tongue. They would have several hours cooped up in here. McCready watched the two of them but said nothing.

Porter increased the volume and then glanced at Logan, who couldn't see him as he was staring out of the cockpit at the front. "Gee, I hope I got my mixtures right. These proportions usually work."

At this Logan turned round. "You better had, laddie, or I'll find you in this life or the next."

McCready sighed. "Okay guys, let's keep this down."

Then to Logan. "He's just winding you up, Mac."

Then to Porter. "Porter."

"Okay, guv, no problem." But there was a massive grin across his face. McCready shook his head. It was going to be a long few hours. He then pulled out an iPad from his shoulder bag, switched it on, opened an app, and a graphic of the ring main appeared. A green mark showed their current position and a red square indicated the position of the vault. A readout showed a figure of 5.4 miles—the distance to the vault. "Okay, transponder's locked on."

Suddenly Richards' voice came over the comms. "DSRV, this is Deep Rover, do you copy, over?"

McCready grabbed the mike. "Loud and clear. Go

ahead, Craig."

"All systems check. Ready to go on your mark."

"Roger that. We have a position fix on the vault. Follow us out."

"Roger that," replied Richards.

McCready turned to Logan. "You ready, big guy?"

Logan finished the final checks. "All check, ready to roll."

Porter glanced up. "So I guess that's a Big Mac to go then!"

"What was that, Porter?" snapped Logan.

"Are you hungry, because I'm—"

"Leave it, guys!" ordered McCready.

The subs submerged and headed into the darkness of the tunnel. As they left the brightness of the access chamber, spotlights flicked on lighting the way ahead.

In the chamber, Matthews checked the system on the laptop. He watched as the markers for the submersibles slipped into the tunnel.

With everything under control he managed to relax a little. He glanced at the cold water a few feet away and hoped this wouldn't be the biggest mistake he had made in his life.

Half an hour later he was bored. He stood up and stretched, then took a walk around the facility. As he passed the window to the office he glanced in and saw the woman staring out at him, following his every move. She shouted for him to release her, but he turned away. He had enough problems of his own keeping the operation on track. There was too much that could go wrong. After crossing the small metal bridge over the pipe and checking out the massive shutters that sealed the chamber, he walked back to the laptop and looked at the display.

The subs were approaching the first of the crossover tunnels.

In the DSRV, Logan fine-tuned the controls. While there was currently zero water flow, there was the occasional anomaly and eddy that he had to contend with to keep the sub from banging into the side. He was glad the flow was stationary though. If it increased, the subs would have a very bad day. At full power the DSRV wouldn't be able to make headway against the water, and if it was going with the flow, so to speak, it would only just be able to steer itself away from the walls.

He glanced ahead and saw the tunnel curve slightly to the left. The water was clear and the lights extended into the distance as though they were in outer space. At least London Water's filtration system was working perfectly.

As he rounded the curve, the first of the doors they had to navigate came into view. "First crossover tunnel door dead ahead," he called out.

McCready clicked the comms. "Paul, we're at the first door."

The reply came back immediately. "Yep, got you there. Opening now."

And as if by magic the door opened in front of them. The series of blades of the iris started as a small hole in the middle and grew larger until they were retracted into the wall of the pipe allowing a clear passage through.

Logan eased the throttles forward and the sub moved down into the angled tunnel that descended further into the earth. As this pipe didn't have to cope with the large flow rates of the ring main, it was smaller in width and a tighter fit for the DSRV, but Logan was fully aware of the issue and kept the sub in the middle of the narrow passage. Richards followed in Deep Rover, his lights casting an eerie shadow of the larger sub across the tunnel wall, making it appear as though a giant mechanical monster was leading them into the depths.

Twenty minutes later they reached the second door. This again was opened by Matthews as though on cue.

They now found themselves at a crossroads in the tunnels.

The system had been designed to be able to move water from one part of the ring main to another and this intersection was a vital component of that. Logan activated the left side thrusters on the sub. It pirouetted gracefully and turned to face the next door that led up into the second crossover tunnel to the right, and the location of the vault. Five minutes later and they were through the third door and on the final leg to their destination.

While it was straight all the way, it took them half an hour before McCready checked the iPad and called out to Logan. "Okay, Mac, should be about two hundred feet ahead on the left."

"Roger that," replied Logan. "Just a thought, but you'd better be right, else when we blow through, someone's going to have a pool in their basement they never planned for."

McCready glanced at Porter. He was busying himself with his equipment. He'd opened the inner hatch door and was preparing a loop of explosives attached to a frame the exact size of the outer hatch. He connected two wires from the loop to a small transmitter located on the side of the frame.

"You ready?" asked McCready.

Porter carried on, focused on the job in front of him. "Almost, guv." Then he paused. "Now, is it the red wire or the blue wire?"

There was muttering from the cockpit and Logan turned to glance at McCready. McCready sighed. "I'm sure he knows what he's doing." He took another look at the iPad. "Thirty feet, Mac."

In the cockpit, Logan slowed the forward movement to a trickle and edged closer to the side of the tunnel.

McCready watched the display intently. "Twenty … Ten … Five …" The iPad bleeped. "That's it!"

Logan stopped the sub. "Moving to lock on."

The sub inched closer to the wall.

In the rear McCready grabbed the secondary collar controls and rotated it to three-twenty degrees so that it would butt up against the wall at the exact position to blow through into the vault.

When he'd studied the plans on the computer there had been two options. The first had been to go in at waist level, but that had run the risk of being too close to the tunnel base where it would have been difficult for the sub to achieve the position. The second had been to go in closer to the top of the vault, which was halfway up the tunnel. At least there was a better chance of blowing a clean hole through, and it would also provide a more acute angle for the slide, which they would need to transfer the gold from the vault to the sub. They'd chosen to go for the second option. At the end of the day no one knew if it would even work. They were all putting a lot of faith in Porter.

From behind the DSRV Richards had a perfect view of how things were going. He hung suspended in the middle of the tunnel. Being a smaller machine and more maneuverable, he was less at risk of colliding with the tunnel walls and the journey so far had been somewhat enjoyable, but now the hard work would begin. He watched as Logan nudged up against the wall. A few seconds later and four metallic bolts shot into the side of the tunnel with a report like simultaneous gunshots. He could see the DSRV was now firmly locked on.

He clicked the comms.

"Looking good from out here, John. Good luck."

"Thanks. Probably better stand off a bit. Don't want us both going down if things go sideways," replied McCready.

"Roger that." Richards nudged the joystick control in front of him and the small sub backed off to a safe distance.

Inside the DSRV Logan switched off the main thruster controls and turned to the rear compartment. "Okay, all locked on." He glanced warily at Porter. "Over to you. And we'd better all be here in five minutes!"

"I'd better be bloody good then, hadn't I?" replied Porter, looking pointedly at Logan. Logan shook his head and turned away.

Porter hummed away as he connected the final wires. Once complete, he moved across into the collar that extended out from the sub and reached over to the outer door handle. "He paused for a second and glanced back at McCready. "Anyway, if the collar doesn't hold, you'll be drowning before I can blow you up!"

From the comms came an indignant Richards. "It'll hold!"

"Guess we're about to find out," countered Porter. "Here we go."

And with that he yanked open the outer door and let it fall to one side. For a moment water sprayed in, but it was only from the small pool that had collected between the outer hatch and the wall of the tunnel. Once it had cleared they could see the clean wall of the pipe sitting there.

Just beyond, through a foot of London clay and the steel wall of the vault, lay five billion dollars of gold—that was, if McCready had got his sums right.

Chapter 32

Porter moved the explosives loop up into the collar and attached it to the wall of the pipe. The charges had been shaped to propel the blast outwards and so blow through into the vault without damaging the sub—at least that was the theory. Richards had every confidence in Porter. McCready had confidence in Richards, and Logan would rather be somewhere else.

Once the loop was secure, Porter double-checked the remote connection, closed the outer hatch, then moved back into the sub and closed the inner hatch. He picked up the remote detonator and sat there for a second. He looked at McCready. "You know, it's like the first time with some bird. You never quite know what's going to happen!"

McCready and Logan exchanged glances.

"At least this way you know you're always going to get a bang!" And with that he took a deep breath and pressed the little red button on the remote.

A muffled BOOM shook the sub. The metal groaned and a shiver seemed to travel through to its core, but it stayed fixed to the wall of the pipe.

Deep Rover moved closer to inspect any damage. Richards picked up the mike. "It's solid from out here, guys. A few small impact bubbles. Clearing now … Looks like you're good to go."

Inside the DSRV they all glanced at each other—they were still there. Logan turned back to the cockpit. "Well, wonders never cease."

Porter opened the inner door, then moved into the collar and grabbed the outer door handle. "One of those moment of truth moments." And with that, he spun the wheel and yanked it open.

A few dribbles of water splashed in but that was it. He removed the remains of the explosive loop that was now hanging limply in the center of the hole and looked beyond.

As the smoke from the blast cleared, he could make out the expanse of a room at the end of the short tunnel. It was dark. There was no light inside, but the little that shone through from the sub indicated a large space. He glanced back at McCready. "She's set."

McCready grabbed the mike. "Okay, Paul, we're in. Keep us up to date on any developments there, and whatever happens make sure the flow rate stays at zero." There was a second's silence and then a crackly reply came back.

"Great work, John. Will stay on top of things, out."

McCready replaced the mike then grabbed a flashlight and moved forward. "Okay guys, time to make a withdrawal." And with that he climbed up into the collar and pulled himself through the small distance to the vault beyond.

The hole had burst through about two thirds of the

way up the wall. McCready jumped down into the vault, turned on the flashlight and shone it around. There in the middle of the space was the pile of gold bars, exactly as he'd seen them earlier that day. The only difference was that there was now a layer of dust and rubble across the top of them from the blast. The metal gleamed in the torchlight and he could see why so many people had been mesmerized by the substance over the years. In the half-light it took on an almost mystical feel. He was jolted out of his thoughts by a shout from the sub.

"Line coming through," shouted Porter, and a small line with a weight on the end landed at McCready's feet. He grabbed it and pulled hard. Attached to the end of the line was a length of plastic designed as a slide to transfer the gold to the sub. A couple of minutes later and McCready had it set up. He moved over to the pile and picked up the first two bars.

In the access chamber Matthews checked all the readings for the twentieth time. The flow rate was zero; all the iris doors were in the position they should be in. Everything was running smoothly, but every so often he kept checking his watch.

Despite the situation he was in he should have been a lot calmer than he was. And when an urgent buzzing came from the video entry phone and a face that had become all too familiar appeared on the small screen in front of him, he nearly jumped out of his skin.

He glanced at the screen, then over to the shutters across the other side of the pipe. He seemed to be thinking very hard about something.

The entry phone buzzed again. Matthews took a deep

breath and moved to the shutter control. After a moment's hesitation he flicked it to the UP position and with a clattering of metal the door started to move slowly upwards. As it rose it revealed the headlights of a Porsche 911 Turbo. As soon as the door was high enough, the sports car drove into the chamber beneath the rising shutter and braked sharply to come to a stop with a squeal of tires on the smooth surface.

Once the shutters were all the way up a truck drove in and parked next to the Porsche. It waited with its engine running while Rizby and two hard looking guys jumped down from the cab. Rizby then climbed into the truck that had delivered Deep Rover and moved it out of the way. Once this was done he signaled for Fisher, who was driving the new truck, to pull up close to the pipe. Once in position Fisher jumped down and joined Rizby and the other men.

Clare watched with alarm from inside the office.

Matthews had also watched with a certain amount of trepidation. Connor Jennings climbed out of the 911 and looked around the facility. With a quick glance at Matthews he turned to Fisher and Rizby. "Okay, get the suits ready and set up the comms. We've got to get moving."

They turned and headed for the truck. Jennings indicated to one of the other men. "You, with me." And with that he walked over the metal gantry across the pipe. Matthews watched them come.

As Jennings stepped off the last step he looked at Matthews. "Where's the girl?"

"In the office, but don't worry, she's no problem."

Jennings didn't reply but turned to the man following

him. "Lock him in with her."

"Hey, wait a minute. What the hell are you doing?" protested Matthews. "We had a deal."

Jennings barely acknowledged him. "Make sure he's secure." The man grabbed Matthews and was about to drag him to the office when Jennings turned to him. "By the way, sorry, mate, but there seems to have been a problem with the transfer of funds. They didn't go through."

Matthews stared at him. He couldn't have moved if he had wanted to. "What are you talking about? No, you can't mean it. You assured me there'd be no problem."

Jennings just looked at him. "Modern technology, what can I say?"

"But I needed that money for my wife's surgery. Without it she won't survive!"

"Bummer," said Jennings. Then he turned his attention to Fisher and Rizby as they uncovered the back of the truck.

A distraught Matthews was dragged toward the office. There was no fight left in him.

On the rear of the truck, just behind the cab, was a sleek white speedboat with green flashes down the side. It was a Scarab 165. It had a low profile, was just under sixteen feet in length and was completely open with no real foredeck. The controls were set to one side and it could carry five at a pinch that included two on the rear-facing seats at the stern. The really interesting spec, though, was that it was powered by a water jet rather than an outboard. This allowed it to travel in very shallow water. You could also spin it on a dime if you knew what you were doing.

Behind the boat were two Exosuits. They were about seven feet high, white in color, and they gleamed under the lights. They were made of metal and resembled the human form in so much as they had arms, legs, a torso and a helmet with a faceplate. Life-support was provided by a rebreather that recycled the exhaled gas and removed the harmful carbon dioxide and was mounted in a backpack on the rear of the suit. As the suits worked on a one-atmosphere principal, meaning the pressure inside was always the same as the atmosphere on the surface, regardless of depth, it meant that there was no need for any lengthy decompression at the end of a dive. Critical to their operation were the two thrusters attached to the side of the backpack. These allowed motion in any direction, and a three knot forward speed through the water. Couple this with the aggressive array of implements and pincers that could be operated on the end of the arms and you had a formidable tool for use in the deep sea, or, as was currently required, a formidable weapon for use against McCready and his men.

Jennings watched as Fisher lowered the suits to the floor, each supported on small frames.

Inside the office Clare watched everything that was going on and then turned to the door as Matthews was dragged in.

She knew when not to speak.

The man holding Matthews glanced at her, said nothing, then left, locking the door behind him. Matthews just crumpled to the floor. Clare stared at him for a few seconds.

"Who the hell are you?" she asked.

Matthews looked up like he was in another world. When he spoke it was as though all life had drained out of him. "Paul Matthews. I work with John."

"And who are those guys?" She indicated out through the glass.

"They ... they are a mistake. A big mistake."

"Tell me about it! What are they doing here?"

Matthews sighed. "I assume you know a certain amount about what's going on. John spoke very highly of you." At this she seemed to soften a touch, but then pulled herself together. Matthews continued. "They're Mercer's men, here to stop John and get the gold back."

"Are they going to kill him?" She looked at him with horror on her face.

Matthews sighed wearily. "No, of course not." But then he hesitated. "Well, I don't know, not now."

"What do you mean, 'not now'?"

He looked at the floor. "I did a deal with them. I'd give them access if they paid for a procedure for my wife. She has cancer. It appears they reneged on the payment. She's going to die. I know she is." He glanced up at her.

Clare could hardly contain herself. "I'm sorry about your wife, but you trusted them?" Matthews said nothing. Clare glanced out of the window. Her attention fell on the small boat on the rear of the truck. "Where's McCready?"

"They're at the vault," replied Matthews.

Clare took another look outside. "I have to get out of here."

Outside the office Jennings looked over the control panel and Matthews' laptop. He found the control he was looking for on the console. "Okay, John, so you want to play games?" And with that, he turned the small dial that operated the turbines.

On the panel, dials showed an increase in power. Behind him, the water started to froth and boil as movement through the pipe began again. Jennings raised the power to level five—half its maximum. He then glanced over at Fisher and Rizby, who were now sealed in the Exosuits and going through the final checks. He picked up a small walkie-talkie.

"Comms check," he said.

Both men looked up from behind the faceplates.

"Fisher, check," came over the speaker.

"Rizby, check."

"Okay, five minutes," said Jennings.

Chapter 33

The pile of gold had severely diminished.

The slide had worked perfectly and McCready's arms were aching from lifting so much weight. It was like doing a never-ending set of dumbbell exercises. But with each bar he moved he was relieving Mercer of over half a million dollars' worth of inventory and that kept him going.

Outside in the tunnel Deep Rover hovered a few feet away. Richards had been keeping an eye on the hatch connection to the wall, and after realizing it was pretty secure he'd spun the sub round to take a look at the rest of the tunnel.

It was about twenty feet wide, so more constrained than the main ring main but still enough room for him to maneuver freely. He was looking more closely at the construction of the pipe wall when he felt a slight sideways movement of the sub. He glanced around, automatically correcting the controls to bring her back in line. "Hello, what was that?"

Without warning the movement became greater, starting to sweep the sub down the tunnel. He corrected again. "This shouldn't be happening." He grabbed the mike. "John, do you read, over? We've got water movement out here. I'm at half power and just standing still. You need to hurry."

In the DSRV Porter heard Richards' message over the speaker and shouted through to McCready. McCready stopped what he was doing and climbed back through into the sub. "Take over with the gold," he said to Porter.

"Sure thing, guv." Porter climbed up through the collar and into the vault, careful not to disturb the slide that was still in place.

McCready maneuvered himself between the bars of gold, which had been spread out around the sub to ensure the trim and keep it level, but in the process making it look like some sort of maharaja's treasure palace. This, along with Logan compensating for the additional weight with the release of ballast, ensured the sub stayed stable in the water. He grabbed the mike. "Tell me, Craig, what's happening?"

The reply was almost immediate.

"We've got strong water flow out here. Someone's started the turbines. It doesn't look good. You need to talk to Paul."

"Roger that. On it."

McCready switched frequencies. "Paul, what the hell's going on over there? We've got water flow in the tunnel. You need to slow it down." He released the mike and waited for a reply, but none came.

In the access chamber Jennings glanced at the laptop from which McCready's impassioned plea had come.

And then the question was repeated. "Paul, are you

there?" asked McCready over the speaker.

Jennings smiled and picked up the headset.

"Doing a little night diving are we, John?"

In the DSRV there was probably nothing else that could have made McCready pause as he did.

It was impossible.

How could Jennings be in the access chamber? A million things raced through his mind, none of them good. Then gradually the hurricane of thoughts coalesced into their situation, which in the last ten seconds had become dire.

Logan had noted the silence and turned to see McCready pushed back against the side of the sub. The look on his face told him things were far from well. "What is it?"

McCready glanced at Logan. "Mercer's men are in the access chamber." He picked up the mike. He had one priority. "Jennings, what have you done with Matthews and the girl?"

When the reply came, there was a smugness in the tone that made him want to rip the guy's eyes out. "Well now, Matthews has been most cooperative. As for the girl—"

"If you've touched her!"

"John, is that concern I hear there? The thought had crossed my mind, but maybe I'll save her for later. Sort of a bonus for a job well done, if you know what I mean. Of course, she could always be useful in the unlikely event you make it out of there alive."

McCready gripped the mike harder. He glanced up at the hole through to the vault. If there was one thing he did know, it was that they had to get out of there and fast.

"Porter, we have to leave now!"

In the vault, Porter was struggling with four bars of the gold. There was still a layer on the bottom of the vault. He shouted back through the hole. "I've not come all this way to leave a few million quid lying around!"

In the chamber Jennings smiled grimly and reached for the turbine controls. He turned the small wheel as far as it would go. The needle on the gauge rose through eight, heading for the maximum of ten. Jennings watched it rise. It was now at full power. "Let's see how long you can hold on, John."

He glanced at the water in the pipe. Eddies and currents were making it boil.

"Don't you just love water sports?"

With that, Jennings crossed over to the Exosuits. They were almost ready to go.

In the tunnel the effect was immediate. If the water in one part of the system speeded up, it meant it all had to speed up. The first effect was to spin Deep Rover round on its axis and push it further along the tunnel. Its lights illuminated the walls in a crazy dance, like some kind of mad fairground ride.

The other more serious effect was to start to prize the DSRV off the wall. The first sign was a small trickle of water that entered from the top of the hatch and dripped onto McCready's head. At the same time the sub started to shake and judder with the external forces being exerted on it.

McCready climbed up through the collar and into the vault. He stared around at the almost empty space and then looked at Porter.

"We need to go, now!"

Porter staggered over to the slide and sent four more bars down to the sub.

McCready clearly wasn't getting through.

"Now, Porter!"

Just then a terrifying grinding filled the vault. It sounded like the whole submersible was being ripped in two. Porter finally got it. He ran for the hole, leaving a single bar of gold on the floor behind him. He dived through, if a hundred and twenty pounds scrabbling into the tight gap could be called diving. He pulled himself head first down the small tube and landed unceremoniously on the floor of the sub.

McCready wasn't far behind—but it was far enough. As he pulled himself toward the collar and was about to grab hold, a tremendous CRACK came from the hatch and the sub started to rip off the wall.

McCready was halfway through. Porter had hold of his arms and was pulling him hard when the collar broke free. Water crashed past McCready and into the sub.

Behind, water thundered into the vault, starting to fill it fast.

Porter desperately tried to hang on to McCready, but water was now flowing in at an alarming rate. He had to let go to reach the collar controls and turn the hatch so it was facing straight down to stop the water from completely flooding the sub.

"Hang on, guv!"

"Oh really!" retorted McCready.

As Porter reached for the control, McCready could hang on no longer and was sucked out of the collar and into the tunnel.

"Shit, we've lost him!" yelled Porter as the collar turned vertically down. At the same time there was a violent hissing of gas as the auto pressure breech system kicked in, equalizing the pressure inside the sub with the water outside.

The inflow of water stopped.

There was still about a foot sloshing around in the bottom of the sub, but it quickly started to drain away down into the collar.

Of more immediate concern was McCready's life.

The first thing that hit him was the cold, and it was all he could do to prevent the involuntary reaction to gasp for air. The second thing that hit him was the side of the tunnel, as he was pushed into it by the DSRV, which was now barreling along out of control.

The sub scraped noisily along the wall, threatening to rip away the delicate pipes and control systems from the metal hull.

McCready managed to prize himself away from the wall and found himself in clear water. He was completely disoriented and very soon he was going to be out of air.

Richards had heard the exchange over the comms and could see McCready in the water, desperately looking around on the far side of the tunnel. With the DSRV heading further into the distance unable to help, McCready was left floundering on his own. Richards powered up the thrusters and headed over as fast as he could.

* * *

McCready was nearly out of air, but he could make out the lights of Deep Rover as it headed towards him. He just didn't know if it would get to him in time. He could feel himself starting to black out, when something grabbed his foot.

Richards skillfully controlled the claw of one of the manipulators to hold onto McCready's ankle as gently as he could. At the same time he didn't want to lose him. He was sure there would be some significant bruising and no doubt some choice words uttered later on, but the priority was to get McCready back to the DSRV.

Richards grabbed the mike. "Mac, try and stay with the flow and go as high as you can in the tunnel, and keep her steady. I've got John. I'll bring him over to you."

"Roger that," came the reply.

Richards saw the DSRV slow its headlong charge down the tunnel and rise slightly in the water. He made his way over as fast as he could, towing McCready with him. He maneuvered Deep Rover beneath the larger sub, trying to get as close to the hatch as he could.

Two human arms reached down into the water.

Closer and closer he moved. "Come on, John, nearly there." McCready was almost unconscious but he was within reach of the arms. Suddenly they grabbed him. Richards released his grip on the foot, and the arms dragged McCready up through the collar.

The moment McCready was back inside he gasped for air, spluttering water from his mouth, coughing uncontrollably. Porter reached down and pushed the hatch closed.

"Picked a fine time to go swimming!"

McCready gave him a look and then took a series of deep breaths while he calmed himself down. He nodded to Porter who had dragged him in and noted the concerned look on Logan's face from the cockpit. "Thanks, guys." He coughed and retched a couple more times, then reached for the comms mike. He pressed the button. "Owe you one, Craig."

"Oh no, mate, you owe me plenty!" came the gruff reply.

The subs were swept further along the tunnel.

There was little they could do in such a strong current except try to control the forward direction and make sure they didn't crash into the sides or each other.

In the access chamber Jennings stared at the graphic on Matthews' laptop. He could clearly see the two small red blips that represented the subs and their position in the system. It wouldn't be long before they reached the door leading into the main ring main. He moved his hand to a control on the panel. He paused dramatically for a second and then flipped the switch which sent the command to close the door, trapping the submersibles like rats in a trap.

He turned to the Exosuits that were now suspended out over the water by two small cranes. Fisher and Rizby stared out of the high-tech machines. He clicked the comms.

"Okay, go get 'em!"

The suits were lowered into the water.

The two men checked their wrist-mounted displays showing the layout of the system, then, with a high-pitched whirring, the thrusters on the backpacks started up and propelled them forward. The helmet-mounted lights flicked on to light the way ahead as they disappeared into the tunnel.

Chapter 34

The subs moved fast in the flow of water.

If anything the speed had increased slightly, and it was all Logan could do to prevent the DSRV from crashing into the sides of the tunnel.

In front of the larger sub, Deep Rover acted as a scout in case there were any surprises ahead. Richards could maneuver more easily and so could take evasive action if required. If necessary he could warn the DSRV, which might mean the difference between crashing and causing critical damage, or taking successful evasive action.

Richards was looking ahead when he noticed a slight change in the tone of the water. The lights on the sub could only see so far, due to the absorption of light in the denser medium, but the water was definitely becoming lighter all around the rim of the tunnel.

And then he knew what it was and a feeling of dread crept over him.

The iris door that led out to the ring main was closing. The change in tone was caused by the lights reflecting off the surface of the iris as it moved toward the center. He pulled the mike trigger.

"Guys, we've got a big problem."

"Go ahead," said McCready.

"The door's closing. You have to stop—like now!"

In the DSRV, Logan had heard the message. "On it," he said.

He immediately pulled the throttles back and pushed the thrusters into full reverse. There wasn't much else he could do. The tunnel was too tight to turn in. They all stared out of the dome, praying it would stop in time before hitting the door.

Richards had managed to spin Deep Rover and head back away from the door. All he could do was watch as the DSRV headed for the obstacle ahead.

It was slowing but not by much.

And then the door was fully closed, and that was what saved them.

With the blockage across the tunnel the flow of water also slowed to zero, so there was nothing pushing the sub through the water.

They were getting closer and closer. There were only inches to go. The door was filling the entire dome. Then the glass reached the door and gently kissed the surface before being pulled back by the power of the thrusters. There was a collective sigh of relief from the three men inside who had been holding their breath.

"Well done, Scottie," said Porter before turning away from the dome and sitting back down in the main compartment of the sub. Logan glanced at McCready and both raised their eyebrows.

Now though, they had a big dilemma. Do they try and get through the door or do they head back down the tunnel?

Either way, things didn't look great.

In the access chamber Jennings stared down at the display on the laptop. It showed the blips of the submersibles at the now sealed door to the ring main. He smiled grimly. "Nowhere to go, my friend." He then picked up the walkie-talkie. "Fisher, position check."

There was a second's delay before the reply came through. "Approaching the crossover tunnel."

"Roger that." He put the walkie-talkie down, satisfied with their progress.

In the office Clare kicked the desk with frustration. Since their last conversation Matthews hadn't said a word. He'd simply sat on the floor staring into his lap. He seemed to be consumed by the belief that his wife was going to die.

Clare looked around the room. There had to be some way she could get free. Matthews hadn't responded when she'd asked him to help remove the files McCready had put above the shelves, but somehow she had to warn McCready. She didn't know what the machines were capable of that had gone into the tunnel, but one thing was for sure—they weren't going to be spreading good tidings and great joy. She struggled with the handcuffs again and looked down at Matthews.

"Paul, you have to help me …" But there was no response. "Paul!" she shouted. "You only know what they said. Your wife may be fine. Nothing is done until it's done."

Matthews looked up slowly, his expression far away. "And if she isn't fine?" he asked weakly.

"Then deal with it later. Make sure they get what's

coming to them, but staying here isn't helping. McCready may be a son of a bitch, but these guys are in a whole different league. They have to be stopped. I have to get out. If those divers reach the subs, it's all over."

Matthews stared at her lamely. "What are you going to do?" he asked.

"I'll think of something, but I can't do anything if I'm stuck in here now, can I? You have to try and help me get these cuffs off." She rattled the metal bracelets to make a point.

Suddenly Matthews seemed to focus. He looked at her hands restrained behind her back, and then said simply.

"I have a key."

Clare looked at him incredulously.

In the tunnel the two subs sat stationary on the bottom close to the sealed door. There was an open mike between them as they discussed what to do next. McCready was the first to speak.

"Craig, the access chamber is clearly no-go. Jennings knows that and he won't be sitting around waiting for us to come out."

There was a moment and then the speaker crackled. "I agree. He's probably sent someone in after us. Question is, are they coming through the ring main and he just opens the door and we're sitting ducks or are they coming through the crossover tunnels?" asked Richards.

"No way of knowing," said McCready. "Either way, I say we try and get through this door. For all we know he's sealed off the others as well. At least this way there's only one to get through. Then we'll have some options. Stuck here is making me nervous. Looks like we'll have to go to

Plan B."

"Agreed, we've no choice," came the reply over the speaker.

In the DSRV the mood turned serious. This was the worse-case scenario, and there was no way of knowing how things would work out.

"Okay, Eugene, better get your gear ready," said McCready.

This time there was no pithy comeback, and Porter grabbed his case of explosives. Logan glanced at McCready and then turned back to the controls. McCready moved to the rear of the sub and picked up a couple of the gold bars.

In the vault the water had flowed out of the barred enclosure where the gold had been kept and flooded the whole area where the semicircle of safe deposit boxes was situated.

As the boxes weren't waterproof they'd filled with water. Any jewels and coins would be fine, but any notes or valuable documents would probably be ruined. In one box about halfway round the semicircle a small electronic device with a red pulsing light was finally waterlogged. The electronics shorted out and the red light died, but the little gadget had performed flawlessly. It was no longer needed and could rest in peace.

Extending up from the vault were the many electrical conduits and other infrastructure networks that the bank needed to keep functioning. As the water continued to flood in, the pressure forced it ever higher. Finally it filled the whole room and was pushing up against the ceiling. Where it could, it found its way into the systems that led up into the bank above.

Outside the front of Wellings Bank a biting wind swept down Frederick's Place.

Ethel Mortimer was huddled up in a thick woolen coat with a fur collar. She was in her seventies but the years hadn't dimmed her will or her fortitude. She was also not averse to telling her somewhat henpecked husband, Bertie, how things were and how they should be. Bertie was at that moment approaching one of two cash machines at the front of the bank.

"Just got to get some money out, dear," he called back to Ethel, who was huddled up behind him trying to use him as a windshield. She heard the words, though, and couldn't help a barbed jibe.

"Always spending, that's you." He pushed the card into the slot and began typing in his PIN. "Bet you can't even remember your number," she continued.

"No, it's fine, dear, nearly there." He hit the last key and the machine whirred.

"Every chance you get, it's spend, spend, spend. Like water you do," she went on.

At that exact moment a torrent of freezing water erupted from the money slot and drenched the couple. Ethel screamed and jumped back, leaving Bertie to take its full force. He stood there stunned for a second before sidestepping out of the way. Ethel just looked at him.

"Now look what you've done. I told you so!"

Chapter 35

Clare was still staring incredulously at Matthews, when he stood slowly and walked behind her and with a simple click undid the handcuffs. She pulled them off her wrists and rubbed the sore flesh to get the circulation going again. "You had a key the whole the time and you said nothing?"

"I had other things on my mind," he said, not looking at her. She ran to the window, crouching low. Jennings was at the control panel.

"Right, we need a plan. I have to get to the controls."

"Okay," he said slowly, gradually focusing on the present. "On my laptop there's a layout of the tunnels. Transponders from the subs show their position." He paused. "There's also something else you should know."

"What's that?"

"They have a backup plan in case the chamber was compromised and they couldn't get out this way."

Clare wondered what this could possibly be. There was nowhere else they could exit the pipe. She looked at him. He took a deep breath.

"They're going to blow through where the pipe

intersects the underground river. Try to get to the Thames."

Clare was speechless. In fact her jaw literally dropped open. Her mind was racing. It was a crazy idea. Then her expression turned to fear. "It won't work. Even if they manage to get through the wall and down the tunnel, there's a metal grille where the river exits into the Thames. They'll be trapped."

Matthews seemed to accept this as just another part of all the other bad news he'd recently received.

Clare was thinking fast. She glanced out of the window and watched Jennings and his men for a minute. Her eyes again played over the jet boat that was still secured to the back of the truck. There were options, but she had to get out of the office.

"I have to warn them," she said.

Matthews merely looked on, a beaten man. "What do you want me to do?"

In the access chamber Jennings looked at the laptop. He saw the subs were still hard up against the iris door. He'd just checked in with Fisher, and the Exosuits were past the intersection, heading up the tunnel toward them. He smiled. "Not long now, John."

Suddenly there was an almighty crash. Jennings whirled in time to see a chair smash through the glass window of the office and career across the floor. Fragments of glass sprayed through the air. A second later and Matthews was running for the elevator. Both of Jennings' men started for the gantry to cross the water but they wouldn't make it in time. Jennings walked forward and calmly reached under his jacket.

"Stop!" he shouted, but Matthews kept running.

He was almost there.

While everyone was distracted, Clare sprinted to the control panel. She looked at the laptop and took in the position of the subs on the display. She could see they were trapped. There was only one thing she could do. She jabbed her hand down on the DOOR OPEN button for the iris door. She then grabbed the headset and was about to try to contact McCready when there was the sound of a gunshot.

The noise was deafening in the confined space of the chamber. It ricocheted off the walls like a deadly echo, but the bullet's trajectory was true.

She spun round to see Matthews' motionless body lying by the side of the pipe. She stared at Jennings in shock. He still held the small revolver. A wisp of smoke curled up from the barrel. He slowly lowered it and for the first time looked at Clare. For a second he didn't take in the significance of her standing there. Then he glanced at the panel and ran over.

Deep Rover was suspended in the water close to the side of the DSRV. McCready called Richards on the radio. "Good job we brought Deep Rover. Plan B would never have been an option without her."

"So right," replied Richards. "Now we just have to work out a way to get through the—" But he stopped mid-sentence.

"What is it, Craig?"

"I was going to say we need to work out how to get through the door, but look … it's opening."

In the DSRV they all strained to see through the front dome. Sure enough the iris door was slowly opening. Porter looked suspicious. "Yeah, but who opened it? Maybe they want us to go through."

Logan glanced at him. "Not a bad point ... for once." Porter glared at him.

"What do you think, Craig?" asked McCready.

The voice came back over the comms. "It's fifty-fifty but I know I'd rather be out there than stuck in here."

McCready thought for a moment. "Agreed. Okay, Mac, take us out. Craig, you follow behind. Make sure everything's secure."

"Will do." The comms went quiet.

Logan eased the controls forward and the sub started to move slowly toward the door, which was now fully open. There wasn't much room, particularly as he had to make a sharp turn to the right to get into the main tunnel, but they inched through keeping the thrusters and other sensitive equipment clear of the sides.

Deep Rover followed behind after checking on something in the tunnel just behind them.

Jennings stood over Clare at the panel. One of his men held her arms firmly behind her back as he checked the display on the laptop. He winced as he watched the two blips heading through the now open door. He glanced at her, shaking his head, then hit the DOOR CLOSE button. He watched the graphic change on the screen and then turned to her.

"What am I going to do with you?"

The DSRV was through the door and Richards lined up

to follow in Deep Rover when he saw the massive iris blades start to close.

"Oh no! Oh no!"

He pushed the throttles forward. The small thrusters on the sides whirred away, spinning the water into spirals of bubbles, but it was no good. By the time he reached the opening it was no longer large enough for him to fit through. He pulled the mike trigger. "John, the door's closed. Not sure what's going on back there but it looks like you're on your own. I'll see if I can open it from in here, otherwise it's going to be a long … Hang on a minute."

The sub had spun sideways after nearly hitting the door and Richards had completed the turn, allowing the full force of the thrusters to take him away from the obstruction. Now he was facing back down the crossover tunnel and in the gloom he could make out a brightening of the water. It was growing stronger by the second. He heard his radio crackle.

"What is it?" asked McCready.

"Not sure, but whatever it is, I don't think I'm going to like it."

He moved the sub forward and slowly the light ahead of him in the water focused into the beams of four bright spotlights. Out of the haze the two Exosuits materialized like metallic specters in the night.

"This is not good." He clicked the comms. "John, it's two of Mercer's men, and they ain't looking friendly."

There was silence for a second. Then McCready replied.

"There's not much we can do from out here. It's all Mac can do to keep us stationary in the flow. No idea how long it'll take to reach the target."

"Okay, do what you have to. If it works I'll see you on the outside. Just have to deal with these two first," said Richards.

"Okay, I think I know those guys. Give them my regards, right where it hurts. We're out of here. Good luck!" And with that the comms went silent.

Richards adjusted himself in his seat and took a firm grip on the two joysticks, pulling the two manipulator arms into position in front of him. The sub now looked like an angry lobster ready to pounce.

The Exosuits were only twenty feet away and maneuvering to either side of him. Richards smiled grimly.

"Okay, you bastards, come and get it!"

Chapter 36

Deep Rover was an incredibly maneuverable machine, but with two adversaries things would be difficult.

Richards edged back against the wall of the tunnel so there was no chance of one of them getting behind him. It did limit his options, but it was the lesser of two evils.

The first suit moved forward as Rizby rocked his left foot control making the thrusters push the machine toward Deep Rover. At the same time he brought his arms up to try to destroy the vital external systems on the sub. Behind and slightly to one side Fisher maneuvered into a flanking position.

As the Exosuit approached, Richards raised the mechanical arms ready to fend off the attack. The two machines clashed and became locked in a titanic struggle. Richards knew he had the advantage though. The Exosuit arms were designed for small movements, like turning valves on subsea oil installations, or collecting scientific samples. The power of their movement came from the arms of the operator, and they weren't designed for unarmed combat. Deep Rover's arms, though, were mechanical and carried far more strength. Richards knocked one of the metal arms of the suit away, but the second grabbed hold of a metal support on the outside of Deep Rover. Now with a firm grip on the small sub, Rizby rocked his foot back, throwing the thrusters into reverse, pulling Deep Rover away from the wall.

Seeing the gap, Fisher moved in behind. He grabbed the cabling at the rear of the sub and tore it free. There was a fizz and sparks flew from the connections. Richards desperately glanced around inside the acrylic dome.

"Not good!"

He turned back to Rizby, who still had hold of the front of the sub. He brought up the second mechanical arm and grabbed hold of the Exosuit, forcing it to break its grip.

Richards now spun Deep Rover, breaking away from Fisher at the rear. Richards could feel the sweat running down his forehead. He turned the sub and started to push Rizby toward the iris door, hoping to pin him against the structure and then destroy the suit beyond repair, but there was still Fisher to worry about. While his back was turned he was open to attack. The odds were not looking good.

What he needed was a miracle.

In the access chamber Clare had to do something. The man was still holding her but she could feel his grip had loosened a fraction as his attention wandered. She took her opportunity. She slammed her heel down on his shin. He cried out and momentarily relaxed his grip even more.

She wrenched herself free and ran for the control panel. She had no time to try to contact McCready, but doing the opposite of what Jennings had done, had to help in some way.

Without hesitation she slammed her hand down on the DOOR OPEN button. She also managed to turn the flow rate control to reduce the water speed in the tunnel.

A second later and she felt the man grab hold of her again. As he pulled her roughly away, she just had time to see the graphic showing the iris door opening. She also saw the flow rate fall to almost zero. She managed a brief smile before Jennings slapped her hard across the face, knocking her to the floor. She turned to look up at him, contempt written across her face.

Deep Rover still had hold of Rizby's Exosuit, but Richards sensed movement behind. A quick glance showed the second suit closing to his rear. He was pushing Rizby toward the door when he saw the iris blades start to open. This gave him a glimmer of hope. If he could just get out into the flow of the main tunnel, there was more chance of evading the clutches of the second suit as they would be swept along at high speed. He moved forward, pushing the suit toward the opening.

Clare's face was smarting from where Jennings had hit her. She was still on the floor. Jennings shot the guard a disapproving look, then glanced down at the control panel. He tried to work out what she'd done. He glared as he saw the graphic of the iris door. It was almost fully open. He clicked the DOOR CLOSE button and turned to her.

"Nice try, but it won't do you any good."

Behind him, Clare watched in despair as the graphic

for the door showed the blades starting to close.

But Jennings hadn't noticed the drop in flow rate.

What Clare could not have known was that Jennings' action was the miracle Richards had been praying for. He had the Exosuit halfway through the door when the blades started to close.

He thought quickly.

He maneuvered the mechanical arms bringing the suit horizontal in the water and then adjusted the thrusters so the Exosuit was in the middle of the door. As the blades of the iris continued to shut, they wrapped tightly around the suit.

Inside, Rizby could see what was going to happen. There was nothing he could do.

And then it happened.

With a wrenching and grinding of metal, the doors sliced through the suit and then continued mercilessly on through the flesh and bone within. Richards could see the terrified expression behind the faceplate and he saw but couldn't hear the final screams as the suit was cut in half.

Rizby died instantly.

The body, along with the remains of the suit, fell in two neatly severed pieces either side of the door. The upper torso fell into the crossover tunnel. The legs fell into the ring main. The iris blades met in the center with a final clunk. A deep stain of red drifted up into the water.

Satisfied, but with a grim expression, Richards flicked the joystick and the small sub spun round to face the other suit.

"Bring it on!"

* * *

Jennings pulled Clare roughly from the floor and dragged her to the office chair that had been thrown through the window and was now lying on its side, well away from the control panel. He righted it and then grabbed a piece of rope and tied her securely to the chair. He pushed her back against the side of the chamber. The wheels, which had probably never been oiled, whined in protest at the sudden movement. "Feisty little thing, aren't we?" he said. "I just might find a use for you later when all this is over."

"In your dreams!" muttered Clare.

"Oh no, young lady, very much in reality," he said menacingly.

But he still hadn't noticed that the water flow was close to zero.

In the crossover tunnel, it was one down, one to go.

The small submersible faced the white Exosuit. They were about ten feet apart. Both hung motionless in the water, illuminated by each other's spotlights. It was like a meeting of two mechanical gladiators in some crazy science fiction movie.

It was the calm before the storm.

Then, as though from a starting gun, both machines charged straight for each other and both knew there would only be one survivor.

Metal hit metal, and it was like a slow-motion boxing match as Richards parried the blows that kept on coming from the Exosuit.

Deep Rover's manipulators were faster to react, though, as the servos and hydraulics could respond more quickly than the man-powered arms of the suit.

After the fifth attempt at a frontal assault with no

success, Fisher adopted another tactic. He moved around the side of the sub to smash the pipes and cabling that had proved so vulnerable before.

In a double, almost crippling movement, a pincer cut a clutch of cables that led to the main battery, and one of the claws rammed into the left-hand thruster. The plastic propeller was no match for the aggression of the metal claw and the small blades splintered instantly.

The thruster died.

It would now be almost impossible for Richards to maneuver.

Richards glanced around inside the cockpit. Sparks erupted from a fuse box and the acrid smell of burnt wiring filled the tiny capsule. He had to do something soon or he wouldn't make it out alive.

He turned as fast as he could, given he only had one thruster. He managed to grab an arm of the Exosuit close to the torso. He pulled it close to the cockpit, restricting the movement of the suit.

He stared out through the two pressurized surfaces straight into Fisher's eyes. The man was only a couple of feet in front of him. With the Exosuit half paralyzed, he grabbed the other arm, holding it in a vice-like grip.

There was nothing Fisher could do. His only option was to use the thrusters to pull Deep Rover through the water and maybe smash it into the tunnel wall. But Richards was wise to that. Even though he only had one operational thruster, he managed to keep them in the center of the tunnel, well away from any walls.

He stared directly into the face of his enemy and then calmly operated the controls that moved the manipulators apart. They moved out to the sides, the arms of the

Exosuit firmly in their grip.

As they extended, the motors whined with the strain. Fisher was trying to prevent them from being pulled apart, but he was no match for the machine in front of him that was intent on his destruction. He could only watch in desperation as the Exosuit arms were dragged further and further apart. Slowly, inch by inch, the suit started to split at the complex joints at the shoulders which allowed the metal arms to rotate at the extreme pressures of the deep.

Fisher could only stare out in terror.

And then with a resounding CRACK the arms ripped from the suit like wings from a fly. Water thundered in, and what was left of the suit fell to the bottom of the tunnel like a broken rag doll.

Richards stared out, his expression hard. He felt no emotion. He was just glad it was over.

But it wasn't.

Suddenly Fisher slammed up against the bubble of the cockpit. He'd managed to extricate himself from the wreckage. He clawed frantically at the acrylic dome, his eyes wide and desperate—a man who knew he was going to die.

Richards could do nothing to help, and he wasn't exactly inclined to even if he'd been able. He watched in almost morbid fascination as the man's struggles grew less and less just inches from his face, and then finally they stopped.

His lifeless body slipped slowly down the dome to lie spread-eagled on the floor of the tunnel below. Richards breathed a sigh of relief and sank back into the seat. He realized how tense he'd become. He wiped the sweat from his brow, then glanced around the shattered cockpit as sparks flew from raw wires, and failing systems started to power down.

He scratched his head and sighed.

"Where the hell's the Auto Club when you need them?"

Chapter 37

When the iris door had closed, sealing Richards on the other side, the three men in the DSRV had one mission and one mission only. They had to find the section of ring main that passed through the old underground river. If they could do that and blast through, they might be able to make it to the Thames.

McCready had previously looked through various archives on the Internet and had found an old underground survey from the 1970s. It looked like there would be enough room for the sub to fit down the river. It would be tight, and there was no knowing the accuracy of the survey. It had been nearly fifty years since it had been carried out and a lot could have changed, but right now they didn't have much choice.

Using the plans on the iPad, McCready worked out the distance from the crossover tunnel to the approximate location of the old river tunnel.

Things were going to be touch and go.

Porter only had three packs of explosives large enough to do the job. If they missed with all three they were going nowhere fast. The distance was about half a mile and the old river appeared to have a width which varied between about twenty and thirty feet. Even if they did break through, there was no knowing what they would find. Luck as much as skill would need to be on their side.

When they'd set off Logan had thought it would be almost impossible for the sub to make headway against the flow of water in the tunnel. They'd been traveling for about ten minutes and only made a few hundred yards when the flow had mysteriously stopped. He had no idea why but he wasn't complaining.

Since then they'd made good time and Porter was just finishing checking the remote controls on the explosive packs when Logan called back from the cockpit. "Okay, we're approaching the section now."

McCready moved forward to look out through the dome. He wasn't sure what he expected to see. The tunnel was the tunnel. There would be no indication where the river had been, but he felt he had to look.

"So where do you want to start?" asked Logan.

"May as well be the best estimate we have. If that doesn't work, try thirty feet each side. We only get three goes at this."

"Okay," said Logan. "Pulling up on site now."

He inched closer to the wall. As he approached, he moved the collar control to angle the hatch at right angles to the side. He then tilted down a fraction. As the explosive bolts had been used at the vault, there was no way to lock on to the wall. They would have to use the power of the sub's thrusters to push them against the side to try to seal the collar. Hopefully this would give Porter enough time to attach the explosives. Some water would enter the sub, but with a bit of luck it would be manageable. Once the explosives were in place, they'd back off and it was then out of their hands.

McCready turned to Porter. "Okay, you ready?"

"As I'll ever be," came the reply.

"Okay, Mac, take us in," said McCready.

Logan gently nudged the controls to turn the thrusters at right angles to the sub, pushing it sideways and toward the wall.

Porter was all concentration. He picked up one of the packs and checked the suction cup on the bottom. He then eased himself into the collar that was now almost horizontal out to the side. He lay in the collar, ready to open the outer hatch on Logan's word.

A second later and they felt the sub nudge up against the side of the tunnel. Logan increased the power to the thrusters, holding the sub tight against the wall. "Okay, now," he said.

Porter pulled open the hatch. Immediately, water jetted in. He gasped against the cold as it hit his face. He took a second to get over the shock and then fought the flow, pushing the explosive against the wall. He held it firm, making it secure, then let go of it.

But a moment later it fell off.

The suction had failed.

"Shit!" cursed Porter. He grabbed the pack and pushed harder, holding it in place for ten seconds before releasing his grip. He held his breath.

It held.

He double-checked, then shouted "Secure" and climbed back out of the collar.

Logan backed the sub away from the wall, at the same time turning the collar vertically down. The water started to drain out. Porter sat on the floor, panting. He wiped his face and then picked up the remote for the charge. "Okay, we need to be thirty feet before I blow it."

"Roger that," came Logan's reply from the cockpit. He maneuvered the sub back away from the section of pipe. He could see the charge clinging to the wall about halfway up.

A minute later he turned to Porter. "Over to you."

"Okay, stand by," said Porter.

They all braced themselves.

Porter jabbed his finger down.

There was a loud BOOM.

The sub rocked as it was hit by the pressure wave. After about a minute it began to stabilize, coming back on an even keel. Through the dome Logan could see a cloud of bubbles and silt reducing the visibility. It hung there like a shroud of mist, but then slowly as the bubbles rose and the particles settled it started to clear, leaving a dull murkiness in the water.

He edged the sub forward.

"How's it looking?" asked McCready.

"Still not clear," replied Logan.

He moved closer, and then through the gloom he could make out a large indent in the wall—but it was solid.

It was the wrong place.

"It's not here," said Logan, his tone subdued.

"What the hell was that?" asked Jennings.

There had been a far-off rumble as the sound of the explosion had carried down the tunnel. A short while later ripples of disturbance shimmered across the surface of the water.

Both of Jennings' men had looked up. Jennings glanced around the chamber and peered into the tunnel. He then crossed over to Clare. She was still secured to the chair by the wall. "You know what that was?" he asked her.

She shook her head. "No idea. Sometimes the system turbines do a reboot. There can be a juddering and ripple effect." It was the best she could come up with but she was sure he didn't believe her.

Jennings picked up the walkie-talkie. "Fisher, do you copy?" There was static from the small speaker. "Rizby, over?" Again static. "Fisher, Rizby. Either of you, do you copy?"

Nothing but static.

Jennings shook his head and then turned to his men. "Okay, get the boat ready. You need to go fishing."

They crossed over to the truck and prepared to crane the boat into the water. Clare watched with interest. She would only have one chance at this. It was a long shot, but the less time she stayed in the access chamber the greater her chances of survival, even though it would be like jumping from the frying pan into the fire.

She was thinking it through when another BOOM echoed down the tunnel sending ever-increasing ripples across the water surface.

Jennings just looked at his men.

"Hurry!"

After the first charge had failed to locate the underground river they'd tossed a coin to decide whether to go thirty feet further away or thirty feet back down the pipe for the second attempt.

Forward won.

After the second charge the sub had rocked again and the water filled with millions of tiny bubbles. Logan eased the DSRV closer as they waited for it to clear.

Slowly the bubbles dissipated. But again the wall was solid. They glanced at each other.

There was only one shot left.

"Okay, back down the tunnel. One last go," said McCready.

Logan grabbed the controls and twisted the joystick to maneuver the sub. It was just starting to turn when Porter shouted out.

"Stop!"

Logan glanced round.

"There, look!" said Porter.

They all looked out of the dome at the wall where the blast had failed. The water was clearer but there were still some small bubbles left, reducing the visibility.

"There on the right." Porter pointed at the far side of the blast area.

They all peered closely and sure enough there was a small spiral of bubbles that weren't adhering to the laws of physics and rising to the surface. They were heading down a small opening at the side of the damaged section. As they watched, the spiral increased until a large flow of water could be seen disappearing into the wall.

They all looked at each other. Logan was the first to speak. "Well done, laddie."

McCready smiled. "Okay, let's get this done," he said.

Porter readied the final charge while Logan moved the sub past the hole by about ten feet. It should put them exactly in the middle of the old river course. When he was ready, he glanced back at Porter. "You're on again."

Porter repeated the previous action, only this time he added an additional amount of explosive. While there were no more large charges left, he had some smaller ones. As he still didn't know the actual size of the river, they needed as big a hole as possible. Anyway, it couldn't do any harm.

When the charge was secured to the side of the tunnel, he called down for Logan to back away. When they were thirty feet clear, Porter gently pressed the small button on the remote.

They all held their breaths.

A massive explosion reverberated through the water. Debris and pieces of the pipe wall disappeared as they were blown into the old river course beyond. Water thundered down the new tunnel. Now free of the confines of the ring main, it sought freedom in the river below. Immediately, the level in the ring main started to drop, creating a larger air gap at the top of the tunnel.

At all points of the system the water started to flow toward the new tunnel.

The DSRV was caught in the current. The whole sub shuddered and shook, and then it started to be sucked forward. It went into a slow spin. Logan fought the controls, trying to stop it from being smashed into the side.

Chapter 38

In the chamber the third blast had made more of an impression. Small wavelets appeared out of the tunnel. They grew larger and more frequent, their reach extending into the tunnel on the other side of the room. Jennings could also see the water level start to drop. Concern flashed across his face.

Clare had seen it too. She had no idea of the condition of McCready and his team but clearly they'd managed to blow through to the river passage. There could be no other explanation. She had to do something. She had to stop him going down.

The Scarab jet boat was now in the water on the far side of the pipe. It gently rose and fell as the small waves flowed across the surface. Since the previous explosion Clare had been trying to work her hands free from the rope that bound them to the chair. She'd managed to loosen one end and was twisting her fingers to pull a loop through.

Jennings was unsure what to do. He was a man who made calculated decisions on data and information and right now he didn't have any. Clare could see him debating whether to come over to her. "Just a minute longer," she whispered to herself.

Jennings started toward her.

"Not yet," she said under her breath, but he was closer now. She managed to pull the rope free behind her back. She didn't have much time. The boat was only forty feet away but one of Jennings' men was in it, and Jennings was between her and the water.

He'd almost reached her when she decided to go for it.

She leapt up out of the chair, pulling it round with her as she went. The wheels screamed in protest. She hurled it at him, smashing it into his kneecaps.

He hit the floor crying out in pain.

Her focus was now on the pipe. She set off as fast as her legs could carry her. She was almost there, but the other of Jennings' men had run across the gantry. She was only three feet from the pipe when she felt a hand on her arm, and the grip was tightening.

Jennings picked himself up off the floor, pain and fury written across his face. "Bring her here!" he yelled.

The man dragged Clare over. There was nothing she could do. It was like being held in a vice.

Jennings walked to meet her, and this time there was no slap—it was a full-blooded punch to the face with all the strength he could muster. She literally saw stars and crumpled to the floor.

Jennings was breathing heavily. Both his men glanced at him with disapproval. He glared at them. "What?"

Then he looked down at Clare.

She moved slowly.

A hand, then an arm, then her head eased itself from side to side. She started to push herself to a kneeling position, supporting herself on her hands. She didn't seem to know where she was. She looked up and the tall shape of Jennings swam into focus. At first she didn't recognize him. Then the pain in her head started to register and her face creased in agony. Her expression turned hard and she stared up at him defiantly.

"Like beating up on defenseless women?" she managed to say. He raised his hand again but restrained himself at the last second. He turned away and then back again.

"You know what's going on. What were those blasts?"

"I don't know a thing. How could I? I'm here, you idiot!"

Jennings nodded to the guy behind Clare. He pulled her to her feet, grabbed her arm and slowly started to twist. At first it wasn't too bad but as the joint started to move beyond its limits, Clare started to worry.

"I won't ask again," said Jennings. He had calmed a little and the smugness had returned.

Clare remained silent.

Jennings sighed and then spoke to his man. "Twist it till it dislocates." Then he turned away and walked over to the side of the pipe.

As her arm rotated further she felt the tendons stretching. The pain started slowly but very quickly grew to a sharp stabbing throughout the joint. This was for real and the guy wasn't going to stop. Tears came to her eyes as she tried to fight through it, but it was no good. Just as she felt a slight tear from her shoulder, she cried out.

"Okay, okay. Enough!"

Jennings turned from the pipe. "I'm listening."

Clare took a couple of deep breaths and glanced at the man behind her to ease off with his grip. He looked at

Jennings, who nodded. The man let go and she dropped back to the floor clutching her damaged shoulder. But behind Jennings she noticed the second guy had started to bring the boat over to this side of the pipe.

"I'm waiting," said Jennings.

"Okay, okay," said Clare, wincing at the pain from her joint. "They've blown through to a passageway, an old underground river that runs into the Thames."

Jennings processed this, his expression hard. "One little titbit our friend Matthews forgot to enlighten us with."

"Well, at least he didn't have a complete lack of judgment," said Clare.

Jennings merely glanced at her, an annoyed expression on his face.

The Scarab was now pulling up on the near side of the pipe. The man was leaning over the far gunwale to move the fender over to protect the side of the boat when it was up against the pipe.

This was her chance. She wouldn't get another.

She calculated angles and then went for it. She forgot about the pain in her shoulder and leapt up off the floor. It was too fast for the man to grab her, and Jennings had his back to her. He turned in time to see a blur race past him.

"Get her!" he shouted.

The man in the boat started to turn but nothing was going to stop Clare. She leapt into the air, her foot extended forward. It hit the man dead center in the chest, sending him sprawling over the side with a splash into the now fast-flowing water. The engine was already running, so all she had to do was hit the throttle. The water jet responded instantly, accelerating the small craft forward like a startled rabbit. Within a second it was up on the plane and heading for the tunnel mouth.

A second later it disappeared into the darkness.

Clare didn't look back. Even the shattering sound of a gunshot couldn't distract her. She heard the bullet fly past her and then she was gone, hurtling down the tunnel to she knew not what.

The wind from the speed of the boat buffeted her, but as she paused for a second, hardly able to believe she'd made it, a wide grin spread across her face. "That's not something you do every day," she said to herself.

In the chamber Jennings raised both his hands in frustration. He crossed to the side of the pipe and casually kicked Matthews' body into the water, just as his man was hauling himself out. Next he ran to the control panel and hit the button that operated the cowl. He watched with satisfaction as the cover closed like a giant hand, sealing the pipe and trapping all within.

"Only one way out now," he said.

He pulled out his cell and dialed.

When it was answered, he spoke hurriedly. "The inventory could be headed for the river."

He listened briefly.

"Yes, sir, I'll put him on it right away."

Listened again.

"Yes, sir, I'll meet you there."

He clicked off the call and immediately hit a speed dial number. It rang twice and then was answered.

Mark Shannon had won the first three rounds of Texas hold 'em poker and was feeling flush. He'd flown Mercer down to London in the Jet Ranger as the Bell 222 was still having its undercarriage repaired, and he was now sitting in the Battersea Heliport rec room relieving some of the local pilots of their well-earned cash. There wasn't a whole lot for him to do during these sorts of trips, but he always had to be close by, just in case. He was looking to clean up on the fourth round when "just in case" reared its ugly head.

He listened to Jennings on the other end of the phone. A minute later he gave a simple answer.

"On my way."

He put the handset into his pocket, told the other players, much to their relief, that he had to leave, then grabbed his coat and ran out to the helicopter that was parked on the pad next to the river. He jumped in and started the pre-flight checks, the twin blades starting to turn slowly above him.

It had been a strange request—he had to look for a flow of water gushing out from the north bank of the Thames. It should be somewhere not far from Waterloo Bridge.

His was not to reason why …

Once the blades were spinning up to speed, he checked in with the control tower. After receiving clearance, he took off, swung out over the river, keeping to the designated route for helicopters over the capital, and headed east toward the City.

The task couldn't be simpler. He was happy. All the nuts and bolts were in perfect formation—just the way he liked it.

Jennings ran across the gantry to the other side of the

chamber and beckoned to his men. "You two, out of here. We were never here."

He then jumped into the 911 and skidded out under the shutters.

The two men were left to retrieve any equipment and remove the truck from the chamber.

The party was in full swing at the Russian Embassy. Once the official business had been completed, the alcohol flowed freely and many of the guests were enjoying the sumptuous buffet that had been laid on.

Mercer had been chatting with the British and Russian ambassadors when Jennings had called with the far from welcome news.

He moved across to the British ambassador and touched him lightly on the shoulder. "I'm terribly sorry, Sir Richard"—and with a glance at the Russian ambassador—"Anatoli, but if you'll excuse me, an urgent business matter has just come up."

The British ambassador looked at him and frowned. "Nothing too serious, I hope, Malcolm, old boy."

"Oh no, just a slight accounting problem," replied Mercer, and with that he hurriedly left the room.

Mercer moved quickly through the ornate building, collected his coat from a pretty girl in a cloakroom, and by the time he breezed out of the front door, his Bentley was waiting for him.

A few seconds later his driver drove out onto Kensington Palace Gardens. It was still thronged with traffic. Even at this hour the capital was a living, breathing thing that operated all hours of the day.

He checked his watch and drummed his fingers on the

leather armrest between the two rear seats.

In the ring main, things were tense. The DSRV was at least now facing the right direction, but the speed of the flow had thrown it against the side of the tunnel several times. Ahead, the lights picked up a growing reduction in visibility. The haze grew as millions of tiny bubbles filled the view outside the cockpit dome. Logan glanced back.

"Better get ready to hang on. Here we go!"

In the rear, McCready and Porter exchanged glances and then sat well down on the floor, grabbing hold of anything they could.

The sub approached the jagged hole marking the entrance to the river passage.

It was swept in.

As it turned the sharp corner it smashed into the side. Pipes and wiring were ripped from the hull. A violent grinding echoed through the interior. It didn't fill anyone with confidence.

"You do have a license for this thing?" asked Porter.

When Logan replied, there was an edge of tension in his voice. "You better hope so. If I can't keep her straight —"

"What?" interrupted Porter.

"We're longer than the tunnel is wide," explained Logan. "We go sideways, we're staying there."

This seemed to subdue Porter, and he glanced around, a concerned expression on his face.

About two miles further along the ring main, Clare was at full speed in the Scarab. There was barely enough room for her to see over the small wind deflector in front of the controls as the top of the pipe was so low. She was huddled down in the cockpit, ducking every now and then as a fitting on the tunnel above sped past and would have decapitated her had she not been alert.

In the sub Logan wasn't happy. The sides of the old river weren't even. Jagged pieces of rock and old pipes stuck out from all sides. They caused eddies and flows that made it virtually impossible to control the bucking machine, not to mention being obstructions in their own right.

He shifted the angle of the lights to look further ahead into the darkness, and his face turned to horror.

"Oh shit!"

Porter was quick to comment. "Oh shit! What the hell does "oh shit" mean?"

"Hang on," was all Logan replied.

Suddenly the sub juddered and was rocked as it crashed into a protrusion in the tunnel wall. The impact spun it sideways, the water pressure jamming it fast.

The dome at the front hit the rock hard. A massive, jagged fracture splintered out across the center with a noise that jarred teeth.

Logan sat back in his seat. He let go of the controls and powered the system down. He looked round at two expectant and very concerned passengers. "End of the line, folks, and someone better think of something fast!"

At that second another crack splintered the dome. This time its branch-like structure reached out across the full width of the glass.

It wouldn't hold for long.

Chapter 39

The jet boat was doing close to forty knots and the tunnel roof whipped past inches above Clare's head. She knew the distance to the river passage and she had to get there in time to try and help McCready. She also knew their exit to the Thames would be blocked. She just prayed they hadn't already made it into the tunnel.

The boat suddenly started to judder, the bow slapping across small waves on the surface of the water.

Clare knocked the speed down and glanced over the top of the windshield. The water was roughening even more.

She was close to the river tunnel.

She angled one of the spotlights to point toward the wall on the right. A second later and she could see the flow disappearing into the side of the ring main. The subs were nowhere to be seen. Her worst fears were realized. Now she had a decision to make.

Should she go down after them?

She watched the flow for a moment. The passage itself wasn't steep as there was an air gap at the top. It was, though, smaller than where she was now, but at least there was a gap. She would be able to breath.

As she considered her options, she suddenly realized she was being sucked toward the opening. She turned the boat around and tried to accelerate away, but it was no good. The flow of water was stronger than the engine, and with it came a terrifying roar, a mind-numbing, thundering sound that filled the space with its power, a power you couldn't escape from, and with mounting fear she realized she no longer had a choice.

She spun the boat to face the direction of travel, and with eyes wide, watched as she was drawn inexorably toward the gaping mouth that was right in front of her and growing larger by the second.

About five hundred feet away in the DSRV, things were becoming desperate. The water relentlessly pounded the hull. It vibrated and shook with the force.

Then suddenly the sound of another large crack ripped through the air. All three men stared nervously at the dome. McCready tried to peer through to the front. "Mac, how high's the water outside?"

Logan glanced up through the top of the dome. "Looks to be about four feet off the roof."

McCready thought for a second. "Okay, if we rotate the collar upright it might give us some breathing space. Also a way out if things go south."

But Porter didn't look happy. "Don't you think we're at the South freaking Pole already?"

"We have to do something," said McCready "If the dome's going to give way, I'd rather be out than in."

"Agreed," added Logan.

McCready grabbed the controls and operated the

swivel of the collar. It slowly rotated from the downward position, through one-eighty degrees, until it was pointing vertically upright. Hopefully it would now be above the flow of water and well into the air gap.

McCready beckoned Porter over. "Okay, you first."

Porter looked distinctly unhappy. "Why me? He can go," he said, pointing at Logan.

McCready rolled his eyes. "Look, we haven't time for this. We all have to go at some point. You're the closest."

Porter backed up a little, making McCready the closest. "Uh uh. Not going up there."

Logan turned round. "What's the problem?"

Porter was hesitant for a second. They both stared at him.

"I can't swim."

He glanced at them aggressively. "Go on, say it! I don't give a shit! But we're in here. It's wet out there and I can't bloody swim, okay!"

Logan let out a bellow of a laugh. "Don't you be worrying yourself, laddie. There's no way we're getting out of this alive, but if it'll make you feel any better, I'll look after you!"

This didn't seem to make Porter feel any better, but he crossed over to the collar and looked nervously upward.

Clare wrenched the wheel round, but she couldn't stop the boat from smashing into the side of the tunnel.

She was forced up against the roof by an eddy in the flow. She had seen the impact coming and ducked in time, but there was nothing she could do to prevent the collision.

And then she was pulled on again, the flow carrying

her relentlessly forward. The dancing light caused by the movement of the boat made seeing ahead difficult, but she knew the DSRV was ahead of her somewhere. She'd seen a piece of tubing on the side of the tunnel that could only have come from the sub.

A few seconds later and she noticed a dim glow ahead. She adjusted the throttle and glanced up again. The glow became more intense and suddenly her face turned to horror.

Ahead, the DSRV was wedged hard, completely blocking the tunnel, and she was approaching it fast. She grabbed the wheel at the last second and spun the boat around, applying full throttle to avoid smashing into the sub, but it was too late.

She careered backward into the metal side as water sprayed out of the jet at the rear. If there had been a propeller it would have cavitated, providing little or no thrust, but as it was the jet provided propulsion and lessened the collision, but it still hit hard.

Inside the DSRV the impact was met with alarm.

The whole structure shuddered violently. They had no idea what it was. The force of the impact rammed the sub even harder against the sides of the tunnel and with a sickening splintering noise the fracture in the dome finally gave way.

Water jetted in through a jagged crack, which was growing larger by the second.

Porter had just about plucked up enough courage to climb up the ladder when the boat had hit. He jumped back down, looking around with wild eyes.

"What the fuck was that?" It was a sentiment shared by

the others.

"Stay there," said McCready to Porter.

"No problem, guv," came the reply.

McCready climbed the ladder in the collar to look out of the hatch. The water level had dropped slightly and there was now about five feet of clearance above the top of the hatch, but he could hardly see a thing. The blockage caused by the sub forced the water to churn and froth, throwing spray into the air. All around the sound was deafening as the water thundered downstream. The air was thick with a moist haze and he was dazzled by the lights from something upstream.

What the hell was that?

As the spray lessened he could make out a boat, and in it – Clare! His first reaction was one of relief that Jennings no longer had his hands on her, but then with a sickening realization he knew she would probably have been far safer there than the situation she now found herself in. He tried to shout to her but could barely make himself heard above the roar of the water.

"Clare. Jesus! Are you alright?"

"John, yeah, I think so," she managed to shout back.

"Can you get any closer?"

She slowly let the boat ride back toward the sub, expertly balancing the thrust against the flow. McCready grabbed hold.

"There's no way past," shouted Clare.

McCready thought for a second. "Porter might just be able to help with that. Stay there!"

He disappeared back into the sub.

Inside, the spray of water from the cracked dome had become a full-blown onslaught that was fast filling up the cockpit. McCready looked at the anxious expressions on the other two faces. "It's the girl in a boat. Looks like we just found our ticket out of here." He turned to Porter. "Eugene, you have any of your stuff that goes bang?"

Porter grinned. "Is a Scotsman a pain in the backside?"

Logan shook his head, but said nothing.

McCready was all action. He had a plan and it might just work. "Okay, Mac, you first. Get out and over to the boat. Clare will help you." Logan disappeared up the ladder with a final hostile glance at Porter.

He climbed out onto the top of the sub and took in the chaos around him. He had to shield his eyes from the spray but then focused on Clare and the jet boat. It was wedged up hard against the sub. He made his way over and jumped in.

Back inside, McCready had explained his plan to Porter who was working away with his equipment. Now he had something to concentrate on he was all focus and the fear of the water slowly rising in the sub seemed to have been put to one side for now. He carefully laid out his explosives and drew some wires from a pouch. He started to connect them to a small detonator. Once he was happy he had all the components he squeezed the plastic-like explosive around the circumference of the sub just to the rear of the collar track. McCready watched apprehensively.

"We will all survive this?"

"Anything's possible," he said, continuing to work.

The water jetting in from the fractured dome was now up to their knees, and although Porter was focused on the task at hand, he kept a watchful eye on the level.

They were both starting to shiver with the cold when

there was another ominous crack from the dome. He redoubled his efforts.

He connected the wires from the plastique to a small box at the side. It had a countdown display on it, and as he fiddled with two buttons, he glanced up at McCready. "I'm out of transmitters so we're on a timer," he said matter-of-factly.

At that moment the dome finally gave way. There was an ear-splitting CRACK and water thundered uncontrollably into the sub. Porter clicked a switch on the small box. There was a beep and a red light pulsed menacingly. He turned to McCready.

"Sixty seconds!"

They both scrambled up out of the collar and onto the top of the sub, chased by the rising flow of water.

A few seconds later and Logan and Clare had helped them into the boat. It was pretty cramped, and they had to crouch down to avoid being squashed by the roof that was just above.

As McCready knelt down beside Clare, they were only a couple of feet apart. He smiled at her and was about to say something when she slapped him across the face as hard as she could. "Don't ever do that to me again!" There was real fury in her eyes. McCready just stared at her. Porter stared at both of them incredulously.

"Hey, I don't know what you two have got going on, but in about twenty seconds there's going to be a ruddy great bang! And right now we're ringside."

Clare continued to stare hard at McCready.

"Hello!" shouted Porter. She glanced at him. "At least fifty feet, if you want to see daylight again."

Clare reached for the controls and pushed the throttle

forward. The boat started to fight against the flow and they powered up the tunnel. They crouched low as the roof flew past inches above their heads. Clare turned to McCready and none of the hostility had gone. "Where's the other sub?"

"Back at the crossover tunnel," McCready answered seriously, "with two of Mercer's goons. What happened to Paul?"

Clare softened a little. "He's dead. Jennings shot him."

McCready felt the anger rising and clenched his fists. "Jesus, the bastard!"

Then Clare's expression was filled with concern, and when she spoke he could see the fear in her eyes. "John, there's something I have to tell you. There's a grille at the bottom of the tunnel. We won't make it out to the river."

He looked at her seriously for a second and nodded, thinking. "Okay, let's deal with one thing at a time, all right?" He squeezed her shoulder.

"That's enough," shouted Porter. "Everyone down. And if you've got a God, now's the time to use him!"

They squeezed as low as they could go in the boat, waiting for the inevitable. The seconds ticked away.

It seemed like forever.

When the explosion came they thought their world had ended. A massive BOOM echoed round the narrow air space, almost blowing their eardrums out. Debris flew through the air, and if the boat hadn't been wedged up tight against the roof, it would have been flipped clean over.

Acrid smoke hung in the air and the lights from the boat cast a blinding haze like headlights in fog. As the ripples from the blast slowly died, they felt the boat moving beneath them. Suddenly they were accelerating down the tunnel and the smoke and haze was blown out of the way.

The path ahead was clear.

"Okay, let's go," yelled McCready.

Clare wasted no time and pushed the throttles forward. There was a slightly larger air gap now as the obstruction of the sub was no longer backing up the flow.

The explosion had blown the DSRV into a number of pieces, and the rear section swept ahead of them like some sort of aquatic bulldozer.

McCready almost smiled. He was beginning to believe they might actually make it out of this alive, but then Clare's words came back to him and any thought of a smile quickly disappeared.

Chapter 40

He connected the green wire in the fuse box, checked all the other contacts, then sat back and clicked the switch. There was a violent electronic CRACK and sparks flew from the wire accompanied by a thin plume of wispy smoke. Richards cursed and changed the sequence of wires.

Since the encounter with the Exosuits, he'd been trying to rewire some of the circuits to see if he could get power up and running again. They'd inflicted almost mortal damage on the little sub, but he was sure there was some way he could bring it back to life.

The other issue was the cold.

He was effectively sitting in water a few degrees above freezing, and with the power gone there was no heating in the sub. He shivered and double-checked the box for one final go. It had to work.

"Come on, baby, just once!"

He almost winced as he flicked the switch, but this time there were no sparks. Instead there was a low, almost muted hum from somewhere behind him. It increased, and then the lights flickered on … and off … then on again. A couple more flickers and they stayed solid. The displays blinked on, reset themselves and proceeded to go through a start-up sequence. A minute later and all the systems were running. Richards leaned back in his seat and let out a relieved sigh.

"Way da go!"

He flicked on the exterior spotlights and checked around him. Fisher's body lay just below the front of the sub, with the dismembered remains of the Exosuit a few feet behind. He'd never wanted to kill anyone but he'd had no choice.

It had been them or him.

He pulled back on the small joystick and the sub lifted off the bottom. He spun it round till he was facing away from the closed iris door. He would just have to go the long way round.

He pushed the throttles forward and headed down the crossover tunnel.

The graphite colored Porsche 911 Turbo sped through the elegant streets of Belgravia. Jennings had broken every speed limit on the dash over from Hammersmith. He lifted a walkie-talkie and pressed TRANSMIT. "Mark, you found it?"

There was a brief crackle and then Shannon's American drawl came over the speaker. "Coming up on station now. You were a couple of bridges out. She's just downstream of Vauxhall Bridge.

"Okay, monitor any developments and keep me advised."

"Roger, Shannon, out."

* * *

About a quarter of a mile from the Porsche, Shannon brought the Jet Ranger round in a controlled slide to a point on the Thames pretty much opposite the iconic Mi6 building.

He was now hovering next to a large tunnel entrance in the side of the north bank of the Thames. Water thundered out of it, and through the spray he could make out a solid metal grille that barricaded the exit. "Doesn't look like anyone's coming out of there," he mused to himself.

As he maintained the hover, he noticed a large Bentley drive up to a spot on the road just above the outlet and stop. A second later a Porsche 911 arrived from the opposite direction. It was moving fast and for a second looked as though it was going to crash into the other car, but the six piston, fixed brake calipers on the Porsche did their job, bringing the performance machine to a stop mere inches from the fender of the Bentley.

Shannon watched as Jennings jumped out of the Porsche and ran over to the rear door of the larger car. The heavily tinted window slid smoothly down.

Mercer looked out. His face showed concern. Jennings gave him an update. "They should be exiting the tunnel anytime soon."

Mercer was emphatic. "I need McCready. That is priority one!"

"Yes, sir," replied Jennings.

"Enough's gone wrong already tonight. Don't screw this up!"

"No, sir."

* * *

The Scarab was riding the flow in the tunnel. The wreckage of the sub was still ahead clearing a path for them to follow. It was bumpy and Clare had to keep swerving to avoid old pipes and drainage channels that stuck out from the walls every now and then, but at least they were heading in the right direction and an air of confidence filled the little boat.

The tunnel took a turn to the left, and as they angled round the curve they could see they were in big trouble. Across the end of the tunnel were four massive bars laid out like a tic-tac-toe board. They were thick and sturdy and it didn't look like they would break easily.

The sub wreckage hit first with a loud metallic clang. It would only be seconds before the boat plowed into the sub.

"Hang on everyone!" Clare yelled, and with that she spun the wheel, at the same time pushing the throttle into reverse. This made a small curved cowl drop down over the water jet, like the reverse thrust on a jet engine on an airliner. This had the effect of rotating the boat almost on its own axis. Once she was facing back up the tunnel, she applied full forward thrust.

The action helped to avoid killing everyone on board, but still the boat smashed into the wreckage that was now hard up against the grille like a rock thrown against a wall.

They were now facing into the flow, so the boat was riding the water well. The big problem was the wreckage blocking the exit. It caused the water to back up, and the level was rising with every passing second.

The boat was pushed higher and higher until it was almost flat against the tunnel roof. Everyone was now below the level of the gunwale to avoid being squashed between the proverbial rock and a hard place.

Porter took the moment to remind everyone of his condition. "I can't bloody swim, remember!"

Logan couldn't resist a retort. "We don't get through here, it won't really matter, laddie!"

The windshield was now flush against the tunnel and the water was still rising.

On the other side of the grille, about a hundred feet out from the bank and fifty feet in the air, Shannon watched from his vantage point in the Jet Ranger. He could see Jennings at the top of the bank. He pressed the trigger mike.

"I can see wreckage at the grille. The water level's pretty high. Doubt anyone could survive that."

Jennings held the walkie-talkie to his mouth and walked over to the river looking out at Shannon in the middle. "Okay, come and pick me up. I need to be sure. Boss wants McCready alive."

"Roger that," came the reply.

Jennings ran back to the 911 and pulled an M16 assault rifle from the storage area at the front of the car. He ran back to the bank as Shannon maneuvered for a landing. Several passing cars screeched to a halt to watch the helicopter. There wasn't room to land, so Shannon expertly dropped a skid onto the stone wall at the edge of the river, the aircraft suspended by the whirling rotors above. Jennings pulled the rear sliding door open and jumped into the back. He grabbed a comms headset and told Shannon to stand off in the middle of the river, facing the grille.

The chopper lifted up into the night.

On the other side of the grille things were desperate.

The wreckage was still there and the water levels were even higher. Suddenly there was a groan from the metal, but nothing happened. In fact, a piece of wreckage shifted, blocking even more of the opening. The boat made a violent jerk upwards, shattering what was left of the windshield and jamming the boat flat against the roof of the tunnel.

"Oh shit!" was all Porter could manage.

McCready and Clare were lying close to each other next to the controls. Clare's anger from earlier had gone. She fully realized these could well be her last minutes on Earth and she was happy for McCready to hold her and give what little comfort he could. His mouth moved close to her ear.

"I should never have got you into this."

"No, you shouldn't, but at least it makes us quits," she said, just about managing a smile.

McCready looked at her, puzzled. "Huh?"

"Well I should think this qualifies for an apology!" She smiled even more at that, and McCready held her tight.

They were just at the point where all hope seemed to be gone, when a massive groan came from the grille.

They all looked towards it.

Then there was another one, and another, and then finally the overwhelming pressure overcame the aging metal and the bars splintered, sending the grille and the wreckage flowing into the Thames.

The four people in the boat could hardly believe their eyes as they found themselves bobbing on the surface of the river in fresh air again. Gradually they all sat up, glad to be free of the claustrophobic confines of the tunnel.

From the helicopter Jennings watched through binoculars as the boat drifted out into the river. There were four people and one of them was definitely McCready. He spoke into the comms. "Okay, take us down!"

Shannon banked hard right, spinning the chopper round and heading down toward the small craft below.

Clare positioned herself at the controls and made sure everything was working. She was just about to set off when the screaming roar of the Jet Ranger filled their ears.

They all turned to the sky to see the menacing black shape bearing down on them.

Chapter 41

McCready was the first to speak. "I don't think that's a rescue chopper. Downstream, now!"

Clare didn't need any further urging. She slammed the throttle forward and the boat took off like a greyhound after a hare, nearly throwing Porter off one of the rear-facing seats at the back. Logan, who was sitting next to him, managed to grab him at the last second before he fell. Porter glanced fearfully at the dark water flashing past inches away and clung on with a death-like grip to a handle on the side of the boat. He looked at Logan but couldn't bring himself to thank the man. He merely nodded imperceptibly. Logan grinned and turned to look up at the fast-approaching helicopter.

The river was calm but flowing strongly. The wake of the boat spread out like a giant wing behind the speeding craft. The Jet Ranger dived down low and shot past about twenty feet away, the wash from the rotors pummeling the occupants as it flew in close.

Clare skidded the boat away from the chopper, completing a complete loop and heading on down the Thames. The helicopter matched the maneuver and came even closer, trying to force the driver into a mistake.

But Clare knew how to handle a boat. After several minutes of cat and mouse, the helicopter pulled up and tracked horizontally. Moments later, shots rang out in a deafening staccato, zinging into the bodywork of the Scarab. Everyone ducked. Clare tried again to dodge out of the way.

Ahead a passenger ferry made its way sedately along the Thames. Clare raced behind it to put it between themselves and the helicopter.

Shannon expertly slid around the vessel and again the jet boat was in Jennings' sights.

From the bank of the river Mercer watched with increasing frustration. He lifted his walkie-talkie. "I need him alive, Connor!"

There was a crackle and then the reply came through. "Yes sir. Then we're going to have to get them wet."

"Then do it!" was Mercer's curt response.

In the Ranger Jennings clicked the comms to Shannon. "Okay, ditch them!"

Shannon acknowledged and circled round high above the boat to work out his best approach.

In the Scarab, Logan looked up as the noise from the chopper receded.

"Looks like he's given up."

Porter was also watching. "I don't think so."

And before he'd even finished the words the small speck in the sky started to grow larger as it swooped back down toward them.

They all stared fearfully as the chopper skimmed the

water, approaching fast from the rear. Then it was alongside and they could clearly see the whites of Jennings' eyes as he watched from the open door. The rotors were spinning almost directly above the boat and the downdraft buffeted and rocked the hurtling craft. The noise was unbearable, like the screaming of a thousand banshees merely feet away from them. They cowered down trying to take cover from the onslaught.

Clare weaved and turned the best she could but the chopper was so close there was the danger of smashing into the aircraft as it raced alongside. If it were possible it moved even closer, the skids almost brushing the surface of the water.

McCready suddenly realized what he was trying to do. "He's going to flip us!" He looked around desperately and then spotted the anchor in the front of the boat. He moved forward and grabbed it. Porter looked at him with alarm.

"What the hell are you doing?" he shouted.

McCready coiled the line while Porter watched with growing concern. "We're a boat. That's a plane. They don't mix!"

McCready glanced at him. "You got a better idea?"

"I don't like flying, man!"

Logan looked at him. "You can't swim and you don't like flying. What the hell do you like?"

"Bloody big bangs!"

McCready looked at the helicopter. It was now only six feet away. The left skid was almost under the bow. He turned to Clare. "Pull left when I say."

She nodded but looked at him, and he could see the fear in her eyes.

A second later and McCready yelled,
"NOW!"

Clare zipped to the left, just as the chopper rose up, clearly intending to flip the boat with the skid. As it rose, McCready threw the anchor. It looped itself around the skid and pulled tight, locking on to the trailing line that was attached to the bow.

"Away fast!" McCready yelled at Clare.

She spun hard left, the throttle pushed fully forward. The boat sped away from the Jet Ranger, the line from the anchor trailing behind. McCready glanced around. "Hold on everyone!"

A couple of seconds later and the line went taut. The chopper jerked in the air and the boat spun round, throwing Logan off the rear and into the water. He landed with a splash, skidding across the surface with the momentum from the speed of the boat. He went under briefly before swimming up and treading water.

In the Ranger Shannon fought the controls to bring the machine back in line. In the rear Jennings was thrown to the floor.

"What the hell was that?"

"She's not responding," yelled Shannon. Jennings managed to regain his balance and then crawled to the side and looked out of the open door. Below, he could see the rope trailing from the front of the skid down to the boat below.

"Jesus! We're attached to the boat. Take us down!"

But Shannon was quick to reply. "If the boat sinks we'll be dragged to the bottom. I need to climb to reach the shore."

He pulled back on the collective and the machine started to rise.

The result of the helicopter climbing was to raise the bow of the boat out of the water.

Porter clung on in terror, but Clare wasn't so quick to react, and as the angle increased, she fell down to the stern, her foot catching in a rope. The boat suddenly hit the wake of a passing barge and Clare was tossed out of the rear into the water. She was dragged behind the boat by her foot, bouncing roughly over the waves from the passing barge.

The boat was now nearly airborne …

… and then it was.

It swung in an arc across the river, the tip of the jet pipe raking the water and sending out a spray as it cut a deep V into the smooth surface.

This was too much for Porter. As the boat rose vertically, his fear of flying overcame his fear of water and he let go of the handle. He fell past Clare with an "Oh shiiiit!" and landed with a splash twenty feet below.

McCready looked down at Clare. She was hanging upside down below the boat.

"Clare, jump!"

"My foot's caught," she replied.

McCready stood at the bow, holding on to the line to the chopper above, looking for all the world like some sort of vertical figurehead. "Okay, stay there!"

"You think?" came the angry reply.

A few hundred yards behind the boat Porter was flailing around in the water. He was now thinking he should have perhaps stayed in the boat. He was finding it hard to stay afloat and every second breath he gasped in water and came up spluttering. It wouldn't be long before he went under completely.

But suddenly he saw a glimmer of hope, even if it was his worst nightmare. Through the darkness he could make out Logan swimming toward him.

"Help! Help me!" yelled Porter. Logan approached but slowed down before he reached the struggling explosives expert.

"Ach, come on you big wimp. It's only a drop of water!"

But Porter wasn't impressed. "I'll kill you, you fucking tartan Wookie!"

Logan was now right next to him but kept a few feet away as Porter desperately tried to grab hold. Every time he nearly made it, Logan backed off just that little bit so he was out of reach.

"Now, that's no way to talk to the one person on the planet who can save your chubby English ass, now is it?" said Logan.

Porter frantically looked around for any other help, but Logan was it. Logan continued. "Come on now, say it, 'I'm a stupid English twerp.'"

Porter glared in anger and would have ripped Logan's throat out if he could have just reached it. "Never!"

Logan trod water and started to turn back to the shore. "Okay, looks like I'm going this way." He started to swim off.

"Okay, okay. Come on, man. Save me!"

Logan turned slightly back.

"Say it!"

Porter clenched his teeth but there was no other option. "Okay, Okay. I'm an"—and he was really fighting this —"English twerp," he mumbled.

But Logan was still not satisfied. "You missed out the 'stupid.'"

Porter again acted like he was under some sort of horrific World War II interrogation. The words came like teeth being pulled from his mouth. "I'm ... a ... stupid ... English ... twerp."

Logan smiled. "There you go, wasn't so hard now, was it?"

He swam forward and grabbed Porter by the collar, then turned and headed for shore.

Things weren't going so well in the boat. It was now a hundred feet in the air and McCready had climbed down to the transom at the bottom. He looked down at Clare, who was hanging by her foot twenty feet below. He tried to pull her up but it was no good. He glanced to his left and his heart jumped into his mouth.

He could see the famous landmark of the London Eye approaching fast ...

... and they were heading straight for it.

Chapter 42

The London Eye had been built in 1999 in time for the millennium celebrations and was originally designed to be in place for only five years, but with millions of visitors every year it had become one of London's premiere landmarks and tourist attractions. Standing four hundred and forty-three feet tall, it consisted of thirty-two air-conditioned capsules, each capable of carrying twenty-five people.

Most of the capsules were full that evening. Tourists from all over the world were crammed in to view the London skyline at night. What they hadn't bargained for was the view of a boat suspended beneath a helicopter heading straight for them.

In the rear of the chopper Jennings glanced up and saw their predicament. In the cockpit Shannon was looking down through the glass section of floor at the swinging boat below.

"Look out!" yelled Jennings.

Shannon snapped his eyes forward and there was a pang of fear as he saw the spindles of the wheel approaching at speed. At the same time he was blinded by several hundred flashguns firing in the capsules. None of the pictures would likely come out as the flashes would reflect straight back into the lenses off the glass, but that didn't change the fact that the pilot of the helicopter was now effectively blind for the critical seconds it would take to avert a disaster.

Shannon instinctively pulled hard on the controls and the chopper rose, but was it fast enough?

On the boat McCready watched in morbid fascination as his fate was decided in front of his eyes. He saw the massive wheel getting closer and closer. The tourists were clearly visible, and their flashguns fired at such a rapid rate they would have triggered an epileptic fit in anyone who was susceptible.

The impact was inevitable, and then suddenly he was above it rising higher into the night sky. He breathed a sigh of relief, but then his heart missed a beat.

Clare!

He glanced down and could see the look of terror on her face. He thought for a second and then acted. He started to untie the rope that attached her to the boat. She glanced up and then stared with shock.

"What the hell are you doing?"

McCready continued with the knot. "We've only got one chance at this. Look down!"

Clare looked down and all she could see was the four-hundred-foot vertical drop to the hard top of the South Bank below. Her face showed real fear as she looked back at him.

"No, look where you'll be in five seconds," said McCready.

Clare looked forward and could see what he was thinking, but it didn't make her any less scared. The boat was rising and it was going to miss the Eye, but only just. She should be able to make it onto one of the capsules— that was, if she had nerves of steel and all the luck in the world.

McCready had the knot undone and was taking most of her weight. The rope was looped around a fixing point on the boat. "Okay, on three … One … two …"

"Oh shit, John. No!"

"Three!"

And McCready let go.

Clare dropped away. It felt like things were happening in slow motion. Below, the Eye was coming closer and closer. Fifty pairs of eyes from the two nearest capsules stared up at her, unable to believe what they were seeing. She even had time to see fifty open mouths as she twisted catlike in midair to land on the top of a capsule that was two thirds of the way up the giant structure.

She hit hard and bounced toward the edge. There were cries and gasps from inside as she slid toward the drop only feet away. She scrambled madly for anything to grab onto.

The capsule was smooth, except for a tube of metal that ran around the frame that allowed the capsule to rotate as it made its journey around the wheel. She grabbed onto this as if her life depended on it, which it unquestionably did.

She hung there for a few seconds, trying to get her breath back, then climbed slowly up onto the glass roof and collapsed, ignoring the amazed faces of tourists just inches from her own. She was barely able to believe she was still alive.

She had her eyes closed and finally risked opening them. Immediately there was another barrage of flashguns. She had to close them again to avoid being blinded.

Slowly she stood up and looked around. Off to her left she could see McCready at the bottom of the boat watching her. The line still stretched up to the helicopter above. He gave her a brief wave and then started to climb to the bow.

Inside the capsule, all attention was on Clare. She was far more interesting than the London skyline. A little girl in a pink top pulled at her father's jacket. He glanced down. She looked up at him, pointing at Clare. "Daddy, do you think she paid more to go out there?"

Her father looked at her with a smile. "I don't think she actually paid anything at all, sweetie. Not part of the standard tour."

The little girl smiled. "Can we go on that one then next time?" Her father looked at her curiously and pulled her closer to him.

McCready's heart had been in his mouth when he'd dropped Clare onto the Eye. He'd had no idea if he'd be sending her to her death, but he hadn't known what else he could do. There was no knowing what would have happened to the boat if they'd stayed suspended beneath the helicopter, and for all he knew, Jennings could have cut it free, killing both of them.

He now stood at the bow and looked up at the Jet

Ranger above him. The aircraft was stable and appeared to be circling over the river. He also saw Jennings staring down at him holding the M16. He didn't have a choice. He started to climb the line up to the helicopter.

Jennings could see McCready heading slowly up the line below him. He lifted the walkie-talkie and spoke into it. "Sir, the girl's on the Eye and McCready's going nowhere."

Mercer replied quickly and the tone was less tense than earlier. "Good, I'm on my way. I have some questions for him."

Jennings looked over the side and saw McCready had grabbed onto the skid just below the open door. He leaned out and smiled. "Well, John, glad you could make it!"

McCready glanced up but didn't smile. He was exhausted from the climb and didn't have the energy to answer. Instead, he offered his arm for Jennings to help him into the rear of the Jet Ranger. Thirty seconds later, he was inside and collapsed on the floor.

Three hundred feet below and upstream, unseen by anyone, Deep Rover exited the underground river tunnel in the bank of the Thames.

In fact, rather than a sedate exit, it was more like the end of a flume ride, and the small capsule rocked violently in the water until Richards could regain control.

He took a deep breath.

"Wonder when they'll have that at Disneyland!"

He looked around at the river and felt the current as it started to move him downstream.

* * *

Clare had regained her composure and half of the occupants in the capsule had lost interest. They were already making up for lost time photographing the view of the capital.

But now what was she to do?

It took the Eye around thirty minutes to make a full rotation, so it didn't move very fast. She had just passed the apex of the ride and was slowly starting the descent down the other side, and although there wasn't much wind, it was cold and she'd been soaked to the skin when she'd been dragged through the water. What little breeze there was, was cutting through her thin shirt, chilling her to the bone. She wrapped her arms around herself, rubbing her shoulders to try and stay warm. She looked out across the river and could see the helicopter still in the air. It was now hovering high above the water, a short distance from the Houses of Parliament.

McCready leant back against the rear seats of the Jet Ranger. One hand was tied securely with a rope to the metal seat fixings, but he doubted he would have had the energy to do anything even if he was free. After all, there wasn't exactly anywhere he could go.

The noise was unrelenting. With the door open the full engine and rotor scream entered the cabin. Jennings had refused to shut it. He wasn't sure why, but he was sure he was going to find out, and it probably had something to do with him making an unplanned exit if he didn't do what he was told.

He watched as Jennings moved over to the door, leant down and cut the boat free. It dropped two hundred feet to the river below, making a far-off splash that could barely be seen in the darkness of the night. Jennings then clambered back in and gave a comms headset to McCready. He indicated for him to put it on. When it was in place, Jennings spoke. "Someone wants to talk to you." It didn't take much for McCready to guess who it was.

"This is McCready."

Malcolm Mercer's voice was almost jovial, but there was that ever-present air of menace he seemed unable to shake.

"Hello, John, having a nice vacation?"

"Go to hell!"

"Now, that's not really the attitude given your position, is it?" replied Mercer.

"What do you expect, you killed my brother."

"Oh please! You were down there. He was your responsibility."

"You bastard!" was all McCready could reply.

But Mercer continued unfazed. "I have to ask you a few questions, and I need to believe your answers, John, or things will not go well for you, okay?"

"Don't tell me, you'll have your trained ape here throw me out of the door."

He could hear Mercer almost smile through his reply. "Oh, I think we can be a little more creative than that. Let's just say your friend won't be completing her trip on the Eye, shall we." Then his voice sharpened. "Connor, stop the wheel!"

Even Jennings was surprised at the order. "What?"

"Shoot … the … tires!"

Jennings looked incredulous. "Shoot the …?"

"Shoot the tires!"

Jennings looked blank for a moment and then understood. The London Eye had a unique propulsion system. It was turned by a series of large tires, which acted on the frame of the wheel turning it slowly round. In 2008, over four hundred tourists had been trapped in the capsules for several hours when there had been a problem with one of the tires. So, take out the tires, you stop the Eye, and Clare would have nowhere to go.

Jennings told Shannon to move closer to the Eye and hold the chopper steady. He then took aim with the M16. Four shots later and four of the tires on the outside of the wheel had been blown out.

Even though the motion was slow, it came to a stop almost immediately. McCready could see people running around like confused ants at the bottom of the structure. It was unlikely anyone would have heard the shots over the noise of the helicopter, and all they would have known was a series of small pops as the tires blew out— that and the consternation of the occupants of the capsules once they realized they weren't going anywhere.

On the top of the capsule, which was now about a quarter of the way down the side of the Eye, Clare almost lost her balance. She'd been looking over the side to see if there was an easy way down when the tires had blown. She'd heard a series of muffled bangs and looked over at the helicopter. She was sure she knew what had happened, and it wasn't good. It seemed they hadn't forgotten about her and she was still part of their plan, whatever that might be.

She now crouched down, keeping one eye on the helicopter, while trying to work out a way to get down from her precarious position.

Back in the chopper, McCready watched with concern. He was brought back to the present by a voice in his ear. "Now, John, where's my gold?" The tone was deadly serious and left no room for argument.

McCready thought for a moment and glanced at Jennings who raised the muzzle of the M16 in the direction of the Eye. Then he sighed and spoke into the mike. "It's down there with the wreckage of the sub in the river."

"Well, that shouldn't be too difficult to find, now should it?"

"Okay, you've got what you want. Are you going to let me go?"

Mercer's tone hardened even more, if that were possible. "I'm afraid it's not that simple. You were on board *Recovery*. What did you see?"

McCready was quiet for a moment. "I had some things to pick up from my locker. I didn't see anything."

"Don't test my patience!"

"Hey, that's all there was," protested McCready.

Mercer's next reply was directed at Jennings.

"Conner, take out the girl!"

Jennings smiled at McCready and took aim at the Eye. He was breathing slowly, training the sights on the target —and then he squeezed the trigger …

… just as McCready lunged. The restraints held him back, but he did rock the chopper at the exact moment the bullet left the muzzle of the M16.

It took the projectile just 0.3 of a second to cover the

hundred yards from the helicopter to where Clare was standing on the capsule. In that time the disturbance to the trajectory from McCready's action caused it to veer a few inches off target. Instead of hitting Clare in the head, it grazed her shoulder, spinning her round and causing her to cry out.

She rolled over the side of the capsule falling, onto the one below.

There were Ooohs and Ahhhs from the tourists inside, but her momentum carried her over the side and she just managed to grab hold of the rotation rail near the bottom of the capsule.

She had no energy to pull herself up, so dangled there for a few seconds before checking below and dropping onto the capsule beneath. She knelt there in pain, clutching her bleeding shoulder.

She glared up at the helicopter. She had no idea what was going on or if another bullet would be coming her way anytime soon.

In the Jet Ranger Jennings pointed the gun at McCready. "Do that again, I swear to God!"

McCready backed down. There was nothing he could do. Then Mercer spoke again. "Now, what's it going to be, John? Are you going to tell me what I want to know?"

McCready was beaten. Wearily he propped himself up on one elbow and spoke. "Okay, okay. They were transferring bars from a cylinder on the bell. Look, I really don't care what you do with the damned stuff. Just let the girl go!"

"Afraid I can't do that. I need insurance," continued Mercer. "We wouldn't want you running round telling stories, would we? So I want you to listen very carefully. You're familiar with the concept of accidents—you've been around a few recently. They can happen to anyone, anytime. Take your late brother's wife for example—a leg crushed in a car crash, a fire at home. She could even lose the baby. Am I making myself clear?"

A cold sweat came over McCready and he knew he had nowhere to go. Mercer had won. He'd said he would never let anything happen to Sarah and he never would, whatever the cost. But he couldn't go out with a whimper.

"You won't get away with this!"

"Oh, I think you'd be surprised what I can get away with," replied Mercer. "Now, if you want to keep Sarah in good health and not go the way of your girlfriend, you'll keep your mouth shut!"

McCready was confused for a moment. "But Clare's …"

"Really," came the confident reply. Then he addressed Jennings. "I think the girl should have an accident with firearms, Connor."

McCready stared at Jennings as he smiled and again took aim at the girl standing on the capsule on the London Eye.

Chapter 43

Jennings tightened his finger on the trigger.

The crosshairs lined up on Clare. She was still only about a hundred yards away and looking straight at him.

She was completely oblivious of her impending doom.

McCready was desperate. He struggled against the rope that bound him to the seat. He rolled and stamped his feet trying to throw off Jennings' aim and at least give Clare a chance to try and get away, but up front, Shannon was holding the aircraft steady as a rock.

McCready could see the finger on the trigger. He pulled at the bindings one more time. He could feel them start to give. He pulled more and more, now with a glimmer of hope.

Then suddenly one of the ends of the rope came free.

He grabbed it with his teeth, and then a hand was free … and then two.

He glanced across at Jennings. The man's concentration was complete. He was focused solely on the sights on the top of the gun.

It was McCready's only chance.

He lunged.

At the last second Jennings noticed a movement to his right and managed to parry McCready's flying arm. He swung the M16 and hit McCready in the head.

McCready slumped back, dazed by the blow, but he managed to grab hold of the weapon with one hand. They wrestled in the doorway inches from the vertiginous drop.

The movement pitched the chopper from side to side.

In the cockpit Shannon tried to keep the machine stable and flew further out over the river, dropping the altitude.

McCready kicked Jennings back against the bulkhead between the seats and the cockpit. Jennings let the gun go with one hand as he grabbed on to anything he could to try to prevent himself from falling out of the door.

McCready reached for the weapon.

As they struggled he knocked it out of Jennings' hand. It clattered to the floor just as the helicopter lurched to one side, sending it sliding out of the door to fall harmlessly into the river a hundred feet below.

"You're going to regret that," shouted Jennings above the roar of the engine. He leapt forward and threw a punch at McCready's head. He was breathing hard and the punch went wide. He glanced at the cockpit behind him and shouted at Shannon. "Take her in close, and I mean really close. Knock her off her perch!"

McCready threw himself at Jennings again.

Shannon climbed, taking the Jet Ranger round in a wide arc, initially away from the Eye on the landward side. He then lined up on the wheel and sped in straight for it, the river a backdrop beyond.

* * *

Clare had watched the chopper dip and dive over the river and could only imagine what was going on inside. It then disappeared over the buildings to the south of the river and she thought it was going away. But as she focused on her predicament on the capsule, the engine noise increased.

She turned slowly and fear crept into her soul.

The helicopter was coming straight for her.

She was frozen for a second, like a rabbit in headlights.

It couldn't be going to do what she thought it was going to do.

But it was.

Mark Shannon was an expert pilot. His participation in two modern wars had meant flying in conditions few pilots had experienced. He could do things in a helicopter many could not, but a bead of sweat ran down his neck as he lined up to bring the blades of the chopper to within a few feet of the capsules.

Clare almost panicked. The helicopter was coming closer and closer. The occupants of the capsule below were transfixed by the rapidly approaching machine. Clare just prayed they wouldn't set off another volley of flashguns and blind the pilot, as that would almost certainly result in the helicopter crashing into the Eye.

She looked left, right, above and finally below. There was no way she could reach the capsule above, so it had to be below. She took a final glance at the helicopter that was now only fifty feet away and approaching at forty knots.

She jumped.

While she was airborne, she heard, and more significantly felt, the buzz saw of the rotors inches above her head, and then it was gone.

She impacted heavily with the capsule below. As she landed with a thud, the occupants stared up. Some shouted and others banged on the side. It was all she could do to crouch down and stop herself from falling off.

But she had no time to relax.

To her horror the Jet Ranger was coming around for a second pass.

She stood shakily and looked around. This time there would be no escape to the capsule below. Due to the circular nature of the wheel, at some point the lower capsule would be underneath the one above and hidden from view. That was where she was now, halfway down the side of the Eye. She watched in despair as the helicopter lined up on her and headed in.

This time there would be no escape.

McCready had seen the first pass close up and had tried to look out of the door to see if Clare had survived as they shot by inches above her disappearing head. But it had taken a whole loop before he'd seen she was still alive and on the capsule further down the Eye. As they sped in toward her again he could also see that she now had nowhere to go.

He was her only hope. He had to do something.

He looked around the cabin and saw a small fire extinguisher on the wall next to the door. He grabbed it and dived at Jennings. The metal cylinder hit the Global Salvage man hard across the jaw sending him crashing to the floor. Jennings lay there in shock, for a moment dazed and disoriented.

This was McCready's chance.

He steadied himself and then glanced out of the door and the three-hundred foot drop below.

Carefully, he placed a foot on the skid a couple of feet below the door and pulled himself outside.

He was now standing on the skid, but immediately the slipstream tore at him, whipping at his clothes, trying to wrench him from the side of the helicopter.

But he hung on. He had to for Clare's sake.

Slowly he inched his way forward. There were plenty of grab handles on the side of the fuselage, and as he moved toward the cockpit, he could just make out Jennings groggily sitting up on the floor behind him.

McCready moved faster now. Almost a foot at a time, he shuffled his feet along the skid until he was at the cockpit door.

Shannon never saw him until he yanked it open and climbed inside.

But at that exact moment the Eye was dead ahead and the blades were going to cut straight though Clare's body.

McCready dared not do anything in case he made the machine crash into the Eye. All he could do was watch in morbid fascination to see what happened to Clare.

As he watched he could see her turn toward him and their eyes locked for a brief instant. She was only sixty feet away, and as he stared she turned away from him.

On the top of the capsule Clare had made up her mind. There was only one option left and there was no time to think about it.

After she had seen McCready in the cockpit, she at

least knew that he was okay. The chopper was now about three seconds from slicing through her body. She could feel her heart rate accelerating inside her. It was thumping as though at any moment it would leap out of her chest. The whining roar of the chopper was right behind.

She ran as fast as she could to the edge of the capsule and then pushed off in the most perfect swallow dive of her life.

The spinning blades cut through the air her body had inhabited milliseconds before. McCready didn't have time to see whether she made it. They were now flying out over the river.

Below, Clare hit the water hard. She shot down fifteen feet below the surface. She had kept her body position perfectly rigid and clenched her hands together, turning her palms outward so they would punch a hole in the water for her body to pass through. If anything, the cold hit her harder than the impact with the river.

In the cockpit McCready lunged at Shannon. The pilot was secured in his seat by a harness but McCready was free to force the controls to bring the chopper lower. He was about to push on the floor pedals when he felt a violent rushing of air from behind—the cockpit door had been opened.

Jennings stood on the skid and reached in and grabbed McCready. He pulled him out of the seat, aiming to hurl him over the side. McCready elbowed him in the face. Jennings reeled back, almost losing his balance. He had to hang on as the chopper dipped to the right. McCready pulled the door closed and lunged at the controls. The chopper went into a near vertical dive.

Shannon was now desperate and fought to regain control, but McCready had let go and pushed himself back into his seat and fastened his harness. He then smashed Shannon in the side of the head, knocking him unconscious.

The Jet Ranger was still diving.

Outside, Jennings hung on for dear life. The downward acceleration pushed him back toward the rear, but he daren't let go of any handhold for risk of being hurled into the void.

McCready braced for the crash as the Jet Ranger hurtled toward the river.

A second later it hit.

The force of the impact threw McCready forward in his seat, smacking his head on the frame of the cockpit.

He blacked out and knew no more.

Jennings wasn't so lucky. He was thrown out into the screaming rotors, his body flailed in seconds, pieces of diced flesh spinning out in all directions.

The helicopter was now vertical in the water, the tail section pointing high in the air. The whirling rotors were thrashing round half above and below the surface like some sort of demented, aquatic power saw.

A few seconds later the airframe settled back into a more natural position—and started to sink.

The cold of the water woke McCready.

He looked around desperately, not sure where he was. While most of the chopper was underwater, there was an air pocket in the cockpit. He started to unclip his harness, but the force of the impact had caused it to jam. As hard as he tried, the buckle remained locked in place. Only the top foot of the cockpit was above the water and then the helicopter slipped slowly below the surface.

There was nothing McCready could do.

Chapter 44

From the north bank of the Thames, Mercer lowered the binoculars. He climbed back into the Bentley, instructed the driver to head for Heathrow, then picked up his phone. This was going to need a major damage limitation exercise.

The River Thames is about thirty feet deep in the middle, depending on the state of the tide. As the Jet Ranger settled on the bottom, it sent up a cloud of silt into the already murky water. The boom at the rear that supported the tail rotor had split away and the cockpit with its large canopy looked more like some sort of broken sports car than a flying machine.

Inside there was an ever-diminishing pocket of air. McCready was struggling with the harness, but it was firmly secured and wouldn't release. The water was above his waist and he desperately looked around for something to cut the belt with.

The water was entering through the door frame where it had buckled in the impact. He was cold, and now that his body had recovered from the initial shock he could feel the temperature of the freezing water creeping through him.

He urgently looked around the cockpit again. An emergency light had come on with the impact, but it was dim and it was hard to make out anything clearly.

He glanced at the pilot. His face was submerged and there was nothing McCready could do for him. But then, just behind his inert body, he saw a small cutting tool attached to the side of the cockpit. It was presumably for just this sort of scenario. It was similar to those you could buy for cars, where you could slice through the seatbelts if the car overturned and people were trapped inside, or indeed if it went underwater.

He felt a sense of relief.

He was going to be okay.

He reached across, pushing the pilot's body out of the way. He was about to grab the cutter when he came up tight against the harness. He was three inches short. He sat back in the seat and then stretched again, but it was no good. The water was now up to his neck and rising.

He had one last chance.

He gave it all he could and lunged for the cutter. The straps moved slightly but he still couldn't reach it. Instead, the movement rocked the fuselage, and, along with the current from the river, caused what was left of the helicopter to roll over.

There was nothing he could do to stop it.

He sat strapped in his seat as he was turned upside down.

It only took a moment for the air pocket to disappear and McCready found himself underwater with only seconds to live.

* * *

On the surface, Clare had seen the crash and swum desperately over to where the helicopter had disappeared below the surface. She was exhausted from her ordeal on the Eye and was shivering almost uncontrollably, but she wouldn't leave the spot where the Jet Ranger had vanished.

At least she'd be able to direct the emergency services to the position when they eventually arrived.

McCready reckoned he had about thirty seconds of air. He had tried the buckle again, hoping that maybe the new position would have loosened the harness, but it hadn't.

There was nothing else he could do other than wait for the inevitable.

He thought back to the events in the North Sea and realized his brother must have gone through the exact same thing.

He felt himself becoming lightheaded and he wondered what death would be like. Some say you saw a light at the final moment and then you went to wherever you go after life leaves your body.

He could feel himself slowly slipping away. A second before he lost consciousness he saw the faint glow of the light.

The stories must be true.

He almost smiled as his head slumped back and he was no longer of this world.

McCready never knew it, but just after his body hung lifeless in the harness, the light he had seen grew in intensity.

The two halogen spotlights of Deep Rover couldn't penetrate far in the murk of the Thames, but they were enough to show Craig Richards all he needed to know.

After he'd exited the tunnel he'd made his way downstream, keeping as low a profile as possible. He wasn't sure how he'd be able to explain his presence in the river, but the longer he remained invisible the better. He'd turned the lights on the sub off and drifted with the current. He'd watched the drama with the helicopter above, though he had no idea what was going on. He assumed McCready was somehow involved but in what way he couldn't know. However, when he'd seen the helicopter crash into the river, he knew he had to do something. Regardless of who might be inside, they would need rescuing if they'd survived the impact.

He'd pinpointed the position on the navigation system, then descended to the river bed and switched on the lights. It was unlikely anyone would see them from the surface and he needed to find the helicopter as quickly as possible. The navigation screen had given him a direction and he'd pushed the thrusters to full power.

Five minutes later he could just make out the outline of the aircraft in the gloom ahead. As he came closer he could see someone hanging upside down in the front seat of the cockpit. Closer still and he could see it was McCready.

He appeared to be dead.

There was no time to lose. Richards pushed the throttles again and rammed the helicopter at full power, pushing the broken shell into an upright position. He then skillfully maneuvered the manipulator arms inside and cut away the harness that was keeping McCready in his seat.

"Come on, John, not now!"

He then gently grabbed at his clothing and pulled him out of the wreckage. Once on the mud outside the helicopter, he pushed both mechanical arms beneath the lifeless body and lifted. It was as though the machine was carrying a loved one in its arms. He then blew all ballast and headed for the surface.

The sub burst through the water in a rush of bubbles. The whole of the cockpit reared fully above the surface before settling back down. The important thing, though, was that McCready's face was out of the water.

Somewhere to his right Richards noticed a figure swimming fast toward him. When it reached the sub, he could see it was a woman. Where she had come from he had no idea, but she eased McCready off the metal arms, and with a nod through the cockpit glass she started to give mouth-to-mouth resuscitation.

Trying to revive someone at any time using this method was a fifty-fifty operation if you were lucky. To do it while floating in the water was almost a non-starter, but there wasn't any choice.

It was also impossible to provide compressions of the heart, which are normally required for any successful recovery. Clare breathed in hard for two breaths then let the air exhale. She then repeated the operation.

Nothing happened.

From the sub Richards watched on, the pain clearly written across his face.

She tried again—nothing.

But then on the tenth series of breaths there was a splutter from McCready. She gripped him harder, making sure his mouth was well above the water.

Then he coughed and jerked in her arms.

She held on. He took a deep breath, then another. Then he tried to struggle. He clearly had no idea where he was. Clare was almost crying with relief and joy. She turned his face toward her.

"Hey, hero, you okay?"

McCready glanced around, things suddenly coming back to him. He took a look across the river, noted Richards in the sub behind Clare then focused in on her face and for some reason for the first time he noticed she had beautiful green eyes.

He took a number of deep breaths, the strain of the ordeal clearly showing. Then he looked back at her. "See, I told you you'd do the right thing. But I was wrong." And he paused. "You don't have anything to prove."

She leant forward and hugged him. Her look told him how much that meant to her.

Suddenly, from further downstream came the roar of a high-powered outboard motor. They glanced across the surface and saw an orange RIB powering toward them.

Before the lifeboat arrived, Richards disappeared below the surface. He really didn't want to be found around there.

His final image from below the water was of McCready and Clare being hauled into the boat.

What had happened to Porter and Logan, he had no idea.

About five hundred yards away, a large Scotsman pulled a

bedraggled Englishman up onto a stony beach at the side of the Thames.

Logan hauled Porter up onto the stones and laid him on his back. He was exhausted from the exertion. He walked around in a circle stretching his aching muscles and trying to get his breath back before checking Porter was okay.

Porter was still shell-shocked from his ordeal and looked off into the distance as though on another planet. Logan moved closer and slapped him across the face—left side, right side. He groggily came back to reality.

"Hey, what are you doing? I miss something?"

Logan shook his head. "You stupid plonker. Come on, say it!"

Porter looked at him, confused for a second, still not all there. "Huh, oh right, I'm a ..." but then realization hit him and he looked around. He saw the beach, and more importantly he saw the water—twenty feet away.

"Wait a minute, Scottie, I'm back on dry land!"

Chapter 45

They say that opportunities often come your way in life by being in the right place at the right time. That was one statement that Fergus Beasley would wholeheartedly agree with. In fact he'd made a career out of it.

Beasley was a paparazzi photographer and a good one. He prided himself on being ahead of the pack. He had contacts in all the right places and always had a heads-up on which celebrities would be at which parties so he could be there to snap them in various states of disrepair as they staggered home from the clubs at all hours of the morning.

But that night had been different. No one had showed. Two events had been cancelled and he'd been racing around central London like a mad thing on his Honda CB500X trying to find some sort of justification for being out at two in the morning. All he had for his efforts was a Kardashian and a Z-league footballer—hardly worth getting out of bed for, or in his case, not going to bed for.

He'd finally given up hope and had been making his way home over Lambeth Bridge, when he'd seen a low-flying helicopter further down the river. It had seemed to be acting strangely. He'd done a U-turn and followed the aircraft, which had taken him down onto the Victoria Embankment.

He couldn't have known that the events that were to unfold would mean he wouldn't have to get out of bed for quite some time, and there wouldn't be a celebrity in sight.

He'd parked the bike just north of Westminster Bridge and lugged his large camera backpack over to the side of the Thames, almost getting creamed by a late-night cyclist with no lights on the bike superhighway. He never remembered they went both ways.

As he'd watched events develop, he couldn't believe his luck. As soon as he'd seen the implications of the helicopter chasing the boat, he'd pulled out his Canon 5D Mk IV and pretty much kept his finger on the trigger.

But when things had moved to the drama on the London Eye, virtually every moment had been golden. He'd snapped on a white 800mm lens with a 2x converter and changed modes so he was recording on 4K video at thirty frames a second. With the quality 4K could produce, it meant he had thirty 8.8MB still photographs for every second of time. It broke an event down into its primal existence.

Of the thousands of images from that evening, the one that was to pay the bills for several years was a single shot from a series of a hundred and twenty captured over four seconds. The sequence showed a woman on top of one of the capsules of the Eye. Behind her, a helicopter was approaching at speed. She turned away from the advancing machine and dived into the water.

Normally when incredibly dramatic images appear in

newspapers and magazines, the drama is often enhanced by the foreshortening caused by the use of a telephoto lens. In fact, in most cases the drama is actually quite minimal, with the subjects being a considerable distance apart.

In this photo no foreshortening was required. The helicopter was merely feet away.

The money-shot from the series showed the fear on the woman's face as she turned from the spinning blades immediately behind her head. What made the shot possible, though, was that at the key moment a barrage of tourist flashguns had gone off, providing the perfect fill light for the scene.

After the girl had turned, she'd run toward the edge of the capsule. As she'd moved straight toward the camera, so the images showed a change in her demeanor.

It was a remarkable transition that flowed almost seamlessly, from a scared woman about to die, through someone with grit and determination to live, to a person totally concentrated and committed to what had to be done to survive.

The final shot, before she'd disappeared out of frame, was of a human being in complete control of her destiny as she performed a perfect swallow dive off the capsule and plummeted to the water below.

Fergus Beasley had stared at the sequence of images on the screen on the back of the 5D for several minutes, his hands shaking. He knew what he had and he knew no one else in the world had it. He'd glanced left and right down the Embankment to make sure—but there was no one there. He'd then lain the camera down delicately in case a sudden jolt should wipe the images from the memory card.

A few minutes later and he'd transferred the files to his MacBook Pro and checked everything at a larger size. They all looked great. It had taken him ten minutes to get his agent out of bed and send him through the series of shots via the WiFi hotspot provided by his phone.

There had been a tangible silence from the end of the line when they'd come through, and then his agent had started laughing.

Within half an hour the photos had been syndicated around the world and begun to appear on news websites across the globe. They would be on all the front pages of the first editions of the papers the next day.

The photo of the woman with fear across her face and the helicopter blades just behind her head would become iconic, and that brief moment in time would go on to earn Fergus Beasley a quarter of a million dollars.

The following morning in a large farmhouse over four thousand miles away on the sloping hills of Montana, a seventy-year old man gripped the pages of the *New York Times*.

He had silvery hair and a slim body that looked in fair shape for someone of his age, but there was something about his eyes that suggested his mental state wasn't in such good health. It seemed like a part of his soul was missing. There had once been fire in those eyes, but it had gone out long ago.

He stood slowly, still holding the paper, and walked across to a small desk in the corner of the room. To one side a window looked out onto a stretch of garden that had been left to grow wild and had clearly received little recent attention. On the desk lay a pile of books, some papers, a few pens, and an old-style corded telephone.

There was also a photograph that had pride of place in the middle. It showed a beautiful woman with flowing auburn hair and a mischievous smile that would melt your heart just to look at it. Next to the gilt silver frame another frame lay face down.

He eased himself into an old leather chair with a well-padded cushion that had seen better days. He put the paper down on the desk and stared long and hard at the photograph of the woman.

Tears appeared in the corner of his eyes, and this was from a man who never cried. He picked up the paper and looked at the picture, which almost filled the entire front page.

The edges were dark. It had been taken at night, but in the center it clearly showed a young woman on the capsule of the London Eye, seconds away from death. The headline even blared "MOMENTS FROM DEATH" across the banner. The terror was clear on her face.

The man trembled as he continued to stare at the picture. After a few seconds he put the paper down and, still trembling, he moved to pick up the photo that had being lying face down on his desk for the past two years. He lifted it reverently, and paused, almost as though he couldn't bear to turn it over, then slowly he turned the frame to face him.

He stared at it, unmoving.

It showed a fourteen-year old girl in a red swimsuit. She was smiling broadly and proudly holding up a medal for all to see. Next to her was a man he hardly recognized.

It wasn't that he'd changed so much in all those years, at least not physically, but more that he couldn't remember the last time he had felt the happiness, joy and pride he was clearly experiencing in the photograph.

He placed the picture next to that of his wife and slowly picked up the telephone at the side of the desk. He lifted the receiver to his ear, then paused, closing his eyes for a few seconds. His lips moved quickly, as though reciting a number he'd almost forgotten.

He opened his eyes and dialed the number.

The phone rang.

As he waited for it to be answered, his gaze flicked between the two photographs. As it did so, a miracle happened. The hard, emotionless expression that had lived on his face for so long started to crumble.

When the phone was finally answered, it was as though an electric shock had passed through his body, and for the first time in many years he felt scared. He was feeling something he hadn't felt in a long time—emotion.

The voice on the other end said, "Hello."

He didn't know what to say.

Again the voice said, "Hello," and, "is anyone there?"

He finally plucked up the courage. "Hello, Starfish."

There was silence from the phone and then an almost animal-like whimper and a sob came from the speaker.

"Daddy."

And he knew that everything was going to be all right.

Chapter 46

One month later

The paddle dipped into the water, then lifted, then dipped again. McCready pulled the strokes hard, one after the other, feeling his heartbeat rise and the sheer joy of skimming across the water of the small bay. The air was fresh. A slight wind ruffled the surface into a minor chop, but the salt water springing off the bow into his face was invigorating and made him feel alive.

Twenty minutes later he checked the interval time on the stopwatch on his wrist and eased down until he was drifting with the current.

A lot had happened since the events of a month ago. After Richards and Clare had saved his life, he'd spent several days in hospital, as much as anything for precautionary reasons, but the impact of the crash into the Thames had pulled a series of muscles in his back, and this current excursion onto the water was testing how well they had healed. Pretty well, by the way things felt, though there was still an occasional twinge if he twisted his shoulders too far.

Richards had managed to secure Deep Rover away from prying eyes and it had quietly been returned to its home in Aberdeen.

There was, of course, the sad death of Paul Matthews. Although the man had sold them out, McCready didn't hold it against him. He'd only been doing what he felt was right for his family, which at the end of the day was all he'd been doing himself. As a result, McCready had made arrangements for Lucy Matthews to undergo treatment at a hospital in Glasgow. Only time would tell if she would make a full recovery.

The other issue was Malcolm Mercer.

Global Salvage had recovered everything from the bottom of the Thames and Mercer had been promoting the reveal of the gold at the new Mercer Wing of the British Museum. It was due to be broadcast live on a number of news channels later that day.

Somehow, though, something told McCready this part of the story wasn't over yet.

The one thing that had puzzled him was the lack of interest he'd received from anyone official. Since the night on the river, he hadn't been contacted by one police officer or anyone in authority asking him questions about what had happened. He wasn't complaining, but he found it somewhat strange, and something niggled at the back of his mind which gave him cause for concern.

He was brought back to the present by a seagull's cry as it twisted and turned in the air above. He followed its trail as it wheeled down to the rocks at the side of the bay. It was heading for a dead fish on a large, flat slab close to the water. The only problem was the fish had already been claimed by a certain mother otter who was sharing it with her son.

After a quick scuffle the seagull lost. It flew off squawking angrily. The otters finished the fish, glanced around, saw McCready and immediately leapt into the water, prancing through the small waves until they reached the kayak.

It was exactly the tonic he needed.

He watched them approach. They seemed to have hardly a care in the world. He'd always thought that animals lived for the present, and that when things happened, like a death in the family, it would be quickly forgotten, but in the case of otters that seemed only to be for the young.

Several times in the early evening, when he'd been having a beer on the first-floor deck looking out over the bay, he'd heard a soft scuffling from below. He'd looked down and seen Mira walking through the grass over to the grave of her pup. She would look at it for a while, then walk round it several times before settling down and sleeping there for an hour or so. Then she would get up and leave. There had never been any interaction between them. She'd never even glanced up at him, but in a way that was how it should be. He wasn't really part of their world, however much he might think otherwise, which made the moments they still shared out on the water all the more special.

He glanced at the front of the boat, and this time Squeak had made it onto the bow and was snuffling around the top of the front of the kayak. Mira chorkled at him, and after a second he slipped back into the water and they were gone, cavorting back to the rocks where they lived their lives as best they could.

McCready smiled. He took a final look at their departing bodies and then spun the kayak and headed for home.

Back in his world again, he smiled at the prospect of the gathering that would take place at the house later that day, and the chance to again see someone he'd come to care very much about.

Half an hour later he dropped the kayak on the floor of the garage, stood under an outside shower to wash the salt off the drysuit, then peeled it from his body and headed upstairs to prepare for the proceedings to come.

A couple of hours later and everything was in full swing. The weather was sunny and surprisingly warm considering it was still winter. The sliding doors were open between the house and the patio area that led out to the games room. It was still a work in progress but the walls were higher now and three sides were built up to roof level.

Just inside the house, McCready had moved the TV so they could watch the events at the British Museum from inside and out. Even though it might be hard to watch, McCready was interested to see things unfold.

Out on the patio a barbecue was going full tilt and helped warm the air when the odd shudder of a cool breeze swept in off the bay.

Although he'd seen Craig Richards a couple of times since the night on the Thames, McCready hadn't seen Porter or Logan. He was pleasantly surprised to see that a begrudging respect had grown between them since Logan had saved Porter's life. They had even arrived together, and as he watched them chatter away like old friends, he couldn't help but think there was a catch somewhere and that any second an explosion could happen, but maybe he was just being cynical in his old age.

The other person present was the one who had in many ways been the catalyst for everything that had happened. He watched as Sarah laughed and chatted with the guys. She looked great in a loose fitting cream dress, and the bump in her tummy was showing far more now. Porter in particular seemed to be falling over himself to help her out. In fact, it was probably bordering on the annoying the number of times he asked her if she was okay.

He was in the middle of yet another concerned exchange when she told him for the tenth time that she was fine—she was only having a baby. This seemed to confuse Porter, who looked shocked and went over to chat conspiratorially with Logan.

Sarah glanced at McCready and simulated pulling her hair out, but she was smiling and McCready smiled back. It was good to see her like this, and while she would take a long time to come to terms with what had happened, she was healing and that was what mattered. He wandered out and stood next to her. As he approached he noticed a tinge of sadness cross her face, as though his proximity was too much of a reminder of Sean.

"Still hurts, doesn't it?" he said.

She smiled weakly at him. "It always will." Then she looked out across the bay. "Somehow, this place, it's part of him."

"That's why I'll always stay. Just something about this country."

She looked at him, smiled and hugged his arm briefly. Then she glanced up and saw Porter crossing over toward them. She groaned and moved slightly behind McCready. "Save me!"

McCready smiled. When Porter reached them he glanced at Sarah, who was now almost completely hidden by McCready. He looked up at McCready and made a beckoning motion with his head. McCready moved closer.

"Here, guv, is she all right?"

McCready tried to keep a straight face. "Of course, why wouldn't she be?" Porter looked like he was thinking really hard.

"But she's … well … you know, pregnant."

"Yeah, that does happen to women sometimes. She's fine."

Porter seemed to be reassured. "Okay, just keep an eye on her, all right."

"Will do."

Porter turned away and then turned back. "Oh yeah, any more beers?"

"Over in the barrel by the TV."

"Thanks, guv."

Porter walked over to the barrel and started rummaging through the cans and ice. McCready glanced over at Logan. "You guys seem to be pretty cool, yeah?"

Logan grinned. "Ah, the little twerp's all right when you get to know him. Quite easy to train really."

"I heard that, Scottie! Here!" said Porter. A can of Fosters sailed through the air. Logan caught it.

"There you go!" said Logan.

McCready smiled, looked round at his group of friends, and then tapped a fork on the side of his glass. All grew silent and turned toward him. For a moment there was only the sound of the gentle lapping of waves on the shore and the occasional spit and crackle from the barbecue.

"Okay everyone, a toast to Sean, who was taken before his time and by someone who's time has come," said McCready.

They all raised their glasses. "To Sean."

McCready turned to Sarah and looked out over the bay.

"With the wind in your hair and the loch by your side,
the love of your life is never far away.
You only have to look in his eyes to realize he will always be here
and you will always stay."

Sarah smiled, and McCready knew she'd noted the subtle change of words from *her* to *his*.

They were lost in their thoughts for a moment when the doorbell rang. Everyone looked at McCready. He glanced round and then walked back into the house and through to the front door. He was surprised to find his heart was beating above its normal resting rhythm.

He took a deep breath, pulled himself up straight and opened the door.

He hadn't seen her since she'd saved his life. She had been working twenty-four seven to smooth things out at London Water and to try and explain what had happened in a way that didn't incriminate a whole group of people she had come to care about. She'd been told to clean up the mess, oversee any repairs to the ring main, then return to the States in disgrace. She would be dismissed from the company when all the loose ends had been tied up.

McCready hadn't dared contact her, except to let her know about today. She had curtly replied that she would see what she could do, but wouldn't promise anything. So the fact that she was here was a major victory in his eyes.

Speaking of eyes, he hadn't imagined it; they were that gorgeous green he'd noticed that night in the river. They just stood there staring at each other for a few seconds and then she threw her arms around him and hugged him harder than he'd ever been hugged.

He folded his arms around her back and held her close. They stayed like that for a minute. Then she pulled back slightly and he could see a tear in her eye. He looked at her cautiously.

"What, no slap?" he asked.

She returned the stare, a slight smile creeping across her lips. "Didn't know you were that sort of guy."

McCready continued the banter. "There's a lot you don't know about me."

Clare reached into her pocket and pulled something out. She raised her arm in front of him and let one side of the handcuffs drop down. The links gave an innocent jangle as they hung there. He winced slightly. She continued. "I know you had a pair of these and were prepared to use them."

"I seem to remember they rather suited you."

"I seem to remember I had no choice."

"Isn't that the idea?"

She smiled and thumped him playfully on the chest.

"So how have you been?" he asked.

"Oh, you know, up and down. Work didn't end well, so

I've just been trying to sort my life out. I had some good news on the family front. Resolved a lot of things with my dad, which is great. Rescued my puppy from a life of drugs and alcohol, which is also great." He looked at her quizzically. "Don't ask," she said. "But I just need to be away from all that right now."

"Even if it meant coming up here?"

She looked at him and smiled. "Even if it meant coming up here."

He held the look for a couple of seconds and then indicated the house. "Come on, there are some people who want to say hello."

He held the door open and she walked in. She stared around and nodded approvingly. "Nice pad."

"It's okay," he said nonchalantly. She playfully thumped his chest again and nuzzled up to him. He put his arm around her shoulder and they walked through and out onto the patio.

You could almost hear the collective sigh of relief when everyone saw McCready with his arm around Clare. No one had been sure how it would go, but it looked like things were going pretty well so far.

Clare immediately hugged and said hello to the guys, and then McCready led her over to Sarah.

"And this is Sarah, Sean's wife."

The two women stared at each other for a moment and then hugged. There seemed to be a connection between them linked by the events of the previous month. When they broke apart, Clare was the first to speak.

"It's so nice to finally meet you. I'm so sorry for your loss."

"Thank you. John has said so much about you, and

that's a rare thing."

Clare looked at McCready quizzically. "Really?"

Richards had joined the group. "Clare, Ocean Oil is in your debt for the ring main repair. Improved the month's figures no end."

Clare smiled. "Hey, you had the gear, and you did know your way around. I just can't believe you went through all that for nothing though. I mean, Mercer found every bar at the bottom of the Thames."

Logan had also wandered over. "Aye, it was a shame."

Clare looked slightly unsure. They were far too nonchalant. "You guys seem pretty cool about it."

"Ach well, you win some, you lose some," said Logan.

She looked around at everyone and still didn't get it.

Behind them a news anchor appeared on the TV screen. When they heard what she was saying they all turned to watch.

"… and we can now cross live to the British Museum"—a wide shot of the museum appeared on screen—"where the British ambassador to Russia, Sir Richard Hawkins will open the newly completed Mercer wing. The Russian gold will be put on display here for the next six months. Here's Sir Richard now."

The shot changed to the inside of the Mercer Wing at the museum. In the center of the high-ceilinged space was the towering stack of gold. It was arranged in a pyramid, with strategic lighting to highlight the effect. In front of it was a raised platform with two microphones. The world's press were gathered, with a bank of TV cameras and journalists to cover the proceedings. The ambassador walked in and stood at one of the mikes. He looked around, scanning the throng in front of him.

The room fell silent.

"Good afternoon, everyone. It is with great pleasure that I declare the fabulous new Mercer Wing at the British Museum open, and what better way to follow that than with the man himself." He looked over to his right and beckoned with his hand. "Malcolm, if you will just step this way."

Mercer walked up onto the platform. Flashguns fired from the banks of cameras. Around the edge, security guards kept a watchful eye. Mercer waved to the group, allowing them to shoot their images—the ones that would be flashed around the world. Then he walked over and stood at the second microphone.

"Thank you, Sir Richard. Well, it's been quite a trip, and I thought the North Sea was rough." There was a ripple of laughter from the floor. "But we made it, and the gold is here for all to enjoy before its final journey home. I hope many people will take this opportunity to come and witness this small piece of history for themselves. Now, are there any questions?"

Porter scowled at the TV. "Yeah, I've got a few bloody questions!" Everyone smiled and turned back to the screen. The shot panned across the sea of journalists. In the group was Tania Briscoe of the *Sunday Times*. McCready glanced at her business card that was propped up on his sideboard.

This was going to be interesting.

On the screen Briscoe put her hand up and the camera zoomed in on her.

"Yes, down there at the front," said Mercer.

Briscoe thought for a second then looked straight at Mercer. "Mr. Mercer, can you tell us if all the gold really

400

came from the German submarine?"

At this there were murmurs from the room. Mercer looked slightly perplexed but managed to hide any irritation. "I'm sorry, I don't follow you."

Briscoe spoke in a condescending tone. "Okay, let me put it this way. Can you confirm that all the gold behind you is one hundred percent genuine?"

The room fell silent. All eyes were on Mercer. There was now a flick of irritation across his face.

"Yes, of course! Now, if perhaps we can have some serious questions."

But Briscoe wasn't put off. "So you'd be happy to have it authenticated live on television?"

Hawkins began to show his irritation and looked around at the other journalists. "This is absurd, really. Now, are there any relevant questions?"

But Briscoe persisted. "Oh, I think this is highly relevant, Mr. Ambassador."

The room was mumbling now, and a stir went around the collective audience. Mercer could see things might get out of hand and everything was going out live. "Okay, okay everyone. Of course I'd be happy to have it tested. Why wouldn't I be? I've nothing to hide."

At this, Briscoe walked forward, and for the first time it was possible to see she was accompanied by a white-haired old gentlemen in his eighties. He walked with a slight stoop but there was a glint in his eye that indicated an alert and intelligent mind.

As Briscoe led the old man over to the stack of gold, she spoke to the group. "This is Professor Henri Carnegie from the Institute of Antiquities in Vienna. He knows about gold."

When they reached the pyramid you could see a gleam in Carnegie's eyes as he appraised the pile in front of him. He picked up one of the bars and turned it over, rubbing it lovingly, examining it closely.

You could have heard a pin drop.

And then suddenly the gleam in the eyes dulled. He threw a skeptical look at Mercer, who was watching confidently.

On the west coast of Scotland everyone moved that little bit closer to the screen.

Carnegie again looked at Mercer. Then before anyone could stop him, he whipped out a small knife and peeled off an outer layer of "gold," revealing solid lead beneath.

Mercer stared dumbfounded. There were cries and gasps from the assembled group. Flashguns fired. The press surged forward to capture the moment. Hawkins stood and stared at the bars in disbelief then turned to Mercer.

"Malcolm?"

Mercer seemed to be in complete shock.

"Malcolm?" Hawkins asked again.

Mercer suddenly seemed to realize where he was. He looked at Hawkins. "Richard, I am at a complete loss."

Hawkins was furious. He nodded to two of the security guards and indicated Mercer. They moved forward and unceremoniously grabbed the Global Salvage CEO by the arms. Mercer looked confused.

"Richard, what is this?"

"I'm sorry, Malcolm, but this is highly irregular, and it's SIR Richard to you." He looked at the guards.

"Take him away!"

Mercer was bundled unceremoniously from the room.

But as he passed the main TV camera that was following his every move, a certain understanding came over him. Before they could drag him out of shot, he looked straight into the lens and his voice was low but powerful.

"I'll get you, McCready!"

And then he was gone, with the press corps in tow.

On the patio there was silence.

The euphoria of the moment had been tempered by Mercer's final words. They all looked at McCready, who simply shrugged. "Hey, what can he do? The guy's going to be spending some time at Her Majesty's pleasure. Beers are on me!"

Immediately the mood lightened and everyone moved to top up their drinks.

As McCready walked over to check on the barbecue, Clare came up to him, a confused expression on her face. "So, if that's not the real gold, where is it?"

McCready looked at her innocently for a second and smiled. He led her over to the half-built games room and looked at the wall.

"Didn't your daddy ever tell you to invest in bricks and mortar?"

She still looked confused. McCready nodded at the wall. She took a closer look and suddenly her eyes went wide and she gasped. At the corner of one of the bricks, the mortar had come away, revealing a golden gleam beneath. She threw her hand to her mouth and turned to stare at him.

"But how?"

Richards had wandered over and provided an explanation. "We had the fake gold in containers on the outside of the DSRV all the time. Plan B. When things got dicey, we dumped the real stuff in the crossover tunnel. When we went back in to repair everything, we just loaded it back up again."

Clare was stunned. "You're lucky I got you guys to do the repair then."

"Hey, what's life without some risk," said Richards.

They all laughed.

Sarah looked at Clare. "So what will you do now?"

Clare looked pointedly at McCready. "Hmmm, I dunno. I kind of like it round here!"

McCready groaned. "They all want me for my money!"

"Come on, McCready. You can do better than that."

"Yeah, I probably can," he replied. "Well, the spare room's a bit of a mess, but there are options."

She punched him playfully.

Porter moved closer to McCready. "By the way, guv, just found out they've reflooded the moat round the Tower of London—always fancied a bit of bling myself!"

Clare looked up. "No way!"

They all laughed.

Over the laughter there was the sound of a ringing phone.

McCready eventually realized it was his. He pulled it from his pocket and answered it. "Hello, John McCready," he said. He was still smiling.

The voice on the other end was unknown to him. It was friendly, but carried an air of authority McCready had rarely heard. It was a voice that was used to being obeyed without question.

"Hello, John. My name is Martin Steel. We need to have a chat."

"Er, forgive me, do I know you?"

"No, but I have a feeling we're going to get to know each other very well."

"I'm sorry, but I'm in the middle of something right now. Maybe you could call back later."

"Later, that wall of gold at the back of your house might not exist."

He had McCready's attention.

Chapter 47

Martin Steel continued.

"I'm sure you need a second, so let me explain. I've been watching you for a while. I need you to do a job for me. I can't give you specifics right now, but this is not a request, and it's non-negotiable."

McCready was starting to have a very bad feeling about this. "And if I refuse?"

There was a sigh down the phone. "John, I'm not playing games here. If you ask the lady in the light-colored dress ... Sarah, I think her name is, to just move to the right a fraction, you'll see a little red dot on the wall —the one that's not made of bricks."

McCready's bad feeling was off the charts.

He looked over at Sarah and moved around to her side. Past her he could see a small red dot sitting in the middle of the wall. It wasn't moving. It was perfectly stable and it was created by a laser.

Steel continued. "Now, I'm going to make it very clear. I'm standing right next to a nice young lady who I only have to tell to press a little red button and your wall disappears. Can you imagine how?"

"I have a pretty good imagination," replied McCready stonily.

"Yes, yes, you do don't you? That thing on the bridge with the Range Rover, very creative."

McCready was astounded. "You saw that?"

"Like I said," continued Steel, "we've been watching you."

"But why?"

McCready had taken the call away from the group and walked through the house and out onto the deck at the back. He looked out across the bay, trying to work out what the hell was going on.

"We've been investigating Malcolm Mercer for a while now but haven't been able to gather enough evidence. You came across on the chatter and we thought we'd take an interest. You turned out to be very interesting."

"But who are you?" asked McCready, just as a shotgun report echoed from the bikers at the house across the bay. He flinched. He was too jumpy. He watched them for a moment and then concentrated on the call again.

"Ever wonder how all your problems went away after London?" asked Steel.

"That was you?"

"I'm a man who can get things done, John. Now, are you going to help me, or do I have to destroy that very valuable wall of yours? I'd prefer to do it without your guests present, but time is of the essence."

McCready thought for a moment. He didn't have an option. He gazed out over the bracken and fields to the house with the bikers, then he was all focus again. "I don't really have a choice, do I?"

"Always knew you were a smart guy."

"Okay," he said slowly, a thought coming to him, "but I want you to do something for me."

"You're not really in any position to make demands."

"Fair enough. Call it an act of goodwill. Seeing as you clearly need me and are unlikely to jeopardize my cooperation …"

There was a pause.

"Go on."

McCready spent five minutes explaining. When he'd finished, Steel was quiet for a moment. Then McCready could almost hear the wry smile over the phone.

"Okay, if that's what you want, it can be arranged."

"Right, now just get your toy out of here, you're frightening the seagulls." McCready hung up, took one last look at the bikers across the bay and then headed back to his guests. As he went, he threw a glance up at the sky, wondering if Steel's drone had left the area.

When he arrived back at the patio the little red dot was nowhere to be seen.

Chapter 48

It was getting dark when the last of them left.

Logan and Porter had gone first, and the long-predicted argument had finally materialized, centered around which one was going to drive, though whether either of them should have been behind the wheel of a car was debatable. Sarah had said she had to get back as she was tired and had stroked the bulge in her tummy with love and affection. They would talk later in the week. Richards had realized he'd drunk far too much and had sensibly ordered a taxi, which had taken an hour to get there, giving him time to consume even more. He'd swayed slightly before leaving but had confirmed that McCready sure knew how to throw a party, and he wasn't just referring to the day's events.

That had left Clare.

Before she'd arrived she'd booked into a local hotel, not knowing how things would go with McCready. She had to be in London the following day to clear up some final loose ends with London Water. She'd wanted to stay, and there was nothing McCready would have liked more, but since the phone call, he didn't want anyone around whom he cared about. He had no idea what was going to happen but he knew it was unlikely to be good. It had been a strain to see her go. She had said she'd be back once things had been sorted out in London. They'd hugged and kissed passionately and he'd watched her disappear into the night.

He wondered when he would see her again.

He was now dressed in dark trousers, a black turtleneck jumper and a Berghaus climbing jacket. It was going to be cold. He made sure his phone was in his pocket and then pulled on some ex-army combat boots and a pair of Salomon ski gloves.

The phrase was going through his mind, and he knew it would justify his actions over the next few minutes.

Parents shouldn't lose sons and brothers shouldn't lose brothers.

Before he left he needed one more thing.

By the door was the baseball bat. His gaze fell on it for a second and then moved to the shelf above. He picked up a small silver cylinder about the length of a cigar. He hadn't used it since he'd been in the vault at Wellings Bank. He tucked it firmly in his pocket and then opened the door and walked out into the night.

The air was cool and a wind was picking up off the sea, but it was a clear sky and the stars shone like a sparkling carpet across the heavens. He zipped his jacket all the way up and then headed down the side of the house. He passed the little grave in the grass at the end of the garden without a glance. He didn't need to look to feel the emotions he was feeling.

The bracken was becoming damp as the temperature fell, and his boots were covered in dew by the time he came to the small rise that looked down on the building at the edge of the bay. It had probably been a nice property at one point, but years of disrepair and neglect had let the weather do its worse. Now, part of the roof had collapsed and the windows had long since been smashed in. Before he even reached the rise, the music assaulted him on the wind.

In front of the building a fire was burning. Five men and a woman stood around it, beer bottles in their hands. To one side eight Harley-Davidsons were parked in a haphazard array. That meant there were probably at least two more people inside the house.

One of the guys had clearly had too many beers and was swaggering around with a double-barreled shotgun. He was looking out at the grass at the edge of the light from the fire. Every now and then a rabbit would scurry into the zone and he would loose off a barrel. None of them found their target, but as they say, it's the thought that counts.

McCready took a deep breath and started to walk down the slope toward the house. He was about fifty feet away and starting to enter the glow from the fire when one of them spotted him.

"Oi you!" The words were slurred and they carried menace behind them. "Piss off! This is private property."

McCready ignored him and kept on walking. The man's shouts had brought the others to attention though. They were now all watching the stranger approach.

The guy with the shotgun was at the front and held the weapon at hip height pointing straight, well almost straight, at McCready. He wasn't too bothered though. The last two rabbits had narrowly missed taking both barrels and the gun was empty. One of the problems of going to war when you were drunk.

All six of them now formed a semicircle about twenty feet in front of McCready. The girl had retreated slightly behind them.

One of the group, slightly taller than the guy with the gun, stepped forward. He didn't seem to be as pissed as Rambo. "What do you want?"

McCready stopped. "You guys have been causing trouble round here for nearly two years. It's time for you to leave."

There was a stunned silence for several seconds, probably while they computed what he'd just said. Then they looked at each other and the tall guy started to laugh. The others joined in. Even the girl made her feelings felt, but there was a nervousness about her. She had probably seen how these things usually ended, and it would not be good for the intruder.

The guy with the empty gun moved forward and the tall guy spoke evenly.

"Now listen, you head on back to your fancy house over the hill. Yeah, I know who you are, and we'll forget you were ever so stupid. One warning's all you get."

McCready was sure he meant it.

"Okay, guys. This is the last time. Leave or I'll make you leave," he said.

Again the laughter. This time the tall guy pulled off his jacket and advanced on McCready. "Oh yeah, and just how the hell are you going to do that? There's six of us." He glanced at the girl. "Well, maybe five." She gave him the finger and wandered back to the fire.

McCready smiled. "Is that all? You're going to need some more."

The tall guy sneered at him. He looked back toward the house. "Tyson! Garbage! Out here now! Bring the hardware!"

He turned back to McCready. "You're going to get what's coming to you."

"Someone is," shot back McCready.

A minute later and two guys stumbled out of the building. They were clearly high on something, but what was slightly more worrying was that they were both carrying AK-47s, and this time the weapons would no doubt be loaded. Where the hell did people like this get guns like that? While on the one hand in their state they were probably unlikely to hit anything they were aiming at, on the other, with automatics, they were likely to hit everything.

They walked to the front of the group and stood by the tall guy. McCready checked where everyone was. He started to back away from the house. They were too close.

They followed slowly.

The tall guy sneered at him again. "Not so cocky now, are you, you little shit!"

He backed off until they were another twenty yards away. Even the girl had joined them.

McCready stopped.

The group instinctively stopped.

McCready pulled the small, cigar-like metal cylinder from his pocket and held it in his right hand, pointing upward. The tall guy tried to see what he was holding.

"Oh yeah, what's that?"

McCready replied nonchalantly. "Nothing really. Just something that's going to make you see the error of your ways."

The tall guy laughed again and was about to say something, when McCready flicked a switch on the side of the cylinder. Immediately, a pencil-thin beam of red laser light shot up into the night sky.

All the bikers were silent, looking up at the beam. Then one of them guffawed with laughter. "Oh look, it's Luke fucking Skywalker!" They all started laughing.

McCready smiled at them, shook his head and leveled the beam onto the wall of the building.

The instant the light hit the wall it was picked up by the sensors of the Reaper MQ-9 drone circling two thousand feet above. A millisecond later and the targeting systems of the drone had locked on. Five hundred miles away at RAF Waddington in Lincolnshire, Martin Steel watched the monitor showing an image of the building in Scotland. He paused for a second and then spoke softly to the woman in the seat next to him.

"Authorized."

She pressed a small red button.

A millisecond later a Hellfire missile launched from the wing of the Reaper. It barely had time to accelerate to its operational speed of Mach 1.3 before it impacted the building. The high-explosive warhead that could take apart a modern battlefield tank had no problem in almost vaporizing the bedraggled stone-walled property.

The blast spread outwards, blowing debris across a wide area. All of the bikers were blown off their feet. Four of the Harley-Davidsons were smashed into a nearby wall, totally destroying them.

McCready had been ready for it. He'd known what was coming and had even seen the fiery blaze of the missile jet, like some sort of deadly comet, as it streaked for the

414

house. He'd crouched down trying to shield himself, but even he'd had the wind knocked out of him.

He recovered well before the others and walked among them retrieving any weapons he could find.

The haul amounted to ten knives, three knuckledusters, a World War II pistol that barely looked as though it would fire, the shotgun, and the AK-47s. At least this would all be off the streets now.

Gradually the men and the woman groggily woke up to a whole new world. The tall guy's arm was broken and the others had numerous cuts and bruises. They stared around in confusion, stumbling to their feet.

Finally they looked at McCready.

There was no sympathy in his eyes. "Like I said, I won't be seeing you again."

He pointed the laser at each of them in turn.

As they saw the little red dot hit their chests they reeled back as though punched by some unseen force.

A moment later and they were running for their bikes. As only four of them had survived the explosion and one of those had a distorted wheel, they had to double up. They kept glancing back nervously, and whenever they did he fired the laser in case they should get any other ideas.

Two minutes later and they were gone. He watched as the wavering white beams from the headlights disappeared up the grass track that led to the road.

When the final spot of light had gone, he sat down on the hillside and took a deep breath. The adrenalin had been coursing through his body and he was now coming down off the natural high.

He felt drained.

He looked around and was about to stand when his phone rang. He smiled grimly, pulled it out and hit ANSWER.

Steel's voice was clipped and to the point.

"Do we have a deal?"

"We have a deal," replied McCready.

He put the phone away and stood up. He took a last look at the burning building behind him and then started to walk back to the house.

Out to sea the carpet of stars was starting to be obscured by an advancing wall of clouds.

There was a storm coming.

The End

A NOTE FROM THE AUTHOR

Hello,

And many thanks for picking up a copy of *Deep Steal*. I hope you enjoyed spending some time in the company of John McCready and friends.

Depending on when you read this, I am probably hard at work on the next adventure, or maybe even the one after that, but either way, these stories can only continue with the support of readers like yourself, so thanks again, it is much appreciated.

As an independent author, a couple of things that can really make a difference are the reviews and ratings we receive. This is not from any personal gratification point of view - though it's always great to hear if people like your work - but more from the way the online retailers promote the titles that receive high ratings and good reviews, and the information a review can give to future readers in helping them decide whether or not it is for them.

So if you enjoyed *Deep Steal*, and have a couple of minutes, it would be great if you could give the book a star rating and maybe say a few words about your experience.

Also, I hope you will be able to join me on more of John McCready's adventures over the coming years.

If you would like to be kept informed about developments and new releases, just go over to www.mikesearesbooks.com. You can also catch up with the latest news and join in discussions about the publications on our Facebook page at www.facebook.com/mikesearesbooks, or follow us on Twitter at @mikesearesbooks.

Many thanks.

Mike Seares
August 2017